How to Buy a Planet

Planet

D.A.Holdsworth

Squirrel & Acorn Press

FOR POP-POP

1

The world's press were wriggling with excitement.

They fidgeted in a big oblong hedgehog of microphones and cameras, pressed around a semi-circle of nervous-looking policemen. Behind the policemen was a semi-circle of temporary steel barriers. Behind the barriers was an empty podium. And behind the podium was the world's most famous doorway.

No.10 Downing Street.

Above Downing Street a thick blanket of cloud had turned the sky black & brooding. The odd camera flash was going off, and a TV lighting crew was hurriedly putting up a rig directed towards the Prime Ministerial podium. Still more press were gathered outside on Whitehall, jostling to hold cameras on long booms above the black wrought-iron gates. Anyone looking carefully would have seen them trying to maintain social distance. Elbows were trying to avoid elbows, tummies were squeezing past tummies. But it was no use. They were too excited.

Beyond and around them the black cabs and other traffic had perched on the pavements as drivers tuned into their radios. The bustle of Ludgate Circus had evaporated, the Strand was gridlocked, Trafalgar Square was motionless. All of London was at a standstill.

In fact the whole world had stopped.

Breakfast TV in North America, the evening news shows on the sub-continent, the late shows in Australia and New Zealand. Every single broadcast channel and internet streaming service in existence was tuned into Downing Street. Many billions of eyes, and a similar number of ears, were strained in expectation with a growing feeling of both excitement and dread. And all of this achieved with a mere three hours' notice.

And it was just as well that they'd tuned in.

Because today the world would learn that its planet had just been sold.

*

"One pahnd."

"Excuse me?"

"Yer bag o' crisps. One pahnd."

"Oh, of course." Toby started reaching into his pocket, and then remembered why he'd really come to the bar. "Err, can you tell me if there's a Dave here?"

"*Who?*" The landlady was chewing gum with an intensity that unnerved Toby.

"His name's Dave. He said you'd know him? Apparently he always drinks here?"

"Sorry, dahn't knah any Daves," she replied, immediately resuming her work at the bar, while her jaws intensified their gum-chewing. Toby was mesmerised. It was like watching two boxers slug it out under a blanket.

Toby looked helplessly round the pub and wondered

how it was possible, in this day and age, not to know any Daves. The place was full already and more customers were arriving. There were probably several Daves here. At least four or five. The odds were stacked in favour of Daves.

A couple of customers jostled their way in front of him and Toby asked himself for the first time why the pub was so ridiculously busy. He squeezed back a step, trying to maintain a figment of distance. His eye caught the news channel that was playing on the TV. A large clock was showing 11:55. Beneath it, a kind but stern-looking Government official, of the type that had become rather familiar in recent years, was saying something that was obviously very serious, while beneath him a ticker message played in a loop:

"IMPORTANT ANNOUNCEMENT FROM DOWNING STREET AT 12PM GMT, 1PM BST · MAKE SURE YOU ARE NEAR A TELEVISION OR WIRELESS · DO NOT BE ALARMED · IMPORTANT ANNOUNCEMENT FROM DOWNING STREET AT 12PM GMT, 1PM BST · MAKE SURE…"

And on and on.

Toby didn't know it, but *everyone* was getting themselves near a TV. They were alarmed by the word 'alarmed' and they were even more alarmed by the word 'wireless', without quite knowing why. The ticker message had been running for three hours. It had created a strange primitive urge in people to hear whatever was going to said in the company of others. This primitive urge collided with a more modern urge to remain socially distanced… But the primitive urge won. This time, for this news event, people wanted to come together.

Strange, Toby thought, and then re-focussed on his own quest. He had just come here about a flat-share. He scanned the heaving crowd looking for any obvious Daves. *Why did this Dave have to be the only one without a mobile?* He decided to ask the landlady again, for good form. If that didn't work out, he'd forget all about the flat and look for something else.

"Are you quite sure you don't know any Daves?" he said to the landlady, poking his head between two customers without quite touching them. "He was certain you'd know him. He said, 'it's impossible to hide your identity these days'..."

The landlady stopped chewing for a moment and looked him straight in the eye.

"Yer mean *Paranoid* Dave?"

"Err, maybe?"

"Well, why didn't yer say so then. Over there, near the TV" she said, pointing with her elbow, and resuming her chewing. "Black beard, leather overcoat."

"Thank you," Toby squeaked, just as the sea of customers closed in front of him.

Toby edged his way in the vague direction indicated by the landlady's elbow and there, on a settle against the wall, he saw a chubby, bearded figure. He was wearing a black skull t-shirt beneath a full-length black leather coat and was staring intently at another large TV screen. Still half-minded to walk out the pub and forget the whole flatmate thing, Toby nudged his way towards him.

*

"Err, hi, I'm here about the flat, are you—"

The bearded figure raised his hand to silence him,

4

while still staring at the screen.

"BST?" the bearded figure asked.

"Err, yes?"

"What does it mean?"

"British Summer Time?"

"Exactly! *British Summer Time*." Paranoid Dave stabbed a single, pudgy finger into the table. "Why bother telling us that? *Why?*"

Paranoid Dave turned to Toby for the first time. His eyes were small and suspicious, sitting in his pudgy white cheeks like a couple of button studs in an over-stuffed sofa.

"It can only mean one thing."

"Which is?" Toby asked.

"I dunno. I'm still thinking about it." Paranoid Dave turned back to the TV.

"Great," said Toby. "Well, I guess you must be Dave?"

"Who wants to know?"

"Err, I do? Look, I'm just here about the ad. I was wondering if you could let me know what the flat looks like?"

"The what? Oh, the flat? Is that what you're here about?" Paranoid Dave patted the bench next to him. "Take a seat. You should've said."

"Well, I did actually," Toby replied sitting down.

"Did you? Oh right." A thought seem to pass through Paranoid Dave's head and he suddenly looked cowed. "I dunno, man. Not sure how much I'm allowed to tell you. It better wait 'til Charlie gets here from work."

Who's Charlie?

Toby pictured a grizzled creature of startling rudeness. He sank back into his seat with his bag of crisps, only then realising that he hadn't actually paid for them. He looked at the bag, and shook it. It was large, but with disappointingly few crisps in it. *One pound for that?* He pulled some loose coins from his other jacket pocket. They totalled one pound exactly. *Surely a sign?* Toby had just resolved to return to the bar, pay for the crisps, and quietly slip out of Paranoid Dave's life, when the TV started to crackle.

After an awkward transition, the drinkers of the Squirrel & Acorn found themselves staring at a rather familiar doorway.

*

12 noon struck in Downing Street.

Nothing happened.

The press fidgeted a little more. Many billions of people watching at home fidgeted with them, and wondered – fleetingly – if there might just be time to pop the kettle on.

Then at 12:03pm, a small and rather unremarkable man appeared on the pavement to the left. He was wearing an old-fashioned brown janitor's coat and pushing a large black plastic container on four small wheels. The press and their cameras turned towards him, a little uncertain. A few sniggers broke out. *Had Downing Street forgotten to put their rubbish out?*

Unhurried, and apparently oblivious to the attention, the janitor-like figure pushed his strange contraption past the door of No.11, then up to the door of No.10. Here he attempted to execute a right turn – and struggled for a moment with the wheels, in a way that anyone who's ever pushed an ageing airport trolley would understand – managed to correct the direction, and came to a rest just next to the Prime Minister's podium. The janitor took up position between the podium and his contraption and folded his hands meekly in front of him. His bulging eyes blinked in the glare of the world's media.

A few more sniggers. A few camera flashes went off, making a disarmingly old-fashioned clicking sound as they did so.

And then at 12:05pm precisely, the door of No.10 opened, and the Prime Minister strode up to the podium, confident and calm.

The media erupted in a frenzy of flashes and camera clicks, like a flock of wading birds startled by a predator. They watched the Prime Minister plant a few pieces of paper on the podium – he straightened them in a dignified and business-like manner – he paused – he looked around – he sucked in the sheer enormity of the audience watching him and briefly contemplated the even more sheer enormity of the news he was about to deliver. Then he smiled, and brushed his famously floppy brown hair from his brow with one hand.

*

"Sssh!"

"Sorry, he was just trying to—"

"SSSH – it's about to start!"

The Squirrel & Acorn was bursting. The ones at the bar were being shushed by the ones near the bar, who were being shushed by the ones in front of the TV. Soon a shushing sound was passing round the pub like a Mexican wave.

Toby and Paranoid Dave's view of the TV was completely blocked. Paranoid Dave stood up on the bench and Toby did likewise. *What the Hell was going on?*

"Oops!" said a lanky, ridiculously tall ginger bloke, as he biffed his head on one of the beams.

"SSSSHH!"

The ridiculously tall ginger bloke froze in front of the TV, panicked. He rubbed his head and looked round at the pub-full of people staring angrily back at him. He couldn't see were to sit; he couldn't see where to stand.

"Come on, Seamus, you can't be standing there," said a short, dark-haired bloke, who pulled him off to one side by the hand. "You're bang in the way."

"SSSSSSSSSSHHHHH!"

*

"Thank you all for coming. And on behalf of the G7 group of nations, I'd like to apologise for the slightly abrupt nature of this press conference."

The Prime Minister was brisk. *Professional.*

"I don't want to waste your time this morning. I shall get straight to the point.

"The world is in crisis. Politicians are rightly criticised for not always telling it straight. So let me say it straight." He paused, looked up from his notes, and several hundred cameras flashed at him.

"The world is in crisis, and it's a crisis of many colours.

"Let's start with the debt crisis. Across the planet, individuals and corporations are mired in debt to banks, whom they can never hope to repay. Banks are mired in debt to each other. The governments of the world are sunk even deeper in debt, while trying to prop everyone else up. Even countries, which you might not think are running on debt, are running on debt."

The Prime Minister paused. He had plunged straight in, no point in sugaring the pill. He looked up and saw the press corps was transfixed. *Yep*, he said to himself, *I thought so.*

"What is the simplest way to think of this predicament? Even before *you-know-what*, ah-hm…" the Prime Minister faltered involuntarily, "…even before the virus crisis, debt was being passed around the global financial system like traffic on an overcrowded network. It only needed one accident for that network to become gridlocked. It could've been anything. A stock market crisis, a bond market crisis, a currency war, a trade war – an *actual* war. Anything that knocks confidence.

"It turned out to be… It turned out to be a virus.

"To keep money circulating round the economy – to deal with the debt crisis – we created a currency crisis. The Governments of the world were forced to print money they didn't have and to issue bonds they could never repay. We muddled through, but the simple truth is, no-one has any idea where this experiment will end. If the major economies of the world continue towards deflation, we face a future in which these debts *might actually grow*, not shrink. And that's the lucky outcome. The alternative is inflation, probably rampant. If that happens, interest rates will rocket and a large proportion of the debt will simply become unaffordable. *Mortgages* will become unaffordable. Businesses will collapse, households will be bankrupted, governments will default. Inflation will ultimately reduce the value of the debt, but not until the global economy has been trashed, re-trashed and trashed again.

"Inflation, deflation – either way we are damned.

"And so we've reached the biggest crisis of all. A crisis of confidence. The system was built on confidence, the system will collapse without it. Old debts will become due for repayment, so people try to raise new debts to pay off the old ones, but they'll be unable to. When no-one trusts anyone, no-one lends. The world faces economic ruin. *Or worse.*"

The Prime Minister paused, swished his hair again, and looked up. As he stared into the pale and startled faces of the journalists in front of him, just for a moment he felt this astonishing sense of clarity and elation. It was like floating one foot above the ground, like he could somehow see through the camera lenses into the homes of all the people watching him.

Is this what it feels like to speak truth to billions? he wondered fleetingly. *How wonderful.*

*

"Shit", said Paranoid Dave under his breath. "He's telling the truth."

In an unconcscious motion, Paranoid Dave pulled a bag of toffees from his pocket and started unwrapping one, his eyes fixed on the TV.

"But that's a good thing, right? Telling the truth?" Toby whispered back.

"You kidding? This is bad news. He must need something really big from us." Paranoid Dave popped the toffee in his mouth, and took a gulp of ale. "And by the way, you see that plastic contraption, the one next to the Prime Minister?"

"Err yes."

"I'm sure I can see a brand name on it – look at the bottom."

"Oh yes, so there is."

"Biffa?"

"Biffa."

"My God, it's *a wheelie bin*," Paranoid Dave observed. "Why the Hell have they brought a black wheelie bin to the world's most important press conference?"

"SSSSH!"

*

The Prime Minister looked down at the rest of his statement. His truth-to-billions moment had passed. He blanched slightly and pressed on.

"I put it to you that this situation is intolerable. We deserve better. The human race has amazing ingenuity. Our planet has amazing resources. It has sustained us as we developed our civilisation to the highest degree. Why should we be shackled with so much debt and so much doubt when so much abundance lies around us and within us?

"The answer is: we shouldn't be. We all have a *share* in this planet and we all deserve better."

He took a sip of water.

"What if there was a way we could make the most out of our planet *and* eliminate global debt at the same time?

"You may say that this is madness – a dream, a fantasy. But I'm here today to tell you about more than just a dream. I'm here to tell you about *an opportunity*. A chance to eliminate debt *and* take full advantage of our cherished planet. It is an opportunity of dazzling dimensions, and one that will not wait. Which is why we, the leaders of the G7, on behalf of the entire planet, have collectively taken the decision that was needed."

The Prime Minister paused pregnantly. He looked up.

"We have sold planet Earth!"

*

Silence.

Looking up from his podium, the Prime Minister saw a row of mouths falling open. For the first time in their professional lives, the cameramen of the press were forgetting to take pictures. Lenses were lowered, and pale faces appeared from behind them. The sound guys forgot their microphones, the journalists stopped scribbling in their notebooks.

You *what?*

*

In the Squirrel & Acorn, jaws slackened and faces blanched. A pint glass slipped from someone's hand and smashed on the floor.

*

On every phone call, every facecall, every conversation around the world – on every TV channel and every radio station – heck, even on the internet – nothing.

Pure, bewildered silence.

The broadcast media went so quiet that for the first time in a century the entire planet was emitting the

same uncluttered, unbroken signal into outer space.
Silence.

2

Actually, not quite everyone was focusing on the Prime Minister at that precise moment.

In a secret lock-up at a secret location, six remarkably masculine men, dressed in black body armour, were sitting in the back of an unmarked van, assiduously preparing an array of ferocious-looking assault weapons. They sat squeezed on two narrow benches opposite each other. Four letters were stitched onto the left shoulder of their black combat jackets:

T - A - R - P

They all wore black helmets, with a high-tech eyepiece over one eye and an earpiece over one ear. Without talking, all six were cocking and uncocking their semi-automatic assault rifles in a manner that was, on a practical level, slightly pointless, but which nevertheless communicated to each other a reassuring degree of masculinity.

After a few moments, their leader leaned forward and passed round a single photo. Each one looked at it and passed it on.

"Got it?"

"Got it, boss," they replied.

"Time check." He looked down at his watch.

"12:11. Check?"

"Check boss." Five replies.

"Then let's go."

The leader pumped his fist on the roof of the van. The lock-up opened and the unmarked van pulled out, melting swiftly into the labyrinthine heart of the metropolis.

*

The Prime Minister found the silence in Downing Street eerie.

"Now when I say 'sold' it is in fact what's called a 'sale and leaseback' deal. We have sold Plant Earth for – may I say – a tidy profit, and now we're leasing it back from the purchaser at a considerably lower sum. After all, we still need somewhere to live. Ha ha!"

Silence.

"Now of course you will be wondering about the financial—"

"Prime Minister – who did the G7 consult before selling the planet?" A journalist called out from somewhere in the middle of the pack.

"Yes, I'm just coming to that. We appreciate this will come as a shock to many. The negotiations had to be undertaken in the strictest secrecy. That's why it was felt the G7 provided the most suitable negotiating platform. We certainly consulted China, but we didn't—"

"Who else?"

"Well," the Prime Minister started, "we didn't—"

"Prime Minister – by what right have you sold our planet?"

"How can the G7 sell something that isn't theirs?"

A couple of interruptions became a volley.

"Why was no-one else consulted in advance?"

"How come this wasn't brought before the EU?"

"—the UN—"

"—the World Bank—"

"—the Pope—"

"—the Dalai Lama—"

"—Warren Buffett—"

"—Greta Thunberg—"

 "—the Queen?"

"You are joking, aren't you Prime Minister?"

"Is this story an April fool, or are you a complete fool?"

"Why are you making the statement? Where's the Chinese President, the US President? Are you just the patsy?"

The volley became an avalanche. The journalists were starting to yell, screaming out the million questions that this insane situation provoked.

Every question, except the one that really mattered, because even in their anger, no-one dared to ask *that* question.

The cameras flashed, manically.

The Prime Minister soldiered on, his words barely audible: "…we see this very much as a partnership of equals, which will deliver inward investment on a truly – ha ha – cosmic scale. It is frankly a fantastic vote of confidence in Planet Earth plc, and we should be celebrating that…"

*

"Is this guy for real?"

The mood in the Squirrel & Acorn was turning ugly.

"It's *our* planet, you *******!"

People starting throwing bags of peanuts at the TV. Then beermats. Then beer. Another pint glass shattered.

Toby looked at his bag of crisps, thinking perhaps he ought to participate in this moment of spontaneous protest and throw the crisps at the TV.

He turned to look at Paranoid Dave, who turned and looked back at him. His chubby face was as drawn as a flaccid udder. He popped another toffee in his mouth, took another slug of ale, and shrugged his shoulders hesitantly as if to say, *even in my most paranoid moments, I didn't see this one coming…*

Toby gulped, put the bag of crisps back in his jacket pocket and leant back against the wall.

*

In Downing Street, the press corps had turned mutinous. They were yelling so loudly – and in so many languages – no-one could hear a word the Prime Minister was saying.

Then a journalist clambered onto the steel barrier in front of the Prime Minister's podium. He was Scandinavian, slight of build, with a blond, pious face. All cameras turned towards him. He teetered unsteadily on the barrier. He held his footing just long enough to launch himself forward, arms outstretched, towards the podium.

It instantaneously became the world's most famous bar dive.

In a strange moment of synchrony, four burly

policemen dutifully, perfectly caught his outstretched body as it arced through the air, bringing him to rest with his face just inches from the Prime Minister's.

For a few moments, the two men were frozen opposite each other. The Prime Minister – tense, flustered, upright. Just inches away, the Scandinavian journalist – blond, furious, horizontal.

Downing Street sucked in its breath...

*

...and so did the Squirrel & Acorn. Watching the TV, Toby and Paranoid Dave could clearly make out the journalist's high Scandinavian tone, as he rasped his question:

"W h o t h e H e l l h a v e y o u s h o l d o u r p l a n e t t o ? "

*

The question that must be answered.

The world paused in anticipation.

Ignoring them (the world that is), the four burly policemen gently lifted the journalist (who was now looking startled by his own boldness) and deposited him with a disarming delicacy back on his side of the barrier, righting him onto his feet as if they were just returning their Grandmother's favourite porcelain vase back to the mantelpiece from which the cat had knocked it.

The Prime Minister turned uncertainly to the janitor standing to his right, whom everyone had overlooked in the melee. The janitor quietly nodded.

"You will all be wondering to whom we have sold

the planet," the Prime Minister continued as if this was always in his script. "The answer is that we have been in negotiation for the last few years – negotiations that you will understand had to be carried out in the strictest secrecy – with a syndicate of highly reputable financiers.

"The leading counterparty are a race of – ah-hm – aliens…" the Prime Minister didn't mean to pause, but he couldn't help himself, "…ah-hm, aliens called the Za-Nakarians…"

*

"The Za-Na-*who?*"

*

"…and I am thrilled to be able to introduce to you today their chief negotiator, with whom we have signed the deal."

The Prime Minister turned to the janitor.

The janitor then turned to the wheelie bin to his right. He carefully lifted the lid back, and steam started to billow out. He stood on tiptoes, his chin just over the edge, and softly called out a name:

"Woof-lis-Woola!"

There was a moment's silence.

He called again, cooingly:

"Wooooolaaa!"

After a few seconds a strange gurgling sound seemed to emanate from the wheelie bin, and a few puffs of steam spouted upwards.

Silence again.

The entire press corps, the entire planet was holding

its breath. You could hear a pin drop in Beijing, even sitting in London.

Then, to everyone's wonder and astonishment, some soap bubbles floated out of the top of the bin. The bright camera lighting refracted off the bubbles in magical, playful colours of iridescent purple and green. More steam poured upwards and outwards, spilling over the edge of the contraption, in a caressing blanket of warmth. Just to look at it was to be reminded of childhood bathtimes.

Slowly, imperceptibly at first, between the steam and the soap bubbles, a head started to rise up. It appeared to be pale green in colour, hairless, eyes still shut, with a broad white stripe running from under the chin all the way down the slender, slowly emerging and increasingly long neck.

The entirety of planet Earth strained towards a billion TV sets to get a better look.

Gradually the bubbles dispersed to reveal the unearthly apparition. And at that moment, with perfect timing, Woola opened his huge baby-like eyes to reveal two gorgeous globes of softly shining, fathomless brown. They were framed by perfectly curled lashes, each one as long as a child's little finger. He fluttered his eyelids open and shut in the glare of the lights, tilted his head gently to one side and trilled in a quavering voice and the most winning Za-Nakarian accent:

"Hellooooooooo…"

*

From Capetown to Adelaide, from Caracas to Vladivostok, many billion earthlings (including the many dozen in the Squirrel & Acorn) emitted a prolonged:

"Aaaaaaaahhh…"

The world was smitten.

*

Inside, the Prime Minister was pirouetting with relief.

On the outside, he assumed a posture of self-conscious gravity. With his most businesslike, don't-worry-chaps-I've-got-this-covered tone, he launched into the remainder of his statement:

> "It was of course the first duty of the G7 to maximise the value we…"

But no-one was listening.

All eyes were on Woola in his wheelie bin. They watched as he started to dive and plash, he swished to one side, and back to the other. As he surged up, they glimpsed more of his body. At the base of his long neck, his torso broadened out into a chubby, aquiline shape. His skin was pale green and rubbery, like a seal, and he had two forelimbs a bit like arms, but a bit like flippers too. At the end of each forelimb he had three chubby digits and a thumb, all webbed at the base. Woola dived back down into the water, and a moment later they gasped with delight as they saw a hundred soap bubbles jet thirty feet into the air. As the bubbles tumbled back down in all directions, cynical, hard-bitten journalists reached up like children to catch them.

> "…a highly complex valuation model was constructed, using a competitive discount rate…"

Woola re-emerged and used his breath to balance a

particularly large, particularly colourful bubble one inch above his nose. The giant bubble wibbled and wobbled under its own weight, but remained beautifully, precariously perched in mid-air above Woola's nose.

Oooh!

"… every consideration was given to the possible consequences of this sale…"
Woola gently blew the giant bubble towards the back of one of the policemen, using his breath to land it directly on the top of his policemen's helmet, whereupon it burst like a miniature firework into a thousand multi-coloured droplets.

Aaaaaahhh!

"…we have a duty to unlock not only our own potential but also that of our planet…"
Woola bowed playfully with his long, graceful neck and, returning upright, fluttered his eyelids.

Hurraaaaaaaay!

Everyone, but everyone, was thinking the same thing: *So this is what alien life is like? If only we'd met these guys before!*
"Ah-hm", the Prime Minister cleared his throat and repeated more loudly, "I shall now be happy to take questions?"
The press corps finally heard him. The Scandinavian journalist, the one who had bar-dived at the Prime Minister, put his hand up.

"Ah yes, Anders Salvgoda, isn't it? From the Svenska Dagbladet?" The Prime Minister – his confidence fully restored – managed to recall his assailant's name and the journalist nodded. "Your question, sir?"

"What day-to-day changesh will there be, Prime Minishter?" His manner was suddenly docile and he stared lovingly at Woola.

"Very few if truth be told," he replied. "Of course we will all have new friends to play with!"

The world smiled.

"When can we expect global debts to be forgiven?" another journalist called out.

"There are still a lot of details to be ironed out, as you can imagine," the Prime Minister replied. "But I think we're talking weeks not months."

"Will that include all mortgage debt... And credit card debt..." the journalist continued, scarcely able to believe what she was asking.

"Oh yes, all consumer debt," the Prime Minister beamed like an indulgent parent at Christmas time. "And all corporate debt, government debt, lockdown debt. All bonds and treasuries, they'll all get repaid. The whole shooting match."

A few journalists scribbled, most just smiled. A strange, irresistible delirium was seeping into the frozen hearts of the press corps.

"How much was the Earth sold for?"

"1.8 quad-*rillion* Za-Nakarian dollars." The Prime Minister's voice landed on the '-rillion' with satisfying emphasis. "With, may I say, an earn-out clause that allows the possibility of raising that to 2.4 quad-*rillion* dollars."

"What's the exchange rate, Prime Minister?"

"Currently running at two Pounds sterling to one Za-Nakarian dollar. You do the *math!*"

"That sounds a lot, Prime Minister, but to whom will the proceeds actually be paid?" There was a slightly frosty edge to the question. A few journalists frowned.

"You are all shareholders now…" the Prime Minister started. The frowns deepened, and a few shoulders tensed. "…but we will work out how to split the proceeds *in consultation with Woola.*"

Everyone breathed.

"How many interpreters are there, Prime Minister? How many people can speak Za-Nakarian?"

"Err… Actually at this stage just one." The Prime Minister looked reluctantly at the janitor next to him.

"What's his name, Prime Minister?"

"His name is, err…" The Prime Minister hesitated, and looked helplessly towards the janitor and the wheelie bin beyond him for a moment, before a light suddenly went on in his head: "…his name is Biffa."

*

"Actually that's not true."

A voice next to Toby had just spoken, addressing no-one in particular.

Toby looked down. The voice came from a small, elderly gentlemen, who was sitting just to Toby's left on the bench. Toby, who was still standing on the bench, hadn't noticed him arriving. He thought it might be impolite to ignore the remark.

"You mean he isn't called Biffa?"

"Hmm? Oh yes, that's right. That's also not true." The old gentlemen looked up and smiled at Toby. His eyes were twinkling with a sprightly energy, while looking a little vacant at the same time.

"Right, I see," said Toby, not seeing. "So if he's not called Biffa, what's the other thing that's not true?"

"Oh nothing, nothing. Hmm. You see? Only that he's not the only interpreter of Za-Nakarian."

"He isn't?"

"No."

"Of course not. Got it." Toby said, not getting it. "So if he's not the only one who can speak Za-Nakarian, who else can?"

"I can."

*

A hundred camera lenses were focussed on 'Biffa', whose eyes were bulging uncomfortably. He shifted awkwardly from his left foot to his right and back again as the questions re-started – *How come there was only one interpreter? – Could his interpretations be relied upon? – Was the sales contract written in English or Za-Nakarian?*

And then a loud snort from the plastic contraption interrupted them.

All the cameras swung back towards Woola. Miraculously, he was managing to juggle three huge soap bubbles in the air with his breath. By swishing left and right in his wheelie bin, and blowing with exquisite precision, he kept three radiant, heavenly orbs in motion, rising and falling and interweaving in a three dimensional lattice above Downing Street.

Woow…

Ooooohh!

Aaaaaaaaahhh!

Biffa mopped his brow with relief.

"OK – last question?" The Prime Minister beamed reassuringly.

"Prime Minister, when can we expect more Za-Nakarians to visit?"

"Well, there are no immediate plans. Space travel is rather hard you know." The Prime Minister smiled knowingly at the camera. "But we look forward to welcoming Woola's friends just as soon as they can make it."

With that he drew the press conference to a close. Downing Street erupted in spontaneous applause.

And the whole world rejoiced.

*

Actually, not quite the whole world.

On the streets of the metropolis one unmarked white van was snaking its way speedily along, inconspicuous in every particular (except perhaps one, namely that it was the only moving vehicle in a city filled with several million parked vehicles; in point of fact, its movement was so noteworthy that two or three different spy satellites, along with a couple of hundred CCTV cameras, had picked it up and reported its suspicious activity backed to the very authorities who had dispatched it in the first place – such being the daily challenges and petty irritations of running an ultra-secret special forces cell in a country full of nosy people.)

Inside, the TARP leader placed his hand to his earpiece and concentrated for a second.

"Right boys," he said, looking up, "we have a fix on the target. He's two clicks south of here. ETA in zero-five minutes. Got it?"

"Got it, boss."

"This is the big one, remember. They've been tracking this target for the last three months. We have to assume he is armed and dangerous. No cock-ups."

"No cock-ups, boss," they replied. And to deal with the rising tension, they cocked and uncocked their weapons a few more times.

3

Back in the Squirrel & Acorn, the ridiculously tall ginger bloke called Seamus was back in front of the TV. He leaned towards it, found the volume knob and turned the sound down. He turned back around, and looked at everyone in the pub.

This time there wasn't a trace of anger on the faces staring back.

Their expressions were wide with a biblical sense of wonderment, like a flock of the chosen people who had just beheld an epoch-changing miracle. Seamus stared back at them, his own eyes wild and wide. He had just had the pants charmed off him *by an alien*. For a moment the pub was noiseless before he clenched both fists in the air and let out the loudest, most piercing whoop of joy the pub had heard in its 350-year history:

"Whooo – HOO – *H O O O O O O O !* "

The world had just been sold to someone *cute* and the Squirrel & Acorn went crazy.

Someone switched on the jukebox and over towards the middle of the pub a few people started dancing. And then a few more joined them. And then a few more again. People who had been up all night dancing started dancing. People who had never danced before started dancing. People who would never dance again started dancing. Over at the tables, folk spontaneously turned to people they didn't know to share their amazement. The world was healing – first from the virus, now from the crash – and it was time to celebrate. Tentative at first, and then with growing confidence, people dared to *touch* each other. Hands high-fived, voices laughed, bodies brushed against bodies. It was time to dance, it was time to trust. At the bar, someone called out 'Drinks on the house!' – and it just seemed the most natural thing in the world that no-one should pay.

Inhibitions melted, jobs were forgotten, friendship and love surged in every heart, debt no longer existed, and money no longer mattered.

In short: a strange and intoxicating euphoria descended on the Squirrel & Acorn, and indeed everywhere else with a TV set or an internet connection.

Which was, basically, everywhere.

*

Toby looked at Paranoid Dave. He wondered, not without a slight feeling of awkwardness, if this was the moment he was supposed to make an uninhibited display of affection. But, just as he was wondering how he might do something spontaneous, he did something spontaneous.

His heart stopped.

Over Paranoid Dave's shoulder, he saw a vision.

A girl was carefully making her way through the gyrating crowd, in their direction.

She looked like she had stepped off a beach. She had flip-flops on her feet and a canvas bag slung casually over one shoulder. She wore a flowing, ivory-white, linen skirt, which flexed elegantly around the revellers, like a yacht tacking through a summer breeze. Her hair was long and mocha-coloured.

"Oh hi, Dave," the vision said.

Toby dropped his gaze. *Oh my God, she knows Paranoid Dave?*

Paranoid Dave swung round, and stumbled down from the bench. "Oh hi, Charlie," he said looking bashful.

This is Charlie? Toby's thoughts were tumbling over each other like nursery children at playtime. He tried to place her looks. Her skin was lightly tanned, luminous; she had an open, trusting expression. Was she partly Asian? Not Indian, not Chinese, somewhere else.

"What's going on here?" she asked, looking around. Her hand went up to steady a pair of sunglasses, that were perched in her hair.

"You mean *you don't know?*" Paranoid Dave asked incredulously.

"No, I've just woken up. I slept in," she replied hazily, pulling up a stool to join them. "Oh hi – you must be Toby? I've been looking forward to meeting you."

She dazzled a smile at Toby, who smiled back awkwardly and stumbled down from the bench, with all the confidence of a young boy arriving at his older sister's pool party.

"Hi," he squeaked back.

"So what's happened here – tell me? And why the party?"

Paranoid Dave took a deep breath. "OK, Charlie, you're not going to believe this but…"

*

The white unmarked van, glided noiselessly to a halt on a side street.

Inside the leader gave the final briefing. He was holding an extremely sophisticated looking console, with a floor plan marked on it.

"Right boys – there's one main entrance and a side entrance. *Here* – and – *here*. Got it?"

"Got it, boss."

"TARP-2 – you come with me and take the main entrance, *here*."

"Yes boss."

"TARP-3, TARP-4 – you take the side entrance, *here*."

"Yes boss."

"TARP-5, TARP-6 – you take up position outside the front windows, and cover the street…"

TARP-5 and 6 waited.

"…*here*."

"Yes, boss."

"OK team, have we got this one?"

"Hell yeah, boss!"

"Then let's do this thing!"

With that, the leader clenched his fist and stuck it towards the centre of the group. Each member of the team clenched their fist, and stuck them one on top of each other's. A bit like an adult version of one-potato-two-potato.

"ONE – TWO – THREE…"

"*HWUH!*" they grunted masculinely at each other.

The leader then kicked open the back of the van and, like an American football team entering the Superbowl, the TARP team rushed onto the street.

*

"They sold the planet? *Shut up!*" Charlie's hand reached up to steady her sunglasses as if they might be blown away by the force of the news. "I'm so sorry." She turned to Toby, "and on the day you came to check out the flat."

"Oh no, it's quite ok." *Why was Charlie apologising?* "Really, the alien they've sold it to is very cute and everyone here seems very happy about it." Toby gestured vaguely to the whooping mass of pub-goers who were swarming around them.

"Look," said Paranoid Dave inching closer to Charlie and checking his watch, "look, erm, there may only be 30 minutes left before the end of the world and everything. So I was just wondering if – you know – you wanted to slip out the back and fool around a bit? I know where there's a trap door down to the basement. There's a door from there to the—"

"What?" Charlie revulsed. "*Noooo!* Urgh. You can be so disgusting sometimes, Dave."

Charlie turned to Toby.

"I'm so sorry about Dave, he's normally ok. Just that sometimes…" She turned back to Paranoid Dave – "…he can be a real pig…" – and kicked him under the table.

"OW!" Paranoid Dave reached down to his shin. "Well I just thought – you know – that's what people do when the world's going to end in half an hour."

"No they don't. Not in my world they don't," Charlie said firmly, "not even when it's ending."

"Actually, that's not quite true." A voice piped up. It was the old man again, still sitting on Toby's left.

"You mean boys and girls *do* hook up just before the world ends?" Charlie asked incredulously.

"Oh – ha ha! No, no. Yes. Maybe. No, I meant it's not true that we only have 30 minutes before the end of the world."

"Oh good."

"It's like I said," interjected Toby, "the alien is really cute, I think everything's going to be just—"

"Not 30 minutes…" The old man was looking at a remarkably handsome gold fob watch. "More like 24 hours." He looked up, smiled, closed the lid of the fob watch and deftly slipped it back into the pocket of his tweed waistcoat.

Toby, Charlie and Paranoid Dave exchanged glances.

The old man's tone seemed playful and, at the same time, authoritative. Toby looked at him a second time and wondered a second time if he was just a crank. He was was wearing a three-piece tweed suit, which was already a bit peculiar. He had a tidy moustache and a small pointed beard and sitting on the end of his nose were a small pair of gold-rimmed spectacles. They were a half-moon shape, allowing the old man to peer over the top of them at anyone nearby, which he was currently doing. Meantime both his arms were wrapped comfortably around a brown leather briefcase on his lap. It looked like an old-fashioned doctor's case.

Feeling awkward, the others all stared straight ahead at the TV. On the news channel a highlights package of Woola's cutest moments was playing in slow-mo. They watched as a soap bubble burst delightfully above Woola's head. The camera zoomed in to catch the colours refracting off his globe-like eyes.

"Are you sure?" Charlie broke the silence. "I mean,

that alien really is quite cute, I'll give him that. He doesn't look like he wants to end anyone's world in 24 hours' time."

"No, you're right, not in 24 hours…" the old man replied. "If we allow for the length of the –ah-hm – press conference, it's probably closer to 23 and a half."

"I knew it," Paranoid Dave said, shifting on his seat and recovering his poise. He leant back on the bench and folded his arms. "I knew it. These guys have all been taken in." Paranoid Dave nodded vaguely at everyone in the pub. "They've got too used to false predictions of the end of the world. This time, it's really on."

The TV was now showing pre-recorded clips of other world leaders. There was the US President with his trademark grin, seated in the Oval office, pronouncing away, while his message of hope and opportunity was spelled out on the sub-titles below. A moment later, the TV cut to the French President, who was standing with self-conscious dignity in front of a large French flag. She looked statuesque and elegant as she read from the exact same script. A moment after that the Chinese President came on – the same script again.

Toby looked round the pub again at all the excitement and happiness that had broken out. He didn't know whether to party or feel stressed. Or party *and* feel stressed. Most awkward of all, he still hadn't been introduced to the old man.

"Hello – err, my name is Toby."

"Hello. I'm Professor James." The Professor beamed, apparently delighted to meet him.

"And I'm Charlie."

"Pleased to meet you," he replied. The Professor

turned to Dave.

"Hello, David – how are you?"

"You two know each other *already?*" Charlie asked in amazement.

"Might do." Paranoid Dave was playing it cool. "Hello Professor, how you getting on these days?" he asked, casually picking some crumbs from his beard.

"Very well, thank you, David. Yes, very well."

"So, about 23 and a half hours you reckon?" Dave asked, flicking a crumb away. "Yeah, figures."

"More or less. More or less. These things can be hard to judge. Hmm? But looking out the window, we might have a more immediate problem."

*

The TARP leader leant against one side of the doorway, his body tense, his assault rifle clutched vertically against his chest. Opposite him, TARP-2 was leaning against the other side of the doorway. The TARP leader turned to him and started gesticulating in military sign language with his right hand: he held four fingers up, jerked his thumb in the direction of the bar, then clenched his fist and made a vigorous up-and-down motion.

TARP-2 gulped nervously, silently wishing he'd paid more attention during the masculine-gestures module of his elite training course, and gestured back in a non-committal sort of way.

It did the trick. The leader nodded knowingly, then spoke into his headset with thrilling urgency:

"All TARP units – you are *GO GO GO!*"

*

On the far side of the pub, TARPs 3 and 4 were standing in a similar posture, heads tilted, two fingers pressed to their earpieces.

As soon as they heard the command, they looked across at each other and nodded. TARP-3 swivelled smartly to his right and plunged into the doorway. He moved in a kind of crouching walk, with his rifle mounted to his shoulder, that just made him look crack beyond crack.

Adopting the same crouching walk, TARP-4 followed in behind.

*

Under the window, near where Toby and his new friends were sitting, the final two members of the TARP team were crouched low like animals coiled to spring.

They heard the same command, and immediately sprung to their feet. One shouldered his weapon and started scanning the occupants of the pub through his rifle sight, while the other started to jimmy the window open.

*

The Squirrel & Acorn was under attack.

4

But not everything went quite to plan.

The TARP team, whose elite training had covered every form of combat scenario in every form of urban and non-urban terrain, had not thus far been trained for the haze of love, joy, and warm fellow-feeling into which they crouched on this unusual lunchtime in the Squirrel & Acorn.

As TARPs 3 and 4 edged forward, they found themselves quickly surrounded by a crowd, who were looking down at them with a loving curiosity. Some girls, who were still gyrating to the music, tried to draw TARP-4 into their dance. Some others started touching TARP-3's equipment in fascination.

"Are these guys aliens too?" someone called out above the music.

"Hey they might be," someone else replied.

"E-X-C-U-S-E M-E , A-R-E Y-O-U F-R-O-M Z-A-N-A-K?" one particularly attractive girl asked.

"No we're not. We're elite special forces, and would you please let us… Hey stop that!"

The ridiculously tall ginger bloke was leaning down and fingering TARP-3's eyepiece. He was mesmerised.

"Check that out," his friend, the short, dark-haired one, said. "Seamus thinks you have a third eye. Do you? Is it a third eye?"

"No it is not," TARP-3 replied testily. "It's a military-grade, combat-recon HUD Mark 4.6."

"Ah well, never mind. I'm Declan by the way," Declan said holding his hand out. When TARP-3 declined to shake it, Declan simply placed his hand on the barrel of TARP-3's gun and gently shook that instead.

"Peace, yeah?" Declan continued. "We're very pleased to welcome you to planet Earth. I think you're going to love this place. It's in a very good mood."

"Great, but I'm not from... Oh never mind." TARP 3 put two fingers to his earpiece. "TARP-leader, TARP-leader, come in TARP-leader... Boss, I've run into traffic – I can't get through the crowd. They don't seem to be scared of us..."

*

At the other end of the pub, the TARP leader had run into problems of his own.

"Excuse me!" the landlady exclaimed, as the TARP leader barged into her, "watch where yer going!" She just managed to hang on to a half dozen empty glasses which she was carrying back to the bar.

"I'm very sorry," the TARP leader replied, "but I need to get through urgently on Gov—"

"Oh, but look at you," she said, changing her tone as she looked him up and down. She started chewing her gum a little slower. "Well hello, sailor!"

"I'm not a sailor, I'm actually the TARP... Oh never mind, I need to get through on Government business. Excuse me, please."

"*Tarp*, yer say? Well I think yer *cute*." And with that she extracted a cocktail umbrella from an empty glass and slipped it behind his earpiece.

"I'm sorry, I need to get through!"

She yielded only the tiniest bit of room, forcing him to brush past her.

"Oh, like to play it rough, do yer?" she exhaled.

At that moment, the TARP leader heard TARP-3 come through on the intercom. He put his finger to his earpiece. "Yes?... What?... Copy that. I've run into traffic myself."

"Traffic? *Traffic?* Is that what I am?" the landlady pouted. And then, putting the empty glasses down on a nearby table, she laid one hand firmly on his shoulder and swung him back around towards her.

*

Toby looked at the others.

"Err, guys, who exactly are those figures dressed in black? I mean, I think they're carrying *guns*?" Toby was looking alternately at both doorways, where the commotion was brewing.

"Ah yes", the Professor replied, "the men with guns. I was wondering when they might catch up."

"They're looking for *you?* Why?"

"Hmm? Well, I would like to explain. But I'm not sure there's time right now, you see?" The Professor smiled vacantly at Toby, leaving him confused as to whether the situation was frightfully urgent or just a mild hiccup of a misunderstanding.

The Professor leaned across. "Err, David?"

"Professor?"

"Did I hear you mention another way out of the pub just now?"

Paranoid Dave nodded as his pale face blushed.

"Would you mind showing us? I think we're going to need to get out of here – how might one say it? – *urgently?* Hmm?"

"OK – no problem. I knew I'd need it one day." Paranoid Dave stood up purposefully. All his life he had dreamt of having to escape from the authorities. "Come on, follow me!"

The Professor and Charlie started following him towards the bar, keeping their heads low. Only Toby stayed at the table.

"Come on, hurry up! We've got to go!" Paranoid Dave hissed.

"But why?" Toby replied. "I haven't done anything wrong. I just came about a flat!"

"Too late," Paranoid Dave replied coolly. "They've probably already spotted you're with us. You're a marked man."

"*What?*"

Toby was about to protest when he turned to the window and saw two more figures in black right outside. One had managed to force the window open, and the other was starting to climb through it.

"You wanna hang out with them?" Paranoid Dave asked.

"Err, probably not…"

"Well get a move on then!"

*

"Here we are," Paranoid Dave called, as he opened a trapdoor in the floor. "The cellar!"

The four were behind the bar, crouching low. They wriggled behind Paranoid Dave and followed him through the trapdoor and down a dusty, stone staircase beneath. Toby went last, pulling the trap door shut behind him. As he did so, the noise of the pub was muffled to an indistinct *thump-thump-thump* of music through the ceiling above and the rumbling sound of a hundred-plus pairs of feet dancing and shuffling.

They followed Paranoid Dave as he weaved his way through a surprisingly long series of vaulted chambers. In each chamber, a single low-watt bulb hung from the low, arched ceiling, lighting their way darkly. The dank smell of stale beer hung in the air.

Paranoid Dave reached a low-slung door, half-hidden behind a keg of beer.

"Right guys, this is it," he said, as he wheeled the keg out of the way. "This is where they bring the barrels in. Behind this door is a small ramp that leads up to the side street."

Paranoid Dave opened two bolts, top and bottom. He gave the handle a firm twist and, yanking hard, the small door slowly opened, its base grinding hard against the dust of the cellar floor.

"Who wants to go first?" Paranoid Dave stood to one side of the open door. No-one replied. "Me then? I thought so. Here goes."

Paranoid Dave dropped down onto all fours and started crawling up the ramp towards the outside. The others followed, and Toby came last. As Toby reached the pavement, he stood back up and saw Paranoid Dave was gesturing excitedly from the side of the road.

"Guys, look, it's their van!"

"What about their van?" Charlie replied, "and keep your voice down."

"*They've left the keys in the ignition,*" Paranoid Dave squeaked with excitement. "We can take it. It's perfect."

"No it's not perfect. And of course they've left the keys in the ignition," Toby replied, rallying with a confidence he didn't realise he had. "They're some kind of ultra-secret army unit. No-one is dumb enough to steal their van from them. If they had a tank, they'd probably leave the keys in that too. There are some things you don't steal and this van is one of them."

"Why not? If we take it, we get away and they're stuck. It's doubly perfect." Paranoid Dave had already heaved himself into the driver seat.

"It's not perfect, it's insane! Don't you think they might have a tracking device on it?"

"Of course it's got a tracking device. Everything's got a tracking device. But it's fine. It'll be hours before they admit they lost the van. HQ will assume—"

Paranoid Dave was interrupted by radio static. On a small handset on the dashboard a red light came on. The gang all looked at it with horror.

"Come in, TARP-leader, this is TARP-base. Come in, TARP-leader, this is—"

Before Toby could stop him, Paranoid Dave lifted the small handset from the dashboard. He stared at it quizzically for a moment and then pressed down on a black lever. The red light went out.

"Hello, err, TARP-base..." Paranoid Dave started. "This is... TARP... Leader?"

Paranoid Dave released the lever. The red light came back on, but there was no reply.

"You have to say '*Over*'," Charlie whispered urgently from behind Toby's shoulder.

Paranoid Dave quickly fumbled with the lever. "Err, over!" he added.

"Have you secured the package?" the handset replied. "Over."

"Err, yes… Yes! The package is secure…" Paranoid Dave replied, and then added with a hint of bravado, "*the bird is caged.*" He looked down at the others and winked.

"*Excuse me?*" the handset blurted.

"Err, we have the package. Yes. We are heading back to base now. With the package. Over," Paranoid Dave replied. "And out."

"OK, roger that. Over and out." The red light switched off and the handset fell silent.

Paranoid Dave leaned back in the seat, triumphant. "You see? Sorted."

"Actually, for once you might've had a smart idea," Charlie replied. "Professor?"

The Professor shrugged his shoulders and smiled, as if to say it was all one to him. Paranoid Dave leaned across, unlocked the passenger door, and kicked it open with his foot. The Professor went round the front of the van, climbed in and settled himself in the middle of the front bench, carefully placing his leather case back on his lap. Charlie followed in after.

"Come on, Toby", she called, as she squeezed herself in, "there's just enough room for you. Hurry!"

Toby found himself putting one foot on the running board and starting to mount…

But no.

It just wouldn't do.

Charlie's extraordinary loveliness was an excellent reason to come along – but not excellent enough. He wasn't in the business of stealing Government property from a group of particularly well-armed, highly trained and generally single-minded soldiers, whose sole current focus was to pursue them.

And there was the real point.

Them – the others. Or at least, the Professor.

But definitely not Toby.

Heaven only knew what the Professor had done to provoke this. For all Toby knew, he deserved to be caught.

"Sorry, guys, but no. You go ahead. I'm just gonna duck out and take my chances."

"*What?*" Paranoid Dave hissed, leaning forward in the cab and turning to Toby. "You can't just duck out. If we leave you here, they'll catch you!"

"Sorry Dave, but no. None of this is my problem. They're not looking for me, I haven't done anything wrong. I just answered an ad for a flat share. And, anyway," he added, "why are you so keen for me to come along? I don't think you even like me much."

"Yeah, that's probably true…" Paranoid Dave mused for a moment. "But that's not the point. I don't like many people much. The point is: you're *supposed* to come along with us."

"Excuse me?"

"You, me, Charlie, the Professor – this can't be a coincidence. One pub, one planet… I can't explain it… But I *know* we're all supposed to be in this together."

"Yeah, Toby, I think we're going to need you," Charlie chipped in, with an imploring look and her most winning voice.

"Need me for what?" Toby replied. "The Earth has been sold to an alien, who I happen to think is perfectly cute and generally reasonable. Frankly I'm glad they've sold it – the alien can only be an improvement on the current bunch. And actually, I think you agree with me, Charlie."

Charlie looked confused for a moment. Toby took his chance and stepped down. "Sorry guys, but goodbye. And good luck."

Paranoid Dave shook his head, and revved the engine. Charlie cast a disappointed look in Toby's direction – briefly causing his soul to leap out of his body and jump in the van next to her – and then she pulled the door shut.

As the van pulled away, Toby stood on the pavement watching.

*

Suddenly Toby felt detached, like he was watching a movie.

He continued to watch that movie as two of the TARP team ran out of the pub, along the street, and chased after the van, gesturing and yelling. They stopped to raise their guns to their shoulders, but in the time it took them to point their guns, the van had careered round the corner and disappeared from view.

A moment later, another two soldiers ran out of the pub, and then another two. Finally the bloke who must have been their driver wandered out of the pub with a pint in his hand, looking dazed. Toby watched as all six soldiers started gesturing angrily at the driver and each other.

But his mind wasn't on them.

It was on the van, already far away in the tangled heart of the city and somehow carrying a piece of himself with it.

And so what was almost certainly the most eventful half hour of Toby's entire life drew definitively to a close.

5

The fleet controller aboard the Jagamath flag carrier uttered a single command. With enchanting delicacy, she fluted a harmonic chord from eight of her thirteen mouths, the precise nature of that chord communicating a simple instruction to her crew:

"Go!"

The command rippled through the 32 circular galleries of the fleet control room, a space several times larger than the Royal Albert Hall, where it unleashed a hive of activity. Navigators checked the ship's course, engineers checked the ship's sensors, priests said the ship's prayers.

The fleet controller looked back down at her console.

A barcode-like message was flashing. It provided the seven-dimensional coordinates required for hyperdrive navigation. Those coordinates would get her fleet to their drop point on the far side of the Universe. Below the coordinates, in accordance with interstellar travel protocols, was a range of other information about the destination planet, including an image of the primary intelligent species.

The fleet controller looked a little more closely.

A couple of silhouettes were flickering on the screen.

The images were grainy, little was known about the species. The fact there were only two figures suggested the species had – unusually – just two genders. Both silhouettes were a bit blobby, not particularly athletic, and not remotely threatening. There was nothing at all of the Vitruvian Man about them. But – nonetheless – they unmistakeably depicted a male and a female human being.

*

At that very moment, one particular example of that harmless, blobby species was aimlessly wandering the streets of one city on one island of that destination planet, feeling a little dazed and very confused.

Toby was trying to make sense of what had just happened. Of course he knew he was right to separate from the others. They were behaving like lunatics. And now they were being chased by lunatics. And it was all because of some unspecified thing the Professor had said or done at some unspecified moment in the past.

It was pretty hard to see things clearly.

The planet had just been sold to an alien race. That was pretty disorientating. The streets were filling up remarkably quickly with cars and people and bunting and a general sense of euphoria *precisely because* the planet had been sold to an alien race. That was pretty disorientating too. But most confusing of all for Toby was this nagging sense deep within him that he actually, weirdly, somehow *missed* the others.

Even though he'd only known them for half hour.

And they were lunatics.

Toby paused outside an electrical goods shop, where a couple of other passers-by had gathered at the window. Live news footage was playing on about two dozen flat-panel TVs of varying sizes. Woola was arriving at Windsor castle. Subtitles on one of the screens narrated breathlessly how Woola was about to have tea with the Queen of England. *Tea with the Queen!*

The cameras showed a smart dark blue van enter through the main gate. Toby watched the van travel with ceremonial slowness past St George's Chapel and up the hill. Another camera showed it stopping at the top of the hill, where four generations of the Royal family, and several rows of immaculately presented Grenadier Guards, were patiently waiting for their visitor from outer space.

Two Palace courtiers in long, smart frock coats opened the rear doors of the van and fastened the ramp. A few moments later Biffa emerged blinking into the light, and started pulling Woola's wheelie bin down the ramp. Woola was peeping out the top, nervously. You could just see his eyes and the top of his head and, either side of that, his two forelimbs gripping the edge of the bin tightly with all six digits.

Woola was about to meet Her Majesty.

This was it, *the moment.*

The wheelie bin came to a halt in front of the Royal presence. Her Majesty's face looked severe. No-one knew the protocol for a Royal engagement with an alien. Should Her Majesty shake Woola's forelimb? If so, *how?* Her Majesty was wondering, the courtiers were wondering, the world was wondering.

And no-one appeared more terrified than Woola. His six digits twitched and his eyes widened with apprehension, bordering on panic.

And then – in his anxiety – he let out an enormous

hiccup, and a huge soap bubble popped out of his mouth.

It floated high over the Royal party. Everyone stared up at it, mesmerised. The TV cameras zoomed in. The bubble wobbled, it wibbled, it hesitated…

And then it descended decisively towards one of Her Majesty's Great Grandchildren, who promptly reached up and burst it with his forefinger, squealing with delight. Her Majesty's face broke out into a spontaneous smile of disarming warmth. Woola giggled, and several heirs to the throne guffawed.

The bubble was broken, and so was the ice!

Toby heard laughter either side of him. He looked around. A couple of dozen passers-by had joined him at the window.

Back on the TV, the Queen could be seen leading Woola and Biffa on an inspection of the Grenadier Guards. As they moved past the ranks of soldiers, with Biffa pushing the wheelie bin, Woola's head swayed left and right, his eyes wide with wonder and his huge eyelids fluttering. But the Grenadiers stood firm. Apart from a few twitches, the hint of a smile here and there, they remained upright and uptight.

Woola reached the end of the line and was wheeled in front of a hulking Sergeant-Major. Woola tilted his head to one side, as nervous as a debutante, and quavered the words, "Thaaank youuuuuuu", at the burly figure in front of him.

It was too much for the Sergeant-Major.

Beneath his huge bushy hat, and behind his huge bushy moustache, he broke out into a broad boyish smile. And behind him, his Guardsmen did too. Thirty-six grown men, whose last few years had been a relentless diet of verbal abuse and grotesque physical exercise, punctuated by spells of standing absolutely still, were suddenly smiling like cherubs.

The cameras went click and there it was – the money shot – the front cover image for the morning papers, the shot that would be wired, fired, shared, and tweeted around the world.

The TV channel froze on that image. The commentary in the sub-titles was ecstatic. The others watching at the window either side of Toby broke into spontaneous applause.

Everyone but everyone loved Woola.

*

Toby wandered on.

Cars were tooting their horns in the street. Folk were tying bunting to the street lamps. Someone had hung an inflatable ET from their bedroom window. People were flooding back into the open spaces, taking ownership of their world again, coming together. Everything felt so right.

And somehow not so right.

Toby stepped it through in his mind.

Useless politicians sell heavily indebted planet to cute alien – Step 1. *Cute alien rescues planet from useless politicians* – Step 2. *Oh, and eliminates all debts* – Step 3. *Entire human population celebrates* – Step 4.

So far, so good.

But what about Step 5?

Everyone parties for evermore and never has to work again... While cute aliens look fondly on from another planet billions of light years away?

Hmm.

He had another go.

Step 5 – *More Za-Nakarians come over to visit, who turn out to be even cuter than Woola and not remotely interested in doing anything with their investment and... Everyone parties for evermore and never has to work again.*

Hmmm.

Toby came to a halt at a bus stop. No particular reason. Just his legs were a bit tired. He perched on the angled ledge, just beneath the adverts. It was one of those ledges that somehow managed to invite Toby's bottom and to repel it simultaneously. Toby sat awkwardly and looked around.

Neighbours were chatting to neighbours. Strangers were greeting strangers. Children were running freely down roads they normally only saw through a car window. A trestle table was being laid out for a street party.

And all this love and friendliness was happening in Britain. *Seriously?*

Talking to those lunatics in the pub, Toby admitted to himself, felt more real than this.

Then the No.55 pulled up.

Paranoid Dave, Charlie, the Professor – I mean they're crazies, Toby continued musing as he mounted the bus for no better reason than that he had nothing else to do, *but did I dismiss them too quickly?*

6

"What the heck?" Paranoid Dave didn't have the quietest voice. "It's *you* again!"

"Ah yes, right on cue," the Professor said.

"Hey! You should really stop stalking us," Charlie added, smiling. "Meantime, come and sit down." She patted the vacant seat next to her invitingly.

Toby's head was so fogged by shock, at that moment you could've hypnotised him with two swings of an old-fashioned pendulum. He automatically sat down next to Charlie.

"Hmm," the Professor mused, "now what are the chances of this? David?"

"I have absolutely no idea."

"Hang on", Toby spluttered, "what are you doing on a bus? I thought you had stolen a van?"

"Sssh!" Charlie put a finger to her mouth, and nodded towards the throng of other passengers. She nudged Toby in the ribs with her elbow. "Not so loud."

Paranoid Dave cut in. "Well we decided they'd probably figure out our little stunt with the van eventually. So once we were well away from the Squirrel & Acorn, we parked it on a side street—"

"—and escaped *on a bus?*"

"Sure," Paranoid Dave replied calmly. "Firstly, it's cheap. Really cheap. In fact, it's free – they're not taking payment anymore. So, second point, that means there's no payment device for them to track. They could try checking CCTV – third point – but the problem with CCTV cameras: they're everywhere. They've got too many of them. Are they really going to start with the buses? I don't think so."

"It's the perfect getaway vehicle when you think about it," Charlie added brightly. "And now we're heading to the Professor's house. He's going to show us proof that these aliens are up to no good. You coming?"

"Err…"

Charlie, Paranoid Dave and the Professor exchanged a few glances. Paranoid Dave spoke first.

"Listen, Toby. The whole thing is just too good to be true, right? I mean, sell the planet to a cute alien – and he *is* cute, I'll give you that – and solve all our problems. Does it really add up?"

Toby was unnerved to hear his own thoughts spoken out loud.

"I know you think Dave is a bit bonkers," Charlie pressed on. "And that the Professor might be some crazy old guy and I've wondered the same thing. *Apologies Professor—*"

"That's quite alright."

"—but I'm at least going to hear what he has to say, and see what he's got to show us. And I think you should too. Professor?"

"Hmm? Yes? Ah well, the Za-Nakarians. Yes. Well you see the thing is, Tobias, the Za-Nakarians have what you might call, err, *form*. This is very unlikely to be a simple sale-and-leaseback operation. Not," the Professor raised a finger to interrupt himself, "that sale-and-leaseback situations are ever simple. No, they're not. But the point, um, is – ah-hm – the point is the Za-Nakarians have colonised several other planets before. Well, at least several, perhaps more than sev—"

"How the Hell do you know *that*?"

"Ah yes, I thought you might ask that. That might take a little while to explain."

"Well what happened to the other planets they colonised?"

"Yes, that's what I would like to show you. If you would be so kind as to accompany us?"

Paranoid Dave leaned in and spoke with urgency.

"Think about it, Toby. Think about who we've sold our planet to. Forget the liquid eyes and the long lashes for a moment. Forget the cute dimples, the charming personality and the appealing laugh – oh, and the innocent delight he shows every time a soap bubble bursts…" Paranoid Dave paused for a moment, a slightly dreamy look coalescing across his face. Then he shook his head vigourously. "Anyway, forget all that, and what have you got?"

"A still remarkably cute alien?"

"No! A seriously rich alien who loves warm water, and whose name comes out something like 'Ruthless Ruler' if you just get rid of the w's and cut out the lisp."

"But lisps are when you can't pronounce an 's'."

"Whatever. You know what I mean."

Toby mouthed Woola's name to himself. *Woof-lis-Woola*. He substituted the r's for w's, and mouthed the name to himself… *Roof-lis-Roola…*

"Fine", he said. "But it's hardly Woola's fault if his name comes out that way in English. And seriously, what has any of this got to do *with me?*"

"What? You mean apart from the crazy coincidence

of you happening to get on the very same bus as the people you're trying to get away from, which obviously means – and call me a soothsayer if you must – that you should probably stop trying to get away from them. You mean apart from that?"

"Err, yes, apart from that."

"Well then, PR." Paranoid Dave leaned back and folded his arms.

"Excuse me?"

"PR."

"Meaning?"

"Public relations. Isn't it obvious?"

Toby stared blankly.

"Look, at some point, we're gonna learn the truth," Paranoid Dave continued. "And then, amongst other things, we're going to have persuade all these people" – he gestured at the folk on the bus – "that it is the truth. And when that moment comes, who's gonna believe me? No-one, that's who. I'm not dumb, I know everyone calls me paranoid…"

Charlie and Toby were about to protest, but Paranoid Dave waved his hand deprecatingly. "Don't worry, I've learnt to accept it. Being right all the time comes at a cost. Then there's the Professor. Well, you can see he's not exactly the persuasive type. *Apologies Professor*—"

"That's quite alright."

"And I'm a girl", said Charlie. "Let's face it: I might get taken seriously, but it's less likely." Charlie could see them about to protest. "Come on guys, how many female world leaders are there? How many female government ministers? Or spokespeople? One in ten? One in twenty? I don't think we'll have time to play those probabilities."

"Oh come on. That can't be true", Toby kicked in, finally finding his voice. "Aren't you the only one here with a job?"

"Actually, I quit yesterday. That's why I slept in this morning." Charlie looked away, her spirit suddenly looking crushed.

"Oh."

"So we need *you*," Paranoid Dave pressed home his advantage. "Someone so ordinary, so uninspiring, so *uninspired*, so without an agenda, that if we have to persuade all these ordinary people to look beyond Woola's extraordinary charm – and we probably will – you're the man to do it."

"Thanks," Toby replied, "so flattering."

"Don't mention it," Paranoid Dave replied, leaning back against his seat in the manner of a man who's delivered what needed to be delivered. "Like I said, *PR*."

Toby swallowed.

He looked around the bus. Two children were playing in the aisle, swishing and swaying in a Woola-like way at each other, while blowing soap bubbles from a small plastic tube. At the far end, he could see a toddler, sitting on her father's lap, clutching an inflatable space rocket.

Toby took a deep breath and looked Paranoid Dave in the eye.

"You're rude and unpersuasive," Toby said, "pretty hopeless really—"

"Look I didn't mean to—"

"—so I'll do it. If you're going to be that offensive, I can at least try to contribute a little politeness to proceedings."

"Alright!" Paranoid Dave threw Toby a high five,

which he didn't quite spot in time, and missed rather awkwardly.

"But I'm still not convinced. And if anybody points a gun at me – or a taser or a laser or even a… whatever – *then I'm out.* Clear?"

7

Imperceptible at first, the Jagamath flag carrier started to nudge forward from its extra-lunar moorings. A few more squirts from the bow thrusters, a gentle buzz from the aft-mounted ion engines, and this colossal beast of the interstellar plains edged its way out of port. Small drones and service modules from the local harbour contractor darted out the way, like frightened birds from the hide of a waking rhino.

A few seconds later, and the rest of the Jagamath haulage fleet started to edge their way out of port. From docking bays that stretched in a continuous circle the entire way around the port moon, all 377 bulk carriers started to move outwards and away. Some minutes after that, they started accelerating towards cruising speed. They would spend another half hour at cruising speed, just long enough to gather into formation and to shake off any smuggler craft hoping to cadge a lift in hyperdrive.

After that, hyperdrive.

The Jagamath fleet on the move was a spectacle to behold. But although colossal, that wasn't the truly impressive thing about them. *Reliability* was what they were really about. The Jagamath were stand-out the most reliable hauliers in the Universe. By far. In the last 100,000 Earth years, they hadn't dropped a single cargo. They hadn't dropped one portion of a single cargo. If it was on the manifest, it was as good as delivered.

One thing that helped was the sheer strength of each bulk carrier. The outer skin was a 100-yard thick lattice of obdurite, a high tensile nano-alloy of obscurium and the toughest known substance in the Universe. The main nightmare for space hauliers, apart from the usual piracy issues, was passing through an uncharted asteroid belt at speed. So the Jagamath spec'ed their carriers to survive a full-frontal impact. What made obdurite so extraordinarily suitable, especially when constructed in a self-reinforcing lattice, was not just that it was unbreakable – which of course it was – but also it was a tiny bit *squidgy*. Not squidgy if you were to punch it – that would break your knuckles – but squidgy if it collided with, say, a large chunk of intergalactic debris. The obdurite would yield, absorb the impact, and then bounce back into shape, sending the unfortunate object off with a flea in its ear, while the crew would be largely oblivious to any collision. Just a yard thickness of obdurite lattice was enough to defend most spaceships against the most brutal of impacts. But 100 yards? If truth be told, the Jagamath fleet on the move *was* an asteroid belt. The fleet controller, in both her hearts, felt sorry for anyone, or anything, trying to cross it.

As to the size of an individual Jagamath bulk carrier, the best way to imagine that is to picture one passing overhead. Imagine for a moment being on a planet, where a Jagamath delivery happens to be due. Then imagine, say, having a picnic in the countryside on this planet when a Jagamath bulk carrier starts to pass overhead. Say the carrier is moving at a typical tropospheric idling speed of around a hundred miles per hour. If the carrier started to pass overhead as you unwrapped the starter, you wouldn't see the back end of it until you were dabbing the crumbs from your mouth at the end of the cheese course. Really long in other words. And quite chubby too.

The fleet controller looked with satisfaction at the reports filing onto her console from around the control room. The course plot was confirmed, the navigational risks had been mitigated, the fleet was performing well. She pulled a large and rather theatrical lever to her right and watched as the lights on the panel around her started flickering from amber to green. One after another the 377 carriers confirmed their hyperdrive status. Soon all had turned green. All bar one, which she spotted from her left ventral eye. *There was always one.* She tapped her toes with a slight mew of impatience as it switched to green, then amber again, and eventually green.

I shall have to look into BC144, the fleet controller made a mental note to herself.

Then with some relief she fluted the final order and the Jagamath fleet switched up to hyperspeed.

The 377 bulk carriers wove a metallic thread through the very fabric of space-time, bearing as they went their unfeasibly large payload towards its wholly unwitting recipients.

*

"Ah, do come in my dears, please do come in!"

As the large oak door swung back, they were greeted by a warm Scottish voice.

"Good day, Mrs B. You are well? Hmm?" The

Professor asked with a chuckle as he entered, his eyes brightening.

"Oh yes, very well, thank you," she replied. "Now do come in dears, you'll catch your death of cold!"

Mrs B ushered in Toby, Charlie, and Paranoid Dave, who crossed the threshold in several states of wonder. They were wondering at the Professor's large and beguiling house, especially when they were expecting a shabby and dimly lit bolthole somewhere. They were wondering why they might die of cold since it wasn't especially cold outside.

And, lastly, they were wondering what on Earth the Professor was doing with a hedgehog.

As they entered the hallway, the Professor promptly knelt down, reached into his leather case, extracted a small hedgehog and placed it carefully on the floor. The creature padded towards Mrs B with perfect self-composure. As the hedgehog reached her, it raised its nose and flattened its spines a little, whereupon the Mrs B gently patted it behind the head.

"Oh, there you are, Carruthers," Mrs B said cheerfully, leaning down. "You're a wee dear, aren't you dear?"

Mrs B was ready with a few small sticks of carrot in her hand, one of which she held out towards the hedgehog. The hedgehog proceeded to nibble the extended carrot with unruffled poise, betraying not the slightest alarm at his unconventional journey to the house nor the three unfamiliar faces staring at him. He had dark chocolate eyes and a fetching white fringe of fur around his forehead and cheeks. He looked, it must be said, as amiable as a hedgehog could look.

Toby looked up from this strange scene, blinking and very much needing a dose of normality.

He was to be sorely disappointed.

As he looked around the large hallway he had just entered, the first thing he noticed was a suit of armour in the opposite corner. The glint of steel looked particularly fierce against the polished wood panelling behind it. Either side of it were two large tropical plants, bursting out of gleaming brass tubs. They had deep green, pendulous fronds and ravishing purple flowers. Either side of them, large archways led to other rooms and, over to the left, a wide wooden staircase swept magnificently upwards to the first floor.

"Oh I think he's missed me, Professor. Yes he has, the dear wee critter," Mrs B said warmly, standing back up. "Now, Professor, a quick check. You werenae followed here, were you?"

"No, no, I don't think so."

"And you took the usual precautions?"

"We took the bus."

"The No.34?"

"No, the 55. We varied the route."

"Oh that's good. Did you pay with cash?"

"No payment needed at all."

"Perfect."

Perfect? Toby thought. *Seriously?* Toby had to say something. Mrs B – whoever she was – had to know they'd stolen a van from people *who had guns*.

"Professor, I don't mean to be rude," he said, "but is there any chance that the people who were chasing us, they maybe know your address anyway?"

"Oh no, haha!" the Professor laughed, while Toby wondered what was so funny. "I'm very discrete about this address. It's not even registered to my, umm, name. It's my little hideaway."

"It's true," Paranoid Dave added. "I had no idea the

Professor lived here. I thought you just lived in that dingy flat on campus."

"And, just to be safe, the Professor hasn't visited here once these last three months," Mrs B added, "not during daylight hours."

"Err, right…" Toby replied indecisively.

"Oh good," Mrs B said, as if to say the matter was settled. "Now, none of us have been introduced properly. Professor?"

"Ah yes, of course. Yes, indeed. Please do meet Mrs B everyone. Mrs B is my, ah-hm…" The Professor trailed off, vacantly.

"I keep house for the Professor," Mrs B continued unselfconsciously. "Oh, Professor, you're no use at all. Now, you must be David? Halloo. And you're Charlotte? How do you do." Mrs B very deliberately reached out and shook each of their hands. "Ah, and *you* must be Tobias."

Mrs B took Toby's hand in both of hers, and looked him closely in the eye, lingering in the handshake just a little longer than customary.

Mrs B was in her sixties, with greying hair pulled back into a tidy bun at the back of her head. She cut a bustling figure, a little portly, but with an irresistibly rosy complexion on her friendly face. Her manner put Toby at ease, despite the fact that she had no business knowing his name, and despite the fact she was still holding his hand.

"Now," she said briskly, as she broke away. "I imagine our guests will be wanting a drink. Would fresh coffee do?"

Mrs B scanned the small semi-circle of nodding faces.

"And where would you like me to serve it,

Professor?"

"Ah yes, perhaps in the conservatory? I have a little job to complete."

"Why of course," Mrs B beamed at the group. "It's such a pleasure to have company in the house. It's been far too long you know, Professor," she tutted cheerfully over her shoulder as she disappeared off through one of the archways.

"Well, very good. Perhaps we should, err... Perhaps we can..." the Professor dithered at the others, looking strangely awkward. "Ah! Let's follow Carruthers. This way, hmm?"

The trio looked speechlessly at the tiny hedgehog, who was padding nonchalantly towards the other archway that led from the hall. He walked calmly past the suit of armour, under the arch, and round a corner, with the Professor just behind.

Paranoid Dave, Charlie and Toby looked at each other, shook their heads in disbelief, and set off after them.

As Toby was leaving the hallway, he glanced briefly behind. One thing momentarily caught his eye. It was the main doorway, through which they'd entered – or, more particularly, a large stainglass window above it. *Who has a stainglass window in their house?* Sunlight was streaming through the window, illuminating what looked like a knight on horseback. There was some kind of creature at the feet of the horse, with mountains and forests stretching behind.

At least that's what Toby thought he glimpsed. An instant later he was passing through a couple more astonishing rooms, and then into the conservatory.

*

The TARP leader replaced the receiver of his satellite phone, and digested the information he'd just been given with a thoughtful expression.

With two tours of Helmand under his belt, and five years as a TARP operative, he wasn't naturally prone to giving up. He surveyed his team and quickly assessed what equipment and weaponry they still had with them.

Then he looked up and down the street at the slow-moving mass of vehicles, tooting and celebrating their way along the road, and he made a decision.

The situation wasn't perfect but it wasn't lost either. Far from it. He almost relished the challenge that his quarry had laid down. This was going to be harder than he thought, but that would make the outcome all the more satisfying. The truth was, the TARP-leader lived for the chase.

"What is it, boss? What do we do now?" TARP-2 asked nervously.

"Follow me", he said, "we're going to settle this the old-fashioned way."

8

Toby watched the Professor at work.

Humming quietly to himself, he was cutting open some small brown seed pods with a paring knife. He was seated at a large round wooden table in a sort of clearing towards the middle of his conservatory. To one side of the table was an old-fashioned black stove, from which a flue extended all the way to the roof. There were a few seed packets and some gardening tools scattered across the table and, just at the Professor's elbow, Carruthers was curled comfortably in a tiny basket. His head was resting on his forepaws on the lip of the basket. The hedgehog's eyes were half-closed and his snouty face had what Toby could only describe as a contented look.

"Oh hello," the Professor said, looking up. "Do, err, have a look round the conservatory if you like, hmm? I shan't be a… I shan't… Yes, no I shan't…"

The Professor lost his thread, as he carefully prised open another seed pod.

"Toby! *Psst!*" Charlie called quietly from between some bushes a few yards away. "Come and look!"

Toby walked down a narrow pathway to join her, passing between gorgeous orchids on either side and brushing palm-like fronds from his face as he went. This was no ordinary conservatory. For one thing, it was long. It stretched the entire length of the Professor's surprisingly large house. And for another, it was tall. Two storeys tall. Toby could see the windows of the first-floor bedrooms looking *into* the conservatory. Above that slender iron spars rose towards a central ridge. The roof of the conservatory was supported by a line of graceful iron pillars that ran its entire length.

"Look!" Charlie said, touching Toby's arm, "up there!"

Toby followed her gaze upwards and saw a pair of cockatoos, perched on the branch of a palm tree, staring down at them incuriously. Their plumage of bright white and yellow was brilliantly illuminated in the slanting sunshine.

"Dave," Charlie spoke to her other side, "why didn't you tell us the Professor lived in a place like this?"

"I already said, I never got invited here before," he replied defensively. He was gazing up at the palm trees, clutching his black leather coat bashfully around his tummy. "I guess I didn't know the Professor well enough. I didn't even know he was so… wealthy."

"Come to think of it, Dave," Toby started to ask, "how *do* you and the Professor know each other?"

But before Toby could get an answer, Mrs B reappeared.

*

"Coffee everybody!"

Mrs B set down a tray with five mugs and a large porcelain jug on the round table, as the others came over to join her. The aroma the freshly ground coffee wafted across the conservatory. Toby looked across at Carruthers and could swear that his nose was twitching in appreciation.

"Yes, Carruthers," the Professor said, looking at Toby over the top of his half-moon spectacles. "Yes, he has a tremendous sense of smell. Quite exceptional, you know, hmm? Even for a hedgehog."

Toby nodded at the Professor, while wondering how well an average hedgehog could smell, let alone an exceptional one.

"He can detect the slightest variations in scent," the Professor said as he resumed his work. He was now grinding the seeds with a small pestle and mortar. "And in the most unlikely of circumstances. On one occasion, when we were travelling down to West Sussex together, he could even smell me accidentally starting to fill the car with petrol. Not diesel, you see, but petrol. Yes, he can smell danger a mile off... Petrol, you see..."

The Professor's voice trailed away, as he carefully tipped his finely ground powder into a tiny round silver dish.

"Ah, perfect," the Professor exhaled, as he hinged shut a tiny lid over the tiny dish. "Done. Now where were we? Ah yes, these seeds, you were asking about them—"

"Was I?"

"—they come from this little fellow," the Professor continued, gesturing to a shrub just to his left. "I picked these pods six months ago, and have been letting them dry. Yes, this undistinguished bush is called *Bella claudianum*."

"Excuse me?"

"*Bella claudianum* – named after Great Uncle Claude. Named *by him* in fact. Haha!"

"So why are you collecting them?" Charlie asked.

"Oh, they have special properties – they're a mild hallucinogen. They induce the so-called 'reverse truth' effect."

"What does that mean?" Paranoid Dave's eyes narrowed.

"What does that mean? Yes… It puts the user at a certain detachment from things. They allow you to resist hypnosis, to see through—"

"Oh Professor, you must stop telling stories," Mrs B interrupted. "I think you had something urgent to tell your young guests?"

"Oh yes, yes of course." His tone changed. "Yes, I do." The Professor pulled his gold fob watch from his tweed waistcoat and looked at it pensively. "Yes, we must get to the matter of the Za-Nakarians."

He snapped his fob watch shut again and, as he did so, Charlie, Toby and Paranoid Dave snapped out of the reverie that had overcome them since entering the Professor's house.

They stared at him, while he carefully removed his half-moon spectacles, polished them with a small chamois cloth, and replaced them on his nose. As he did so, he looked around at each of them.

He drew his breath in. It was time for the truth.

*

"I believe the Za-Nakarians plan to develop our planet as a tropical tourist resort."

The Professor paused to let his words sink in.

None of the youngsters reacted.

"Hmm? Oh, they plan to do some of the more usual colonial activities too – a little mineral extraction here, dump some of their more troublesome pollutants there. That kind of thing. No, but mostly, to begin with, they believe the Earth has great potential as a tourist destination."

"So…" Toby glanced around the table, looking for support, "…where's the big deal?"

"Right…" Charlie began tentatively, "…so they basically want to do the things we like doing already? Polluting and partying. Right?"

"Actually, it sounds quite cool," Toby added, warming to the idea. "It sounds harmless."

"Ha ha! Yes, yes, harmless – I completely agree with you," the Professor replied amiably. "Unfortunately, we're both wrong. You see, they want a tropical resort. Very warm, very humid, lots of beaches."

"You already said," Charlie replied. "And?"

"They love daylight."

"Ok… Still sounds harmless."

"Minimum sixteen to twenty hours continuous sunlight each day. They're highly evolved, you see? They only sleep three to four hours per night. They don't like spending long hours in the darkness. They get scared."

Charlie looked across to Toby and they both shrugged their shoulders.

But Paranoid Dave's eyes gradually lit up.

"No way… You mean…?"

"Yes, David, I do."

Paranoid Dave pumped his fist into his other palm. "*The dogs.*"

"What is it? I don't get it?" Toby asked.

"Think! Where do you find eighteen hours of daylight?" Paranoid Dave stood up and started pacing round the table.

"Scotland maybe – during the summer," Toby ventured, swivelling in his chair to follow Paranoid Dave. "Perhaps England for a short while in late June and early July?"

"And where else?"

"I dunno, maybe New Zealand, during their Summer?"

"Exactly. But never in the tropics – always around twelve hours there."

Paranoid Dave sat down, stared at the Professor, and stabbed a single pudgy finger into the table. "They're gonna try to fix our climate, right?"

"I'm afraid so."

"Turn the higher and lower latitudes into a tropical paradise, while the two poles melt and the tropics just – I don't know – *burn?*"

"Something like that. Effectively a return to the late Cretaceous period—"

"—when sea levels were what, like—"

"—fifty metres higher? Correct."

"*Damn.*"

Paranoid Dave threw his body back against the chair and stared upwards. "It's just what I thought. They like it warm, they like it wet, and they're ruthless."

He looked at the gorgeous greenhouse around him, with wonder and horror written simultaneously on his chubby features. Then he promptly leaned forward, urgently unwrapped a toffee, popped it in his mouth and took a slurp of coffee. "And they're gonna do all this just because they can't get enough daylight hours in the tropics?"

"Correct again."

"And a 50-metre sea-level rise?" Paranoid Dave

stood up again, restless. "Holland would be a complete write-off. So would large chunks of Belgium. Ditto England. But the Highlands of Scotland—"

"—would become the most lovely of tropical archipelagos," the Professor took over from his horrified former pupil. "Is that what you were thinking? Hmm?"

"Just a minute you two. Just stop for a second." Charlie joined back in, trying to grasp the situation. "Let me try to get this straight. You're saying that the Za-Nakarians love warm, wet, tropical conditions?"

"Correct," the Professor replied.

"And they like holidays, they like to travel?"

"Correct again."

"And they like sunlight, say sixteen to twenty hours a day?"

"Exactly."

"So to achieve all that, they've bought planet Earth, they're going to trash our climate and turn the northern and southern latitudes into a tropical resort? Just so they can enjoy tropical conditions *for a few extra hours per day*?"

"You've got it!" The Professor clapped his hands together with delight.

"Great. Got it. I understand what you're saying." Charlie lent back on her chair and folded her arms. "But I don't believe it. I'm sorry, Professor, I'm not buying it. It's madness."

"Yeah, me neither." Toby exchanged a supportive glance with Charlie. At that particular moment, getting into Charlie's good books seemed a much better option than believing his planet was about to be trashed for a few extra hours of sunbathing.

"Guys, listen." It was Paranoid Dave. He had

stopped his pacing on the opposite side of the table to Charlie and Toby. He dropped his voice and leant towards them. He jabbed a single pudgy finger into the table. "Think about it. It's economics."

"Meaning?" Charlie asked.

"Let's look at this the other way round," Paranoid Dave replied. "You're both saying that it's totally absurd that the Za-Nakarians would come and trash our planet for a few extra hours of sunbathing per day?"

"Exactly, absolutely, makes no sense."

"Right," Paranoid Dave replied in his most reasonable voice, "the way it's absurd that we go and trash a tropical island somewhere, just so we can take it in turns get the occasional week of sunshine during the winter months. Absurd like that?"

"Exactly! No, wait, hang on, no…" Toby stuttered. "That's not fair, that's totally different."

"Oh it is? Because – let me think now – because we haven't just trashed one tropical island, but lots and lots of them? In fact, pretty much all of them. Plus the coastline of a whole bunch of continental tropical nations too. Because of that?"

"No! Because… Because at least we're not trashing their climate!"

"True, we just disrupt the local economy and build over environmentally sensitive areas, while the profits are mostly repatriated back to the same rich countries that are sending the tourists over in the first place. But the CO_2 from our long-haul flights – which kinda does affect the climate actually – I guess you're saying at least that affects our climate as much as theirs? Is that it?"

Paranoid Dave arched a single eyebrow and stared at them both. Toby and Charlie found themselves wilting in front of it.

"Look," he continued, "I'm not trying to make you feel bad. I'm just saying that when you mix wealth with opportunity, people do selfish things, right? Often without even realising. So I think we should hear the Professor out."

Toby turned to the Professor.

"OK, OK, let's just suppose you're right, Professor. And I'm not saying you are, but let's just suppose you are. Why, oh why, bother with this whole purchase arrangement? And why bother with the charm offensive? In fact, why bother being *so damn cute?*"

"Exactly," Charlie chimed.

"Why not just send in their warship-spaceship thingies and zap everyone, and then build their resort?"

"Oh my Heavens – they couldn't possibly do that." The Professor was shocked. "They're peace-loving."

"They're *what?*"

"Peace-loving. And anyway, there are strict rules against that kind of thing. It would never pass at the United Inter-Galactic Council."

"The *who?*"

"The United Inter-Galactic Council – it's like the um… Err… Like the UN. But for the whole Universe. They meet regularly on the Senate Moon in the Aranoid Cluster. They ensure that the laws of the Universe are obeyed. Not the physical laws – no, haha! They keep breaking those. No, I mean the legislative laws. You have to understand, the Earth has, ah-hm, protected status."

"It *does?*"

"Oh yes, we've been designated 'EIA'."

"Eh?"

"Endangered Indigenous Aliens."

"Err right…" said Toby wondering again how someone as vague as the Professor managed to keep bamboozling him. "But if we've been given this protected status, why aren't we being protected?"

"Oh but you are. The Za-Nakarians applied for permission to purchase the planet before approaching the G7. They argued that they – as owners – would be best placed to defend Earth from less reputable colonisers."

"And their plan to screw our climate?" Paranoid Dave asked.

"Oh, that's been cleared too. I've not seen it, but I understand they've submitted a full environmental management plan. You see? They've argued they're returning Earth's flora and fauna to its original – that's to say, late Cretacious – state. The planet as it was prior to the K-T extinction. Something like that. My source wasn't totally specific."

"Who's your source?"

"What's the K-T extinction?"

Toby and Charlie looked at each other, bewildered.

"The Cretaceous-Tertiary extinction," Paranoid Dave replied. The Professor nodded approvingly. "The last major extinction event on Earth. The one that wiped out the dinosaurs."

"But what about all the damage they'll do, Professor?" Charlie asked. "Are they sick or something?"

"Well you have to understand", the Professor continued, "most Za-Nakarians will be unaware of the damage. And in any case, I understand they have many established charities on Za-Nak to help displaced populations from their colonies. They're very caring."

"Professor, I really don't mean to be rude. But this

could all be complete hokum." Charlie's eyes were flashing. Toby looked across with admiration. "I mean, it sounds plausible when you say it – but what actual *evidence* do you have?"

"Oh my dears," Mrs B called out. She was standing at the entrance to the conservatory. "It's your alien friend. He's on the television and he's not where we thought he was... They must've put him on a plane. You better come and look."

9

Woola surged and dived and plashed. He pirouetted, he somersaulted and as his aquiline – but ever so slightly tubby – torso disappeared beneath the water, audiences around the world gasped in delight at his clumsy grace.

Watching a Za-Nakarian swim was like watching a cherub fly.

"Give us a wave, Woola!" yelled the paparazzi.

"Smile!"

"Blow us a soap bubble!"

"Flutter those eyelashes!"

With each cry from the press, Woola did his best to oblige.

"Do the Nessie look, Woola!"

"Yeah, a little bit mysterious, pal!"

Nessie?

Woola had been briefed by Biffa on this one.

He took a deep breath, disappeared underwater, and stayed there. The paparazzi went quiet. They waited.

And waited.

The excitement rose.

Where was Woola? Was he ok?

Suddenly one of the TV cameras picked up a line of air bubbles tracing a path fifty yards out over Loch Ness and disappearing. "Over there!" someone yelled, and the cameras started flashing again furiously.

Then the bubbles faded.

Nothing again.

Stillness.

Just when folk were starting to get properly anxious, and the nearby rescue boat was about to power up, and everyone was wondering who would inherit the Earth if Woola died and whether in fact a will had been made at all and, if it had, would it be valid outside of the Earth's jurisdiction… Just when everyone was fretting in other words, a head broke slowly, mysteriously through the still waters of the loch. It was about a hundred yards away. It rose higher and higher, twisted slowly to the left and slowly to the right. A foot or two behind his neck, a short length of Woola's back emerged, describing a gentle arc above the water.

The Loch Ness monster itself.

Woola held the pose for a few seconds, before diving down again, bobbing back up and swimming triumphantly to the shore.

Another perfect photo-shoot.

As Woola returned to the pontoon and clambered up the ramp out of the water, the whole crowd erupted in cheers and whoops and whistles. Viewers around the world wanted to laugh, they wanted to cry. They were captivated. It felt like Nessie existed after all. And if a childhood fairy tale like that could be true, what wasn't possible in this brave new Universe?

*

One of the TV cameras stayed on Woola as he clambered back up onto the pontoon. He was shivering slightly. Woola turned to Biffa and said something in Za-Nakarian.

The words had an electric effect.

Biffa turned to the attendants around them and started issuing instructions. One attendant rushed over with a large white towelling robe and draped it over Woola's shoulders. Another turned a hairdryer on and blew it towards Woola's face. Two more rushed down the pontoon to fetch the wheelie bin. They pushed it back towards Woola as quickly as they dared, with the warm, steaming water inside sloshing and spilling. Another attendant came running behind with a set of wooden steps. They stopped in front of Woola, and the steps were positioned against the wheelie bin.

Woola flippered his way up the steps, paused at the top, turned to Biffa and spoke in Za-Nakarian. There was a scowl on his face and his words were quite clear this time:

"Bume-lvak-menla-fring? Lala-fkng-frafra!"

With that, he discarded the white towelling robe, and slipped into the steaming water inside the wheelie bin, emitting a long sigh of relief as he did so.

*

"Bume-lvak-menla-fring? Lala-fkng-frafra!"

The Professor repeated the words to himself, musingly. "Hmm… Interesting."

"You can't actually translate that, by any chance, Professor?" Charlie asked.

"Hmm? Oh yes, yes, I think so. Ha ha!" The Professor chuckled to himself. His eyes wandered back to the TV. Woola was being wheeled carefully back along the pontoon towards the press corps.

"Well, could you then?" Charlie turned the sound down on the remote. "Translate it, I mean?"

"Hmm? Oh I see. Well, it's a little rude actually. But it comes out something like this: *'Are you sure it's not always this cold? That was BLEEP-ing freezing...'*"

The Professor paused to chuckle at the way he had avoided any rudeness. "Something like that, anyway."

Toby, Charlie and Paranoid Dave looked at each other uneasily. As evidence, it was nothing. A scowl, an expletive – it proved nothing. Who wouldn't find the deep dark waters of Loch Ness freezing?

And yet.

"Of course that's not what I brought you here to see. No, no," the Professor continued, "you must see some *real* evidence. Now... Let me see, where did I put that envelope.... Haha! Funny the things one misplaces... Now let me see..."

The Professor started rooting around on his cluttered desk for what was, at that particular moment, the most important envelope on the planet.

They had all moved to the Professor's study to watch the television. As the Professor searched for his envelope, Toby's eyes wandered round the room. It was all leather furniture and bookshelves. In fact there were books everywhere. Floor-to-ceiling. Shelf after shelf. Leather-bound books, antique books, hardbacks, paperbacks, folios. Against the wall opposite the Professor's desk, Toby spotted a gleaming brass staircase that spiralled up towards a mezzanine gallery. The gallery was also lined with shelves upon shelves of books.

Charlie meantime was still staring at the TV. She was perched against a small table in the centre of the room, absent-mindedly fingering a large antique globe next to her, as she watched Woola greeting the crowds.

Toby took a seat just a couple of yards away on a studded green leather sofa. It was a little hard, a little uncomfortable, but terribly distinguished. Toby felt important just from sitting on it, like he was privy to the great affairs of state.

And then Toby had a thought.

He *was* privy to the great affairs of state. Kind of.

"Ah!"

Toby gave a start.

"Found it! Yes, yes, here we are. Now…" The Professor brandished a large brown envelope, "do please come and look!"

Paranoid Dave, Charlie and Toby gathered round him at his desk. He extracted a single photo. He laid it down carefully on his desk, just next to Carruthers' basket. The hedgehog looked up contentedly, sniffed the photograph approvingly, and laid his head back down.

The image in the photo was spectacular.

"Yes, yes, you see. Here we have a planet known as, let me think now, Halitron B, I believe. It's in a charming little spiral arm galaxy in the Gamma quadrant of the Trop-D232 cluster. Is that right? Yes, look it says so in the corner."

The photo showed a verdant, lush, blue-green planet, with a few cloud formations here and there. A single well-defined ice cap was visible at one of its poles. The shape of the continents was different to Earth – more landmass, less ocean – but otherwise it looked similar.

"This photo was taken as the planet was sold to the Za-Nakarians. Looks rather nice, doesn't it? Rather inviting. Never been myself…" The Professor fished for a moment in his envelope and extracted a second photo. "Now here's a shot of the same planet. You see? Look at the time stamp in the, err, on the… Just here. You see? Taken at the same time of day, in the same season, and from the same location. But five years later…"

He laid the second photo next to the first.

"Doesn't look too bad?" Toby blurted out with relief.

"No… No, wait. Look again…" Charlie said. She stared at it intently. "Look, the ice cap has mostly retreated. There are dense cloud formations – low-pressure storm fronts – but weirdly, they're concentrated over what must be their equator."

Charlie was leaning right over the picture, absorbed.

"If you look carefully, I think the coastline has retreated in a few places. Makes sense if that ice cap was continental. And look, a broad desert belt has appeared either side of the equatorial region, here and…" Charlie paused.

"And what?" the Professor urged her on.

"Well it doesn't make sense. There seem to be dense cloud formations – storm fronts – over the northern and southern oceans, but not over the land. Strange. Maybe it's just coincidence, when this photo was taken, or maybe—"

"Hang on," Toby cut in, "how do you know all this stuff?"

Toby felt an elbow land sharply in his ribs. It was Paranoid Dave. He hissed in a low voice, " *B e c a u s e s h e s t a r t e d a P h D i n A t m o s p h e r i c C h e m i s t r y, t h a t ' s w h y* ."

"Oh, OK. That's great," Toby whispered back. "So why are we whispering?"

Paranoid Dave held a finger to his mouth, and

mouthed back under his breath: "*B e c a u s e   s h e
n e v e r   f i n i s h e d   i t .*"

"Oh right, sorry, got it", Toby whispered back.

"No, it's alright guys." Charlie had heard anyway.
"That's all in the past now." She paused for an instant
as a cloud passed over her face. Then she turned back
to the Professor.

"Professor – looking at these two photos – and
assuming they really are just five years apart – I would
guess this planet is suffering a catastrophic warming
episode. Although some aspects of it still don't quite
add up. But anyway, that's my opinion."

"Ah yes, yes, spot on," the Professor replied, his
eyes twinkling. "Now look at this photo, taken thirty
years later."

He laid a third photo to the right of the other two.

The gang gasped.

"Please tell me that's not the same planet?"
Paranoid Dave

"Oh my God. It is, isn't it?" Charlie's hand went up
to her sunglasses.

"I'm afraid so."

The gang were looking at a reddish globe. The ice
cap had disappeared completely. The oceans were still
there, in vivid blue, but it was the continents that were
most changed. Colours of brilliant red and gold.
Martian. And not a cloud in sight.

"Thirty years, you said?" Charlie asked the
Professor.

"Thirty years."

"Biologically inert?"

"More or less. Some primitive life forms on land,
clinging to the coastline, hmm? It's actually the oceans
that were most affected, so I'm told. They're almost

completely lifeless, which is why—"

"—they're such a brilliant blue." Charlie finished the Professor's sentence. "Just like the Permian extinction."

But there was more. The Professor pulled out another set of photos from the envelope. They showed another planet before, during and after a Za-Nakarian occupation. The same process. A gorgeous, living planet turned first into a strangely storm-ridden planet, and then into an inert globe of deserts. They stared in silence. The Professor pulled out another set of three photos. The same again. He was about to pull out another set.

"Oh my God… Just stop for a moment, Professor, please?" Charlie was overwhelmed. She stepped away from the desk and returned to her perch on the arm of the sofa. "I just don't get it. What are the Za-Nakarians trying to do? They turn up the temperature, they kill the planet. It's obvious."

"Yes, it does seem a bit silly, doesn't it?" The Professor mused. "But in the meantime, they get anywhere between twenty and fifty years of premium tourist resort."

"No, no, no," Charlie cried out, her hand resting defensively on the Professor's antique globe. "That just can't be right. Injecting that much heat into an ecosystem. That's bound to have thermodynamic repercussions. You can't just turn the temperature up and start sunbathing. There'd be uncontrollable storms, tidal waves, and Heaven knows what other unintended consequences from melting the poles and effectively *frying* the tropical belt."

"Eye yng-yng tsk lol, me drr. Kanga jm oh-la-la lrr… Oh sorry, I slipped back into Za-Nakarian. I was just saying, *you shouldn't worry about that my dear*. There are whole civilisations that have dedicated themselves to studying environmental control. It's one of the most sought-after services in the, err, in what you might call the Universe. Hmm?"

The Professor leaned back in his chair, and closed his fingers together meditatively over his tummy.

"Think of all those advanced civilsations on over-exploited planets," the Professor continued. "They're crying out for these services. Oh yes, yes. No, the Za-Nakarians will hire the best environmental consultants. Of course they will. They will make sure that all the excess climatic energy is directed away from what they call the, err, the 'resort belt', either into the poles or to the equator."

"But *how?*"

"Oh, they'll have computer models, chemicals, a fleet of drones I should imagine. Hmm? The drones will constantly patrol the relevant latitudes to contain the problem. Hence the storm belt that we just saw in those photos, do you see? All the excess energy is contained within defined latitudes."

"Hang on," Paranoid Dave cut in. "You're not seriously suggesting the Za-Nakarians will try to control the weather across the whole planet? That's insane."

"No, no, you're completely right, yes, it's insane," the Professor conceded, smiling, "but perfectly possible. For a while at least. We already have primitive climate control technologies of our own. Just imagine how the technology could evolve over a few thousand years? Hmm? And then imagine a few million years. Perfectly possible."

"It's true, Dave," Charlie said listlessly. "Chemicals

are used regularly here to seed rain clouds, where rain is wanted. Or to make it rain in one place, so rain is avoided in another. As technologies, they're clumsy, they're controversial. I wouldn't for a moment imagine they could be used across a whole planet, but…"

Charlie's voice faded away, sounding defeated. She walked slowly towards the window. She sat down on the low sill, her pretty mouth hanging open in disbelief, and stared up at the sky.

"Oh my God, it's true. They're really going to do it. The Za-Nakarians are going to stuff our planet. And the worst bit?" she said, addressing no-one in particular, her large, intense chestnut eyes glistening like two pools of sorrow, "we invited them in to do it."

*

The room fell silent.

The tick-tock of the Professor's grandfather clock became audible, even loud.

The gang didn't know where to look or what to think.

His eyes wandering, only then did Toby notice that Mrs B had taken a seat at a small desk beneath the gallery. There was an anglepoise lamp just next to her and she had an eyepiece in one eye, the kind watchmakers use. She was working hard on something, deep in concentration, he couldn't tell what. Whatever it was, it didn't seem to matter much now anyway.

The grandfather clock struck three, with a deathly gong that made Toby shudder.

He looked back at the TV, which was playing on mute. The cameras showed Woola in his warm wheelie bin, being guided back to the bus. The subtitles reported that the bus was going to take him back the airport, and from there he would be jetted back to London. Someone had put a big floppy tartan hat on his head – the kind with a bobble in the middle and a fringe of comedy ginger hair around the base. Woola was smiling and waving and the crowd were going wild, their faces contorted in a silent frenzy. Hundreds of them, maybe thousands, had coalesced out of nowhere to this remote section of Scotland. They were pressed up against steel barriers, either side of the road, their arms stretched vainly forward, like they were reaching for a prophet.

10

At precisely 15:00 Greenwich Meantime a huge rending in the fabric of space-time was experienced within a cosmological whisker – a mere 100,000 miles – of the planet Earth. The source of this disturbance? All 377 bulk carriers of the Jagamath fleet were arriving out of hyperdrive.

The fleet of bulk carriers re-emerged into the four familiar dimensions of the observable Universe like so many rubber ducks bobbing to the surface of a bath. Space-time bulged around each ship momentarily, before closing behind the stern with the cosmic equivalent of a *plop.*

Safely out of hyperdrive, the bulk carriers glided smoothly into four orbiting rings around the Earth. One ring of carriers set off to orbit around the equator. A second around the Greenwich meridian. And two more were spaced evenly between the others, orbiting diagonally around Earth. The four rings of carriers criss-crossed each other at two points above equator: over the Gulf of Guinea, just off the West coast of Africa, on one side of the planet, and over a large garbage patch in the Pacific Ocean on the other.

There was a balletic synchrony in the movement of these hulking vessels. In the tentacles of lesser navigators, there could've been carnage at the crossing points. But such was the skill of the Jagamath, they handled the navigational dynamics with well-rehearsed expertise, and the bulk carriers glided past each other like well-behaved traffic on the roundabout of a mid-sized and generally sober English market town. The odd hiccup or cross face, the occasional toot of a horn, but nothing to give serious concern.

*

"Listen, guys…" Paranoid Dave stood up to break the silence. "We can't just give up because we've found out the truth. Or at least some of the truth."

He turned to the Professor.

"OK, Professor, I think you've convinced everyone here that the Za-Nakarians are up to no good. Charlie's obviously convinced. Toby?"

Toby put his hands up defensively and nodded.

"So now we know *what* the Za-Nakarians plan to do. That's already something, right? Question is, *how* are they going to do it?"

"Ha! That's what we need to find out. You see? My source could only confirm that action typically starts within a day of the new purchase."

"*24 hours…*" Charlie repeated the words in a trance-like state.

"Err, more like 21 now," Toby offered, staring at the grandfather clock.

"When their victims are still enchanted by the prospect of new rulers," Paranoid Dave added, staring at the TV.

"Yes, that's right, during the, err – *what would you call it?* – honeymoon period. Haha!" the Professor chuckled.

On the TV, Woola could be seen waving from the window of his bus as it pulled away.

"I guess this is all this is a well-rehearsed charm offensive?" Paranoid Dave asked, gesturing at the TV.

"Yes, I'm afraid it is."

"Well, we need to know their plan if we're going to stop them," Paranoid Dave continued. "So how *do* we find out?"

"You know what, Professor?" Toby cut in. "I think you already know what we need to do. Yes. I think you've already thought out our next move and I'd like you to share it with us." Toby's face was frowning, but inside he was a little bit pleased with his decisiveness.

"Haha! Well, perhaps I might have…" The Professor chuckled, apparently pleased that he had been found out. "I think we shall have to join AAC."

"Fantastic!" Toby clapped his hands together in appreciation of the simplicity of it. "Err, what's the AAC?"

"The Alien Advisory Council."

"And they are?"

"When we first made contact with alien intelligent life, a body was formed to advise the President. I was, well, part of it. Back then. It was called the AAC."

"Cool…" Paranoid Dave looked at the Professor with appreciation.

"Ah yes. Rather cool as you say, in the early days. But then I was thrown off it, you see? Three months ago. I didn't quite agree with… Let's just say I didn't think it was a good idea to sell the planet."

"But if you were thrown off the AAC, isn't it going to be impossible to get back in?" Charlie asked.

"Ah yes, it will be rather tricky, haha!" The Professor appeared to find the dilemma mildly amusing. "But actually they kept my ejection very secret. I think they're rather – ah-hm – embarrassed. That's why they've been pursuing me so assiduously. On the plus side, most of my former colleagues on the AAC aren't aware that I've been, err… *ejected*. Do you see? They were told I was poorly, or some such. That's the great thing about frightfully secret organisations. No-one knows what's going on."

The Professor brought the fingers of his two hands together and leaned forward.

"It's a little naughty, but… If we can forge some passes, we can pretend to be on the AAC, get close to Woola and his, err, entourage. And then find out what they're going to do. Hmm?"

The Professor leaned back and let his words sink in.

"Forge passes – gain access to Woola – find out what the real plan is – stop them doing it – save the world." Toby counted the stages on the fingers of his left hand. "Sounds great. Brilliant. And Step 1 – forging passes to the world's most secret committee – that should only take only take, what, a couple of weeks, maybe months?"

Toby folded his arms, daring to feel a little pleased with himself again.

"Actually, dear, it's already been done."

"Excuse me?"

Mrs B had suddenly planted herself in the middle of the room. She placed her hands on her hips and stretched her back stiffly.

"Oh, but I'm not as young as I once was… I was a wee slip of a girl once, can you imagine?" Mrs B lamented in her Scottish brogue, as she stretched her neck from side to side. "Yes, dear, while you've all been taking your time, refusing to believe the

Professor, I've been busy on your passes. And now they're done. I just need a photo and thumb print. Come along, we dinnae have much time left."

Mrs B beckoned to Charlie first. Charlie nervously followed Mrs B back to her workspace under the gallery. Next to her desk, Mrs B had created a makeshift studio. There was a tripod-mounted camera, and a small lighting rig, positioned opposite an empty chair with a white sheet behind it.

"Now, just sit yourself down here," Mrs B said as she guided Charlie, who looked dazed and uncertain. Charlie cast a glance back at Paranoid Dave as if to check this was ok, and Paranoid Dave nodded back at her. Toby felt a little rush of jealousy.

Mrs B flicked a switch and the lighting rig illuminated.

"Right, I shall need a minute or two to finish the set-up," Mrs B said, as she started adjusting the equipment. "So please talk amongst yourselves."

"OK, Professor…" Paranoid Dave started. "We get the passes, but then what? I mean the Za-Nakarians are presumably keeping their plans secret from the AAC. Right? So if they haven't found out the truth, how can we?"

"Ah yes, good point" the Professor replied agreeably. "But then I've always found the truth leaves a breadcrumb trail, hmm?"

"So are you thinking the direct approach?" Toby asked. "Go up to Woola and just ask him? Appeal to his conscience?"

"Heavens no. Why would we ask him?" the Professor replied. "The Za-Nakarians aren't the dangerous ones. They probably don't even know the full picture."

"They're not? They don't?"

"No, no, the ones you want to worry about – the ones who are calling the shots – they're a much darker bunch." The Professor's brow furrowed.

"Who then?" Toby and Paranoid Dave looked at each other uneasily. "And do they have anything to do with the Za-Nakarians?"

"Hmm? Oh yes. Yes, they have *everything* to do with the Za-Nakarians." The Professor was staring into the middle distance.

"Well, *who* then?"

"Why, their bankers, that's who."

11

The Jagamath loved their job.

They were the nomads of the known Universe. Ever since their own planet had died beneath a pall of smog and exhaust fumes, they had lived purely on their bulk carriers, plying their trade and minding their own business.

It hadn't all been plain sailing.

For a century or two after the Great Departure, they felt rootless and regretful. But then – quite surprisingly and quite unexpectedly – they found happiness. A simple, uncluttered happiness. Stripped of responsibility, and owning only what they could squeeze into their cabins, they discovered a strange bliss in criss-crossing the Universe. No deep commitments, no real worries. They came to see their job differently. They came to cherish their customers and to delight in visiting new planets. They thrilled at seeing old friends, and they loved the release of hyperdrive, the experience of departing the material dimensions to travel through the higher ones. And lastly, they just loved being hauliers – fulfilling that underated but utterly crucial first step in constructing anything great. Throughout the Universe, greater civilisations than their own depended on the Jagamath to help them build, construct, *create*.

Sadly, however, this particular job was different.

Very different.

On this particular job, the Fleet Controller had more than the normal number of reasons to be suspicious about her payload. She looked down again at the supply contract in her tentacle. The arrival instructions were quite specific. Prior to delivery, the Jagamath fleet must deploy its full arsenal of surveillance probes and counter-measures. They were to evaluate the delivery site, investigate threats, seek out targets, defend themselves if necessary, and attack if instructed. Their client had provided a list of potential targets, which had been pre-programmed into the probes.

The time had come.

Releasing a heavy sigh from her dorsal voicebox, the Fleet Controller pressed a large red button under her console. Within an instant, 10,000 probes were launched from the flagship. They started hurtling down towards the Earth's atmosphere, fanning out around the globe in a menacing lace of technology. Bristling with sensors and weaponry, each one was the size of a large flowerpot.

The Fleet Controller looked again at the contract, and looked again at the name of the clients who had signed it. She sighed again. These people paid well, they were reliable. But her people lived to help create things, not destroy them. And in all her working life she had never known anything good to come from making a delivery on behalf of the *Golgothans*.

*

"Oh my Heavens, you are quite the most bonny

creature I've seen in this house in years. Too bonny to be British. Is one of your parents from across the seas, dear?"

"I am British, Mrs B. Quite proud of it actually," Charlie replied quietly in a tone of gentlest rebuke – so gentle that Mrs B missed it. "But, yes, my mother is from Java."

"Ah, I thought as much." Mrs B gently pulled a few loose strands of Charlie's hair back over her ears. "Well, you'd be even prettier if you just smiled a little."

"But Mrs B…" Charlie started, smiling a little despite herself, "I'm struggling to follow the Professor. Is he trying to say the fate of the planet rests in the hands of *bankers?*"

"Hasn't it always?" Mrs B replied, as she looked in the camera's viewfinder. "Smile please. Imagine you're petting Carruthers—"

Click.

"Ah, lovely!"

Mrs B looked at the photo and then looked up with satisfaction. "Oh my dear, I'm sure all the young gentlemen struggle to take their eyes off you." Mrs B cast a glance at Paranoid Dave and Toby, who both looked down hurriedly. "But perhaps a tiny bit naïve, bless your wee socks. We'll come to all that soon enough. For now, let's have a thumb print on this pad here…"

Charlie, still smiling a little, dutifully leant over an electronic pad and pressed her thumb onto it.

"Wonderful! Done. Your card will take a minute or two to print. And that," Mrs B clapped her hands together, "is just enough time for a wee story. Are we sitting comfortably?"

Mrs B was perched against the table. She looked across at the gang, who were all sitting on the sofa opposite. Toby glanced at the clock, fretted about the time that was passing, but bit his tongue.

"Good, I'll take that as a Yes. So to start: which of you can tell me about the *Wow!* signal?"

"August 1977. Radio frequency of 1420Mhz. The SETI project." Paranoid Dave said without drawing breath.

"Err, SETI project?" Toby asked.

"Search for Extra-Terrestrial Intelligence."

"Exactly, David, very good. The *Wow!* signal was our first proven contact from an alien race. Correct. A radio transmission that originated from outside the Solar System. It lasted only a few seconds but it was without any doubt generated by aliens."

"*Seriously?* How can you be sure?" Toby asked incredulously.

"Three reasons. The signal was strong. It was transmitted uninterrupted at a very precise frequency – not something found in nature. But most important of all, it was transmitted at 1420Mhz. That's the exact frequency at which hydrogen emits radiation. People much cleverer than us predicted, long before the signal had ever been received, that that's the frequency at which we might expect one civilisation to reach out to another."

Mrs B paused to let the information sink in.

"Who knew about this?" Toby asked.

"Everybody, dear. Everybody who was paying attention," Mrs B smiled benevolently. "What people didn't know is *who* sent the signal."

Toby, Paranoid Dave and Charlie looked at each other and shrugged. They were starting to wonder just what kind of a housekeeper Mrs B really was.

"The Za-Nakarians?" Charlie ventured timidly.

"No, dear. An understandable guess. But no. It was from a civilisation known as the Golgothans."

"The Golgothans? Who are they?" Toby asked.

"Well they, I'm sorry to say, are the bankers. The ones who've got us into all this mess, *but—"* Mrs B held her finger up abruptly before any conclusions were jumped to. "We didn't know that yet. You see there was no actual information in that first signal."

"You mean, it was just, like, a blank whistle?"

"That kind of thing. The *Wow!* signal was just the Golgothans clearing their throats. Like tapping a microphone before a concert, and saying 'testing, testing'. They were getting our attention."

"But there was no follow up, right?" Paranoid Dave's small eyes were wide enough to pop. "I mean SETI waited and waited but there was never a second signal was there?"

"Ah yes. How folk like to pull the bedclothes over their head when they hear a noise in the night..." Mrs B's eyes wandered off wistfully into the middle distance, as if recalling a more innocent age. "Who were we kidding? Ask yourselves, who would only send *one* signal? It's not as if radio waves are expensive. If you have the technology to send one, why not send another – you know, just so that anyone listening could be sure it wasn't a fluke."

"*I knew it*," Paranoid Dave punched his fist into the palm of his other hand. "So what happened next?"

"You see this was the problem: the Golgothans were *livid*."

"Livid? But why?" Charlie asked

"They listened to our own radio chatter, and they

were livid the signal got so much publicity. They wanted to make contact *discretely*. They made their views clear in their next signal."

"But surely it arrived in some weird language, like Golgothan or something?"

"Oh no, they wrote in English – they'd heard enough of our radio broadcasts to figure English out years before. That second signal is a bit of a legend amongst those who know about it. It was of course the first ever intelligent communication – the first ever *message* – from an alien race. Now where is it? I jotted a copy down in case you asked me this…"

Mrs B fished for a moment in the front pocket of her apron.

Charlie, Toby and Paranoid Dave looked nervously at each other on the sofa, waiting what seemed like an age, while Mrs B extracted her spectacles from another pocket in her dress and carefully perched them on her nose.

"Now what did they say…" Mrs B continued, leaning back from the scrap of paper to get a better focus. "Ah yes. The first ever message received from outer space was: *'Patch me through to your boss, you cretin, and this time keep your clapper shut.'*"

"Oh," Paranoid Dave remarked, "nice."

"Yes, wasn't it? You see, the Golgothans wanted to speak to the President of the United States. Needless to say, he was soon looped in and broadcast back at 1420 Mhz. There's been a dialogue ever since. Between the Golgothans and the President. A few other world leaders were in on it too of course."

"The G7?"

"That sort of thing. In recent years they've let the G20 know too. I'm afraid the Golgothans didn't get any more polite with time. Our leaders found it rather trying."

"Right… But the SETI project is still running – I mean those guys are still looking for extra terrestrial intelligence, right?"

"Oh no, that's just a sham. They're employed to keep the public convinced space is empty. I mean they have a job. They still scan every known radio frequency of course. But their real job is taking down messages from the Golgothans. They've taken to calling themselves the SET-C project."

"SET-C?"

"'The Search for Extra-Terrestrial Courtesy'. You'd be looking for it too if you had to deal with the Golgothans every day."

*

On the streets of the capital, among the many hundreds of thousands of vehicles that had taken to the road again, one particular vehicle weaved between the others with particular purpose in pursuit of a very particular goal.

It was the TARP team.

They had a new means of transport and they had a new location for their target.

In the back of their new vehicle, the team quietly re-checked their equipment and their weapons (the ones they still had). They didn't talk. This was not a team accustomed to missing their mark and they had no intention of doing so twice in one day. They knew the stakes and they were determined to make up for the morning's mishap. This time there would be no underestimating of the opposition.

The TARP leader snapped shut his console.

He looked out of the window and made a quick note of the streets they were passing. Then he looked around the vehicle they were in. The route looked OK, the vehicle looked OK, and their new driver – he looked OK too. Not special forces, but he'd do.

As the TARP leader looked at him through the rear-view mirror, the driver turned his eyes and looked back with a calm, even gaze. The TARP leader, catching the stare, shifted uncomfortably.

The eyes looking at him were young, but the soul was very old.

12

The Professor leaned down over his desk and watched Carruthers very carefully. Mrs B watched on anxiously. The hedgehog's nose was twitching nervously, up and down. He seemed to be sniffing in a particular direction, back towards the hallway. He got out of his tiny basket, walked around it three times restlessly, got back in, sat back down on his bottom, his nose still twitching.

Toby watched Mrs B watching the Professor watching Carruthers and wondered what the heck was going on.

"Trouble?" Mrs B asked.

"Yes," the Professor replied simply. "Trouble."

"How long do you think we have?" Mrs B asked.

"Fifteen minutes. Possibly less."

Mrs B looked back towards the hallway and then up at the Professor. "Professor, are you sure you werenae followed here?"

"Hmm? Followed? Really, I don't think so."

*

"Charlotte your pass is ready," Mrs B said briskly, holding Charlie's new ID out to her. Mrs B had just extracted it from a machine on her desk. "Quickly dear, time is against us."

Charlie took it promptly, a little awe-struck by the forgery in her hand.

"Right, David – your turn, dear. Quickly please." Mrs B ushered him without ceremony to her makeshift photobooth. "These cards aren't too bad, as forgeries go," Mrs B continued, while adjusting the tripod for Paranoid Dave and re-setting the lighting rig. "Of course the magnetic strip doesn't work, and the chip is a fake. They wouldn't get you through the barrier at a tube station, never mind where you're going. But it's the best we can do in the time."

"You're not really a housekeeper, are you, Mrs B?" Paranoid Dave's eyes narrowed.

Mrs B was quite unfazed. "Oh, my dear," she replied, still working as she spoke, "can't I be a housekeeper and other things as well? I mean you're not just a student who didn't finish his studies, are you? Smile!"

Paranoid Dave gurned awkwardly at the camera.

Click.

"So, yes, I've done other things, "Mrs B continued, "I *do* other things. Right now, I'm – how shall we put it? – the historian of alien contact. Self-appointed, I'm afraid. But I do think it's important someone is keeping a record, don't you? Thumb print here, please dear."

Mrs B briskly directed Paranoid Dave's bewildered thumb to the digital pad.

"It's all been so hush-hush until this morning. And since the Professor has been kind enough to share what he knows with me, I thought I better fill the role… Thank you, dear, you have a lovely thumb. You can sit down again now.

"We only have a few minutes, we better use them

wisely. You need to know about the Committee you've just joined. So" – Mrs B clapped her hands – "the Alien Advisory Committee. Who are they? What do they do?"

Mrs B perched her ample backside against the table again, and scanned her young audience.

"There are dozens on the AAC, hundreds. They advise the G7 leaders on anything and everything to do with alien contact. They're responsible for looking after Woola while he's here on Earth, and they're the ones who advised that we sell the planet. They're a pretty hopeless rabble to be frank, but" – Mrs B raised a single finger – "they weren't always like that. In the early days, there were just six. A scientist from NASA, a radio specialist, a diplomat from the State department – he handled communications with the other world leaders 'in the know'. That's three. Let me see, who else…?"

Mrs B looked towards the Professor, who made a strange exploding motion with his hands.

"Oh yes, a military advisor from the Pentagon – he was forever wanting to fire missiles – and a top biologist makes five. And then finally, a linguist. That was the Professor."

Mrs B cast an admiring glance towards the Professor.

"The Professor has many accomplishments. Theology, history, mathematics. A true polymath. But in case you're wondering why they chose him, it's because he's also a linguist. He's fluent in over twenty languages from eight different language groups. He can read a dozen more. Look at the books around you. If anyone could master an alien language, it was the Professor."

"Of course," Charlie said. "And so now he's mastered Za-Nakarian?"

"Tsk-kyck-ta-rarararara-ck-tss, mi drr," the Professor chuckled from behind his desk. "Oh, haha – that means *I get by well enough, my dear.* I could hold a basic conversation, buy bread in the shops that sort of thing."

"They have bread?"

"They have *shops*?"

"My God, Professor, have you actually travelled in outer space?" Toby asked.

"Oh no, I've never traveled in outer space," the Professor replied reassuringly. "But I have visited a number of other planets."

As Toby cocked his head to one side, wondering how confused he should be, Mrs B hurriedly continued.

"The dialogue with the Golgothans in the early years was a colourful business. It wasn't long before they offered to buy the planet. Naturally our leaders refused. It was absurd. They had no idea who they were selling to. Everyone got very nervous. That was when the men from the Pentagon started twitching. The AAC thought: if they can't buy, they might attack."

"Did they? Attack, I mean?"

"Oh no. No. Things just became rather – how shall I put this? – unusual. *Weird.* They came back again and offered to buy shares in the planet, a partial takeover. Our leaders refused that too. So they suggested a merger. Refused. A leveraged buy-out. Refused. A management buy-out. Refused. So they suggested they lend us money so we could buy shares in other planets. Refused as well."

"That is properly weird." Paranoid Dave whistled between his teeth.

"Yes. Very. Remember – we had just made contact for the first time with an alien race. Imagine! The AAC were ready to discuss the Laws of the Universe, learn about unheard-of technologies, read them Shakespeare, play some Beethoven. All the noble stuff. And instead the aliens were spouting Wall Street jargon. Well, there was a good reason for that, as the Professor found out much later. But in the meantime, we were in a merry wee guddle."

"Well, the planet's been sold now," Paranoid Dave observed bluntly. "So what happened?"

"The financial crisis happened, dear."

"Which one?"

"Does it matter? They always reduce our political leaders to headless chicken, who become strangely dependant on the advice of the very people who got them into the mess in the first place. But since you ask: the Credit Crunch. You see, the world had been brought to its financial knees. The financial system had become like some old building that had to be buttressed. The people inside were still happily making money, while everyone outside was straining and heaving to prop it up. To our politicians, a solution like selling the planet suddenly seemed less outlandish. And thus negotiations with the Golgothans were opened."

"OK – and then?"

"Well then the virus, dear. And the next financial crash. If the financial system was like a creaking old building before the virus, it was now covered in scaffolding. Every wall, every nook relied on government support of one kind or another. But the governments of the world were exhausted. Literally and financially. And that almost sealed the deal in the mind of our leaders. *Almost*."

"You're making me feel sorry for them," Paranoid Dave mused, "*almost*. So what did seal the deal?"

The Golgothans had a couple more tricks up their sleeve."

"Which were?"

"The Za-Nakarians visited. Our leaders met a delegation of them at the height of the crisis, and you can guess the impression *they* made."

Mrs B paused, as the gang nodded silently, picturing the encounter.

"And there was something else. Something the Za-Nakarians brought with them. Something quite… Something quite mind-blowing, to be honest."

"What was it?" Charlie asked.

"Well, it was a present, a very… special present." Mrs B looked uncharacteristically cautious. With a parental, shall-we-tell-the-children sort of expression, she turned to the Professor. The Professor looked back and inclined his shoulders in a non-committal sort of way.

"You see…" Mrs B continued uncertainly. "Oh wait. It's Carruthers again. Hang on a moment, dears."

The gang watched in frustration as Mrs B got up from her perch and crossed the study to the Professor's desk.

*

The vehicle carrying the TARP team slowed to a crawl as it approached the target location, and then drew noiselessly to a halt.

Inside the TARP leader issued his final instructions to his five team members. They didn't need reminding how urgent their mission had become, nor how important.

The rear doors of the vehicle opened and the TARP team, with much greater caution than three hours earlier – with much greater *stealth* – slipped out and made their way to their assault start-points.

*

"We haven't got as long as we thought. Only a couple of minutes, maybe less," Mrs B announced severely. She switched her gaze from Carruthers to her card-forging machine and back again.

Carruthers had curled up tight. His small, inquisitive face had disappeared completely into his tummy, leaving an awkward little ball of white and brown spikes.

Meantime, a plastic card popped out of the printer, glided down a short slide and landed in a small metal basket at the base.

Mrs B grabbed it and turned around.

"David – your card. Take it, please. Toby, your turn, dear. This way. Hurry now." Mrs B gestured Toby briskly to the seat in her makeshift studio.

"Smile—"

Click.

"And place your thumb here... Thank you." Mrs B hit a few keys on her computer and looked nervously at her watch. "That'll take another two minutes to print. This will be tight. Everyone get ready to leave, please."

The Professor touched his hand to his forehead. "Ah! My course notes, I must fetch them."

"Your course notes? Are you sure you need them?" Mrs B asked.

"Oh yes, yes. I should imagine they might be quite handy."

"Oh dear. Well do please hurry!"

Mrs B and the rest of the gang stared anxiously, as the Professor made his way up a set of library steps. From the top, he peered along the topmost shelf, holding his half-moon glasses up with one hand, while the fingers of his other hand ran along the spines of the books.

"No where are you, hmm?" the Professor addressed his missing notebook genially. "I'm quite sure I left you somewhere between Akkadian and Middle Egyptian… Or are you next to the umm… that's to say, the err…"

"Professor!"

The gang were left in finger-drumming suspense as they watched the Professor search. It was only as Toby stood there, drumming his fingers, and staring at the library steps, that he actually noticed the library steps. And then he realised they were in fact the most unusual, the most magnificent set of library steps he'd ever seen.

Toby hadn't seen many library steps in his life and indeed hadn't paid much attention to those he had seen. But this set – now the Professor was on it – was something else. For one thing, they were eight steps high. Running up their left hand side, all the way to the top, was a fluted, wooden bannister. The very topmost step was large, like a small platform. The bannister ran all the way round it and there was even a small red leather bench on one side – just wide enough to seat two.

"Professor…" Charlie broke the silence cautiously, "are you quite sure you need these notes? What course was it exactly?"

"My course," Paranoid Dave said simply.

"*Your course?* Of course…" Toby clicked. "The Professor was your lecturer. What exactly was he teaching—"

"Found it!" the Professor said, turning around on the platform. In one hand he was holding a small, leather-bound notebook. He tapped it with his other hand, smiling triumphantly. "You see the course was about… Oh!" The Professor interrupted himself.

"What? What is it?" Mrs B asked.

"Mrs B – were we expecting the gardener today?" the Profesor asked.

"No, Professor, why?"

"Because I think I saw something move out there…"

"Was it… Was it a human shape?" Mrs B started. "Or *something else?*"

"I couldn't rightly say. Something black I think, and metallic. But I can't be sure…"

"Everybody – on the ground – now!" Mrs B commanded. "Get out of sight of the windows. Professor – come down at once!"

Toby, who had immediately dropped onto all fours like the others, looked up to see the Professor making his way rapidly down the steps, his movements surprisingly spry.

An instant later and Toby's card popped out of the machine and slid into the metal basket. Mrs B's chubby hand reached in and grabbed it urgently. Toby wriggled towards her on his hands and knees.

"Don't lose it!" she said, as she thrust the card at him. "Right everybody – to the doorway, quick as you can. Stay out of sight! We have to get to the corridor.

There are no windows there."

Mrs B started shuffling on all fours towards the door, which was standing ajar. Moving her ample bulk with surprising energy, she passed by the Professor's desk on her right. She paused to scoop up the inert Carruthers into the pouch at the front of her apron, and then continued crawling. Paranoid Dave crawled behind her and Toby behind him, all of them moving at speed, with the floorboards creaking mightily under their weight. Toby found his hands and knees surprisingly sore from rubbing against the Professor's very distinguished but rather threadbare carpet.

Toby made it past the study door and into the corridor, where he waited briefly, still on all fours, for first Charlie and then the Professor to come wriggling round the door to join them. Just for a moment, the five of them remained there in the corridor, panting and motionless on all fours.

"Mrs B – what is it out there? What do you think is happening?" Paranoid Dave asked.

"I dinnae know, my dear, but nothing good," Mrs B replied, "I should imagine…"

Before she could finish, the doorbell rang.

It was an old-fashioned bell. It had an uneven, metallic clang that rose and fell, communicating in a subtle but unambiguous way the mood of the person who was ringing it. The mood of this particular person was impatient. The gang were still on the floor. They shuffled awkwardly on their knees and looked at each other.

"Now what?" asked Paranoid Dave, running his hand through his hair. "There's someone at the door and something in the garden. What the Hell is happening?"

The doorbell rang again, urgently. Twice.

"Professor," Mrs B spoke decisively, "I'll get the door. You have to get our young friends out of here. That's imperative. The fate of the… Never mind, you have to get out. Whoever's at the door, I'll stall them."

"Hmm. Yes, I see. It is all rather urgent suddenly, isn't it?" the Professor observed not sounding particularly urgent. "We might need a little help from Albrecht perhaps?"

"Albrecht? Albrecht. Yes, good idea," Mrs B replied. "You take him, I'll take Carruthers. I have a feeling he might be useful," Mrs B looked down pensively at the curled up hedgehog.

Charlie, Toby and Paranoid Dave looked at each other, feeling slightly baffled and very scared, and then watched as Mrs B stood back up a little creakily – stretched her back for a moment – and bustled off towards the entrance hall, still holding Carruthers in her apron.

13

"Hello? Now you really must stop pulling the bell like that. Oh and you can put away that big... *thing* right now. I can assure you there'll be no need for that."

Mrs B gestured disdainfully with one hand towards a long, cylindrical battering ram that the two figures in front of her were holding between them with a pair of straps.

"I can tell you, you're scaring the daylights out of my poor wee pet here."

Mrs B's right hand tenderly patted the little spiny globe that her left hand was carefully holding with the apron. She was rewarded by Carruthers very slightly unfurling himself. His pointy little nose poked out ever so slightly, and his dark liquid eyes blinked open just long enough to take in the battering ram, the two figures holding it, and the guns slung over their backs. At which sight he promptly curled right back up.

"There, you see? You've frightened the wee beastie half to death."

The TARP leader looked towards his companion, with an exasperated look that seemed to say, *why has nothing about today been remotely simple?* He gathered himself together.

"Madam, I am here to arrest Professor AC James. We have reason to believe he's sheltering in this house.

I have an all-premises warrant to search wherever I have reason to believe he may be hiding. I should like you to step aside so that we can search here."

"I shall do no such thing, young man!" Mrs B replied at her most formidable. "For one thing, there is no Professor James residing here" – Mrs B quickly reasoned to herself that this wasn't exactly a lie – "And for another, I should like to see this warrant that has got you so excited. An *all-premises* warrant indeed."

"The warrant? TARP-2, the warrant?"

"The warrant, boss? Err... Let me have a look." TARP-2 promptly dropped his side of the battering ram to reach for his pocket. The TARP leader, against whose legs the battering ram had smartly swung, cursed noisily.

"And I can assure you there's no need for language like that either, young man." Mrs B pouted with indignation.

"Err, boss... I think the warrant is in the back of the van?" TARP-2 was trembling slightly.

"You mean the van that was stolen this morning? Is that the van you mean?" the TARP leader replied caustically, still nursing his leg with one hand.

TARP-2 nodded nervously. The TARP leader ground his teeth with silent fury. He turned back to Mrs B. "Madam, it appears that the search warrant has been stolen by Professor James. Nevertheless I insist you allow us to—"

"Pah! You're saying this Professor James has stolen his own search warrant? Careful now, you're in danger of reducing an old woman to helpless laughter."

"Madam, I demand you—" At that moment, a voice came through on the TARP leader's earpiece. He pressed a finger to his ear and listened. "...Yep...

OK… Roger that…"

"What's up boss?"

"TARP-5 says he can see a bunch of coffee mugs on a table in the middle of the conservatory. That, Madam, would be five coffee mugs to be precise." The TARP leader looked pointedly at Mrs B. "It seems, TARP-2, that this lady has been entertaining guests recently. One mug for her and *four* guests."

"Oh, so now you're going to invade my house because one of your men, who is presumably trespassing in the garden, has spotted yesterday's washing up?"

"Yes, Madam, we are." The TARP leader spoke into his wrist. "All units, you are *GO – GO – GO!*"

At that point he and TARP-2 shouldered their weapons, brushed past Mrs B and, adopting their crouching-down-pointed-gun posture, stormed into the house.

*

"Professor?"

On the corridor wall, opposite Toby, was a portrait of one of the Professor's more buxom ancestors. The Professor was pressed against the portrait, almost hugging it, and running his hands up and down behind it.

"Professor, I don't think this is the moment to be eccentric," Toby said urgently. "*Professor?*"

"Just a moment… Wait… I can almost feel it," the Professor gasped awkwardly, his cheek pressed against the ancestral bosom.

"Aaah!" he sighed with satisfaction, "sweet release…"

Ping.

Just to the side of the painting, a part of the wooden panelling sprang open.

It was a secret door.

A dark passageway beckoned.

"This way, gentlemen, Charlotte, if you please? Hmm?"

The Professor stood to one side and beckoned them in with a look of quiet triumph on his face.

An instant later and the distinct sound of splitting wood could be heard from the study. Someone had forced open one of the windows.

With no further hesitation, Paranoid Dave dived into the secret passage, followed in short order by Toby and Charlie and lastly the Professor. He swung the door shut behind him, and it clicked back into place.

The four of them barely had a moment to adjust to the dark world they had just entered before they heard heavy but careful footsteps in the corridor they'd just left, and the sound of two men whispering furtively.

After a few heart-stopping seconds, the footsteps continued on down the corridor and away.

What are the odds? Toby thought to himself. He had never before hidden in a building from intruders, and today it had happened twice before teatime.

"*F o l l o w   m e !*" whispered the Professor.

The Professor switched on a small pocket torch and brushed past them as he set off into the darkness. The others followed behind. The secret passageway materialised ahead, illuminated with each step by the comet-shaped light from the Professor's pocket torch. The passage was narrow and surprisingly cool. Toby could feel grit and a few loose stones beneath his feet.

They walked for fifteen, maybe twenty yards, penetrating deeper into the house. After a few more yards, the passageway turned to the right, and a few yards after that it narrowed until it was little more than the width of their shoulders. The group slowed down as they started to shuffle along sideways.

"Professor," Paranoid Dave said, breathing heavily, "seriously, how do you come to have a secret passageway running through your house?"

"Oh, that's Great Uncle Claude for you. He inherited the Victorian taste for melodrama, I fear. Now please be careful," he called softly over his shoulder, "there should be a few steps coming up here, if memory serves."

Gingerly the gang stepped carefully down eight or nine stone steps, which they could just make out in the quarter light of the Professor's pocket torch. They had moved forward another dozen yards or so when the Professor raised his hand to halt them again.

He gestured up above his right shoulder.

The gang could see a small ventilation panel. The Professor placed a finger to his mouth, and spoke in the faintest of whispers.

"*The dining room.*"

The gang froze. The sound of creaking floorboards slipped through the ventilation panel like an unpleasant vapour – at first just faint, but very soon they could hear the unmistakeable shudder of someone heavy trying to move silently. Through the metal lattice, Toby could just make out two pairs of black, military-grade boots stalking stealthily through the dining room.

How many of them are there in the house? Toby asked himself, before remembering the attack on the

Squirrel & Acorn. *Six.*

The sound of footsteps rose and rose…

And then receded.

The Professor started to move off again, but with renewed urgency. Moving with less hesitation now, he led them around a couple more corners, down a couple more steps, before they came to a door. The Professor scanned with his torch and located a small handle. He yanked it a couple of times and swung it open.

The three stepped tentatively out of the passageway. Toby rubbed his eyes and blinked a couple of times.

"What on Earth is *that*?"

"Gentlemen," replied the Professor, "may I introduce Albrecht?"

14

For a young man in his mid-twenties, Aftab had seen more of life than most. He had lived on different continents, he'd mastered languages with no common roots, he'd seen men kill and he'd seen men die. He hadn't sought this out – far from it. It came from growing up in a war zone. When the family got the chance, they fled to England, and then London became his home. He studied hard in school, he got good grades, and he continued to see some pretty strange things but – *thank goodness* – much less killing.

Aftab liked the English.

He liked their cricket, he liked their vintage cars and he liked their amateur spirit. Where he came from people might die for being from the wrong tribe, or following the wrong religion, or even for following the right religion wrongly. The English, by contrast, just bowled him the occasional racist insult and expected it to hurt. *Amateurs.*

Aftab fiddled with the settings on his radio and the static crackled in a disarmingly old-fashioned way. He had recently bought this old cab and loved its eccentricities. He'd had to replace the engine to meet modern emissions standards – bit of a nuisance and very expensive – but not the radio. The regulations couldn't touch that. The antiquated device reminded him of the cars he knew as a child.

Aftab fiddled some more. After a couple of false turns on the dial, the static gave way to the cricket commentary from Lords, resonant and clear. Aftab smiled quietly, and settled back into the comfortable embrace of his cab. This was the kind of reassurance he needed given the day that he, along with the rest of the planet, was having. He looked left and right at the calm, leafy street on which he'd parked and agreed with himself this was a very satisfactory place to pretend that nothing had really changed.

He leaned back, half-closed his eyes and allowed the sounds of the match to wash through him like a cool glass of fresh lemonade. The soothing crack of leather on willow. They might stop the cricket for the rain or poor light – but not for a minor alien invasion. Quite right too. All doubts about his current fare drifted out of his open window, no more consequential than a cucumber sandwich…

*

Crack!

Aftab looked up with alarm.

Two wooden garage doors burst open on the opposite side of the street and a magnificent old car in burgundy red came bumping out awkwardly. It lurched to a halt in the middle of the road. With the momentum of the exit, the garage doors were thrown wide open; the doors bounced on their hinges and clattered unhappily back together behind the car.

The car lurched forward a few more yards and stalled. *Wrong gear*, Aftab thought to himself. He recognised the model immediately of course: a 1949

Daimler DE36. German brand, British made. Very rare. He could see the driver, who was a wild hairy fellow – *could he possibly be Afghan?* – look down at the gear stick, and then frantically work it back and forwards with his arm. The engine came to life again, and the car jerked awkwardly forward towards the opposite pavement. The driver heaved hard right on the steering wheel, just avoiding a rather magnificent beech tree, but turning the car directly towards Aftab's stationery cab.

Aftab screwed his eyes tight and braced for impact. His mind made one of those lightning fast calculations that happen occasionally at moments of high drama. The weight of the oncoming Daimler, its speed and its likely turning circle meant impact was inevitable. The size of the probable repair bill flashed across his mind, uninvited.

But they didn't collide.

By some miracle, the old Daimler had a tight turning circle. Just like a cab. Its front bumper clipped Aftab's front bumper, sending a little shudder through the cab. A small dent but nothing worse. For an instant, Aftab could just glimpse the occupants a yard or two away through the windows. They looked wild-eyed, raving. And as the car powered past, Aftab saw a pretty girl in the back seat. As he watched her flashing past him, she seemed to mouth the word *Sorry*.

Aftab knew that wild-eyed look only too well from his childhood. He instinctively lowered himself in his seat, and turned the radio up a notch.

*

Screeeech!

So much for the cricket. Staying as low as possible, Aftab turned his head to look behind.

The Daimler had juddered to a halt just fifty yards away. One of the back doors opened, and a nondescript, young-ish sort of a fellow jumped out and ran back down the street toward the house they'd just left. Just as he reached the front door, an older lady came to meet him and handed him something. The young man took it carefully in his hands, appeared to say thank you, and then started to trot back to the car.

What on Earth is he carrying? Aftab wondered. He could swear it was a hedgehog, only he knew it couldn't be, because that would be absurd.

He didn't wonder for long. At that exact moment, the street was filled with the sound of shouting.

"Oi, you! Stop NOW!" yelled a voice. Six men, dressed in black, burst out of the garage and set off after the Daimler. "Come on lads!"

Here come my fare, Aftab thought to himself.

Aftab saw the ordinary-looking young man glance back at the soldiers, tuck the animal under his arm and sprint towards the Daimler. Meantime the Daimler started to pull away with the back door still open. The young man caught up with it, passed the animal to someone inside – *it really did look like a hedgehog –* and then started running alongside. Aftab saw him try to step in several times, but each time he stopped to lift his leg, the car had already moved past, and he had to run to catch up again.

CRACK!

A gunshot was fired. The violence of the noise reverberated down the leafy street.

Aftab recoiled. But he didn't panic. He'd heard too much shooting as a child for that.

Up ahead, he watched as the hapless young man – *terrified* – seemed to grasp the roof of the car with both hands and, in a heroic effort, jumped and pulled himself inside the moving vehicle all in one movement.

Impressive, Aftab whistled to himself.

The Daimler sped away.

He looked back at the soldiers. Their leader had lowered the gun of one of the soldiers towards the pavement. The shot had gone into the ground. The leader mouthed angrily at the soldier for a short while, and then turned round towards Aftab's taxi. He pointed directly at Aftab, shouted an order, and then in an instant all six soldiers were sprinting towards him, gesturing wildly.

*

"Are you *mad?* They had their guns out, Dave. One of them *fired* at me. Why couldn't you just—"

"Well done, Toby!" said a quiet voice.

"—slow down and let me back in?" Toby blundered on breathlessly. "I mean I might've been—"

"That was amazing." Charlie spoke again, looking at Toby with admiration.

"—killed." Toby's voice faded away. "It was?"

"Uh huh."

"I mean, what was amazing?"

Paranoid Dave peered round over his shoulder. "The way you went back to fetch Carruthers. And then launched yourself into a moving vehicle. Amazing."

"No, no, I agree, Tobias," the Professor added. "Amazing."

"Really? Oh. Well that's OK then. I guess." Toby shifted awkwardly in his seat. "Thank you."

He had never been shot at before. And he'd certainly never been told he was amazing before. It was unsettling.

The Professor turned to Charlie in the backseat. She had Carruthers on her lap, where she had been gently petting him.

"Oh yes, Professor, you want your hedgehog back." Charlie gently stroked the spines behind Carruthers' head and held him up to look in his eyes. The hedgehog's nose twitched a couple of times. Charlie twitched her nose back at him, which the hedgehog seemed to like. His front paws wriggled and the eyelids over his intense brown little hedgehog eyes fluttered. And so did Toby's stomach as he watched the two of them together. For no particular reason, except that he was falling hopelessly in love.

"He's come out of his ball," Paranoid Dave observed, looking in the rear-view mirror.

"He certainly has," Charlie said, as she passed Carruthers reluctantly back to the Professor. The Professor took him, gave him a gentle pat on the head, and then placed him carefully back in his leather briefcase.

"Are you sure he can breathe in there?" Charlie asked.

"Oh yes, this case has been specially adapted." The Professor tapped some air holes that had been punched through one end, and gently clicked the case shut.

"OK, well, I guess that went OK, all things considered." Toby spoke. "So now we need to locate Woola, right?"

"Yes, yes, that's our starting point," the Professor

replied amiably.

"Great, so how do we go about that?"

But before Toby could finish his question, Paranoid Dave banked the Daimler into a screeching left-hand turn. Everyone in the car lurched to their right.

"Dammit, Dave," Toby squawked, with his cheek against the glass. "Do you have to drive like a madman?"

"Back window," Paranoid Dave said tersely, as he yanked the car violently out of the turn.

"*Whaaat?*" Toby cried, as his body was flipped back the other way, landing against Charlie. "Sorry, Charlie."

"That's quite alright."

"Back window," Paranoid Dave said again.

"What's wrong with the back window?"

"Oh no, it's them again," Charlie said, as she stared out of the back window. "The soldier people. They're following us."

"Correct," Paranoid Dave said, as he spun the steering wheel hard right, lurching the car round a tight bend. "Black cab, three cars back."

Toby looked round just in time to see a black cab, three cars back, accelerate towards the oncoming traffic, overtake a car, and then weave back into their lane just in time to avoid colliding with a van. Now it was two cars back.

A moment later, Paranoid Dave spotted a small turning to his right and, at the last moment, spun the Daimler into a 90-degree turn, slipped between the oncoming traffic and shot down a narrow side street.

Oh great, Toby thought as he righted himself in his seat, *here we go again.*

*

"We need to call in a chopper. The radios are down, mobile networks are jammed. TARP-2 – get me HQ on the satellite phone."

The TARP leader sounded firm, decisive.

TARP-2 reached awkwardly into his backpack and produced a largish contraption, with a splendidly old-fashioned handset. He leaned across the TARP leader to dangle the small antenna dish out of the taxi window.

At that moment, the taxi lurched sharply to the left. TARP-2's body was thrown against his leader's head, which in turn was thrown against the window. The TARP leader found himself with his cheeks pressed between the window and TARP-2's underarm.

"Y o u   a r e   s q u a s h i n g   m e . . . " the TARP leader said through gritted teeth, his lips protruding in the manner of an expiring cod.

"Oh, sorry boss!"

At that moment, the taxi came out of the turn and lurched sharp right. Both of them were thrown off the window and against the pile of other TARP bodies in the back of the cab.

The TARP leader was just preparing some choice expletives for the driver, when the cab screeched to an abrupt halt and he was thrown forward, clean off his seat and into the arms of TARP-6, whose large frame was perched on the small jump seat opposite.

"My apologies for the most abrupt halt," Aftab spoke softly, as he applied the handbrake.

"You've spotted their car?" the TARP leader called out in a jaded voice from somewhere near the bottom of the footwell into which he'd collapsed.

"Yes, yes, I did spot the magnificent burgundy red car," Aftab called back, as he turned around in his seat and opened the connecting window. "But I think I may have lost it again."

The TARP leader swore under his breath. Amidst a clattering of equipment and sweaty man-grunts, the TARP team righted themselves in the back of the cab. Seated more or less comfortably, TARP-2 chirped up again.

"Err boss… The satellite phone, it's ready. I think?"

The TARP leader took the old-fashioned handset and started trying to speak into it.

But it was no use.

*

They couldn't know this, but their satellite phone didn't have a buttercup in a farmyard's chance of connecting to any satellites. The phone was fine, the problem was the satellite. Because that particular satellite, which had helped them with such exquisite precision a couple of hours earlier, had just bounced off the underside of a Jagamath bulk carrier in the manner of a shuttlecock flying accidentally into an articulated lorry. As they tapped away on the phone's keypad, the satellite was spinning prettily (albeit with one of its solar arrays flapping in a slightly irregular manner) on a new trajectory towards Mars.

Interestingly, a back-up satellite was available – but as the majority of the planet's satellite communications were now being routed through it, it had crashed. Metaphorically, not physically. Some extremely clever, but slightly frazzled operators would bring it back online in the next fifteen minutes, but, to avoid another crash, all non-essential traffic would be blocked and the bandwidth reserved for the Pentagon, GCHQ and a bunch of other agencies who were frantically, secretly trying to find out what in heck had entered the Earth's orbital zone. And while TARP communications ought to have been part of that reserved bandwidth, the TARP team were in fact such a secret cell, controlled by such a secret Government agency, that almost no-one knew of their existence, and the few that did weren't authorised to re-route their communications.

In other words, the TARP team were on their own.

15

"What is *that*?" Paranoid Dave spluttered, hitting the brakes hard.

"Wow!"

"Shut up…"

"Hmm. Interesting."

The Daimler, which had been flying down a side street, came to an abrupt stop at a T-junction. Passing in front of them, down one of the main thoroughfares towards central London, was a carnival parade. A vast, seething, infinitely colourful mass of humanity was on the move, singing, shouting, whistling, dancing, rejoicing.

"OK, wasn't expecting that…" Paranoid Dave said to himself. He turned in his seat, "Guys – what do we do now?"

"Quickly, drive on," Charley replied urgently. "They'll catch us otherwise. They're probably just round the corner."

"Yeah – but the traffic, that procession, it's almost static. They'll catch us there."

"Not if they don't see us," Toby joined in. "They'll think we just crossed the procession, or took a turn somewhere. Do it, Dave – quickly!"

"Ah, hiding in plain sight," the Professor chuckled approvingly, "the best place for it."

"Okaaaay…" Dave said under his breath as he edged the Daimler into the crowd. The people in front and the people behind happily made space. For them, at that particular moment, it seemed like the most natural thing in the world to see an old 1940s Daimler in gleaming burgundy red joining their carnival. The Daimler was soon swallowed up amongst them and proceeded to roll forward at a couple of miles per hour.

Toby gazed out of the window.

All along the route, burger vans and stalls had sprung up. Office windows had been thrown open, and rainbow flags were draped haphazardly from windowsills. A huge banner was strung across the street:

We sold the Earth, but we found Heaven!

"Amazing isn't it, hmm?" the Professor was the first to break the silence in the car. "The speed at which people can throw a party."

"People want to come together again, Professor," Charlie replied. "Not virtually, but *really*."

"Well, there's no debt anymore," Toby chipped in. "That must help."

"If you ask me, it's suspicious as Hell," Paranoid Dave spoke. "Are we sure it was just the AAC that were in the know? Look around."

Toby and Charlie turned in the backseat and looked through the rear window. A short way behind were a couple of dozen clowns on stilts. The clowns had comedy smiles painted on their faces and were gurning in all directions as they blew small soap bubbles that danced across the parade.

Toby followed one of the bubbles with his eyes, as it danced on gusts of wind, blowing it higher and higher…

And then he gasped.

He and Charlie found themselves looking up at a giant inflatable model of Woola. It was so tall, they had to press their faces to the rear window to see to the top. It swayed gently in the afternoon breeze, turning a little to the left, a little to the right. The base was tethered to the back of a flatbed truck, while the head looked out over the six-storey buildings on either side of the road. Each of Woola's dark eyes was the size of a small car, and he had an inane grin on his face that must have been visible for miles around.

How did they manage to make that thing in the last few hours…? Toby wondered.

*

How did they manage to make that thing in the last few hours…? Aftab also wondered.

After losing the Daimler, he had turned the cab around, gone up the side-street where he last saw it, guessed the next few turnings and accidentally entered a huge, bewildering carnival parade. He now found himself staring at the backside of the largest inflatable figure he'd ever seen, and wondering how the world had managed to turn quite so crazy quite so quickly.

He glanced in his rear-view mirror.

The soldiers were still bickering and fiddling with their daft equpiment that never seemed to work.

"Do you think that maybe the Daimler is maybe also joining this parade?" Aftab politely suggested to the TARP leader.

"*What?*" The TARP leader looked up from the satellite phone with an irritated expression, and then glanced at the slow-moving parade around them.

"Don't be ridiculous. No-one would be that stupid. TARP-2 – give me the handset back!"

Aftab quietly shook his head and switched his trusty radio back on. The cricket was still playing – thank goodness – and he settled comfortably back in his seat.

*

"Here's the question I've been wanting to get straight all day," Toby said, grabbing his chance. "Professor – Dave – you two. How actually do you know each other?"

"Haha! Yes, I was wondering when you were going to get to that."

"Well?"

"Well it goes back to the AAC, hmm?" the Professor continued. "You remember I told you about all the years spent trying to persuade the AAC to drop the idea of selling the planet?"

"Yes."

"Well, as it was becoming clear I wasn't winning the argument, I did the next best thing. I set up a course. A university course. I thought, if the authorities are determined to sell the planet, I should at least educate a new generation in the perils of, ah-hm, interstellar finance. Don't you think? It was a master's degree but a rather unusual one. You see…"

The Professor paused for a moment to try to summon his words. He stared out the window and then turned back to them.

"You see, I couldn't let my students know *why* they were going to study it." The Professor gestured with his right hand. "And I couldn't let the university know *what* they were going to study." He gestured with his left hand. "And I didn't have much idea *how* they were going to study," he concluded, waving both his hands enthusiastically.

"Rather unusual, no?" the Professor asked. "But what can you do when you're trying to educate people about a dangerous secret which you cannot reveal?"

"So what did you do?"

"Ah, yes, yes. I called the course 'Astro Financial Mechanics'. Hmm? It worked, for while. There was just one small problem. It only attracted a single student. Which is where…"

"I come in," Paranoid Dave said quietly.

"OK…" Toby said. "But, Dave, why would you want to do a course on astro-financial mechanics?"

"Well, I thought the course was about the mechanics of space travel…" Paranoid Dave shifted uncomfortably, and looked in the rear-view mirror to see the other two staring at him. "What? I love mechanical things. It was an innocent mistake."

"Yes," the Professor continued, "everyone sees what they want to, hmm? Astro-financial mechanics… David thought it was a course on mechanics. The University thought it was about methods for funding space exploration. But it was actually about, erm, well, interstellar finance."

"I never found out about the *interstellar* bit. You just presented a lot of finance stuff…" Paranoid Dave added sheepishly. "I mean, Professor, you didn't breathe a word about *all this*." Paranoid Dave gestured vaguely with his arm at the carnival around them. "The Za-Nakarians, the Golgothans, outer space, the exciting stuff. I mean, God, if I'd known, I'd have paid more attention."

"Hang on," Toby interrupted, "now I'm properly

confused. You sat a course on interstellar finance, but didn't know it was about interstellar finance?"

"Yeah. Pretty dumb, huh?" Paranoid Dave sunk a little lower.

"Ah!" the Professor continued. "But that was my intention. It was important to cover the basics of financial mathematics first, in the Autumn term. Hmm? No need to scare my students with any reference to the wider Universe."

"So what did you learn? In the Autumn term?" Toby asked.

"Well," Dave replied, looking thoughtful, "the first module was on financial compounding and discounting. I think? Then there was stuff on bond valuation and... equities. That's right and then the Professor went on to derivatives and it started to get properly complicated. The next modules were on short positions, I remember that..."

"And then swaps, options, and securitisation, hmm?" the Professor continued helpfully. "The more exotic modules were due to start in the Spring term. That was when they'd find out what was really going on, once my students had passed the Autumn term exam. Once they had proved themselves... How should I say?"

"...worthy." Paranoid Dave answered morosely. "Only I didn't, did I?"

"What happened? What went wrong in the Spring term?" Toby asked.

"Oh, everything started fine in the Spring term," Paranoid Dave replied, looking at the Professor. "Except that I quit—"

"—and I went into hiding," the Professor added cheerfully.

"Quit? Hiding? What did you do to each other?" Toby asked.

"I wasn't going to sit the Professor's exam," Paranoid Dave replied defensively. "I'd just have flunked it. So I quit, ok?"

"You quit?" Toby started "After just one—"

"Hey! Leave him alone," Charlie interrupted sharply, instantly crushing Toby's soul. "There's nothing wrong with quitting." She leaned across and placed a hand protectively on Paranoid Dave's shoulder. Her voice turned half-tender, half-defensive. "Failure can be ok. You close a door, another one opens... Well, that's what I'm hoping anyway..." Charlie's voice trailed off.

"And as for me," the Professor continued cheerfully, "the problem wasn't David. It was the AAC. That was when they threw me out. I had become a risk to the sale process. They've been hunting for me ever since."

*

"Well now," the Professor spoke up, after a silence which everyone found extremely awkward except him, "where do you think we shall find our friend Woola?"

"Actually, I did have an idea about that," Charlie replied.

"You did?"

"Sure. He's the most important person on the planet right now, and we know he's heading back to London. It can't be that hard. Why don't we find out the old-fashioned way?"

"Which is?"

"Switch the radio on? Every channel will be talking

about him."

The Professor inclined his head in agreement and leaned down to switch on the old radio below the Daimler's dashboard. It crackled with static for a moment, and then the cricket commentary came on.

"Ha!" exclaimed Paranoid Dave. "Every channel except that one. Try another station, Professor."

"No wait!" It was Charlie. "Turn it up for a second."

"Certainly…" the Professor adjusted the knob.

Thwack!

"…Oh marvellous shot! Straight through mid-off. That looks like it's going to be… And it is! Four runs. Marvellous!

"Now as I was saying, my Woola cake. We've been sent the most marvellous confection this afternoon, shaped exactly like…

*

"…our favourite alien. It's come from Mrs Huggins in Pontefract…"

Aftab smiled to himself. There was nothing quite like the cricket commentary for relaxing the mind. Although he did wonder for a moment about Mrs Huggins from Pontefract. He was pretty sure Pontefract was in Yorkshire. *How had Mrs Huggins found time since the press conference to bake a cake and have it delivered to a commentary box in London?* Shrugging that thought from his mind, he looked in his rear-view mirror. The six soldiers in the back were still bickering and elbowing each other.

Then he looked out through the windscreen at the front. He could see the giant rubbery bottom of the giant inflatable Woola. Pressing his face close to the windscreen and looking up, he could make out the back of Woola's huge head, lurching about above the top of the buildings.

"There's a message written in icing, 'Happy 1ˢᵗ Earthday, Woola!' Lovely! Of course Woola isn't far from us here at Lords. He's already back from Scotland and heading to a concert in Trafalgar Square…

*

"…and after that to Downing Street for talks with the Prime Minister. What a simply marvellous day to be a cricket fan…"

Click.

Paranoid Dave turned the radio off, and looked up in the rear-view mirror.

"We have our answer. Trafalgar Square anyone?"

"Yeah sure," Toby replied.

"Let's do it," Charlie said.

"And if that doesn't work, we can try Downing Street after," the Professor added, smiling sweetly as if nothing could be simpler.

*

Aftab gently turned the radio off and stroked his fine black beard meditatively.

By now the traffic had crawled to a standstill. His hand lingered on his beard as he thought for a moment.

And then he made his decision.

Very quietly, he applied the handbrake, removed his keys, opened the front door and slipped out onto the street. The wonderful thing about a street, Aftab thought to himself, is that they're one dimensional. There's only one way to go.

16

"Now it's my turn for a question," Charlie said firmly. The Daimler was still crawling along in the procession, inching towards the left-turn they needed up ahead. "Professor – Mrs B mentioned that the Za-Nakarians brought a special present with them. When they first visited Earth. Something that helped persuade our leaders to enter the sale negotiation."

"Yes, yes, that's quite true. It was very persuasive."

"What was it?"

"What was it?"

"Yes, what was it?"

"Ah, well, I see… Yes, hmm…"

"Professor!"

"Well… It was… a 'Personalitron'."

"A *Personalitron*?"

"A Personalitron."

A Personalitron… Charlie rolled the word around inside her head.

"Well, ok… What's that?"

"What's that?"

"Yes, what's that?"

"Ah, yes, *that*. Well, that is… It is…" the Professor fumbled vaguely. "A Personalitron is a means of travelling across space. To anywhere where's there's another Personalitron. They link up to each other in a kind of network."

"You mean like… *teleporting?*"

"Hmm, yes… And no. But mostly yes."

"No way. *Seriously?* They brought one of those?" Paranoid Dave took his eyes completely off the road.

"Quite serious, yes. But no, they didn't bring one," the Professor replied, smiling. "They brought two."

"*Get out of here!*" Paranoid Dave exclaimed.

"*Shut up!*" Charlie's hand reached for her sunglasses. "Oh, sorry, Professor, it's just an expression…"

"Not at all, my dear, not at all. They quite dazzled our leaders. You can travel light-years in a few Earth minutes. There are, however, a few complications… For example, they don't teleport the *whole package.* No, they don't…" The Professor trailed off for a moment. "But let's not overcomplicate things. No, no. The main point is this: Personalitrons are quite good for conveying small objects like humans across large distances like space and, since 2008, we now have two of them."

"But where are they? In Washington DC? In the Pentagon?" Paranoid Dave asked.

"Oh no, they're just a few miles away," the Professor answered matter-of-factly.

"Where?"

"Under Downing Street."

"*Downing Street?*"

"Downing Street."

*

"Boss… Err boss?"

"What is it?" the TARP leader replied tetchily, as he

continued fiddling with the satellite phone.

"Boss, I think our cab driver has gone," TARP-2 replied nervously. "And he's taken the key."

"Fine, fine, just find anoth— You *what?*"

"Have a look, boss. Vanished."

"*What the…*"

*

"When you say the Personalitrons are in Downing Street, Professor—" Toby started.

"I didn't say *in*, I said *under*."

"Right, *under* Downing Street," Toby corrected, "do you mean the Downing Street in London? The one where Woola is heading after Trafalgar Square, and where we might be going too? *This* Downing Street?"

"Yes, *that* Downing Street," the Professor replied.

"*This* Downing Street and *that* Downing Street – from our point of view, are they connected in some way? I mean, it's just a coincidence, right?"

"Oh, I should think so," the Professor replied, not clarifying which of Toby's questions he was answering.

Tap, tap.

Toby gave an involuntary start. True, the car was surrounded by a throng of people, and all the noise of the world's most spontaneous, and largest, street carnival. But sometimes quiet noises can cut straight through loud ones, and the sound of someone tapping the rear passenger window of the Professor's old Daimler was one of those.

Toby looked up to see a young, handsome, bearded face a few inches away, smiling calmly at him. Toby wound down the window.

"Excuse me?" the stranger asked very politely.

"Err, yes?"

"I'm sorry to disturb, but I am needing to check something. You are heading to No.10 Downing Street, aren't you?"

"Err, well, funny you should ask. We might drop in on Trafalgar Square first. But probably. Hang on, why am I telling you this? Who are—"

"Thank you, that is all. Goodbye." The stranger smiled politely.

"Goodbye."

The stranger made to leave, but turned back. "Oh, and by the way, very nice jumping."

"Excuse me?"

"When you jumped into this marvellous car as it was moving. This was very good jumping. Amazing actually."

"Thank you," replied Toby, who was too startled to say anything coherent.

"And you did it without any further damage to your very fine Daimler. I am very pleased. Wishing you good day."

"Good day," Toby replied automatically.

And with that, the stranger started to walk away.

"*Tobyyyyyy…*" hissed Charlie on the back seat. "That's the taxi driver. The one who's driving the soldiers around. I recognise him!"

"Call him back! Quickly, before he disappears," Paranoid Dave added urgently. "Maybe he can tell us what they're up to?"

Still half-hypnotised, Toby obediently leaned out of the back window and called out to the stranger, who was fast merging into the crowd.

"Excuse me!" he shouted. "Hellooo…"

Miraculously, the stranger heard him, and turned back towards the Daimler.

"Yes?"

"Err, what's your name?"

"Aftab."

"Aftab? Nice, to meet you, Aftab. I'm Toby." Toby stuck his hand out of the window, in a way that left his elbow poking out to the side at a strange and rather awkward angle.

"Nice to meet you." Aftab didn't shake Toby's outstretched hand, but graciously pressed it between his two hands in a manner that seemed to Toby rather – well – *spiritual*.

"Excuse me, Aftab, but are you, erm, are you…" Toby turned to the gang in the car, who were chattering umpteen instructions at him. "*Sssh,* I can't think."

He turned back to the stranger, who was still holding his hand.

"Excuse me, are you trying to kill us?"

"Oh no. Not at all."

"You're not? That's great then. What a relief." Toby withdrew his hand gratefully back into the car.

"But I do have six trained assassins in the back of my taxi. I think maybe they are thinking to kill you?"

"Oh, I see."

"I truly hope they don't. But you see, I am accepting their money. I am bound by honour to delivering them where it is they want to go. And they have asked to go wherever you are going. And so it is."

"Oh right…" Toby thought for a second, finding Aftab's words both strangely calming and slightly alarming at the same time. "But do you have to accept their money? Could you take them some place else, you know, for free?"

"They are my guests."

"Oh right. I see." Toby didn't see, of course, but he had the feeling he'd been told something profound that couldn't be argued with. "Well, is there anything you could do to – you know – slow them down a bit, or put them off in some way? There must be something?"

The stranger thought for a moment.

"Yes I do believe there is something."

"Oh wonderful."

"I shall pray for you."

The stranger smiled beatifically. "Wishing you good day."

And with that he left, disappearing genie-like back into the crowd from which he'd emerged. Toby watched him go, and turned back to the others.

"Well, what's he going to do? How's he going to help?" Paranoid Dave asked.

"He said he's going to…"

"Going to what?"

"…pray for us."

*

Aftab slipped quietly back into his cab. He turned the key in the ignition, and eased the cab forward a few yards to catch up with the procession that had nudged forward.

He looked in his rear-view mirror.

All six soldiers were staring in his direction, open-mouthed.

The TARP leader spoke first.

"You've just been to see them, haven't you? The suspects, the people we're pursuing."

"Indeed," Aftab replied calmly.

The TARP leader nodded, chewing some gum and trying to look casual.

"Find out anything, did you? Where they're heading, anything like that?"

"Indeed."

"Uh-huh, that's good," the TARP leader replied, still chewing. "And where might that be then?"

"They are going first to Trafalgar Square and then to the very seat of Government. To No.10 Downing Street."

"Oh?" the TARP leader gulped, almost swallowing his piece of gum. "Close by, are they? The old Jaguar, I mean."

"Yes, they are close by. Their car is just the other side of the giant, blow-up alien."

"Is that a fact? Interesting. Don't you think TARP-2? The people we're trying to hunt down, who may very well be assassins, are now heading to No.10 Downing Street. Interesting isn't it?"

"Yes, boss, that's really interesting."

"T H E N   G E T   Y O U R   B L O O D Y   A R S E S   O U T   O F   T H E   C A B   A N D   G E T   A F T E R   T H E M !" the TARP leader exploded. "*N O W !*"

The TARP team bundled out of the cab as fast as their equipment and bulk allowed. Which wasn't in fact very fast at all, but certainly looked urgent.

Aftab watched them leave.

"But one important point you missed," he said in a quiet voice as they disappeared out of the cab. "It is not a Jaguar. It is a Daimler. The DE36 model. First manufactured in 1949, and with a V8 engine if I'm not mistaken."

Aftab wagged his finger and tutted.

"Schoolboy error."

But the TARP team were gone, forcing their way through the crowd towards the inflatable Woola.

*

"Oh no, what now…"

Paranoid Dave looked in his rear-view mirror. He could see a commotion in the crowd behind him, and then suddenly the TARP team burst into view. They looked menacing and predatory in their black uniforms as they emerged from the mad colour of the carnival.

"Daaave," Charlie screamed, "*Daaaaaave* – hit the pedal!"

"I'm trying!" Paranoid Dave replied, as he banked the Daimler into a sharp left turn, down a side street and away form the main carnival. "But Christ, there's people in front. I can't just mow them down."

"Well use the horn!"

"OK, OK, obviously! I'm not stupid," Paranoid Dave replied. "Err, where's the horn?"

Paranoid Dave's left hand started fumbling with every lever and knob it could find, while his eyes stayed fixed on the pedestrians in front. With all its lights flashing on and off, and the windscreen wipers squeaking against an entirely dry windscreen, the Daimler started to gather speed – but not fast enough.

The TARP team bounded up to it and ran alongside. They started banging on the bodywork and yelling at them to stop. Toby looked to his right and saw one of the soldiers running right next to him. He noticed a patch on his upper arm: 'TARP-2'. TARP-2 was alternately looking ahead and then looking sideways at Toby and yelling. At that moment a jet of water squirted directly into TARP-2's eyes. Paranoid Dave's hand had crashed against the lever for the screenwash. TARP-2 lost a yard or two, rubbed his eyes clear and bounded level with Toby's window again, looking even angrier than before. Toby's brain, whose thoughts he was having less and less success at controlling, reacted slightly bolshily. He wondered why TARP-2 was so angry. *After all I'm the one being chased constantly, and for no good reason*, Toby reasoned to himself, *I have much more reason to be furious.* Just for a moment Toby even found himself wondering what TARP-2's children (assuming he had any children) would say to TARP-2, if they knew that he was trying to arrest the very people who were trying to rescue the planet for their benefit and everyone else's. He imagined they'd give TARP-2 quite an earful.

As Paranoid Dave's hand frantically crashed against another set of levers, the Professor leaned across and pulled a knob on the dashboard. The Daimler's horn gave off a deep, ear-shattering noise, the kind you might hear from a huge ship passing by in the fog. It momentarily knocked the TARP team off their stride.

The pedestrians ahead scattered out of the way.

Paranoid Dave floored the pedal and the Daimler pulled away from its pursuers.

17

"HELLO LONDOOON!"

The crowd responded with a huge whoop and cheer that surged like a sea swell, and faded again.

"H E L L O   P L A N E T   E E A A A R T H !"

An even louder surge.

The pop superstar knew how to whip up a crowd, he'd been doing it for decades. Nothing was easier than a festival crowd and, although this wasn't a strictly a festival, the atmosphere was totally festival. He adjusted his pink-tinted glasses. He cupped the mic in both hands, pressed his face against it – just off centre – and let rip.

"H E L L O O O   U U U – N I I I I I I – V E E E E E R R R R S E !"

The crowd went wild. In his skin-tight black leather trousers, the pop superstar strutted off to his right, mic raised in one hand above his head, his other hand clapping against it rhythmically. He strutted back to the centre, whipping the crowd even more.

And he hadn't even got to the climax yet.

He paused centre stage. He let the noise subside. He dropped his voice.

He was going to work them back through the gears.

"We have a guest for you tonight…" he said quietly, theatrically.

Pause.

A few off-beat whoops rang out in the silence.

"…uh-huh, we do… Oh yeah… A VEEERY special guest…"

A longer pause. More whoops. The audience held its breath.

Could it be true? Was it possible? Were they going to see…

The pop superstar erupted into the mic:

"…W E   H A V E   W o o o o o o o o o o o –
L A A A A A A A A A A A A A A !"

Woola was wheeled onto the stage as a screaming, baying vortex of sound rose from the crowd – a noise so powerful, so visceral, Toby felt physically lifted by it. It rushed in through his ears, it penetrated his skin into the hairs on his arms, it travelled along the ground and up through his legs. It passed into every crevice of his frame, it ripped up and down his spine like an electric shock. The lighting rig on stage went haywire as beams flashed in all directions. Powerful searchlights had been mounted behind the audience and they hurled purple and yellow beams through the half-light of dusk onto the National Gallery, Admiralty Arch, Nelson's column, every corner of Trafalgar Square, and high into the sky above it.

Back on stage, the pop superstar approached Woola and gave him a fist bump, which Woola met with a clenched forelimb and just a hint of cool. Woola was wearing a black, floppy beanie on his head and a few bracelets on his forearms. The pop superstar handed Woola the mic.

The mad swell of noise subsided fractionally. Woola leaned towards the mic to speak.

But even that gesture sent the crowd into a

screaming ecstasy.

Woola leaned away from the mic and smiled quizzically at the pop superstar. The pop superstar nodded and went to centre stage. He put a finger to his lips and made an exaggerated gesture for quiet.

Eventually the crowd quietened. Woola leaned towards the mic again.

"*Hellooooo...*" he trilled in his trademark greeting.

A swell of noise from the crowd rose and fell.

Woola continued.

"*Woola loves you... L O N D O O O O O O N !*"

The audience screamed.

It was a mad, hysterical, frenzied, ecstatic scream.

And a new, deeper note entered the polyphony. It was a base tone, a kind of animal moan. As if Woola had released some craving, some strange intoxicating mixture of desire and desperation. The hysteria was infectious, pervasive. And it didn't just express itself in noise. The audience pressed together, stranger against stranger, skin against skin; they heaved, they writhed, they jumped, they screamed. The months and months of maintaining social distance, the agony of confusion, all melted away in this moment of shared ecstasy. Thousands of arms stretched and rubbed and reached frantically towards the stage, fingers splayed, in a collective mania of longing.

It was only when he felt a hand come down calmly on his shoulder that Toby realised he was screaming too.

He looked round. It was Paranoid Dave, who was staring at him firmly, his hand still on Toby's shoulder. Toby blinked a couple of times, and felt himself coming back down to Earth. He looked to his right and saw Charlie, who was still staring at the stage, transfixed. Her pretty mouth was half open and her eyes shone with an intensity as they thought Toby-wasn't-sure-what thoughts. Or maybe they weren't thinking any thoughts at all, which was perhaps the whole point.

Paranoid Dave placed his other hand on Charlie's shoulder, and she turned towards him with a start. Paranoid Dave gestured with his head, and all three of them looked behind to see the Professor. He had his usual bemused look on his face. He mouthed some words to them – which were totally inaudible in the din of noise – and beckoned with his hand.

It was time to leave, they weren't going to get anywhere near Woola here.

The gang wriggled their way back through the hysterical crowd. As they reached the edge of the Square, Toby looked back up at the stage. Woola was being wheeled off again. A tribute band were getting ready to play. Toby glimpsed Woola's wheelie bin disappear behind the stage towards his minders.

They would have to try to catch Woola at his next stop. Although Heaven knows how they were going to manage that.

*

Words are flowing out like endless rain into a paper cup...

Fifty yards to go.

...They slither wildly as they slip away across the Universe...

The song playing in Trafalgar Square boomed powerfully all the way down Whitehall, clearly audible beneath the hysterical screaming. Toby could feel the bass notes and the drum beat travelling along the road and up through his legs as he walked.

Left and right, revellers were making their way towards Trafalgar Square, drawn by the noise and the the growing desire to throng together with other people. There was no traffic. The streets belonged to the people now. London was one big party.

"Professor – isn't there like a rear entrance? Somewhere more private. Wouldn't that be an easier way in?"

Toby was trying to recover his sense of normality. It didn't help that his ears were ringing and his own voice sounded muffled and detached like someone else was speaking. It also didn't help that they were fast approaching the main gate to Downing Street with the Professor apparently totally unconcerned as to how *utterly and completely insane this was.*

"Hmmm? Oh no, the front way in is much easier. Far less security. No machines to read our passes. It'll be fine."

Nothing's gonna change my world…

Twenty yards to go.

"Professor," Toby hissed. "Seriously, Professor, this is *nuts* – we'll never get in there. We'll get arrested and put in jail and then the whole planet will be stuffed."

Nothing's gonna change my world…

Fifteen yards.

"Professor, seriously, can we stop and think about this?"

"Hmm? Ok. Very well." The Professor stopped in his tracks.

"Oh. Great." Toby was pleasantly surprised, someone had actually listened to him. "So we'll try the back way?"

"Oh no. We'll go in the front way," the Professor replied sweetly. "I just wanted to give you some time to compose yourself. Hmm? Otherwise you'll spook the policemen. And that's unfair, don't you think? They've probably had a very trying day."

The Professor smiled at Toby.

"Ready?"

"Err… Ready, " said Toby. Wrong-footed again.

"Excellent."

And the Professor set off again in his strange ambling gait. Toby watched him for a moment as he half-walked, half-floated across the ground. His body was turned almost sideways to his direction of travel, as if he was being blown along by a gust of wind and as if one more gust might carry him clean away. Toby looked ahead to the massive and utterly impenetrable security barrier in front of Downing Street and wondered how someone so slight was going to get them past an obstacle so massive.

…Thoughts meander like a restless wind inside a letter box…

Ten yards to go.

Five yards.

Four – Three – Two…

One yard.

"Evenin', Professor," one of the policemen said in a gravelly cockney accent, and with a hint of deference. "You keeping well?"

"Oh, yes, perfectly well, thank you, Peter," the Professor replied courteously.

"Card?"

"Here you are." The Professor held out his card as if it was the most natural thing in the world. "And you? Your two boys in good fettle? Hmm?"

"Oh, they're proper little rascals, those two," the policeman smiled as he handed the card back having barely looked at it. "I see you've brought some friends with you. AAC?"

"Yes, that sort of thing."

"Card!" the policeman grunted in Toby's direction without even looking at him. Toby reached down mechanically into his pocket, retrieved the card and held it out. "Come to think of it, Professor, haven't seen you round these parts for a few months. How's that then?"

"Oh I've been busy," the Professor smiled.

"Course you have. Cards, you two!" the policeman barked at Charlie and Paranoid Dave. "You must have been busy with all this rumpus, Professor. We've had a lot of your colleagues through today. It's a funny old business."

"Oh yes, very strange."

"Mind you, 'spect it will all blow over soon enough, don't you think?"

"Oh, I should think so," the Professor replied agreeably.

The policeman turned to his colleague behind him in the small security hut.

"All clear, Rogan. You can let these four through."

Toby, Paranoid Dave and Charlie stepped through the gate, their eyes wide with disbelief. They had just entered Downing Street under false ID in pursuit of an alien. The Professor was following behind through the gate, when the policeman's voice rang out .

"Hang on, hang on – just a minute!"

Toby's heart stopped.

Damn.

This was too cruel.

He looked round, ready to put his hands in the air, surrender in a quiet manner, dignified. He'd seen the war movies.

The policeman leaned towards the Professor with a stern look on his face. Then he whispered to him, conspiratorially.

"This whole malarkey, Professor," the policeman said. "*Do* they know what they're doing? Do they really?"

"Hmm, ha! Yes, yes, well," the Professor stroked his beard and paused. "Yes, that's what we intend to find out, you see?"

"You do? Well, if there's any fishy business, we'll be depending on you to set them right." The policeman tapped his nose and straightened back up. "On your way now, gentlemen, miss. They'll open the door for you as you arrive. See that you close it behind you as you go in. It gets quite draughty there in the evenings."

The policeman winked as they left.

*

By 'door' the policeman of course meant *that* door.

Toby's eyes fastened onto it as he started walking down Downing Street. He felt a strange, sparkling, tingling sensation in his skin. It was the feeling he got sometimes when he entered a room, where a party has just been held, as if the guests had left some of their energy behind.

It was the same feeling now as he crossed Downing Street, times by ten. Or perhaps twenty. Some of the crowd barriers were still scattered around. A few busy, preoccupied-looking officials were criss-crossing the street. The lighting rigs were still up, and here and there a scattering of reporters were speaking to camera.

As they approached the world's most famous door on the world's most famous street, sure enough it opened for them as if by magic. The Professor stepped through it with his usual smiling unconcern. Paranoid Dave followed behind, clutching his leather overcoat around him. Toby and Charlie lingered behind just for a moment, looking around at Downing Street and trying to take in the sheer bizarre madness of it all. And then Toby turned back towards No.10 and, leaving Charlie a moment longer with her thoughts, he stepped in.

Another door, another threshold.

18

"You've enjoyed your day?"

"Yeah, not bad, not bad. Pretty good actually, as these things go."

"I'm thrilled to hear it."

"Cold up in Scotland though. *Brrrrr.* How do those people put up with it? I mean *seriously?*"

"Haha!" The Prime Minister laughed ingratiatingly. "They're quite tough up in Scotland. They cope. Best to leave Scotland to the Scots, that's what I always say."

"You think? I think the place has potential," Woola mused in accentless English, crossing his upper flippers under his head to make himself more comfortable.

"But you'll let us know if you have any suggestions? You know, changes we can make down here? On Earth I mean. You bringing a fresh pair of eyes and all that. Haha!"

"Yeah?" Woola cast his eyes briefly towards the Prime Minister. "Well, you could start by warming Scotland up a few degrees."

"Haha! Oh you are funny."

"Excuse me, Prime Minister, Woola" an orderly addressed the pair with formality. "Three minutes to departure."

"Three minutes? Sure thing," Woola replied nonchalantly. He shifted a little on his gurney and started whistling *Scotland the Brave*. One of his lower flippers tapped along. He had learnt the tune from a bagpiper outside Holyrood.

The Prime Minister was on the gurney next to Woola, looking anxious. He wasn't yet comfortable with the idea of lying naked on a stretcher on wheels in the middle of the Personalitron departure terminal, while a stream of orderlies and operators bustled to-and-fro around him. All of them were wearing white, full-body hazmat suits while he just had a small white towel, draped across his middle, to preserve his modesty. His slightly pudgy torso had gone noticeably paler, and a thin film of sweat was forming. Which was strange because he actually felt rather cold.

"You look ill. You ok?" Woola looked across, just realising something for the first time. "Say, have you actually been in one of these things before?"

"Err, no actually. This is the first time."

"Ah, there's nothing to it. But you should relax. That's important. Relax. Reduces the risk of fragmentation."

Woola resumed his humming.

"Fragmentation?"

"Hmm? Oh yeah, fragmentation. That's when your personality breaks up in transit, so not all of you arrives on the other side. Fragmentation."

"I'm sorry… I'm not sure I follow?" The Prime Minister spluttered.

"Well look, they're sending over a package, right? Not your actual body – that stays here – but all the information that's needed to make a perfect, functioning copy of you. Your genotype, your phenotype, your memories, your personality, your soul, ya-de-ya. It all goes over. As a package. So stay cool and enjoy the ride."

"Right, yes, of course." The Prime Minister said to himself, crossing his hands over his tummy and staring fixedly at the ceiling. "Stay cool, enjoy the ride."

"Two minutes to departure," the orderly announced.

The Prime Minister drummed his fingers on his tummy for a few seconds.

"Just out of interest," he asked Woola, "do they send *everything* over? I mean, I've been having a little err… A little runny tummy… Will the err…?"

"Will the germs get sent over? 'Fraid so. Everything that goes in that tube gets copied and sent. You, your germs, the lot. Heck, they'll even copy the gurney." Woola nodded at the stretcher on which the Prime Minister was lying. "There's dozens of those things at the other end, it's a hoot."

"Ah? Lots of gurneys. Haha," the Prime Minister laughed, as another piece of him died inside. "So how do you stay so calm?"

"Oh it's easier for me."

"Because?"

"Well remember, I'm on a *return* journey. That's easier. I'll just be slotting back into my own body on Za-Nak. This is London Woola. That's Za-Nak Woola. *This* Personalitron will send all the information across to *that* Personalitron, and hey presto – Za-Nak Woola gets updated with the new stuff. The new memories, the new relationships and so on. It's just a mental package that gets sent back, actually. So any bugs, germs, diseases I might've picked up, they stay here. I wake back up in Za-Nak feeling just the way I do now, but physically not a day older than when I left." Woola smiled. "Easy."

"And London Woola?" The Prime Minister gulped.

"Goes into a body silo. Same as London you."

"London me? Body silo?"

"Yeah, those things over there," Woola thumbed casually towards some mysterious looking structures, barely visible in the half light. "And then on *your* return journey, they will take your body back out of the silo, pop it into one of the insertion tubes, your personality and so on will be re-inserted and – hey presto – you're home. Re-insertion is always a lot easier than ejection," Woola mused.

"Got it."

"One minute to departure," the orderly announced gravely. "Are you both ready?"

"Born ready," Woola replied, winking at the orderly.

The Prime Minister turned slightly to the orderly and gurned a false smile. He tried to quip a casual joke but found himself strangely unable to speak.

He laid his head back down, defeated, and started drumming his fingers again.

"Will this take long?" he asked Woola after a few seconds. "I mean the, err, crossing?"

"Haha, now you're asking! We haven't got time for that debate. I mean, what is *time?* Journey time, that's simple. Somewhere between five seconds and five minutes. Nice and quick. But time *as you will experience it?* That's a whole big can of worms. So many variables. Curvature of space-time. Alignment of the galaxies. Gravitational fields. *Relativity.* But you know what?"

"What?"

"It mostly comes down to the weather."

"The *weather?* But I didn't think there was any weather in space?"

"Oh, there's weather in space alright. In the 5th and 6th dimensions especially. Calmer in 1 to 4, true. And if you can use the 7th dimension, that's nice and smooth. Actually, you want to use 7, that's just great. But this old bit of junk," Woola added, nodding at the machine in front of them, "this thing stays firmly in 5 and 6."

"What do you mean junk, I mean why do you call it—"

"Excuse me Prime Minister, Woola." The orderly interrupted firmly. "Zero hour. Towels please!"

At his command, two more orderlies whipped the towels smartly away from the Prime Minister and Woola. Before they, or anyone else, could get too surprised by the sight of their completely naked bodies, another two orderlies pushed the gurneys forward, conveying a totally disorientated Prime Minister, and a much calmer Za-Nakarian Chief Negotiator, into the two ejection tubes of the London Personalitron.

The gurneys clicked securely into the position, and the orderlies smartly closed the two circular glass doors behind them. They placed their hands on the large circular steel locks and spun them shut.

*

"Guys, guys – did you see who was just behind us?"

"Who?"

"The TARP team people, or whatever they call themselves," Charlie whispered. "I looked back through the door of No.10 as they were closing it, and I saw them just running up to the gate of Downing Street."

"Can you be sure?" Paranoid Dave whispered back.

"Not a hundred percent. They were the other side of the railings, it was hard to see. But how many guys dressed in black combat gear are we expecting in Downing Street around now?"

"Damn. They've caught up with us already. I wish they'd stop doing that," Toby joined the whispering. "By the way, why are we whispering?"

"I dunno, maybe this lift is bugged or something?"

The gang were travelling down beneath Downing Street in a stainless steel lift, that was shiny and futuristic-looking. On entering No.10 they had been greeted by a flunky who recognised the Professor and thought it the most natural request in the world to be taken to see Woola. The other three had followed behind in a state of disbelieving awe as they were guided through a warren of windowless corridors and hallways. No.10 had a tardis-like quality: modest on the outside, maze-like on the inside. At every turn, the whole bewildering diversity of Government seemed to brush past them – men in suits, women in military uniform, humourless looking security guards, cleaners, a couple of dudes in shorts and t-shirts, even a small clutch of children briefly appeared and disappeared again. Eventually they arrived face-to-face with a stainless-steel lift door. The flunky had inserted a key and the lift doors opened. The flunky had leaned into the lift, entered a code, and then pressed a large button labelled 'P'. And so here they were, taking a surprisingly long descent beneath Downing Street.

"Professor…" It was Paranoid Dave, looking at his watch. "How deep does this lift go? I thought we were just going down to the basement?"

"Well, we are. In a manner of speaking," the

Professor replied evasively. "It's just that Woola may in one of the, erm, lower sections of the basement."

"Professor," Paranoid Dave's eyes were at their beediest. "Has this got anything to do with the Personalitron?"

"The Personalitron?" Charlie repeated in alarm, like a tripwire going off. "So we are heading to *that?*"

"Professor…" Toby started. "We have the TARP team behind us and, as far I can tell, the Personalitron in front. And this lift is *still* travelling down. What's going on?"

"Well, yes, it's true that the Personalitron is kept beneath Downing Street, hmm? About fourteen floors down. In a manner of speaking. Of course, there aren't really thirteen floors between Downing Street and the Personalitron."

"Well what is there then?"

"More like a couple of basement floors and a lot of rock. Anyway," the Professor clapped his hands, "with a bit of luck we'll catch Woola in time before he, errm, departs. Yes?"

"And if we don't?"

"Ah yes, well then," the Professor stroked his beard, "we may have to devise an alternative strategy. Yes."

"Like following him?"

"Conceivably."

"Into space?"

"Perhaps."

"Oh God…" Toby said, as he put one hand against the side of the lift to steady himself, "I knew it."

"Into *outer* space?" Paranoid Dave asked in a tone of awe.

"Yes," said the Professor.

"Wow," said Paranoid Dave.

"*Shut up!*" said Charlie.

"Hmm, yes, but look on the bright side. We shall escape the TARP team… Owp! We've arrived," the Professor added with a hint of relief, as the lift doors swivelled open.

*

"Passes!" a stern voice called out.

Before Toby and the others could rally against the Professor, they found themselves standing meekly in line behind him at a security checkpoint in a surprisingly large subterranean hallway. They were in a very different world to the one they'd left fourteen floors higher. The checkpoint was located at the entrance to an octagonal hallway, from which corridors ran off in four directions. It was all bright lights and spotless surfaces. Every chrome fitting screamed top-secret-high-tech facility.

"In the machine, please," the stern voice said again in a rather uncompromising and not-easily-charmed sort of way. The voice belonged an imposing looking lady in her fifties, who sat hunched over a computer terminal by the security barrier. She was large and squat, and wore an old-fashioned grey woollen uniform that looked just a touch incongruous amidst all the high-techness. On her chest, a large name badge proclaimed: Dorothy Overend, Head of Security. Bottle-end glasses were wedged implacably onto her nose and strict waves of steel-grey hair curled around her head like coils of barbed wire. Two very polished looking marines were stood to attention behind her, looking equally humourless and about a hundred years younger.

The Professor placed his card into the machine.

A red light went off.

"Card not recognised," the security woman said. "Officers, please escort this man back to ground level and see that he finds his way out of Downing Street. Either that or arrest him. Up to you."

The two marines started to advance on the Professor like a pair of Dobermans towards a juicy steak.

"Well, of course, you must do precisely that," the Professor said in his most agreeable voice. "But I must say, Dorothy, it is a little strange. I had no trouble at the main entrance to Downing Street."

The security woman held up a hand and checked the marines' advance.

Very slowly she leaned back in her seat, removed her bottle-end glasses and polished them with a small cloth. *Oh God*, Toby thought, *she's enjoying this.* He shifted uncomfortably in the queue and wondered whether to do a runner back to the lift. *She's not just going to arrest the Professor, she's going to watch those marines eat him. And then they'll start on us.*

She slotted the glasses back into the deep red furrows on her nose from which she had withdrawn them, and leaned slowly – very, very slowly – towards the Professor.

She blinked slightly.

"Artemas? ...*Artemas?* Is that you?"

"Oh yes, Dorothy, it's me. Well, it was five minutes ago, when I last checked, hmm? And probably will still be in five minutes time. Although perhaps not if I get in that Personalitron of yours!"

"Oh, Artemas, you are a wit," Dorothy broke out in titters like a schoolgirl. One hand involuntarily went up to straighten her iron grey curls. It was purely a symbolic gesture. The chubby fingers prodded and plucked, but the curls didn't yield.

"Well, Professor – I suppose I should call you 'Professor'" …more titters… "You best let me see your card."

The Professor passed it to her.

"Well, what a fine photo that is…" Dorothy continued coyly. "You say you had no trouble at the main entrance?"

"Yes, yes, Peter was very helpful," the Professor replied. "How frustrating for you. Have you been having a lot of trouble with your machine recently?"

"Well, now you mention it, it was making a strange humming sound a couple of months ago… I shall have it looked at. Through you go," Dorothy added, leaning under her desk and pressing a button.

She turned and saw the two marines looking at the Professor suspiciously.

"What are you gormless muffins staring at?" she said, returning to battleship mode. "Professor James has been on the AAC since before you were born, so you can both get back in your kennel right now."

The two soldiers retreated a yard, looking chastised.

She turned back to the Professor, her face lighting up again. "Your young friends are with the AAC as well? Of course they are," she added without waiting. She buzzed the security barrier open, and the three of them stepped through.

"Oh but you will be careful in the Personalitron, won't you Professor? I've heard it's also been a little temperamental recently."

"Hmm? Really? Oh yes, quite careful, quite careful," the Professor replied. He turned and waved, "Goodbye Dorothy!"

"Goodbye Arty!" Dorothy replied, holding up one hand and coyly wriggling her fingers at him.

*

"Artemas… I never even knew his name," Paranoid Dave muttered to himself.

"Artemas?" Charlie nudged Paranoid Dave in the ribs. "*Arty* more like!"

"The sly old dog," Toby added. "Has he got girlfriends everywhere?"

Toby, Charlie, and Paranoid Dave were trailing behind the Professor, who was gliding – wafting – along the subterranean corridor, looking thoroughly at home and thoroughly out of place at the same time.

"Professor Artemas C James," Paranoid Dave muttered to himself again. "I wonder what the 'C' stands for?"

*

The Prime Minister's last thought on Earth – if thought you can call it – was to stare with a kind of numbed focus at a medium-sized patch of rust on the upper section of the cylindrical tube in which he was now entombed.

This thought was not to be confused with his penultimate thought on Earth, which was quite different. That thought had been more along the lines of *Get me the Hell out of here, you imbeciles*, as he banged desperately on the glass hatch which had been shut behind him. But no-one had replied, nor even thrown him a sympathetic look, and after a minute of banging he had collapsed back onto his gurney, quite spent.

Was it really a patch of rust? he wondered to himself.

What in fact is rust?

Perhaps rust is a good thing?

Yes, that's right. Rust is a good thing. Rust is a wonderful thing. Where there's rust, there must be iron. And everyone knows that iron is strong and good.

And where there's rust, there must be oxygen too. And oxygen is… Oxygen helps… Oxygen…

And then he was gone.

Quite gone.

Pfft.

Not physically, of course. The pale, slightly corpulent form of the Prime Minister was still very much there, unchanged. But mentally, spiritually, consciousness-wise – *personality-wise* – the Prime Minister of Great Britain and Northern Ireland and 1st Lord of the Treasury had departed this Earth.

19

Toby felt a very queasy sensation come over him as he read the sign over the double doors:

Decontamination unit
Personalitron travellers and authorised personnel only

He watched the Professor's hand reach up and press the entry button.

The door opened and in they went.

For the next fifteen minutes or so, Toby's body ceased to belong to him. Along with the others, he was suddenly mobbed by orderlies in white, full-body hazmat suits. It was all too reminiscent of when *you-know-what* was sweeping through the country. Only this wasn't on TV, this was happening to him right here, right now. He was ushered into a cubicle and his clothes taken from him. He was thrust into a shower and scrubbed down by a strange machine with an unusually pungent detergent and a particularly severe scrubbing brush. He was pushed onto a rotating pedestal in a drying chamber, while hot, filtered air was blasted over his body. At each stage he passed further and further down the decontamination unit towards a huge pair of high-security glass doors at the far end of the room.

As the drying fans whirred to a standstill, two orderlies manoeuvred him onto a gurney, placed a small hypoallergenic towel across his middle and wheeled him in front of the large glass doors. Lying flat on his gurney, he spotted an orderly opening a locker, into which he placed their clothes, along with the Professor's leather briefcase. Carruthers must still be inside. Toby looked to his left and could see the Professor lying on another gurney, also watching the briefcase but looking perfectly calm. Just beyond him, he glimpsed Charlie on her gurney; to his right was Paranoid Dave, his scraggly black beard suddenly looking strangely clean and fluffy and blow-dried. A moment later and a red light above the door pinged green, the huge glass doors wheeled opened, and four orderlies pushed their gurneys forward by three yards, until they stopped again in front of an identical set of large glass doors.

"Excuse me," Toby managed to squeak to the orderly behind him, "what's happening? Where are we now?"

"Airlock. You're entering a one hundred percent germ-free environment," the orderly replied through her breathing apparatus. "The other side of the lock will open in two minutes. Bon voyage!"

And before Toby could reply, the orderly had disappeared. An amber light started flashing and a mechanical warning sound went off. An automated voice announced over the tannoy in a rather alarming American accent:

"The airlock is closing. The airlock is closing.

"Authorised travellers only.

"The airlock is closing. The

a i r l o c k   i s   c l o s i n g . . . ."

The huge glass doors wheeled shut behind them. And then Toby felt a deep visceral thud, as of two large weights meeting each other in a rubber-tinged embrace.

The airlock was secure.

Suddenly, they were in a sealed environment that was completely and utterly noiseless.

Toby felt queasy enough to vomit.

He briefly wondered how that would go down in their hundred percent germ-free environment. He looked between his toes at the glass door in front of him and the departure chamber beyond. He could see a large steel machine with two circular glass doors. Above the left hand door was a sign reading "Ejection tube 1". And above the other, "Ejection tube 2".

The Personalitron.

"Damn," Paranoid Dave interrupted the silence, "is that the Prime Minister? Look!"

Toby peered between his feet just in time to glimpse a body being wheeled out of Ejection tube 1. He could momentarily see the face in profile, before the seemingly lifeless figure was wheeled away.

"It certainly looks like him," Toby replied. "My God, he looks dead."

"Not dead, hmm? Just inert," the Professor added.

"*Inert?* Is that what you call it?" Paranoid Dave responded.

They watched as Ejection tube 2 was opened. They saw Woola's limp figure being pulled out and wheeled away.

"He looks so harmless like that," Charlie mused. "To think of the damage he's going to cause… And he's probably not even that bad an alien."

"Professor…" Toby spoke, "what exactly did

Dorothy mean earlier, when she said the Personalitron had been temperamental recently?"

"Hmm, temperamental? Did she say that? Well, probably just the weather."

"What do you mean the…"

THUMP!

The gang nearly jumped out of their skins.

THUMP – THUMP!

Charlie started, her hand instinctively clutching her towel over her chest. Paranoid Dave looked round in confusion. Huge thudding sounds continued to shudder around the airlock.

THUMP – THUMP – THUMP!

"Behind! Look behind!" Paranoid Dave called out.

They all swivelled awkwardly on their gurneys, clutching their towels over them, to see two of the TARP team on the other side of the glass doors – still in black, still armed – yelling and screaming. One was trying to prise the doors apart, while the other thumped against the glass. From their shoulder badges, they could it was the TARP leader and TARP-2. As their mouths moved and contorted, not a sound reached the gang inside the airlock, but with each thump on the glass, Toby, Charlie and Paranoid Dave instinctively flinched.

"Oh, it's just our friends again," the Professor observed with perfect calmness, and lay back down. "They really should stop that thumping. They won't make any impression on those doors…"

Toby, Charlie and Paranoid Dave, who were sitting propped up on their gurneys, exchanged a look of relief.

"No," the Professor continued, "those doors are designed to withstand a radioactive meltdown in the Personalitron core. So they can definitely cope with a couple of chaps banging. Nothing to worry about."

"Nothing to worry about," Toby replied, now worrying what a radioactive meltdown in the Personalitron core might look like. "But can't they force the staff to open the airlock?"

"Hmm? Not really. They can only open those doors once this other set has been opened and re-sealed. And by then we'll be safely inside the departure chamber, hmm? Of course, they can follow us in, provided they spend their two minutes in the airlock, but they'll need to go through decontamination first. Undress, shower, dry and so on. I would say we have ten minutes. Plenty of time to make our escape. Haha!"

"There's no other way into the chamber?"

"No. Only one way in."

"So hang on," said Paranoid Dave, "let me get this straight. The longer they spend thumping and making prats of themselves, the longer it will take to decontaminate them and the longer they'll take to reach us?"

"Hmm? Yes, that sounds about right."

"Right then," Paranoid Dave announced with firmness. "Let's be 'avin' yer."

"Excuse me, Dave?" Charlie asked, "what are you planning to…"

Too late.

Paranoid Dave made a stop gesture with one hand,

as he took in a deep breath, and composed himself. Then he turned round to the TARP leader immediately behind. Raising his fingers to his lips, Paranoid Dave blew their leader a huge, pouting kiss. And then, with an even more pronounced pout, he blew a kiss at TARP-2 as well. He wiggled his bare chest at them for good measure.

"Dave…" Charlie called out, "have you gone mad?"

"I reckon I've just bought us an extra minute. Watch."

They turned to see the two TARP team members staring at each other in disbelief, before erupting in an orgy of shouting and banging. It was like watching a couple of angry wasps in a jar. Orderlies crowded round, hopelessly trying to restrain them.

"Oh look, they're so angry," said Charlie. "They're actually quite cute. Look at that one – his little face is all screwed up. I think he might be crying."

Charlie was pointing at the TARP leader, who was indeed close to tears. He was slamming the palms of both hands against the glass wondering how an elite special forces operative with fifteen years' experience in the field, including two tours of Afghanistan, could be frustrated so often in one day by a small group of clowns and what – but what – would it take to finally arrest them? Because as he stared at them through the glass doors, and stared at the Personalitron beyond, he had this horrible sinking feeling that he would have to follow them across the Universe.

The amber light started flashing. The automated voice rang out:

"The airlock is opening. The airlock is opening.

"Prepare for departure.

"The airlock is opening. The airlock..."

The large glass doors in front of the gang started to wheel back. A small gap of a few inches opened. Then a few inches became a few feet, and then a few more feet, and then they were fully open.

In front of the gang was the Personalitron. Behind them were two armed assassins from the TARP team.

Outer space it would have to be.

20

"What are *they?*" Charlie asked.

"Ah yes, those," the Professor replied. "The body silos."

"Ok… And what's a body silo?" Charlie asked.

She and the Professor had been moved to a dimly lit section of the departure chamber, off to the right. She was sitting up on her gurney, her towel wrapped carefully around her, staring at a very strange sight. Disappearing into the darkness, right to the back of the departure chamber were several rows of large cyclinders. Each one was about fifteen foot tall and about four foot in diameter. Except for the fact they were made of frosted glass, they looked like rather sinister missile silos.

"Look carefully, you'll see."

Charlie squinted.

"Oh my God!"

"What? What is it, what's gone wrong?" Toby called out, sitting up on his gurney. He and Paranoid Dave had been parked opposite the two ejection tubes. They were going to leave first.

"Do please try to stay calm, sir," an orderly rebuked Toby. "You'll have a much smoother flight."

"Right, yes, calm, got it," Toby replied, lying back down. He paused for a moment and then shot back up.

"But seriously, what the hell is a body silo?"

"Two minutes to departure."

"What is it that you've seen, Charlie?" Paranoid Dave called out from the neighbouring gurney. He was looking much more composed.

"Well, I can't be sure, but I think it's the President of the United States… "

"The President of *where?*" Toby called out.

"UNITED STATES…" Charlie replied. "Is that even possible, Professor?"

"Oh yes, quite likely in fact."

"And just next to him is the French President. But I can't be sure because…"

"Because what?" Toby asked.

"…because I've never seen them naked before."

Through the frosted glass Charlie could just make out the face of the US President. His body was floating in a clear, viscous liquid, turning and bobbing slightly. Large bubbles were drifting up through the liquid and plopping to the surface a foot or two above his head. His face seemed to be smiling in a way that was both serene and a little gormless.

About half way down the room, Charlie could make out a crew lowering another body into an empty silo. She guessed it must be the Prime Minister. Next to him was the unmistakeable shape of Woola's body.

"How come you're so calm, Dave? Aren't you at all nervous?" Toby had turned to look at Paranoid Dave, who was staring straight up at the ceiling.

"Me? Oh, I feel great," Paranoid Dave replied slowly, almost dreamily. "I can't believe I'm going into space. I mean, *space.* I've fantasised about this since I was a little boy. It's just so cool, right?"

"Well, I suppose when you put it like that, it is quite

cool," Toby replied. "That's quite calming actually, thank—"

"Now I don't mean to alarm you," the Professor interrupted. He was suddenly standing above them, his towel wrapped around his waist. "But we have a slight problem."

"What? What is it?" Toby asked.

"One minute to departure."

"The TARP team. They seemed to have bypassed some of the protocols, hmm? I don't know how. Very peculiar. But they're going to make it out of the airlock in the next – oh, I don't know – sixty seconds or so."

The three of them turned round to see the TARP leader and TARP-2 in the airlock. They weren't even pretending to follow protocol – they were standing up, white towels around their waist, hands on the glass doors, waiting for them to open. Their bodies rippled with a rather uncompromising set of muscles. Their faces were puce.

"The airlock is opening. The airlock is opening..."

The doors started to open and the TARP team immediately inserted their fingers in the gap.

"Hmm... Better make that thirty seconds."

"Prepare for departure. The airlock is opening..."

"Tobias, don't look down and don't let the orderlies see this," the Professor was suddenly very close and speaking directly into Toby's ear. There was an uncharacteristic urgency in his voice. "But you'll need this."

Toby felt something being pressed into his hand. It felt metallic, maybe a very fine chain, with a small box attached. Toby felt the Professor's old, ornery fingers close his own around the object. It was very small, the Professor must've kept it concealed in the palm of his hand during decontamination.

"What is it?"

"It's a locket. It contains a powder. Now you must take it when you arrive on Za-Nak. Hmm? Most important. You do understand, don't you?"

"Yeah, ok, sure," Toby replied. "Arrive on Za-Nak. Take the powder."

The Professor visibly relaxed.

"But hang on," Toby suddenly had a thought. "Doesn't Dave need it too?"

The Professor looked at Paranoid Dave, paused thoughtfully for an instant, and then looked back again.

"No, he'll be fine."

Behind them the doors of the airlock were still opening. There was a gap of about a foot, and the TARP leader had already inserted his shoulder into it. His face was livid with effort as he heaved at the doors.

"Excuse me, Professor, please return to your gurney." It was one of the orderlies. "Zero hour. Towels please."

The towels were whisked from Toby and Paranoid Dave's torsos and two orderlies started pushing them into the ejection tubes.

"But Professor, Charlie," Toby called out, as his feet started to disappear into Ejection tube 1, "will you be OK? Won't the TARP team arrest you?"

"Oh we'll be fine. Don't worry about us," the Professor called out in reply. "There's only two of them down here. They won't try to arrest us."

"OK, great…" Toby replied, as his head disappeared into the ejection tube.

"They'll try to arrest you instead," the Professor

continued. "That's their pursuit protocol. We'll be fine."

Pursuit what?

C L U N K

The circular glass door closed behind Toby's head.

At the same moment, the airlock had opened just enough to allow the TARP team members through. Both of them burst into the departure chamber and immediately dashed towards the ejection tubes.

As Toby lay on the gurney inside the ejection tube, his last thought was what a wonderfully elastic thing the human mind is, especially in moments of high drama. He somehow managed to split his attention three ways. He thought about the Professor's last words, and the prospect of being pursued by the TARP team through space. He thought about the strange creaking sound behind his head, which he correctly imagined to be the TARP leader trying to wrestle open the ejection tube. But most of all he just stared at the metal cylinder into which he had been inserted, pondering the curious medium-sized patch of rust above his eyes.

Could that really be rust? I mean rust is what you find in old, disused things, not in a—

And then, *pfft.*

Gone.

Toby, like several world leaders before him, had departed this Earth.

21

Charlie stepped out of the rear entrance to Downing Street.

The air was warm and close.

Night had fallen.

In front of her was Horse Guards Parade. Beyond that was St James' Park. It was mostly quiet except for a few stray revellers, wandering about drunkenly, and the sound of the rock concert passing over the rooftops. She looked behind and saw the Professor a couple of yards away, straightening his suit.

The pair stepped out onto Horse Guards, quite alone. Charlotte felt strangely nervous stepping into such a large open space, so famous and now so empty.

"Are you alright, Charlotte? Hmm?" the Professor asked.

"Yes. Yes, I think so."

"You've managed to bring away everything you brought here?"

"Yeah, I've got everything," Charlie replied. "And you, have you got Carruthers OK?"

"Oh yes," the Professor replied, giving his briefcase a couple of gentle pats.

"Great. But do you think the others are OK? I mean they're *in space* now. God," she added, touching her sunglasses, "I can't believe I just said that."

"We have to hope they'll be OK, we have to hope. The Personalitron is not the most, ah-hm… It's not the, err, the most, err… Yes, indeed."

Charlie didn't like the way the Professor's voice faltered. She was learning to be suspicious whenever he didn't finish his sentences. Which was increasingly often. Her mind wandered back to the events a short while earlier. After Toby and Paranoid Dave had been ejected from the Personalitron, there had been a chaotic five minutes in the departure chamber under Downing Street. As soon as the orderlies had withdrawn their two motionless bodies from the ejection tubes, the TARP leader and TARP-2 clambered into the tubes themselves. They were livid. As the Professor had predicted, they were sticking to their pursuit protocol.

Meantime she and the Professor had been able to quietly make their way out of the Personalitron facility without any fuss. The other members of the TARP team had melted away, and they'd been able to retrieve their clothes and the Professor's leather briefcase. They exited Downing Street via the rear gate, and so here they were above ground again, on Horse Guards.

"Well, we better quietly, ah-hm, melt away," the Professor said. He gestured vaguely towards St. James Park beyond and the warm, embracing anonymity of London. "Albrecht still needs to be collected. Shall we?"

"Sure," Charlie replied simply.

And she set off with the Professor, into the darkness.

*

Toby started to dream.

The dream was powerful and simple and very real.

It started out of blackness. There was no lead-in and no narrative. Toby found himself in a black space, lit dimly by some unseen source – like an old-fashioned mime artist illuminated on an otherwise entirely black stage.

And then, out of the blackness a dagger passed through his heart.

He didn't feel he had been stabbed, there was no pain, and no violence in the movement. He didn't see anyone wield the dagger. It just passed into his chest effortlessly, with an uncanny smoothness. The handle sat there, pointing out of his chest, barely visible in the darkness.

In that instant, Toby knew he must die.

No-one can survive a dagger passing into their heart. Obviously.

The sensation was both intense and strangely emotionless. He felt no panic, no pain, no sorrow, no anger, no relief, no release. No memories surfaced, nothing flashed before his eyes. There was just one plain, absolute and quite awesome fact: that he must die, and do so in the next few seconds. And that after that, for better or for ill, he must surely discover what death is.

His consciousness started to ebb away, and with it his life. He felt himself shutting down. The light that was illuminating the dark scene became dimmer, his awareness of this simple, dark world ebbed. No thoughts rushed in to replace them. He was fast approaching a void.

And then nothing.

His dream, which arose out of blackness, returned to blackness.

*

Time passed.
Time that couldn't be measured.
Time like a circle, with neither beginning nor end.

*

Toby was in a state devoid of colour or detail.
A formless, wakeless state.
Oblivion.

*

And then – like a match being struck at the base of a dark and fathomless cave – some flicker of awareness lit up in his brain.

This thought, if it could be called that, had neither shape nor purpose nor language. It was almost nothing, this thought. At most, it was some basic awareness of being.

The thought grew a little.

Like a flame flickering to take hold on a match, the thought started to push and probe in different directions.

This thought knew that it belonged to a living entity. Or at least to an entity that had once been alive.

It acquired a basic sense of time. And a little language too.

And so it asked, very calmly: *Am I dead? Is this death?*

The thought grew a little more.

I may be dead, I may be alive, but I must be

somewhere – where am I?

Who am I?

And then it grew a little more. The thought started to access memories. Its owner started to become aware of being its owner.

I've been here before. I've woken from a deep, deep sleep like this before. If I stretch out my right hand I will touch something – then I can start to identify where I am.

The owner of the thought tried to stretch out its hand, and pat a few things nearby.

Only there was no right hand. Or at least, not one that was prepared to stretch out.

That gave the thought's owner the nudge that was needed.

Like a match that's been applied to a hurricane lamp – and a hurricane lamp that's being held aloft in the deep, fathomless cave – awareness grew and the single simple thought started to multiply into many thoughts.

Toby became aware he was Toby. That helped him prise open the gateway to memory. His mind went back to the last thing first. A strange dream of dying. A dream in which a dagger, passed into his heart. *But that was just a dream.*

Wasn't it?

Dream memories and wakeful memories were jostling with each other, intertwined. Toby couldn't sort them one from the other. Not yet.

He tried to discipline his mind and to focus on the present.

I don't think I'm dreaming – am I? Because I'm thinking logically and that doesn't happen in dreams.

But at the same time, I can't see or sense anything, and I can't move. And that does *happen in dreams.*

So, logically, I must be dead.

But then another memory surfaced.

Once in his life Toby had had a *lucid dream* – a dream in which he was aware he was dreaming. A dream in which he had some conscious control over his thoughts even while being asleep. The body didn't respond to commands, but the mind did.

That's it, Toby thought, *that's it. This must be a lucid dream. Perhaps I* am *still alive?*

Toby looked around. After all, things are never *totally* black. There's always a chink of light somewhere, a shade of darkness slightly lighter, or darker, than the shade next to it.

Sure enough, after focussing for a while, Toby made out tiny, static flecks of light in the distance. That was something.

He. strained his attention a little more, and more little flecks of light appeared. A few moments later and he could see flecks of light all around him. Some were scattered loosely, but others were clumped together.

They almost looked like stars.

Oh my God...

And then everything tumbled into his consciousness at once.

They *are* stars.

22

Charlie stopped to rest.

She and the Professor found a bench and sat down. Charlie watched the Professor lean into his case and extract his hedgehog. Then she leaned back and stared up into the sky. She started thinking about Toby and Paranoid Dave and the sheer crazy, astounding, perilous, unthinkable journey they had embarked on.

"Amazing to think they're up there, somewhere in space," she mused out loud. "I mean, not just in space, but in another dimension. Do they dream as they travel? Or are they conscious? Are they awake? *Madness.*"

Charlie paused for a moment as something occurred to her.

"Must be a cloudy night, Professor. I can't see any stars, the moon, nothing. In fact… I can't even see the usual glow from all the street lights? Strange."

"Hmm? Yes, that is strange…" the Professor said. "And here's another strange thing. Carruthers always loves his diced carrots at this time of day and yet he's not eating tonight. Most unusual." The Professor was staring at his hedgehog, who was ignoring his treat and fidgeting on his front paws, looking left and right.

"I mean, what can it possibly be like to travel in another dimension, without your own body?" Charlie continued, returning to her theme. "The implications of it. Does it mean the human soul *actually exists?* Or does it mean the opposite?" And then another thought occurred to her. "Professor – if something happens to Toby and Dave over there, I mean something bad… Would it be possible to bring their bodies back to life? The ones they've left here under Downing Street?"

"Ah, yes…" the Professor replied. "But no. I'm afraid not. It's been tried before, many times, but without success. If the individual experiences death then it seems that some, err – *how would one say?* – some vital essence has been lost. Anything in a body silo, whether the original or a duplicate, is, ah-hm… Well, it's quite useless, alas."

"Oh," Charlie replied. "A vital essence… So perhaps the soul does exist… *God*, but it really is dark tonight."

Charlie peered a little harder at the sky above, trying to spot the moon, or a star or two or something. After all, nothing is ever *completely* black, she reasoned to herself.

"Now why are you looking at me, young man, hmm?" the Professor asked Carruthers, whose moist little nose was pointing upwards and twitching. "Are you trying to tell me there's trouble? But I already know that, hmm?"

"But if it's such a cloudy night, why can I see the glow of street lamps over there, but not over here?" Charlie asked out loud, still looking up.

"But you're not looking at me, are you?" the Professor said to Carruthers, turning his head upwards to follow his hedgehog's gaze. "You're looking at the sky…"

Charlie started.

And so did the Professor.

In the same instant, this one peaceful moment in their day was shattered. The Professor and Charlie stared at the same time in the same direction at the same patch of apparent sky.

"Professor?"

"Charlotte?"

"Yes?"

"Yes?"

"What the Hell is *that?*"

"Yes, that. Oh dear. I have absolutely no idea."

*

Before I started dreaming, I was deep beneath Downing Street. I was fleeing from the TARP team and I was about to get into the Personalitron.

I did *get into the Personalitron.*

Oh my God, so right now I must be in…

Toby stopped. He couldn't bring himself to say it, to acknowledge it. Not yet anyway.

Toby tried to take his mind off the stars. It was insane. So instead he took his mind back again to Downing Street. He retraced events step-by-step.

He was pushed into the Personalitron, he went into one tube, Paranoid Dave into the other. Before that, the Professor had whispered something to him. Before that, he was lying on the gurney listening to Charlie telling them about the body silos. She and the Professor didn't get in the Personalitron. They were left behind with the two members of the TARP team…

Charlie.

Was she ok? Had she been arrested? Or had she escaped with the Professor? For sure the Professor would be looking after her. Toby hoped she wasn't worrying about him.

Suddenly there she was.

In his mind's eye he could see her, complete and clear. Her body, her person, her personality, *her soul*. Complete and unclouded. Neither beautiful nor not beautiful, just her. His thoughts became curiously unselfish. He found himself thinking about her not as an elusive, half-glimpsed object of desire, but as the person she actually was. Vulnerable, intelligent, inquiring, loyal, protective.

Thinking about her seemed to give him the strength to open his mind again. To the stars that were all around him.

What had once seemed like total blackness was becoming almost comically *not* black. There was a great milky spread of stars in front of him, and they weren't even static now. He could see them moving. And then colour. *Colour.* Toby had never spent much time thinking about space and he certainly didn't associate it with colour. But over to his left, he saw a giant, exquisite purple cloud, a cloud so vast there were scores of stars scattered within it. The cloud hung in space like an escaping pool of dense gas. It moved past him on his left.

Only it wasn't moving at all. Toby knew that. He knew it wasn't moving, because he realised *that he was*.

Ahead to his right, three huge, brown-ish columns hung suspended in space, like biblical pillars of dust. The pillars were connected at the base. As Toby drew closer, he could see stars were scattered around and throughout, illuminating patches of the dust-brown pillars in beautiful vapour-like shades of ochre and russet. Toby drew closer and closer. He found himself passing between two of the pillars, like a voyager in classical times passing through the pillars of Hercules. He was awe-struck by their simple majesty.

Toby was travelling through space.

He could say it to himself now and it was just fine. Whatever had happened had happened, whatever was going to happen was going to happen, and right now there was only right now.

And right now was, frankly, amazing.

Toby felt neither cold nor heat, he felt neither weight nor motion. He felt instead an astonishing, liberating, overwhelming sense of… Something different, something he had never felt before.

He passed whole galaxies to his left and right. Some were just tiny splashes of light in the far, far distance, others were biscuit-size; one over to his right was close and huge, a vast swirling spiral of sparkling lights..

And then a planet came into view.

It was a beautiful, apple-green planet. It looked so vibrant in the darkness of space. Toby started to decelerate as he drew closer to it, without quite knowing how. He could see first one, then two moons orbiting it. Beyond was its sun. It was intensely bright and yet Toby could look directly towards it without pain.

As the planet started to fill his field of vision, he felt this sudden rush of curiosity and empathy.

Was there life on the planet? If so, was life still early in its journey, or had it evolved into something complex and intelligent and amazing?

He found himself asking simple, obvious questions. If there was intelligent life, were they at peace? Or were they fighting wars? Had they learned to be kind to each other, or were they ruled by dogma and insecurity?

Issues that seemed so clouded and confusing in his old life were now effortlessly simple. Were they nurturing their fragile planet? Or were they draining it? Had they built a civilisation? And if they had, was it bringing joy and wonder? Or were they slaves to it?

Were they, in fact, *happy?*

And then, as if drawn by the pure force of empathy, Toby was suddenly racing through clouds, down and down towards the planet's surface. As the landscape beneath him came into view, he swerved out of the descent, and flew in a generous arc above the land.

Beneath him was a scene of Elysian beauty.

Directly below was a mountain range. As he crested the last line of peaks, he found himself flying over a huge forest that swept downwards from the mountains in a tide of green. He spotted a river descending from a gash in the mountains, and snaking through the forest. He swept over the forest, following the line of the river. He could see it beneath him, visibly growing in width. To either side he could see thin, fragile trails running like undulating pencil lines between the trees, passing from one small clearing to another. Rising from the clearings he could see little plumes of smoke, providing the faintest hint of an intelligent species at work.

Further on and the forest gave way to expansive, sweeping water meadows, through which the river flowed, calmer and wider. A patchwork of sunlight fell between the clouds, illuminating the meadows in different shades of quilted green – here a patch as luminous as emerald, there a patch of shaded verdigris. To one side of the river, the land rose up towards a gentle plateau, dotted with trees and small villages. He could see livestock grazing peacefully, small black flecks against the green sward. As the miles flew by, the villages became larger, with crop fields arranged in rectangular grids around them. Tidy grey roads appeared in between.

Further on still and a beautifully ordered town came into view, close to the mouth of the river. Around it he could see a town wall, with steeply gabled houses tucked tight behind the fortifications. At the far side of the town was a harbour and beyond the harbour was a stunning archipelago of islands, sitting around the coastline in a haphazard semi-circle like a fractured jigsaw puzzle.

Sailing boats were heading to and from the harbour, but moving so slowly they looked motionless – as if painted against the water. Toby could see a few larger and more intrepid boats, square-rigged sailing ships, venturing beyond the archipelago into the open ocean.

Toby, pulled along by he-wasn't-quite-sure-what force, started to sweep back upwards, over the ocean, through the upper atmosphere and back towards space.

Toby asked himself again – *Am I, in fact, dead?* – even calmer this time, almost hopeful.

Because if this was death, it was fine. It was OK. It was a little daunting, but not frightening. In fact, Toby was feeling something he'd never felt before. Not having felt it before, he wasn't quite sure what to call it.

And then it occurred to him.

Peace.

Perfect peace.

23

The Professor and Charlie squinted hard at what they thought was the night sky.

Only it wasn't the night sky.

About 10,000 feet above their heads, Bulk Carrier BC144 of the Jagamath fleet was breezing past at the regulation tropospheric cruising speed for a bulk carrier under full load in a near-planetary drop-zone. Everything on board was running smoothly, but for one tiny detail. A rather sloppy Cenaphian sub-contractor had forgotten to close the lower ventral docking bay. It was a modest-sized entrance, about thirty by forty yards, but it was positioned on the underside of the vessel and light flooded out of it in a vaguely rectangular pattern.

Looking up at this solid rectangular block of light moving overhead at the speed of a fast-moving cloud Charlie and the Professor's brains were in overdrive trying to figure it out. And the longer they squinted, the more detail they could make out. Their eyes started to pick out the texture around the hatch. And then they started to realise that the grey-ish darkness above their heads wasn't quite the same shade as the darkness over towards the horizon. And then, like a car crash in slow motion, their brains collided with the reality above their heads.

"Oh my God…" stuttered Charlie.

"Oh dear," replied the Professor.

"It's a spaceship isn't it?"

"A rather large one."

"Like in that movie?"

"I hope not."

"Should we tell the authorities?" Charlie ventured, still looking up at the sky.

"I rather think they've already noticed," the Professor replied staring in the same direction.

"But they have been a bit useless up until now."

"True. But perhaps not that useless." The Professor turned his face back down to the ground. "I think we might need a slightly different plan at this point."

"What have you got in mind?"

The Professor stroked Carruthers meditatively.

"Charlotte," he said at length. "Do you perhaps remember someone called Dr de Haan?"

Charlotte blushed in the darkness.

"Yes."

She had learnt to stop being surprised by what the Professor knew and who the Professor knew.

"Yes, I do."

"I'm sorry to bring his name up…"

"It's ok, Professor – just ask what you need to ask."

"I rather need you to take a message to him. But it will need to be delivered personally. And by someone he trusts, hmm? You understand?"

"Of course. What's the message?"

The Professor was scribbling onto a small piece of paper. It took a minute to write it down.

"Here," he said, folding the paper as he spoke, "this is it."

Charlie took it from him.

"Dr de Haan," he continued, "must receive that message tonight."

*

As he approached home, the Professor switched Albrecht down into second gear.

He glanced left and right through the side windows of the car. The street was lined on both sides with old-fashioned gas lamps. Wrought-iron pillars supported globe-shaped lanterns that illuminated Cleremont Avenue with a warm white glow like moonlight.

An hour earlier, after saying goodbye to Charlie, he had collected the old Daimler from the side street where they'd left him that afternoon. As he drove slowly down the street, the Professor felt the familiar feeling of peace wash over him that he always felt on returning here. The Professor could remember when the lanterns were still tended by lamplighters. Every day, their appearance with long poles would announce the arrival of dusk. No.55 had been in the Professor's family since it was first built by his Great Uncle Claude. Back then it was one of the first houses on the street. That was a time when all of London lay in one direction, and the open countryside in the other.

As the car rolled past the front door of No.55, light from the main hall shone out through the window above it. This evening of all evenings, the stained glass window, showing St. George and the dragon, looked particularly striking. The Professor braked gently and pulled left into the garage. The door had been left open for him. As he stepped out of the car, he saw Mrs B waiting.

Mrs B approached the Professor and placed one

hand on his arm. She looked at him closely.

"Are they come, Artemas?" she asked. She gave a faint nod in the direction of the sky.

"Yes, they are come," the Professor replied simply.

Mrs B held his gaze for a couple of seconds, nodded and dropped her hand again.

"The study?"

"Yes," the Professor replied.

The pair made their way quietly through the house. The familiarity between them required few words. When they reached it, the study was illuminated by the soft light of an old banker's lamp on the Professor's desk, and the glow of a small fire that Mrs B had lit in the grate. The Professor made his way to the set of library steps that had caught Toby's attention earlier. He paused with one hand on the rail and turned back to Mrs B.

"Is the house being watched?"

"Not that I can tell," Mrs B replied. "Except perhaps by satellite?"

"Oh, I don't think we need to worry about that."

The Professor chuckled a little as he made his way to the top of the library steps. Once there, he knelt down in front of the small padded bench, and lifted the seat with both hands. It hinged upright. The Professor spent a few moments intensely studying whatever was concealed underneath. When he was satisfied, he hinged the seat shut again and made his way back down the steps.

"Is it ready?" Mrs B asked.

"Yes, yes," he replied, as he settled himself into a studded leather armchair by the fire. He looked up at the old Grandfather clock, whose hands were approaching midnight. "I think I shall take a couple of hours rest here, hmm? Charlotte shall be along presently and then we must take her to… To Ormilu. You see?"

"To Ormilu?" Mrs B repeated. "Ay, Ormilu. That makes sense."

*

Charlie pulled up in a taxi onto another quiet street in the capital. Her senses were sharpened and her pulse had quickened. The fatigue that should be expected to descend on a young person towards midnight on the most eventful day of her life so far had completely failed to appear. Almost the opposite. As she stepped onto the street, she was aware of the distant thud of music and the glow of lights over the centre of the city. It was both thrilling and menacing, like being a few miles from the front line of an artillery battle.

She paid the taxi driver and made her way along the street that she had passed many times to the house she had never actually entered. She stopped outside the door and attempted to gather herself together. So many things in her life, Charlie reflected, just seemed to happen to her. Falling in love with her PhD supervisor was one of them. She didn't ask for it, she didn't want it and – even worse – he didn't want it either. And yet it had happened. Hopelessly so. So much so that quitting her studies hadn't felt like a choice either. Even today, even this crazy adventure that she now found herself part of, was scarcely a choice; and the Professor sending her to her supervisor's house – well he'd offered a choice, but of course she had no choice.

And so here she was. Outside Dr de Haan's house. The lights were still on in several of the rooms, it looked like there might be guests. She felt inside her pocket for the Professor's note, and her fingers closed around it for security. *At some point*, she thought to herself, *I'm going to start making choices of my own.* And then she dutifully pushed the door buzzer.

After a few seconds, a middle-aged lady opened the door. She had a handsome face and an open, trusting expression. She seemed puzzled, but not perturbed, to be getting a visitor at this hour on this day.

"Hello, can I help?" she asked.

"Yes, I'm here to see Dr de Haan."

"Of course. He's in. And what's your name?"

"Charlotte."

"Oh." The middle-aged lady stopped dead. "Charlotte. As in… *Charlie?*"

"Yes."

"I see."

"I'm here to deliver a message for Dr de Haan," Charlotte continued quickly, her hand was clutching the piece of paper inside her coat pocket. "It's from Professor James."

"Of course." The middle-aged lady drew in a deep breath and composed herself. She patted her hands self-consciously against her hips as if to flatten her dress, then she opened the door fully and stepped aside.

"I think you had better come in, Charlie."

*

Toby looked up.

That doesn't look good, he thought to himself abruptly.

He was heading to a strange formation of clouds suspended in space ahead of him. The clouds were a little like the purples ones he'd passed earlier, except these were dark grey and they were shaped in a kind of swirl, focussed around a tiny black point at the centre.

Toby sensed himself accelerating. As he got closer and closer to the dark grey clouds he could see they weren't static at all. They were in constant motion, broiling and seething around the small black central point. It was a vortex, and Toby knew with a gnawing inevitability that he was being drawn into it. He suddenly didn't feel so peaceful anymore. The acceleration accelerated, the vortex approached.

Strangely, Toby's last thought as he approached the void was *Paranoid Dave... I forgot about Paranoid Dave – where the Hell is he?*

And then he passed out.

24

In the Personalitron terminal on Za-Nak a strange scene was playing out.

Any casual visitor from Earth entering the terminal for the first time would have seen plenty of familiar things to relax the travel-weary mind. The room itself was relatively normal – it was of about middling height, with a floor, a ceiling, and a couple of doors. There were some old strip lights on the ceiling, that looked like they had seen better days. Over against one of the walls were a number of ambulance-style stretchers, or gurneys, that looked perfectly familiar (although perhaps it would seem a little strange to find so many stacked on top of each other). Then there was the Personalitron itself, which was also reasonably familiar, assuming that the casual visitor had already seen the same machine back in London. And the other point of familiarity were the people. In fact, they weren't just familiar, they were *very* familiar.

The only thing a casual visitor might have found unsettling was the way those familiar figures were behaving. They were arguing – vociferously.

"Ah tell yu – ah am not moppin' ze floor again! Yu mop – Ah shall sweep with ze b*rrr*ume."

The first figure with the haughty French accent folded her arms around the broom handle and pouted.

"Now listen, doll, you may be something swell back

home – but raat here, raat now, we're somewhere *democratic*." A second figure with a Southern American drawl stubbornly held out a mop. "And it's your turn is all. So you just get raat along 'n' start moppin'."

"Ah take your mop," the first figure said, taking the mop, "and Ah reject it. Ah *repudiate* it."

The first figure threw the mop contemptuously against a large metal machine behind her.

As the mop landed against the Personalitron, an amber warning light on the machine started rotating and flashing.

"Now will you just look at that?" the second figure said. "I think you darn gone 'n' broken it."

"Vill you two stop ze bickering!" a third figure demanded in heavily accented German. "Zis light, zis does not mean zat ze machine is broken. Verdammt old, yah? But noch nicht kaput. Nein, nein – I believe zer are more arrivals about to arrive."

"There are *more* coming?" It was the figure with the Southern American drawl. "But I thought we had everybody already?"

"Yah, me too," replied the German. "Here zis morning, it iz like ze Charing Kross!"

The German was seated at the controls of the machine, on which the amber light was flashing. He started pulling at some levers and knobs. Meantime, the machine started to shake. Its metal feet rattled against the floor in a rather alarming way.

"What in the name of Jesus is that there machine doin' now?"

"Yah, yah, we don't panick, yah? Zis is ze *body formation*. You zee ze leetle picture here in ze leetle display: ze leetle hands are going on with ze teeny tiny

202

fingers!"

A few seconds later, the machine paused for a moment. And then broke into a throaty chugging sound, not unlike an old tractor engine coming to life.

"Darn! And now?"

"Yah, yah, gar kein panick, yah? Otto is calm," the German figure replied. "Zis is ze eency teency head."

A minute later and the Personalitron transitioned into an intense whirring sound. Like an old washing machine moving into a spin cycle, the Personalitron was shuddering and rattling with alarming energy.

"Now that don't sound none too healthy. What's there left to add to a man after his head and his brain?"

"Pah! 'Ow do yu know it's anozer man?" the French figure pouted. "If they are sending a b*rrr*ain over, it's p*rrr*obably a woman."

The Personalitron's rattling accelerated by another degree of alarmingness. It was now visibly shaking left and right, and a small puff of steam shot out from one of the upper vents at remarkable velocity.

"Actung Alarm!" The German figure slipped his right hand under his shirt and started massaging his chest, while his left hand mopped a sweaty sheen from his hairless and very broad brow. "I vonder if maybe ve should do ze panicking now?"

"Well look 'ee here…"

The figure with the Southern accent was staring at the controls with unruffled curiosity, oblivious to the panicking next to him.

"I do believe this must be the personality download. Yessir I do."

*

Where the Hell am I?

Toby blinked a few times, and opened his eyes.

He was lying on his back. As his eyes adjusted to the light, he was aware of a strange restlessness in the wall of the tube that surrounded him. He refocussed just in time to spot forceps and scalpels and all manner of unpleasant little tools scurry back into their burrows like fleeing animals. Metal lids slid back over the top and they were gone.

The tube suddenly looked smooth and clean. Well, mostly clean. Toby could see a few patches of rust here and there. He gave a shudder.

Oh yes, the Personalitron.

Toby's mind, in the time since he had left London, had become rather agile in adjusting to new realities. He was pretty sure that he'd travelled through space, but he couldn't be totally sure. So he reasoned to himself quite reasonably: *Either I am still in London, and I never left because this whole thing is a hoax.*

In which case, *Phew.*

Or, more likely: *I have in fact arrived in the ejection tube of the Personalitron on Za-Nak.*

In which case, *Wow.*

The thing he was most conscious of was how great he felt. His mind felt clear as a bell. Totally refreshed. His body – if it was in fact his body – felt amazing. Zingy.

He was on the same gurney as when he had left London – assuming he had actually left London. His hand went up involuntarily to his neck. The Professor's locket was still there, or at least a very good facsimile of it. *What was it the Professor had said about the locket?* The Professor had seemed terribly serious…

Toby heard a scraping sound coming from behind

his head, and instinctively twisted his head round to look. It was someone unscrewing the door lock. The door swung back, slightly creaky on its hinges, and a head, a distinctly human head – in fact a rather Chinese-looking head – inserted itself inside, just a couple of inches from his nose. The face was a little pudgy, with a slightly blank, slightly friendly expression, like a teddy bear.

The face opened its mouth to say something – thought better of it – and closed again. And then it disappeared as abruptly as it had arrived.

A moment later, a set of pressed clothes was thrust through the hatch and landed unceremoniously on Toby's face.

"Err, thank you, that's very kind," Toby's muffled voice replied.

There wasn't remotely enough room to get dressed. Toby would have to get out first. The gurney was locked in position and it didn't look like anyone was coming to help. Toby tentatively extended his arms above his head, gripped onto the outer edge of the hatch, and pulled himself awkwardly outwards. He grabbed the clothes he had just been given and held them over his middle to preserve his modesty, and then he eased his legs out of the machine and onto the floor.

Well, he thought to himself, *that went as well as could be expected in the circumstances. So which is it – London still? Or Za-Nak?*

He turned around to assess his new environment.

Ah...

Immediately in front of him was the President of the United States, leaning against a mop in a kind of homely way. He was wearing a strange kind of pyjama suit: a floral, Hawaian shirt with matching shorts. Next to him was the President of France, wearing a matching pyjama suit and clutching a broom. Over on Toby's left was – Toby had to pause for a moment to think – but it was almost certainly the German Chancellor. Or at least a lookalike. He was seated at the controls. And then on Toby's right was the oriental gentlemen who had given him his clothes a moment earlier. Toby wasn't all that hot on world leaders, but the oriental figure looked familiar and, given who the others were, he reckoned it must be the Chinese President.

As they stared at each other, another figure came to join them. He was buttoning up his pyjama top as he walked. Toby had no trouble recognising this one, it was the Prime Minister. The Prime Minister took his place in the small semi-circle around Toby, and all of a sudden there they all were. The world's most powerful leaders, all of them wearing the same matching pyjama suit.

OK... Toby thought. *I'm mostly naked and I'm standing in front of the most powerful people on Earth.* Although they were probably not on Earth. *But even so.*

Meantime, the Personalitron had broken into a slightly alarming, rather hoarse chugging sound. *Funny*, Toby thought, *sounds like a bit of old farm machinery...*

"Hi, I'm the President of the United States," said the US President, holding out his hand. "Welcome to Za-Nak, son."

"Bonjour, je suis la Présidente de la République de France. Je vous souhaite la bienvenue à Za-Nak", said the French President in a silky female voice, while holding out her hand.

"Very pleased to meet you both," he said, as he

shook their hands. He wasn't used to being greeted by Heads of State. He made a quick policy decision to treat this all as perfectly normal. *Za-Nak rules*. He could adjust.

"And you represent vich country?" the German chancellor asked with polite curiosity.

"Oh, nowhere important. Nowhere you've heard of," Toby blustered, not sure what to say. And then decided to come clean. "Actually, I'm British".

"Ach nein, imposter!" the German Chancellor shrieked. "He zinks he iz ze Prime Minister of ze Great Britain. Achtung, personality svitch! Sound ze alarm!" He turned to his controls and started thumping buttons.

The amber warning light on the Personalitron started flashing again.

"Now just wait a moment," said the Prime Minister of Great Britain. "I'm the Prime Minister of Great Britain! Nothing's been switched."

"It's true he really is," Toby chipped in. "I'm just on the, err, AAC. I do the, umm, Public Relations. PR, that's me."

"Na ya? Ze PR, not ze PM? You are sure?" Toby nodded and the German Chancellor drew in deep breaths of relief, massaging his chest as he did so. "OK, OK. Otto is calm again. Pleased to meet you. I represent ze Germany."

"Pleased to meet you," Toby said, holding out his spare hand. "Look, this is wonderful to meet you all, but would you mind terribly if I were to, you know, get dressed?"

"Sure, son, you go raat ahead," said the US President, still leaning on his mop and not budging an inch.

"Err, right, thank you," Toby replied. He stared

awkwardly at the semi-circle of world leaders around him, who stared right back, apparently unconcerned.

At that moment the Personalitron behind him started vibrating energetically. As their attention was momentarily diverted, Toby turned his back on the world leaders. He dived down and yanked up his shorts as fast as he could humanly manage, reliving that loss of dignity that every young boy experiences on the beach when instructed by their mother to put their swimming trunks on.

"Looks like another one on the way," the British Prime Minister observed. "But who are we expecting? Japan and Canada both stayed home. Italy doesn't want to be involved. Hey, I know – maybe it's Russia?"

"Ah do not know, and Ah no longer care," the French President replied theatrically. She turned her attention back to Toby. "Pity me, jeune homme. Ah am stuck 'ere, forced to work wiv zis *imbécile*, who thinks only of ze b*rrr*ume, when 'ee should be 'appy wiz ze mop." She gestured dismissively towards the figure next to her.

"Now excuse me there, Madame," the US President replied with indignation. "There's no need to adopt that kind of tone. There's many young ladies back home would be mighty happy to do a shift in my company."

Toby looked at the pair for a moment dumbfounded by what he was hearing. His dumbfoundedness was interrupted only by a loud clatter.

Over on his left, the hatch of the second Ejection tube burst open.

"BUGGER ME!"

Paranoid Dave's voice echoed from the inside of the tube, loud and resonant.

"Err, Dave…" Toby tried to make himself heard

without shouting. "You might want to—"

"TOBY, YOU THERE?" Paranoid Dave bellowed, still inside the tube. "I JUST MANAGED TO UNLOCK THE DOOR FROM THE INSIDE. CLEVER, RIGHT?"

"Err, yes, very. David, you might want to… You perhaps ought to…"

But Toby's voice wasn't audible above Paranoid Dave's heaving and grunting, as he dragged his body out of the machine.

"David, I really think it would be a good idea to…"

Too late.

All fifteen stone of Paranoid Dave stumbled out of the machine. He stood up, straightened his body in all its glory, and pulled his thick black hair back from his eyes with both hands.

"…put some clothes on first?" Toby said, his voice fading away.

"Excuse me?" Paranoid Dave replied. "Oh, clothes? Yes, right. Absolutely."

As he smoothed his hair back over his head, he turned to look at each of the figures arranged in the semi-circle before him. The smile on his face became increasingly forced as he recognised one President after another.

"Clothes," he repeated redundantly. "Err, pleased to meet you, everybody."

"Enfin," came a silky voice. "A *rrr*eal man at last." The President of 5th Republic looked Paranoid Dave up and down as she rolled the *r*.

"Well, Madame," Paranoid Dave replied, doing his best at diplomatic protocol, "I must say I'm most humbly flattered. But I'm not really—"

"Don't! Whatever yu are about to say, don't say it.

Do not dest*rroy* this beautiful moment," the French President turned away theatrically, placing the back of her hand to her forehead in a swooning gesture. "Yu are a fine man, a bold man," she continued. "Not like this one 'ere."

She thumbed at the figure next to her.

"Now you just hold on there a second," retorted the US President.

"The years have battered his bodee," the French President continued regardless. "He is so fat, he can scarcely mop ze floor. 'Iz face and 'iz neck and 'iz chest are *rrrr*olling into one. 'Ee iz blob," she concluded.

"Now listen here, missie…"

"*T o b y y y y y . . .*" Paranoid Dave mouthed across, during this exchange. "*W h a t   t h e   H e l l   i s   g o i n g   o n ?*"

"*I   h a v e   n o   i d e a,*" Toby mouthed back, doing up the last buttons on his floral pyjama top. "*Z a - N a k   h a s   h a d   s o m e   w e i r d   e f f e c t   o n   t h e m ?*"

"*Y e a h   b u t   w h a t ?*"

"Well this is all very jolly, I must say," said a lugubrious English voice at the back of the room. "But would you mind terribly if you got dressed?"

A new figure appeared from behind a screen at the back of the Arrivals room. *Oh God,* Toby thought, *who now?*

*

The voice came from a Za-Nakarian. He appeared in a shiny chrome *thing*. Toby wanted to call it a wheelie bin but it wasn't that. The wheelie-bin-like-thing glided to a halt near the gaggle of world leaders. The Za-Nakarian had one elbow propped up on the edge, and was leaning his face on his forelimb, looking very bored. He looked a bit like Woola, but not very. Older.

"Oh," said Toby, "are you... *Woola?*"

"Woola, Woola, Woola – would you people ever stop going on about that brat? Woola's already left, OK. I'm the one stuck here looking after this dump of a terminal."

"I do apologise. And your name is?"

"My name is... Oh you'll never remember. I'm Woola's dad, let's just leave it at that. Now," Woola's dad continued, looking at Paranoid Dave. "While it's terribly nice to meet you, I really don't need to meet *all* of you."

"Excuse me?" Paranoid Dave replied.

"Your clothes? Could we put them on please?"

"Oh, err, sure."

"Thank you. That's quite enough excitement for one day," Woola's dad announced. "President Fu – please bring our new arrival his pyjama suit. The rest of you – back to work now! Come on, chop chop!"

Woola's dad clapped his forelimbs. To Toby and Paranoid Dave's astonishment, the world leaders set to work like scolded children. The French and US Presidents immediately started mopping and sweeping the floor, the Chinese President went to fetch Paranoid Dave's new clothes, the British Prime Minister picked up a duster, and the German Chancellor turned back round to the control panel on the Personalitron.

Woola's dad came over towards Toby and Paranoid Dave in his chrome wheelie bin.

"So you two say you're not world leaders?"

"That's right."

"You promise?"

"Err, yes?" Toby replied warily.

"Thank God. What a bunch of dupes they are." Woola's dad leaned forward conspiratorially, and spoke behind a cupped forelimb. "You see that one, the German?"

The three of them turned to look at the obese and rather anxious figure of the German Chancellor, as he sat hunched over the Personalitron.

"Ya, ya, ze little buttons," the Chancellor was muttering, "Otto is calm, Otto likes ze little buttons."

"*Fragmentation,*" Woola's dad whispered. Toby and Paranoid Dave looked confused. "The whole package didn't quite arrive. Know what I mean?"

Woola's dad pointed one of his digits to the side of his head, and made a corkscrew motion, while whistling in a this-one's-a-bit-crazy tone.

"Oh I see. That doesn't sound good," Toby replied politely.

"I tried to get him to do the dusting, but he kept breaking everything. So I just let him sit there instead."

"Isn't that a bit risky?" Toby asked. "I mean, he's clumsy and he's sitting at the controls of the Personalitron?"

"Heavens no. I disabled the controls. They're not needed for arrivals. Only for departures. I'll switch them back on later."

"Oh I see."

The three turned back to Otto, who was happily humming a little tune to himself as he pressed the various buttons:

> "Ach yaaa! Ze leetle Button 1
> Ve press you for ze fun,

Ze leetle Button 2
Ve love to pressing you,
Ze leetle Button 3
Iz bizzy like ze bee,
But ze leetle Button 4 – ja, ze leetle Button 4 –
Ze leetle Button 4
Ve don't like you at all! Hahaha!"

The German Chancellor chuckled with delight, as he started thumping one of the buttons. Toby and Paranoid Dave assumed this to be the unfortunate Button 4 of his song.

"Err, can I ask a question?" Toby turned back to Woola's dad, shaking his head to try to clear the image of the German Chancellor from it.

"Sure, what's up?"

"Do you happen to know where Woola went?"

"Oh I think he was off after that ghastly Golgothan," Woola's dad replied.

"Biffa?"

"Who's Biffa?"

"Is Biffa a Golgothan?" Paranoid Dave asked.

"Err, never mind," Toby quickly interjected. "But do you know which way the Golgothan went?"

"Search me", Woola's dad replied, starting to look bored again. "Probably the Mutu-Lulu Resort. That's where most Golgothans stay when they come over here."

Toby remembered the TARP team. "And have you seen two, err, two other humans come through yet?" he asked, looking totally concerned in the way that only someone trying to look unconcerned can look. "They're not world leaders. They're just sort of… Ordinary, like us, you know?"

"Nope – all the humans on Za-Nak are in this

room… I think?" Woola's dad leaned back and yawned. "Look, I'm off for a nap now. See this lot don't slack, would you?"

"Sure, no problem," Toby said.

Woola's dad swished away in his chrome wheelie bin.

"Excuse me," Paranoid Dave called after him. "Just one more question before you go. Woola – your son that is – what's his job over here?"

"Job? Don't make me laugh. That brat doesn't have a job. He's on his gap year. Byyye."

And then he was gone.

*

Meantime back in London, two other familiar figures were playing out an equally unfamiliar scene. Mrs B was in the library of No.55 Cleremont Avenue, gesturing to Charlie encouragingly, urging her forwards.

Charlie approached cautiously. Tentative, like a gazelle approaching a watering hole, she stepped forward. She placed her foot on the bottom-most step.

"That's right, dear, just another couple of steps."

Charlie paused.

"Mrs B – I thought you said we needed to go to Ormilu?"

"And we do, dear, we do."

"Then why aren't we going there then?"

"Oh we will, dear, we will."

Charlie was suspicious. It was five in the morning, she'd had all of two hours sleep, maybe three, and now Mrs B was acting strangely. Charlie looked around her. They were in the Professor's study. Mrs B was a couple of yards away and the Professor a couple of yards beyond her. He was kneeling down on a small platform, where he seemed to have opened the seat of a small bench and was busy fiddling with something beneath it.

"Mrs B, I'm confused."

"Oh, didn't you sleep well, dear? Was the bed not properly aired? Do come a little closer."

"The bed was fine, and I slept fine, thank you. Well, sort of," Charlie replied. "But if we're going to Scandinavia, why are we dawdling here, on Cleremont Avenue? Why aren't we catching a flight? I mean, I can't see how we've possibly got time to go to Scandinavia, but if that's what we have to do, could we please get on with it?"

"And we will, dear, we will," Mrs B replied. "Just come a couple of steps closer, it's more comfy here."

"Mrs B! Please stop being so mysterious." Charlie was losing patience. "We are nowhere near an airport and nowhere near Scandinavia. We're on a set of *library steps.*"

25

Toby and Paranoid Dave found themselves in a hall of unimaginable vastness.

Light was flooding down from a ceiling so high above their heads they could scarcely see it. It was a honeycomb of glass and metal. The air around them seemed cool and air-conditioned, even while a sky-blue sky was beaming down on them. Opposite was a huge, curved wall – again, a honeycomb of glass and metal – that described a vast arc in front of them. And it wasn't a simple vertical wall: it bowed outwards at the centre. Turning round, they could see the door they had just walked through was itself part of a huge, gently curving wall behind them.

Everywhere, everything was curved, round, confusing.

"Torus," said Paranoid Dave in amazement, his eyes bright with wonder.

"Excuse me?" replied Toby.

"Damn, it's a giant bloody torus," said Paranoid Dave, not hearing and still looking around in wonder.

"OK, it's a torus. And what's that?"

"Eh?" Paranoid Dave said, finally hearing Toby. "Oh, just think doughnut."

"You mean, like a jam doughnut?"

"No, the other kind. The one with a hole in the

middle. Behind us, this big pillar-thing where we've just come from, that's the centre of the torus. Where we are now, we're in the main section. See how it bulges in the middle, and curves round to the left and right? Doughnut. *I think.*"

"So if we set off in this direction, and follow the wall round, we'll eventually come back to where we started?"

"Yep, that's what I'm guessing."

"OK – fine, amazing…" Toby replied. "But can we get back on mission now? We need to find a friendly Za-Nakarian and get directions to the Mutu-Lulu Resort. I mean there are thousands and thousands of travellers here, someone must be able to help."

A short while earlier, after finding out from Woola's dad where Woola was probably heading, Toby and Paranoid Dave had slipped away from the Personalitron terminal. They waited for Woola's dad to disappear for his nap, and then pushed on the first door they could find. They had assumed it would be locked, but not a bit of it. The door opened freely – no buttons, no passcode, no high-tech security – just a pair of slightly squeaky hinges. The pair had wandered down a nondescript corridor, pushed open another door, and now found themselves here.

The pair started looking around for a friendly Za-Nakarian to ask. There were travellers in mind-boggling numbers before them. In the distance, running along the inside of the walls, they could see walkways and balconies, along which tiny speck-like figures were moving in their hundreds. Huge, long gantries criss-crossed the hall at all angles, with more travellers streaming along them. Small aerial craft of various descriptions were buzzing and weaving in between.

And directly in front of the pair, on the main concourse, a river of alien beings flowed to-and-fro in their thousands. They all looked busy, exotic, unapproachable.

"Well, here's the thing," Paranoid Dave said after scanning around for a short while, "I just can't see many Za-Nakarians? In fact, I haven't seen any since we got here. Apart from Woola's dad."

"Me neither..." Toby said, still looking around. "Right, I'm just gonna ask the alien nearest us... There! Up there. That... *person* looks helpful. Come on."

Toby led Paranoid Dave up a short staircase to their left. It led to a low walkway on their side of the hall.

*

"Va klk klk mssggi vrrm vrrm vlala?"

"Errm, I'm terribly sorry," Toby stuttered. "Me no speak Za-Nakarian. Me from far away."

The alien creature tilted her head to one side and looked at Toby with an inquiring expression. She had large, imploring eyes, with long curling lashes that would look attractive in any species.

"Ah!" she said after a short pause. "You're English? Oh that's lovely. My name is Za-Farka. How are you?"

"Err... Wow?" Toby said, too amazed to be amazed, and more just confused. "You speak English? I mean, hang on... *How?*"

"Oh, that's simple. I've had a speech transponder implanted so that I can better service my clients." She fluttered her eyelashes and smiled prettily at Toby in a way that he still found attractive, even despite her green skin and the way her three nostrils flared slightly.

"Speech transponder? Implanted? Excuse me?"

"Yes, a speech transponder. It can automatically translate my voice into any one of millions of different languages."

"OK… But how do you – how does *it* – already know English? There have only been a few visitors from Earth and they're all holed up in a weird, dingy room back there?" He thumbed vaguely in the direction he thought he had come from.

"Oh, my colleague and I have been getting visitors from Earth for years." She gestured towards another hostess a few yards away, who was standing next to Paranoid Dave. "You look so uncomfortable, do please take a seat?"

Toby was so confused, he obeyed her instruction unthinkingly, allowing his arms to flop randomly onto the four arm rests available. He was still wearing the floral pyjama suit he'd been given by the Chinese President.

"Va klk klk mssggi vrrm vrrm vlala?"

"Eh?"

"Oh sorry!" Za-Farka giggled. "I was asking if perhaps sir would like his upper shoulders massaged?"

"Err, OK, that's very kind," Toby replied, wondering where his lower shoulders might be. "I don't actually have any money. Is this expensive?"

"Oh no," the hostess replied. "This is a service that the hyperspaceport is pleased to offer all travellers."

"Ah, ok," said Toby, thinking he was starting to get somewhere. "So we're in a hyperspaceport? What does that mean exactly?"

The hostess giggled a spontaneous, disarming giggle, as she started to massage Toby's shoulders.

"You're very sweet," she said. "You've arrived here

but don't know where here is."

"Haha," Toby laughed back, in a slightly forced way. "Basically, no."

"Your brain is confused by the journey, that happens. Well, this is the Bodytron terminal of Port Dharma-Ka. That's Za-Nak's premier hyperspaceport."

"Great, great," Toby replied. "But surely you mean *Personalitron* terminal?"

This time the hostess broke off from the massage to laugh so loudly, you would have to call it a guffaw. Toby found her amusement just the wrong side of polite.

"*Personalitron?*" she giggled, prettily putting the back of her forepaw to her mouth to suppress her amusement. "No-one has used those in generations! Oh they keep a few rusty ones out the back in case of a powerdown in the Bodytron terminal. But that *never* happens," she added cheerily.

"Haha, silly me," Toby said. "No-one would be so dumb as to use a Personalitron. But my brain is a bit confused as you say. Just remind me of the difference between a Bodytron and a Personalitron?"

"Well, a Personalitron only sends your personality between terminals, while a Bodytron is a second-generation teleportation device. It sends your whole body. So your whole body travels to wherever it wants to go. You just need a Bodytron to send it and a Bodytron to receive it. Unlike a Personalitron, where you have to create new bodies and leave old ones behind. Biological 3D printing. So inconvenient."

"Yeah, what a drag," Toby replied. *So why did they install two of them under Downing Street?*

Toby looked across to check on Paranoid Dave. He was trying to communicate with the other hostess. He was silently mouthing words in English with extreme contortions of his face, while making alarming gestures with his hands in a sign language that he had just made up.

"Dave…" Toby called across, "Dave…"

"Sssh, Toby – not now. I'm trying to make myself understood," Paranoid Dave replied over his shoulder as he continued to gesture.

"Err, Dave, actually they speak English?"

"Eh? English? Don't be ridiculous, of course she doesn't…"

"You speak English?" Paranoid Dave's hostess asked him, smilingly. "Perhaps sir would relax for a moment, and I would be happy to massage him?"

"Ah, English eh? Well, that's alright then," Paranoid Dave replied, dusting some fluff from his shoulder. "Yeah, I had pretty much figured that out anyway."

Toby leaned back. The hostess' forepaws were kneading Toby's shoulders with increasing pressure. It felt fantastic.

"So that's your role? To greet weary arrivals at the hyperspaceport, and offer them a massage?" Toby asked, giving into the pleasure of it.

"That's right," she replied, smiling. "They normally come down these plastic tubes, drop into the seats – *plop!* – and I'm there to receive them. This is the arrivals side of the hyperspaceport. Over there is the departures side," she added, gesturing to the curved wall opposite.

"But you don't look Za-Nakarian? Actually, come to think of it, not many creatures here do."

"Oh, Za-Nakarians make up only about five percent of the population. People just *love* to come and settle here. Me, I'm from Ma-Boosh. It's a small planet, just a few million light years away." Toby looked up at her. A shadow of sadness seemed to pass across her face.

"So how did you end up here? Were you doing this job on Your-Boo... I mean, on your home planet?"

"Oh no! Back home I was the Chief Scientist."

"Chief scientist?" Toby replied, sighing comfortably. "That sounds good. Like in a school? Or a company?"

"No, no. Chief Scientist. On the planet. It was my job to advise Governments on the major scientific developments of the day. Hyperspace travel, dark matter mining, AI-AI, that sort of thing."

"AI-AI?"

"Oh that's when you design autonomous robots who can design other autonomous robots. It's a little risky, but we designed effective protocols."

"Ok... But your planet, it was just a small one right?"

"That's right. Just twenty billion."

"Twenty billion and *you were their Chief Scientist?*" Toby swung round to look at her.

"Uh-huh."

"Well what, if you don't mind me asking, are you doing here working as a hostess?"

"Oh but I love it here," she replied frankly. "The Za-Nakarians are so lovely, they pay me well, and..."

"And?"

At that moment, a distinctly unpleasant face, purple with another three nostrils, appeared directly in front of Toby's. It looked at him threateningly, before throwing the same look at Za-Farka.

"Let's just say, things didn't work out so well back home," Za-Farka said timidly, dropping her gaze. "By the way, please meet Za-Charma. She's just woken up. She's my other head."

Toby looked at Za-Charma. Her head was attached to a long, umbilical neck and, when Toby followed it to its source, he could see it was attached to the same body as Za-Farka's. Toby waved nervously. Za-Charma stared back suspiciously. And then Toby remembered with a jolt. *Mutu-Lulu Resort.*

"Excuse me," he started, "can either of you tell me where to find the—"

"MUTU-LULU RESORT?" A loud, bored and slightly irritated voice called up to him loudly from the main concourse below. "I expect you're looking for it?"

It was Woola's dad.

Next to him were four bulky looking guards of some undefined species. They wore heavy armour and were carrying gun-like things.

Oh dear, Toby thought, *we've gone and blown it this time.* He looked across at Paranoid Dave who was far, far away in a massage-induced stupor.

"Well come on then," Woola's dad continued. "Are you going to hang around there all day?"

"Err, are you arresting us?"

"What?"

"Those guards. I mean, are they here to arrest us?"

"What, these halfwits? *Nooo*, they're here to escort you."

"Escort us?"

"You want to find Woola, right?"

"Err, yes actually we do…" Toby replied.

"Good. Because he's expecting you. I got a message. So irritating. Would you please hurry up, or I'll miss my favourite show?"

"Right. Good. Well that's OK then." Toby turned to Za-Farka, as he got up from the chair. "Thank you for the massage. I think this is where we say goodbye?"

"Oh no need for that," Za-Farka replied sweetly, "we're coming too."

26

"Hey Seamus, check it out! And look, it's my size too."

Seamus and Declan had been staggering through the streets of London. Dawn was breaking. Like everyone else in the Squirrel & Acorn – in fact like everyone else on the planet – they had figured that if yesterday was a day to remember, last night better be a night to remember too. So they hadn't gone to bed. And now they were drunk with joy, fatigue, and a few other things besides.

The market was open early. They had stumbled in and stopped to browse the first stall they reached. It was selling t-shirts, cards, books and bric-a-brac.

"Does it look good on me? Does it?"

Declan was holding up a t-shirt against his chest. Seamus stared at it and a broad happy smile spread across his freckled complexion. An image of Woola had been photoshopped to show him sitting atop a temple. He was in the lotus position, with a chequered loincloth around his waist and the palms of his flippers pressed together in the prayer position. The early morning sun was rising over mountains behind him.

Declan turned the shirt around with a flourish. On the back it read:

The Age
of
Za-N'Aquarius
is
Dawning

"I think I should get it! Now… I wonder if they're still bothering with money here?" Declan added, fondly remembering the sequence of bars they'd visited the night before, where the fun was free and money a thing of the past.

"Ay-up, these shirts look just grand on you. But then it's a grand day to be alive, eh?"

A short, tubby figure approached the pair. It was the owner of the stall. He had overheard the two partygoers as he was putting some books out on a stand.

"Ma name's Morley. Pleased to meet you both," he said holding out five stubby, potato-like fingers, which Declan assumed to be his hand.

"Pleased to meet you," Declan replied, as he shook hands. "I'm Declan, this is Seamus. Err, these shirts. Can we take them?"

"Ay, you can take 'em soon enough, fella," Morley replied, drumming his fingers against his chubby tummy, while his jocular face creased into a smile. "Same as Ah took 'em from the last fella. But we maat need t'exchange a few sovereigns in the process like."

"Err, does that mean we have to pay?"

"Hahaha, oh-ay, you're a funny one you are."

"So is it free?"

"No."

*

Toby was the last to step out of the hovershoot. It bucked a little as he transferred his weight to the docking platform, the way a small boat might as you step off it.

Toby was just getting ready to admire this striking vehicle – *he had absolutely no idea what kept it in the air* – when he was struck by something else instead. The air. As he stepped into Za-Nakarian outdoors for the first time, the warm, tropical humidity hit him with a cloying whoosh.

If they like warm, humid air so much, why do they use so much air conditioning indoors? Toby found himself wondering.

Down below him lay a stunning resort. It was a vast, beautifully manicured array of sparkling blue lagoons, connected by a shimmering network of streams, walkways and bridges.

"Welcome to the Mutu-Lulu Resort and Spa Complex!" It was Za-Farka talking. "I shall be your hostess for today. It's my job to ensure your time here is as relaxing as it possibly can be. Please follow me."

The leaders of the USA, Britain, China, France, and Germany all followed obediently, like well-behaved school children. Toby and Paranoid Dave fell in line behind them.

"Say, what's your name, honey?" the US President asked their guide.

"Za-Farka."

"Za-Farka? Well ain't that just the prettiest name! And your, err, second head," he continued, "does she have a name too?"

"Of course, that's Za-Charma."

Za-Farka smiled back disarmingly, while Za-Charma glanced back at the group with a suspicious scowl.

"*Za-Charma?* Fooled me," Paranoid Dave whispered to Toby.

"Sssh! Keep your voice down," Toby whispered back. "And try to keep up."

As Za-Farka faced backwards towards the group, and prattled away, her other head – Za-Charma – was facing forwards, leading the way. It was, Toby had to acknowledge, a spectacularly efficient arrangement for a tour guide. One head for navigation, one for the commentary.

"...so you see Dharma-Ka is the largest city on Za-Nak," Za-Farka continued, "and this is the premier leisure facility in the city. Your hosts have spared no expense. Over here to your right, you can see one of the 34 pools in the complex. The Za-Nakarians love nothing more than to relax in warm water..."

Toby looked across and saw a scattering of Za-Nakarians lounging round the edge of a luxurious-looking rock pool, while beings of various descriptions brought them food and nibbles. Next to the pool there were a couple of thatched bars, at which several more Za-Nakarians had parked themselves, while they sipped on exotic-looking cocktails.

"...and do you see the large domed building ahead to your right?" Za-Farka continued. "That's where your conference suite is. That's where you will find out what the Za-Nakarians really have in store for your planet," she added, still smiling sweetly.

*

"Have you seen the dawn this morning?" Morley asked Seamus and Declan. "Ah've never seen 'owt like it, not in London, not in thirty years in the Dales…"

Morley might have wanted payment for his goods, but apart from that little commercial detail, he was as much infected as everyone else by the joy and euphoria of the previous 18 hours. He was now staring upwards at the breaking of what was indeed an amazing dawn.

Seamus and Declan rubbed some of the bleariness out of their eyes. They weren't sure if they had ever actually noticed dawn breaking over the city before, but they could now and it was breathtaking. A morning mist lingered over the great park to their right, which the soft yellow light of the rising sun illuminated in subtle hues of luminous violet and turquoise. They were spellbound.

"Wow…"

"Yeah, like, seriously, wow…"

"Woooooooow…" continued Seamus just slightly longer than was strictly necessary, lovely though the breaking dawn was.

He tugged on Declan's sleeve.

"Wooooooooooooooooow," he said again.

"Thanks, Seamus, I get it. It's a lovely dawn," Declan replied, removing Seamus's hand from his sleeve. He turned back to Morley. "By the way, what's that book you're holding?"

Morley looked down.

"Oh ay. This is a bit special. Early-bird discount for you fellas. Here, have a look…" Morley held it out and Declan took it from him.

The cover image showed Woola blowing soap bubbles, with the famous black door of No.10 in the background, artistically out of focus. The title read:

My Story
by Woof-lis-Woola

Just an Ordinary Za-Nakarian

"Ah-mazing…" Declan exclaimed. "Now how did they manage this? The fella's only just got here and he's already published his autobiography?"

"Ay, it's a bloody miracle," Morley replied.

"Woooooooooooooooooooow…" said Seamus again, tugging on Declan's sleeve again.

"Not now, Seamus, I'm talking." But Seamus persisted. He tugged his friend's sleeve again and pointed at the sky. Not to the east, where the dawn was breaking, but to the north.

And then Declan looked up.

"Ooh…"

"…maaa goodness," added Morley, also looking up.

The three of them stared.

And then stared some more.

A bulk carrier from the Jagamath fleet was just starting to pass overhead. It was following the exact same north-south orbital used the night before by the bulk carrier, which the Professor and Charlie had seen from more or less the same spot. At the moment that the three onlookers turned their gaze upwards, the vast bow planes were just drawing into view, cresting the hill at the top of the park. The sight was awe-inspiring. Like watching a huge nuclear submarine pass overhead, only many thousands – hundreds of thousands – of times larger.

Small, involuntary gasps escaped from their throats as they stared. They knew this was connected with the events of yesterday. They didn't know why or what, but they sensed in an instant that something had just gone terribly, terribly wrong.

The spaceship glided forwards serenely. The breaking dawn was blotted out, the ship's shadow passed across the market.

The three of them stared, uncomprehending, for a few more seconds and then dropped their gaze.

An uncomfortable silence reigned.

Seamus chased around a loose pebble with his foot. Declan whistled aimlessly. Morley found a little dust to sweep off his bookshelf.

This sight, this spacecraft – it was utterly and completely beyond their frame of reference. Its size was so colossal, its means of propulsion so inexplicable, its purpose so uncertain, and the implications of its arrival so momentous, that their sleep-deprived minds were performing giddy little pirouettes trying to comprehend it. The way your brain might if you, say, walked out of your front door one morning to find your car levitating in the air, chatting to the lamppost.

It was just easier to block it out.

In the midst of the awkwardness, and searching for something else to look at, they all fixed on an eccentric who was passing by, wearing an old-fashioned sandwich board.

The End

Of The World

Is Nigh…

The eccentric stared back at them, puzzled. *He* was normally the thing everyone tried to avoid looking at. He stopped, turned around, and stared up in the same direction they had been staring.

Oh.

He looked back down.

And up again.

And down again.

And scratched his head.

He looked across to the three of them. He nodded in a sort of fraternal way and they nodded back. A brief moment of understanding passed between them all, which – to the eccentric – was very special. And then he continued walking.

The back of his sandwich board came into view:

…and it

Feels Great!

A moment later Declan realised, with a muffled spasm, that he was still carrying Woola's autobiography.

"Yep, well, I might just pass on this," he muttered, embarrassed, quickly giving the book back to Morley.

"Of course," Morley replied, taking the book – before dropping it onto a bench next to him, like he'd touched an electric eel.

The two partygoers nodded sideways at Morley and shuffled off. Morley directed a non-committal grunt at the pavement, cleared his throat and went back to his things.

*

Out on the street, the passers-by passed by other passers-by. Everyone walked with their heads down, no-one's eyes met.

It suddenly looked like any other normal day in the big, anonymous city.

Except that an enormous spacecraft was gliding overhead.

27

Woola was staring lovingly at the leaders of planet Earth.

He was feeling that dreamy, hazy feeling of affection that was habitual to most Za-Nakarians (except for his dad, who was an awful grump). Only today he was feeling it even more than normal. Things were going well. The leaders of planet Earth had arrived safely on Za-Nak, and they all seemed terribly nice. They were frightfully nervous of course – but so sweet, so eager to please.

As Woola stared, he took in the full breadth of the room. Za-Nakarians, with their large, globe-like eyes, had a stunning, 270° field of view. If any human could have seen the world the way they did, they would've been amazed. This 270° field of view was rendered in their mind's eye as a wide, horizontal frame, as if life was constantly playing before them at a slight distance, like a movie in a widescreen cinema. Below the horizontal frame was just blacknesss. But above the horizontal frame… That's what humans, and many of the Za-Nakarians' other vassal species, would have loved to see.

Above Woola's main field of view was a second, much smaller one. It was oval in shape. Within this oval, Woola's imagination was playing out. Within this oval, Woola could see whatever he chose to see, and he could see it not in some vague, half-distinct way, but with absolute crystal clarity.

So even while Woola looked hazily at the nervous gathering in front of him, he was imagining them in a very different mood. In his second field of view they were jubilant. Still in their bright, floral pyjama suits, they were high-fiving, they were clapping, they were stamping their feet.

They were *celebrating*.

*

Why is Woola staring at me in such a funny way? was Toby's last coherent thought. Not his last coherent thought ever, but his last one for the next half-hour or so. Which, to be clear, would turn out to be a rather significant half-hour for the fate of the planet.

"So is everyone enjoying their time on Za-Nak?" Biffa asked. "You all had a good journey here? You're enjoying your new bodies?"

Biffa smirked slightly, as he scanned the room.

"I certainly am!" came the voice of the US President.

"Oh tais-toi, imbécile," scolded the French President, before turning to Biffa. "Mais oui, we are very 'onoured to be guests 'ere on Za-Naque."

"Good, I'm glad to hear it."

Biffa was sitting behind a desk. He stood up and walked round to the front, and perched his backside against it. On a bar to his left were a pyramid of champagne flutes, empty and gleaming. In front of him was a low circular table, with a large, doughnut-like hole in the middle. Beyond the table, the world leaders were sat in a semi-circle, with Toby and Paranoid Dave sat behind them.

The assembled group were looking at Biffa with renewed interest. *Who was this guy, really?* He clearly wasn't just the interpreter or janitor. Shorter than average height, and a bit plump, Biffa had a face that *bulged.* Bulging lips, bulging cheeks, and bulging bulbous eyes, which had an unfortunate habit of darting left and right like a lizard's. There was a strange nervous energy in his movements and an air of repressed aggression in his demeanour, like he might snap at any moment. In short: there was little doubt this was a face that had been bullied at school – probably badly – and was going to spend the rest of its life working through its issues.

"Great. OK, so let's summarise the situation," Biffa continued, happily soaking up the attention and respect that he was now commanding. "You guys have sold planet Earth to the Za-Nakarians for 1.8 quadrillion Za-Nakarian dollars. Congratulations. That was a smart move…" Biffa's gaze returned to Woola, who was sitting just to his right, "…*by us*. Haha!"

Biffa looked at the startled faces staring at him.

"Hey, don't look so worried. I'm just messin'. So," he continued, "we've got the population of planet Earth in the right place now, emotionally. The sale transaction went smoothly and the PR has been good – excellent in fact. Thank you, everyone, thank you, Woola. He's shown us a textbook case of how to buy a planet."

Biffa nodded towards Woola, who inclined his head in acknowledgement.

"As I see it, everyone on Earth thinks – one – that

Woola is cute," Biffa numbered the items off against his fingers. "Two – that he can't speak English – three – that the Za-Nakarians are gonna do a better job of running planet Earth than you guys ever did. *They probably got that right.* And – four – that I'm just the interpreter-stroke-janitor. Can you believe it? I brokered this, I'm the investment banker who cut a 1.8 quadrillion dollar deal, and they think I'm just a guy who pours hot water into a wheelie bin? Dumb schmucks."

Biffa started laughing.

No-one else joined in.

"Oh come on!" he said, slapping both hands on his thighs and still laughing. "It's funny, right? Me, just a janitor? Have a little laugh at my expense, come on, loosen up!"

Woola put his flipper to his mouth and his shoulders started convulsing slightly, as if the hilarity was too great to suppress. That was too much for the US President. He started giggling too and, looking round the group, thumbed in the direction of Biffa as if to say, *Can you believe that guy? What a gas!* The British Prime Minister took his cue from the US President and started guffawing, which got the Chinese President laughing, and then they were all laughing. Even Toby got caught up in it, and found himself flowing with the merriment. And the more the group laughed, the louder they got, and the louder they got, the more they laughed. Until they were bellowing and buckling up on their chairs and slapping each other, and a slightly hysterical note could be heard.

"Ach ya," the German Chancellor spoke up, between lungfuls of laughter, "Otto is finding this very amusing, ja!"

"OK, enough already!"

Biffa made a sudden cut-it-out gesture with his hands. Everyone fell silent.

"This is a serious business. You've just sold planet Earth to planet Za-Nak. We're talking about the fate of two planets *forchrissake*. Wise up."

The room fell silent. Otto stared down at his feet.

"That's better. OK. You've all seen a little bit of Za-Nak now. You probably think you're experts. But you're not. Let me tell you a thing or two about Za-Nak."

Biffa picked up a remote and clicked a button. Over the table in the centre of the room, above the large hole, there now appeared a holographic image of Planet Za-Nak that filled the centre of the room. It was a stunning, mesmerising 3D image, complete with clouds and mountains. It was shimmering and radiant and, as the image rotated, the iridescent colours refracted and sparkled against the hypnotised eyes of the visitors.

"The Za-Nakarian civilisation is two million years old. Did you know that? When humans were just starting to climb down out of the trees, these guys already had cities and public drains. OK, true, they've had to swap planets a few times since then – a few dozen times actually – but after some practice they developed climate control technologies that have kept Za-Nak-34 *in great shape*. They've been on this planet for two hundred thousand years already. For all that time, this exquisite ecosystem has been kept *in balance*."

In the centre of the room, the holographic display had changed to show images of early Za-Nakarian civilisation. One moment they were looking at a sepia-tinted image of Za-Nakarians in wooden hot-tubs, being pulled up and down a street on carts – the next, grainy colour footage was playing, showing the first Za-Nakarian astronaut climbing into a primitive-looking rocket.

"Of course it helps that they've outsourced their industry to other planets. The most polluting thing you'll find on this planet is an aquapod. And those things run on compressed deuterium batteries, that never need replacing. Which is another way of saying: *there is no pollution* on Za-Nak. Because, let's face it, the Za-Nakarians are an extraordinary people, a special people. Did you know that they are the ones who first invented the Personalitron? No? Well, now you do."

The holographic display changed to show the earliest Personalitrons.

"Did you know they have a seat on the Inter-Galactic Council? …No? Well, yes they do. In fact they *founded* the Inter-Galactic Council."

Now the display showed a debating chamber with creatures of all descriptions yelling at each other. A Za-Nakarian figure, his aquapod perched loftily above the chamber, remained impassive as a fight broke out beneath him.

"We, the Golgothans – and I'm a Golgothan, as well as a human, in case you hadn't figured it out already – we are *honoured* to serve such an extraordinary civilisation."

Biffa's voice started to rise.

"Given what they've contributed to the Universe, I think it's reasonable for this civilisation to expect something back. I think we can all agree that this is a people who deserve to have a holiday planet or two. Or twenty. OK, about two hundred, but anyway, somewhere for them to relax, to unwind. And I think we can agree that if a little race like humankind has to make a few sacrifices so that a great civilisation like Za-Nak can flourish, then that's a sacrifice we're *happy* to make. Am I right?"

"You damn right you right!" the Chinese President shouted.

"Too right you're right. Right on!" the British Prime Minister added.

"The Earth, my friends, is an irrelevance, an off-chance purchase," Biffa shouted, reaching his climax, "what really matters is Za-Nak... *A m I r i g h t ?* "

"Hell yeah!" said the US President, high-fiving the French President.

"Bien sûr!" said the French President

"You betcha!" said the British Prime Minister.

"Damn right!" said Toby, despite himself, despite everything.

"Jawohl!" the German Chancellor added enthusiastically.

"Enough already!" Biffa made his cut-it-out gesture again.

The room fell silent again. So silent in fact, that Biffa almost caught the end of what Paranoid Dave was saying.

"*What's got into you?*" Paranoid Dave whispered into Toby's ear, "*why are you going along with this nonsense?*"

"Excuse me?" said Biffa leaning to his right, and eyeballing Paranoid Dave round the side of the hologram. "Did you say something?"

"Damn right I said something," Paranoid Dave replied boldly. "I said—'"

"What did you say?"

"Damn right!'"

"You did?"

"Damn right I said *damn right!* I said," Paranoid Dave continued, "let's screw the Earth. This is about *Za-Nak*! Hell yeah!" Paranoid Dave pumped his fist in the air.

"OK… Well that's alright then."

"Damn right!"

"Yeah, you can stop now, thanks," Biffa said, looking suspicious. He turned to the others, recovering his poise. "It's time to tell you what this purchase *is really about*."

Biffa clicked his remote again. The image of Za-Nak faded, and was replaced by an image of planet Earth, in the familiar, beautiful hues of azure blue and apple green. The image rotated on its axis.

"The Earth and Za-Nak are both on Standard Universal Time, S.U.T. The details are a little complicated, way beyond you lot, so let's just go with this: in six hours from now, S.U.T. – and despite what you think you know about relativity, it really will be six hours from now – we will be taking irreversible action to turn Earth into a resort paradise for the Za-Nakarians. Hell, it will be paradise for humans too…" Biffa added, clicking on his remote again, "…for those that survive."

A series of small oblong shapes started to stream across the face of the Earth. They spread down and around the planet, until they formed four continuous rings, encircling the planet.

"On behalf of the Za-Nakarians, we have hired the Jagamath fleet of hyperspace bulk carriers. These vessels are big, by the way. They look like little blips on the image here, but each one is actually big. I mean, like, screw-you big."

Biffa clicked the remote again. An image of a bulk carrier replaced the Earth for a moment. It was displayed vertically. At its base, a small-ish mountain could be seen next to it.

"Here's a mock up, showing a bulk carrier next to Mount Everest. Like I said, big. But you know what? That's just a detail. Here's the really good bit..." Biffa clicked back to the image of the Earth. "There are 377 of them. Circling the Earth. Right now."

Biffa started walking round the Earth.

"At 12pm GMT on Sunday they will start to release their payload. The operation will last about six hours. What is their payload? Oh just 3 teratonnes or so of compressed CO_2, that's all. Currently sitting in liquefied form aboard the bulk carriers, but once released, it will expand into 1.5 quadrillion cubic metres of gaseous CO_2. Or 1.5 *quintillion* litres. Haha, I like big numbers, did you notice? I should stop showing off. Fact is, these carriers are only using a fraction of their carrying capacity. This is just a little drop-off job for them on their way to their next pick-up. At midday, they'll release the payload and the atmospheric concentration of CO_2 will be roughly doubled, providing a nice, cosy blanket around your darling little planet and you guys never need feel chilly again. Just watch while I play..."

Biffa clicked the remote again.

"...a time-lapse movie. Things are gonna change."

The room fell silent as they watched planet Earth transforming before their eyes. Clouds started to gather and swirl over the equator, forming vortex-like storm systems. While over the northern and southern latitudes – over Europe, Siberia, Canada in the north – over New

Zealand, South Africa and Argentina in the south, the clouds retreated, leaving an almost eerie calm. As the seconds ticked by, slithers of Northern Europe disappeared beneath fingers of blue ocean. The fingers widened and whole countries splintered into small islands. In the far North, the Arctic ice cap disappeared entirely and the Greenland icesheet dwindled to a rump.

"What you're seeing is the northern and southern latitudes being turned into a resort paradise, where your new Za-Nakarian guests can enjoy sixteen to twenty hours of uninterrupted sunshine – in the northern hemisphere during the northern summer and in the southern hemisphere during the southern summer. Meantime all the excess climatic energy is confined to the equatorial regions and the poles, using the best climate control technologies that money can buy."

Biffa hit another button, and the image froze.

"This, my friends," Biffa continued, "is what paradise looks like."

Silence.

Total, stunned silence.

And then, from out of that silence, the sound of two hands pressed together in a solitary clap.

And then another.

And another, and another.

Clapping.

It was the US President.

"Alright!" he said, looking round for support. "Liking that! Hey, you got my vote!"

The British Prime Minister took up the clapping with enthusiasm. "And mine. Bravo! Excellent presentation!"

Woola joined in, flapping his flippers together enthusiastically. Biffa beamed as the rest of the room took up the clapping and started whooping and punching the air. Toby – again – found himself carried along on the tide. Without quite knowing what he was doing, he joined in the clapping and whooping.

"*What the Hell are you doing?*" Paranoid Dave hissed into his ear, while attempting an awkward smile and clapping himself. "Are you serious? Has something *happened* to you?"

"What do you mean? Everything's cool," Toby replied, "these guys are smart, look at them, they got it covered. Maybe we – maybe *you* – need to lighten up a little."

Paranoid Dave looked furious, he was about to punch Toby. And then his face changed, like something had struck him.

"Hang on – Toby – did the Professor give you something before we left?"

"*What? I* can't hear you!" Toby broke off to put two fingers in his mouth and release an ear-piercing whistle. "Damn, I couldn't even do that with my old body!"

Clapping even more enthusiastically, Toby straightened in his chair to get a better view of Biffa, who was picking up what looked like a magnum of vintage champagne. He started to shake it vigorously.

"You better appreciate this, you schmucks," Biffa shouted. "You've no idea how hard it is to smuggle this stuff through the Bodytron terminal!"

"You mean ze Personalitron?" the German Chancellor asked.

"Hey? What's that?"

"Ze Personalitron? Zat iz ze machine, yah?"

"Can't hear ya!"

"Ze machine is called ze Peronalitr…"

POP went the cork!

"WHOOP!" Biffa shouted as champagne spouted and frothed from the bottle. Great gobs flew in all directions, onto his shirt, his sleeves, onto Woola, and through the holographic image of the Earth onto the table below.

"Now, Woola and I have to leave shortly," Biffa continued breezily. "We have some business to conclude on Golgotha – a few last financial details to iron out. But I want you guys…" he continued, as he poured the bottle into the pyramid of champagne flutes, "to enjoy yourselves! Drink yourselves stupid, have a party. In a few hours you go back to Earth and once you're there…"

Biffa paused for a second as he drained the bottle and picked up the top glass of the pyramid for himself.

"…you'll know what to do. Some folk might be a little jumpy, seeing all those spaceships. Reassure them, calm them down, tell them it's all part of the plan. Which, by the way, it is."

Biffa raised his glass.

"Santé – Mazel tov – *Cheers!*" he called out, draining the glass down his throat.

Paranoid Dave pinched Toby's arm viciously.

"*D i d   t h e   P r o f e s s o r   g i v e   y o u   s o m e t h i n g   b e f o r e   w e   l e f t ?* "

"Hey? You're hurting me." Toby yanked his arm away sharply. "No. He gave me nothing. Oh, thank you very much!" he said to Za-Farka as she handed him a flute of champagne.

"Thank you, that's very kind," Paranoid Dave said, hurriedly taking his glass as well.

Za-Farka moved on to serve the US President, whose other hand was resting mysteriously on the French President's knee, and then to the French President, who – strangely – was allowing the Presidential hand to stay on her knee. Meantime, Za-Charma swivelled on her long, articulated neck to stare at Paranoid Dave.

Paranoid Dave lowered his voice and said with all the emphasis he could muster, speaking out of the side of his mouth, "*A r e   y o u   s u r e ?*"

"Yes!" Toby replied, not a little irritated. And then he glanced at Paranoid Dave's eyes, which were wearing an intense, pleading expression he hadn't seen before. Which made him feel bad, so he had another think.

"Oh – no, wait. There was something…" Toby's hand involuntarily went up to his neck where the small locket was hanging. "Yeah, he gave me this."

Paranoid Dave abruptly leaned across, yanked the locket from Toby's neck, snapping the chain.

"Ow!"

"Shut up!"

Paranoid Dave opened the locket carefully to reveal a little mound of chalky grey powder. He leaned forward, until he was completely obscured by the German Chancellor's ample bulk and, taking Toby's champagne flute, he tipped the powder into it.

"Drink," he said. "*Now!*"

Toby looked at Paranoid Dave with a hurt look on his face. He reluctantly took the glass and knocked the contents back. He stared directly ahead for a few seconds, while Paranoid Dave watched him anxiously.

He wasn't the only one watching. While Za-Farka was circulating with the champagne, Za-Charma was craning on her neck, trying to get a better view of the pair.

"Oh," said Toby.

"*What?*"

"I see."

"What do you see?"

"Sorry."

"What?"

"We're here to save the planet aren't we?"

"Maybe so," Paranoid Dave replied warily. "Which planet are you thinking of saving?"

"Earth?"

"Thank God."

"And not to glory in its destruction?"

"The Professor's reverse-truth drug... It actually works."

"Sorry."

"Forgiven."

"Shall we go now?"

"Yes!"

28

"And where do you think *you're* going?"

Za-Charma swung right in front of Toby. It took all his breaking power to stop his slightly pink, slightly sweaty face slamming into her very purple, very dry one. Her expression was menacing.

"Hey! Leave off him. We just came out to get some air, that's all," Paranoid Dave retorted protectively.

"Oh yeah, and who asked you to speak, fat face?" Za-Farka, supposedly their friend, swung her green face right in front of Paranoid Dave, throwing him a death stare at six inches.

Toby and Paranoid Dave had just found their way back to the entrance of the resort building. They needed to get back to Port Dharma-Ka *fast*, but they had no idea how. They had burst through the doors, and now the two-headed hostess was in their way.

"We think—" Za-Farka continued.

"—that you're trying to escape," said Za-Charma.

"Well I don't think—" Toby started.

"—that's any of your business," Parnoid Dave finished.

The pair looked at each other, a little troubled.

"Hang on," said Paranoid Dave, "did you just—"

"—finish my sentence?" finished Toby.

"That's actually kind of—"

"Freaky?"

"Yeah."

"Excuse me!" Za-Farka resumed.

"What is it?" Toby replied, irritated.

"I hope we're not interrupting here?" said Za-Charma.

"Well actually—" Toby started.

"—you are," Paranoid Dave concluded. Without moving his gaze from Za-Farka, he held his palm out flat and Toby – who didn't move his gaze from Za-Charma – slapped him a high-five.

"Well tough," Za-Charma continued. "Because if you're going to get back to the Professor you'd better get a move on."

Toby and Paranoid Dave looked at each other again and then back at their hostess.

"W – W – h – h – a – a – t – t ?" they both said, more or less in unison.

"Professor James?" Za-Farka said.

"Professor Artemas C. James?" Za-Charma amplified, like she was talking to a nitwit.

"You both *know* him?" Paranoid Dave asked in amazement.

"Actually, do you happen to know what that middle 'C' stands for?" Toby asked. "We were kind of like, you know, wondering?"

"Urgh. You are trying to save your planet, aren't you?" said Za-Farka. "The way we couldn't save ours…" she added under her breath.

"Sure we are, yes," replied Paranoid Dave. "But *who are you?*"

"We are friends of the Professor," Za-Charma replied, "and we've been feeding him information for months," Za-Charma continued.

"You remember how I told you back in the hyperspaceport that we had to leave our planet, Ma-Boosch," Za-Farka asked Toby. Toby nodded. "Well that's because the Za-Nakarians screwed that over too."

"Oh my God…" said Toby slowly, the scales falling from his eyes. "You're the Professor's 'special source'!"

"Affirmative," replied Za-Farka.

"The ones who told the Professor about the Za-Nakarians' history with previous resort planets?" continued Paranoid Dave. "You gave him the photos, the before-and-after pictures?"

"Correct," replied Za-Charma.

"OK…" said Toby. "But why didn't you tell us straight away who you were, when we first met?"

"Because we couldn't be sure who *you* were," Za-Charma replied. "Not until I spotted the Professor's locket."

"Ah, I see…" Toby said as more scales fell away.

"The Za-Nakarians find a different way of stuffing each planet," Za Farka said. "But now we know what they're going to do to yours, you need to get back to the hyperspaceport *fast*—"

"—back to Earth—" said Za-Charma.

"—and back to the Professor!" said Za-Farka.

"OK," Paranoid Dave replied, "actually, that's what we were trying to do."

"Then it's just as well we've left a hovershoot on standby for you, right…" Za-Charma swung her head round and nodded towards an aerial vehicle twenty yards away, "…*there*."

Toby and Paranoid Dave threw each other a look

which said, *maybe we misjudged these two?*

"Err, ok, well then, err, thank you," replied Paranoid Dave. "Sorry if we've been a bit rude…"

"…we didn't realise you were on our side," Toby added. "We're just a little on edge, you know how it is."

"Just one last question—" Paranoid Dave started.

"—the Professor's middle initial," Toby continued, "the 'C'. Seriously, what does it—"

"Go—"

"—*now!*"

*

On a small planet, many many galaxies distant from Za-Nak, Mrs B crunched through snow, making her way towards a woodshed. She was briskly hugging herself as she walked, flapping her arms to stay warm in the chill air. The Professor followed behind, perfectly at ease in his three-piece tweed suit, and looking unconcerned as ever.

"Will young Charlotte be OK by herself here?" Mrs B asked, as she closed the shed door behind them.

"Hmm? Well she's not by herself. There's Jaakko."

"That's what I'm worried about."

"Hahaha, yes, I see, yes. But no. We don't need to worry about him," the Professor replied. "His criminal days are behind him, hmm? And anyway, if we twiddle the settings just right, you will only be gone a few minutes. And I'll be back soon enough after that."

"Hmph," Mrs B grunted sceptically, as the two of them entered the woodshed. The Professor made his way to a set of controls and fiddled with them for a few moments.

"Ready for the off?" he asked breezily.

"Ready."

"Well then, here we go."

*

Toby and Paranoid Dave were back in the main terminal of the Dharma-Ka hyperspaceport.

They scurried around the vast, curved concourse, looking not unlike a couple of travellers rushing for their connection. They were moving in that run-stride-run rhythm, that Toby knew all too well from being late at railway stations, when trying unsuccessfully to find a balance between urgency and dignity.

"Damn – where is that door to the Personalitron terminal?" Paranoid Dave panted. "Do you think we already passed it by accident?"

"Not sure…" Toby panted back. "And when we do find it, will they actually let us use the Personalitron?"

"Woola's dad…" Paranoid Dave sucked in a quick lungful of air. "He doesn't seem to like the Golgothans much. Nor his son for that matter. Maybe he'll help?"

"Yeah, maybe. But we're kind of fugitives now. That can't help."

Paranoid Dave stopped for a second and leant against a counter in the middle of the concourse. "Anyway, one thing's for sure, we're not going to find any more answers on Za-Nak," he wheezed. "God, but this is a big room."

Paranoid Dave paused to look around the main terminal of the hyperspaceport in all its intimidating majesty.

"Dave…" Toby started. "Do you think we've got

any chance at all? We've only got, like five hours before they release the CO_2. Everything's stacked against us."

"I dunno," Paranoid Dave replied. "We've just got to get back to the Professor and pray he can think of something. Come on, let's get going—"

"Wait!"

"What?"

"*Don't move!*"

Toby had frozen to the spot.

He had just seen two familiar faces. Two horribly familiar faces. The last two people that he'd want to see on Earth or any other planet.

"*W h a t   i s   i t ?*" Paranoid Dave hissed. "*W h a t   h a v e   y o u   s e e n ?*"

"Don't look, but I've just spotted the TARP team behind you," Toby replied, "and they're doing something... God, *but what are they doing?*"

"What? What is it?"

"I dunno... Urgh. What are they *doing* to that creature? I think they're... Could they be... I think they're administering a..."

"What? What is it? What are they... *administering?*" Paranoid Dave's face was drawn wide with horror as he imagined the worst.

Toby peered over Paranoid Dave's shoulder at the TARP leader and TARP-2. They were both wearing white surgical uniforms. Behind them, a tall gaunt-looking alien seemed to be issuing instructions. In front of them was another alien, stretched out motionless on a couch, as the two TARPs seemed to probe at it with various instruments.

"I think they're delivering..." Toby continued, "...*a pedicure.*"

"A pedicure?"

"Actually, it's a manicure," another voice interrupted. "Those are hands, not feet. But a forgiveable mistake, hmm?"

"*PROFESSOR!*" Toby blurted out.

"What? Who?" Paranoid Dave said, swinging his head left and right. "Oh my God, Professor! You're *here?*"

"Hmm, here? Yes, yes, I'm always present," the Professor replied, smiling affably. "From my point of view."

Waves of relief washed over Toby and Paranoid Dave. The Professor was right *there*. In front of them. Wearing his three-piece tweed suit and, as usual, looking entirely comfortable and entirely out-of-place at the same time. In one hand, he was holding a strange-looking glass with a strange-looking liquid in it. In the other hand, he was holding a couple of coats.

"Mrs B thought you'd want these back," he said, passing a coat to each of them.

"Oh thank God!" Paranoid Dave said, gratefully putting his black leather overcoat straight back on, over his floral pyjamas. "But how did you get here?"

"And are the TARP team going to arrest us, or attack us or something?" Toby asked, putting his jacket back on too. As he straightened it, he heard the familiar rustle of cellophane. The bag of crisps, from the Squirrel & Acorn, was still in his pocket. That and the one pound in loose change he was supposed to have spent on them.

"Oh no, I don't think so," the Professor replied equably. "They seem to have signed on as trainee staff at this beauty salon. In fact one of them just gave me a quick shoulder massage. And a cocktail too, hmm?

Cheers!"

The Professor raised his glass to them both and took a short sip of the purple and green concoction.

"I'm sorry, Professor, I don't get this," Toby persisted. "I thought they were on a mission to follow us across the Universe and arrest us. You called it their 'pursuit protocol'?"

"Oh that? Yes, I see," the Professor replied, taking another sip of his cocktail. "Do you know, that really is delicious? Anyway, yes. No. It appears they changed their mind about that. Hmm? I think they had a rather transformative experience during their Personalitron journey. TARP-2 was telling me about it."

"Seriously?" Toby replied. "Actually, to be fair, the journey was…"

"…fairly special," Paranoid Dave concluded.

"You too?" Toby looked at Paranoid Dave.

Paranoid Dave nodded.

Toby nodded back.

"Is that so? Oh good," the Professor said amiably, looking at them both. "Never tried it myself. But I think our two friends may have given up on their old ways. Mmm, yum," he concluded as he sipped on the cocktail again.

The Professor turned to look at the two members of the TARP team, who were busy filing the claws of their rather corpulent client. They happened to look up and, seeing the Professor, they wriggled their fingers at him. The Professor waved back. Toby involuntarily found himself doing so too. Until Paranoid Dave's hand grabbed his arm and pulled it back down.

"Well, this is all very pleasant," the Professor said pleasantly, replacing his cocktail on the counter, "but I rather think we need to get out of here, don't you? And then you need to tell me everything you've learnt?"

The trio started to make their way out of the massage area, but Paranoid Dave suddenly spun back around.

"Sorry, Professor – one last thing." Paranoid Dave called over to the TARP leader. "You! TARP man. Yes, you! I've got a question for you."

"Sure anything," the TARP leader replied, as he looked up and calmly put down the claw file he was holding.

"What… *What*…" Paranoid Dave hesitated for a moment, and then launched in. "What does TARP stand for?"

"Sure, that's easy," the TARP leader replied, smiling. "'Tactical Armed Response Protocol'."

"'Tactical Armed Response Protocol'? Pah. That's daft," Paranoid Dave replied dismissively. "Doesn't even make sense. How can you refer to a team of people as a 'protocol'?"

"*Daaave*, don't be rude." Toby had caught up with his friend and grabbed him by the shoulder. "Come on let's go…"

"Hey, it's ok. Your friend is posing an interesting grammatical question," the TARP leader replied with an unflappable, slightly uncanny friendliness. "If we called ourselves TARPs that wouldn't work. But actually we always referred to ourselves as a TARP *unit* – so it does make sense."

"Hmm… Still just says TARP on your jacket!" Paranoid Dave continued to eyeball the TARP-leader as Toby physically shoved him away. "Just a minute… Wait, if you spell it backwards, it comes out as… It comes out as 'PRAT' – ha!" he called over his shoulder triumphantly, as Toby bundled him off.

"Haha-*ha!*"

*

Toby, Paranoid Dave and the Professor made their way along one of the upper gantries that curved around the main wall of the terminal. They were at a dizzying height. Beneath lay the concourse of the hyperspaceport in all its enormity. As the Professor glided along the gantry almost effortlessly, Toby and Paranoid Dave were on either side of him, rushing to keep up.

"Yes, that makes sense," the Professor said, as the pair finished telling him all they'd learnt on Za-Nak. "Yes, yes, it all adds up. Charlotte and I saw one of their bulk carriers, as you call them."

"You did? What was it like?" Toby asked, out of breath and a little excited despite himself.

"Rather awe inspiring, if I was being honest," the Professor replied coming to a halt. He turned to face his two young friends. "377 of them you say?"

"Yes," Paranoid Dave replied. He was doubled over with his hands on his knees and rasping for breath. "All of them full to the gunnels with compressed carbon dioxide."

"I see." The Professor turned to peer at a display on the wall. "Ah yes, this is our Bodytron. Look – there are our names!"

The Professor pointed to some squiggles on the screen that made no sense to Toby or Paranoid Dave.

"Bar-Za-Nakarian," the Professor said simply. "Not an elegant script, I must say, but terribly efficient. Do you know that in Bar-Za-Nakarian you can squeeze the *Complete Works of Shakespeare* onto thirteen sides of

A4? Yes, yes you can, hmm? Now, I asked Za-Farka to reserve a departure slot. So if I just place my hand here…"

The Professor placed his hand against the screen. A laser beam scanned his palm up and down, in a pleasingly sci-fi kind of way. A moment later, three arch-shaped doors in front of them slid open. As they did so, they gave off the kind of slick, high-tech, pneumatic whirr that most doors can only dream of.

"But Professor, I'm confused. Great that we're travelling in a Bodytron. But I didn't think there were any Bodytrons on Earth. How can we possibly land there?"

"Oh, but we're not going back to Earth."

"We're not? But we need to warn the authorities – so they can shoot down the bulk carriers with missiles or something."

"Heavens, we don't want to do that."

"We don't?"

"Of course not. Can you imagine if they actually succeeded?"

"Well then, great… Right?"

"Wrong. All the CO_2 would escape. Gentlemen, please?"

The Professor gestured to the three open portals. Confused, Paranoid Dave and Toby each entered through the small portal in front of them and sat down on a small seat inside. The doors whirred shut in front of them. Toby could still hear the Professor's voice through the thin partition on his left, in a way that made him feel slightly awkward – like he was chatting to someone in the next door toilet cubicle.

"But it's a moot point," the Professor continued, "because we'd never succeed. It would be like shooting arrows at a tank. No, we're going somewhere quite different."

"Where?"

"Golgotha."

"*Golgotha?*"

"Yes. We'll follow Woola and Biffa."

"But what can we possibly achieve there?"

"Hmm? What are we going to do on Golgotha? Isn't it obvious?"

"No, Professor, it isn't."

"We're going to buy the Earth back, that's what."

29

"Professor – did something just *happen*? I have the distinct feeling something just *happened*."

"No, nothing much. But we are on Golgotha now."

"What?" Paranoid Dave cut in. "You mean *that's it?* Just like that, and we've suddenly travelled across who-knows-how-many light years?"

"More or less."

"No dreams? No crazy at-one-with-the-Universe sensation, nothing?"

"Nope, I'm afraid not. The Bodytron is most efficient."

"Pah, that's modern technology for you." Paranoid Dave leaned back and folded his arms, in the manner of a man who expects better.

The three of them were sitting in what looked like an almost identical chamber to the one they had just left, with low lighting, and wire mesh on all sides.

Toby was just getting ready to join in the complaining when his seat tipped forward. Or, more like, lurched forward.

He found himself sliding down a shoot in total darkness. He automatically splayed his feet and hands but there was nothing to grab hold of, just a smooth plastic-like material on all sides. A few moments later and he was passing through a short length of transparent tubing.

Toby shot out of the tubing and landed with a bump onto a padded seat.

Ah, Toby thought to himself, adjusting quickly to his new reality and taking a moment to breathe in deeply*, the Bodytron arrivals terminal. This must be the bit where a female alien, hugely attractive to her own species, and still slightly attractive to others, offers to fetch me a drink and massage my upper shoulders. That should compensate for—*

"Papers?"

"Excuse me?"

"Papers?" repeated the gruff, impatient voice. "Where are your papers?"

"Errm, I don't think I have any," Toby replied casting about with his eyes to see where the voice was coming from. "Do I need them?"

"Haha, funny," the voice said, without laughing. "Papers or prison. Make a choice."

The figure tapped impatiently with his cane against the ground. The vibration in the floor caused Toby to look down at his feet. And that's when he saw his interviewer. Standing in front of Toby, no higher than his knee, was a Golgothan immigration official. He wore a black frock coat down to his ankles and had gold horn-rimmed glasses perched menacingly on the end of his nose. Toby looked at him in disbelief. The official was tiny and yet, at the same time, every part of him was huge. He was barrel-chested, with a large, round head, and wispy flaxen hair. His smart frock coat was pulled taut over a stocky pair of arms and legs.

Toby looked around for the Professor and Paranoid Dave. He glimpsed them being pushed through a doorway by a couple of guards who were very not tiny.

"Really, I don't have a choice," Toby pleaded with the official, "because I don't have any papers. But I don't plan to stay long. I've just come here to buy my planet back, you see. Do you think you could—"

"Haha, you're a real laugh," the Golgothan immigration official said, still not laughing.

He removed his spectacles for emphasis.

"You realise every schmuck wants to come here, get rich, be a hero? What would happen to Golgotha if we let that happen, huh? I'll let you ponder that one in the detention centre. Welcome to Golgotha. Guards!" he called out, as he thumbed dismissively over his shoulder, "Take him away!"

*

Charlie looked out over the side of the sled at the snowscape through which they were gliding. The cold, the scenery – it was exhilarating. She felt a sense of renewal.

"Mrs B," she said, turning to her companion in the back of the sled. "How come the Professor knows Dr de Haan? And why did he need me to deliver a message to him so urgently?"

"Ah, Dr de Haan…" Mrs B replied meditatively. "Yes, Dr de Haan is a member of a rather important Council. Same as the Professor. Important, but a little secretive. Messages must always be delivered in person."

"Council? You mean Committee – the Alien Advisory Committee?"

"Not exactly, dear. Something else."

"I don't understand?"

"Yes, it is all a little confusing, isn't it?" Mrs B

lapsed into silence and stared straight ahead for a moment. Charlie looked sideways at Mrs B and bit her lip. She figured if she wanted an answer, she better stay quiet.

On the bench in front, a large figure sat cloaked in animal skins and hunched over the reins. He made a hooping sound that pierced the icy stillness of the air. Charlie watched as he gave the reins several flicks to encourage the team of huskies that was pulling them along.

"Let's just say," Mrs B resumed eventually, "that at some point very soon we're going to need to have all the world's major leaders gathered in one place. To stop all this nonsense."

"Nonsense?"

"Yes, dear."

"You mean the sale of the planet? The deal with the Za-Nakarians?"

"Oh no, not that. They can't be trusted to sort that out. I'm afraid that's down to us. No, I meant if – and it's a big *if* – we get out of this mess, then things will need to change. And by that, I mean the way the world is…"

Mrs B's voice trailed off.

"The way the world is… What?… The way it's run?" Charlie offered tentatively.

"Sort of. The financial system. Capitalism. It's got itself into a pickle, don't you think?"

"Well, yes, I suppose…" Charlie replied.

"Now there are very few organisations that can gather the world's leaders at short notice. The UN is one, of course, but we have no connection there. It just so happens that the Council is another, just less well known. A large number of world leaders are in London anyway, on account of the whole Woola business. We just need to gather them together at a venue of our choosing, and on our terms. The Council can help with that."

"Which is where Dr de Haan comes in?"

"Correct. He's one of its most respected members. He's the world's foremost climate scientist, it's hardly surprising."

"OK… But if the Council is all about climate change, environmental protection, how's that going to—"

"Oh it's about so much more than that, dear." Mrs B replied, folding her hands over her lap. There was a finality in the gesture that made it quite clear she wouldn't be yielding any more information on that particular topic.

Charlie leaned back in her seat, and looked around.

The sled passed into a deep forest. The broad snowy vista tapered to a darkly sparkling world. Slender icicles hung from densely packed trees, and the crunch of the snow beneath the sled echoed back in the stillness.

"Now it's my turn for a question, dear. Dr de Haan," Mrs B said, turning towards Charlie. "Were you very much in love with him?"

*

"Oh dear," the Professor said, "that didn't go quite to plan."

The Professor was seated on the floor of a rather dank cell next to Paranoid Dave and Toby, whose expressions looked as miserable as the room they were in. The floral pyjama suits, which Toby and Paranoid

Dave were still wearing under their coats, looked incongruous against the morose greyness of the cell and their faces.

"Damn it, this is hopeless," exclaimed Paranoid Dave. "They only need to keep us here. Every extra minute that ticks by brings the apocalypse closer."

"Too right," Toby replied, kicking a small pebble across the floor in frustration.

A sullen silence descended on the trio.

"Professor…" Paranoid Dave said after a few moments. "Do you still have your notebook with you? You know, the course notes? I mean, if we're just gonna sit around, I might as well find out what I missed out on?"

"Of course, David. Here you are," the Professor pulled the leather-bound notebook from his inside jacket pocket and passed it to Paranoid Dave, his eyes twinkling. "I recommend skipping straight to the last module, hmm? You can work backwards from there."

"The last module…" Paranoid Dave mumbled as he leafed through the notebook "…ah, got it." He read out loud: "'Nine ideas for rescuing capitalism from itself, of which there are nine here but may be others'."

"Snappy title. Sounds fascinating," Toby said sarcastically. He was about to indulge in some gratifyingly pointless cynicism, when he was interrupted by a loud grunting noise, almost like a snore.

He looked up.

They had a cellmate.

Whom they had somehow managed to not notice.

Which was strange, because their cellmate was enormous.

Sleeping on the upper bunk, and wearing a grey

jumpsuit that was uncannily matched to the grey walls of their cell, was a huge ogre. Its legs extended beyond the end of the bunk right up to the wall, while the opposite wall was pressing the ogre's head forward over its enormous chest. Its huge torso was pressed up against the ceiling, such that each time it breathed out, its tummy – with nowhere else to go – bulged alarmingly to the side, like a burger from an overstuffed bun.

"What is *that?*" Toby whispered, alarmed. Visions of being roughed up in jail by a thuggish alien suddenly flooded his mind.

"Oh him? I shouldn't worry about him, hmm?" the Professor replied. "His type are forever forgetting their papers. He's a Cenaphian engineer."

"A *what?*"

"No, no, not a *Wat*. Now that would be alarming. No, a Cenaphian engineer," the Professor corrected. "Hmm? They spend half their working lives in detention cells. Most port authorities are quite pleased really – they normally have some plumbing that needs fixing, or some wiring. The Cenaphians help out and then get released. It's all quite civilised, you see."

"So he won't beat us up or anything?"

"Heavens no. They're quite charming fellows, some of the gentlest. Just a little absent-minded, you see? And surprisingly timid."

"OK, that's great," Toby said. "But excuse me, Professor, *how do you know this stuff?*"

"Ah yes," the Professor replied, "I'm quite well travelled you see."

"Yeah, about that," Toby replied, a hint of suspicion, "that's another thing that doesn't add up. You never told us how you got here? I mean not here, but to Za-Nak? You say you've never used a Personalitron. But if not that, then *what?*"

"Ah yes, that is confusing, I see your point," the Professor mused sympathetically. He lowered his half-moon spectacles and peered at Toby. "What else don't you understand?"

"Eh? Err, well, since you ask... Why did all the most powerful leaders in the world travel out to Za-Nak at the same time? Why did they agree to it? I mean it was so obviously risky. What if they all get kidnapped, or ransomed or something?"

"I can only assume the Za-Nakarians persuaded them," the Professor mused. "From their perspective, it's perfectly logical, hmm? The Za-Nakarians wanted our leaders out the way when the bulk carriers arrived in the Earth's atmosphere. To minimise the risk of resistance."

"Makes sense."

"Just a nicety really. I'm afraid there's nothing our leaders could have done, you see? Indeed, there was probably nothing they wanted to do."

"Right. Because that's my next question: what's gone wrong with them? You should have seen them, Professor. They were *pleased* that the Earth was going to be trashed. It's like they were hypnotised. Come to think of it, I wasn't much better..."

"Well, I think you've answered your own question, hmm?" the Professor replied. "They probably were hypnotised. The Za-Nakarians do seem to have some hyper-evolved ability in that regard... Quite astonishing really."

"Which is why I had to take the powder," Toby continued. "Your reverse-thingy thingy?"

"Reverse-truth drug. Correct."

"But you don't need it Professor. Nor you, Dave."

"Hey?" Paranoid Dave looked up from the Professor's notebook, in which he'd been completely absorbed. "What's that?"

"Tobias was just saying, you weren't fooled by the Za-Nakarians?"

"Oh yeah, that. Ha! Well, I'm paranoid, remember?"

"Still, very impressive," the Professor looked at his former student with a hint of pride. "I always suspected you might be immune, David. Yes. But when we met again in the pub, I was sure of it."

If Paranoid Dave's pale face could have blushed, it would have. But it couldn't, so he changed subject instead.

"Actually, Professor, I'm the one who's impressed. Your notebook – these suggestions for reforming capitalism – they're so simple, so obvious..." Paranoid Dave stabbed a pudgy forefinger onto the page. "I love them."

"Really? Why?" Toby asked.

"Well, some are about ensuring financial stability and just seem so obvious the way the Professor writes them – but I'd never thought of them before. Like there's one here, Number 7, on how to limit the size of banks and so limit the risk they pose. But the clever bit is to do it using market forces, not just compulsion. The bigger the bank, the more capital it has to hold – so the less profitable it's likely to be. It creates an incentive for banks to de-merge and stay small – which means less risk for all of us. Less chance of a single bank bringing the whole global economy to its knees. *Finally.*"

"OK... Not sure I completely get that... What

else?"

"Most of the others are about making capitalism more... more likeable. And less damaging. Like there's one here, Number 4, on the 'stakeholder triangle'. Directors of larger companies should be equally responsible to not just shareholders, but to their staff and the environment too. All three should be represented at boardroom level."

"Ah, yes, yes, one of my favourites," the Professor chuckled.

"Then the others are just common sense. Like there's another one – Number 6 – 'Tax justice'. Large multinationals should be taxed on their sales not profits. Makes the tax easier to collect and makes sure it ends up in the right country. So no more tax havens. Everyone knows that makes sense, but no-one's done much about it. In fact, come to think of it, all 9 of them are obvious. Just that I've never seen them all written in one place before. It's almost like a... Like a..."

"A manifesto, hmm?"

"Yes! Exactly."

"Great... Love it." Toby said, who could feel his bout of pointless cynicism was coming on after all. "Just one problem. We don't even have the power to open the door and walk down the corridor, never mind solve all your issues with capitalism. In fact, I'd happily put up with all those issues, if we could just get out of this cell and buy our planet back. But we can't."

"True," Paranoid Dave sighed and closed the notebook. "And we haven't even mentioned our other problem."

"Our other problem?"

"So," Paranoid Dave continued, "even if we can somehow get out of here and even if we can find Biffa, and even if he's remotely interested in selling us our planet back – which, by the way, I think is pretty improbable given that he's like the most evil person in the history of history... But even supposing all this can somehow happen..." Paranoid Dave said, spreading his two palms open "...what are we going to pay him with?"

Paranoid Dave leaned back, both impressed and appalled by his own words.

"Well, I've got one pound, in case that helps?" Toby said sarcastically, as he examined the loose change in his jacket pocket. "Oh, and a bag of crisps, that I still need to pay for."

"And I've got half a bag of toffees," Paranoid Dave added glumly.

"Some toffees, some crisps and one pound in loose coins? Hmm? Yes, that isn't very much," the Professor replied. "Still—"

He was interrupted.

A small commotion could be heard in the corridor outside their cell. The sound reached them of talking, heavy footsteps, doors banging, and keys being rattled.

*

"This shouldn't be happening, no, no, no," a loud voice echoed in a tone of outrage through the steel door of their cell. The voice seemed somehow familiar. "Guards – open this cell, let these gentlemen out. They should be our guests, not our prisoners. Come on – hurry up will you?"

The Professor, Paranoid Dave and Toby heard a brisk tapping on the steel door of their cell. A moment later a small shutter on the door, positioned at about knee height – just about where you'd find a catflap – was yanked backwards. Through an iron grill a bespectacled face appeared. It was the Golgothan immigration officer.

"You lot, it's your lucky day. Get your things together. You're leaving."

The steel shutter slammed back shut.

"It's the immigration official," Toby said, turning to the others. "I wonder why he's letting us out?"

The steel shutter slammed open again.

"I'm not. It's your friend," the official said, before slamming it shut again.

"Friend? I don't have any friends on Golgotha. Dave, do you?"

"Me? No way. Professor?"

Both of them turned to the Professor.

"Me? Hmm? No, no friends here I'm afraid," the Professor replied. "Except perhaps our Cenaphian cellmate here, but we're scarcely acquainted."

Toby and Paranoid Dave looked up at the bunk bed to see the huge ogre had woken up. He was lying propped up on the bunk, his head squashed against the ceiling, and was staring back at them with fearful, baby-like eyes.

"So no," the Professor continued, "I can't say I have any friends on Golgotha, not unless—"

"Oh come now, Professor, don't talk like that," a distinctly familiar New York voice interrupted him as the steel door of the cell swung open. "Of course you have a friend on Golgotha."

It was Biffa.

He stood in the doorway of the cell and smiled at them.

"You've got *me*."

"*You?* What are you doing here?" Paranoid Dave asked.

"What am I doing here?" Biffa replied nonchalantly. "Well, I might ask you the same. You seem to have developed a knack for following me around."

"We're not following you around. We just want to get our planet back," Toby said impulsively.

"And that's so sweet. I admire that. And you know what?" Biffa paused, like a cat letting a mouse go for a moment. "I intend to reward your tenacity. Yes I do."

"You do?"

"Uh-huh. Yes indeed. As the lead investment banker to the Za-Nakarians, I am officially inviting you to watch the Earth being auctioned. The IPO – that would be the Initial Public Offering. I guarantee all three of you a front-row seat as we auction the Earth on the Inter-Planetary Exchange, the IPE. But why am I confusing you with all this finance talk, huh? IPE, IP-schmo, who cares. The point is, this is a wonderful day for planet Earth, and I want to share it with you. I want you to watch as the Earth is sold to a thousand, thousand investors from all corners of the Universe and I get rich in the process."

"You're selling the planet on?" Toby asked, uncomprehending. "But you've only just bought it?"

"Of course we're selling it on. Trading, that's what we do," Biffa replied. "Bit of a nuisance for you guys, if you ever wanted to buy it back because basically that would become... *Let me think now...* Impossible. But let's not dwell on that."

Biffa opened his arms expansively.

"Come on guys, are you in? The IPO's not for another three hours, I can give you a tour of the City first. It'll be fun. Whaddya say?"

"I reckon…" said Paranoid Dave slowly, "that I would rather be stuck in a phone booth for all eternity with *him*," he thumbed over his shoulder at the Cenaphian, who looked alarmed and drew his bedsheet up around his chest, "than spend five more minutes talking to you!"

"Oh it's like that is it?" Biffa replied with mock distress. "You know what, you're even cuter than I thought. But it's not a problem. I don't have a phone booth for you two lovers, but you can just as easily spend that eternity together right here."

"Ah-hm," the Professor cleared his throat. "Actually the tour sounds like a wonderful idea. We accept your kind invitation. Thank you."

"Professor! What? You seriously mean we have to spend time with this—"

"Yes, David" the Professor said with emphasis, "I think it's an excellent idea."

Biffa smirked and stepped back to let the trio pass through. Just as the guard was closing the door behind him, Toby had a thought.

"Err, Biffa, the big fellow we've been sharing a cell with. He seems pretty harmless, can't you let him go too?"

"That big Cenaphian oaf? Sure why not," Biffa replied. "I expect they've got a toilet that needs cleaning somewhere. Guards – let the fat guy go!" Biffa called out breezily.

Biffa looked back at the Cenaphian's big, grateful face. He was surprised how powerful he felt doing something good, and made a mental note to start hosting more charity galas.

*

Charlie smoothed her windswept hair back from her forehead, gathered it in a hairband, and let it fall in a simple ponytail from the back of her head.

She felt refreshed from the sleigh ride.

Mrs B was making her confront the things she never dared to confront. But for some reason today – *here* – she felt ready for it. Her head was clear.

"Mug of tea, dear?"

"Thank you, Mrs B."

Charlie leaned forward and cupped the enamel camping mug in her hands. The log cabin was starting to warm up again. The steam from the mug and the radiant heat from the log fire seemed to merge together, and Charlie breathed them in, gratefully.

"This place is amazing, Mrs B," Charlie said. "It's bright, it's cold, it's beautiful, it's remote from home, and yet everything back home seems so much clearer."

"Yes, I know. It's a very dear wee planet. We wouldn't give up our little cabin here for the world," Mrs B replied comfortably. And then paused. "So tell me, Charlotte, have you figured out why?"

"Why?"

"Why did you let yourself fall in love with a married man?"

"Oh. That." Charlie stared into the fire. "I dunno, Mrs B. Dr de Haan, he was my supervisor. Pretty dumb, huh?"

"Did he reciprocate?"

"No!" Charlie exclaimed, and then more quietly, "No. He was… perfect. A perfect gentleman."

"Yes, I thought so," Mrs B mused. "So why, Charlotte?"

"Does there have to be a *why*, Mrs B? Can't stuff

just happen sometimes?"

"Oh there's always a why, dear. Always. What was yours?"

30

Toby stared out the window of the hovershoot, disconsolate. The hail was hitting the roof and windshield in a relentless, angry rattle, like the sound of broken machinery that won't stop working and won't be fixed either.

They were travelling along a kind of aerial highway through the heart of Golgotha city. *Always assuming Golgotha city has a heart* – which Toby wasn't sure about. Down below, he could see inhabitants scuttling along the streets, their outerwear pulled tight around them. Toby reckoned he was about thirty storeys up.

Toby switched his gaze upwards.

The buildings were vertiginous. Almost all them disappeared up into the brooding, charcoal-grey clouds above his head. The effect was strange, like the skyscrapers were pillars supporting this roof of rolling clouds. An occasional flash of lightning momentarily illuminated the clouds and the upper floors of the skyscrapers concealed within them.

A couple of seats ahead, the Professor was being surprisingly chatty with Biffa. Next to them sat two hulking stooges, staring ahead. Biffa's bodyguards. *Of course Biffa had to bring minders*, Toby thought.

"And just out of curiosity…" the Professor started to ask a question.

"Yeah?" Biffa replied.

"If we were interested in buying the Earth back, before the auction, would that be remotely possible?"

"Oh remotely? You mean remotely, like is there a tiny chance? Or remotely, like with a TV control?" Biffa replied with a malignant twinkle.

The Professor smiled back.

"I'm being mean. I shouldn't play with your feelings. Sure you can buy Earth back," he replied, leaning back in his seat, settling his hands over his tummy, "sure you can."

"We can?" Toby asked.

"Sure kid," Biffa replied. "I can see this is cutting you up, so sure. You can buy the Earth back for exactly the price you sold it to us. No profit to me, no profit to the Za-Nakarians, honest as the day is light. Yours for just 1.8 quadrillion Za-Nakarian dollars."

"You complete and utter—"

"No wait, Dave, wait," Toby cut him off. "We must still have that money in an account somewhere. I mean not us, but the world leaders, the G7, those guys. They were paid in Za-Nakarian dollars, right?"

"Yes, they were," the Professor chipped in.

"So where is the money now?" Toby asked. "If we can locate it, we can send it back, surely?"

"I can help with that," Biffa said, playing along. "It's at Rakemore Telfer. That's the investment bank I work for. They got clearance from the Intergalactic Currency Exchange to trade in most major currencies in the Universe."

"They did?"

"Uh-huh. The money is all in a Za-Nakarian-dollar-denominated account. Just one single, very big account."

"Oh. OK then. Thank you. Well, maybe we can do this, right?" Toby looked round at the others, his eyes widening. He was daring to hope. "Biffa – can you turn this hovershoot around? We still have time to take the Peronsalitron back to Earth and speak to the—"

"Oh shucks," Biffa interrupted. "Just a second. Did I just say the money was in a Za-Nakarian-dollar-denominated account? Oh no…"

A look of mock sympathy spread over Biffa's face. "Oh that's too bad, really it is."

"What's too bad?" Paranoid Dave asked, his eyes narrowing.

"Just that the Za-Nakarian dollar… There's been a crisis… It crashed overnight."

"Crashed? Are you serious?" Toby asked. "How much crash are we talking about? How much is our 1.8 quadrillion dollars worth now?"

"Oh I don't know… Has anyone got a calculator? No? Hang on, I've got one in my pocket here. Let me run the numbers for a second."

Biffa plugged away on the calculator, mock concern on his face.

"Oh shucks that's not good."

"Give it to me!" Paranoid Dave snatched the calculator from Biffa, and looked at the screen. He looked back up at Biffa, a blood-draining expression of disbelief crossing his face. "One pound?"

"Actually, 89p. I rounded up slightly. But between friends," Biffa replied, "one pound."

"Hang on," Paranoid Dave said, "are you seriously telling us that the money the G7 raised by selling planet Earth now amounts to *one pound?*"

"Oh my God," said Biffa. "When you put it like that, that's just awful. It's a disaster."

"But this can't be right," Toby said, struggling against a drowning feeling. His fingers clenched around the loose change in his jacket pocket. One pound. The cost of a bag of crisps. "We've just been on Za-Nak. We didn't see any crisis?"

"You didn't? That's odd... No wait. I think I know the answer. The reason you didn't see any crisis on Za-Nak is because..." As Biffa continued, his voice changed with each carefully enunciated word from phoney concern to the old nonchalance, "...they use a currency called the Svelt. They haven't used the Za-Nakarian dollar in years."

He paused a moment to let it sink in.

"No wait. Did I say years? I meant aeons. In fact, come to think of it, I'm not sure they ever used it."

"*What?*" said Toby.

"You mean we were paid in a currency that doesn't really *exist?*" asked Paranoid Dave.

"Oh, I wouldn't go that far. But, basically, yes."

"You're trying to trick us." Paranoid Dave uncrossed his arms and re-folded them for emphasis. "I don't believe you."

"Of course you don't. I wouldn't believe me either," Biffa replied, standing up to take manual control of the hovershoot. "Which is why I brought you here..."

The trio followed Biffa's gaze out of the window. The hovershoot pivoted out of the aerial highway and started rising vertically up the side of a huge, wide building. As they reached what they thought was the top, an extraordinary sight greeted them.

Through the front windscreen, the gang found themselves looking at a kind of aerial plaza, forty storeys up. Small figures were scuttling to and fro, pulling their clothing tight against the hail. At the far end was a vast, neo-classical structure. It had a sweeping stone staircase, a grand portico, classical columns. It looked like the Bank of England in mid-air. Except where there should have been a roof, a small-ish skyscraper extended upwards into the clouds.

"The Inter-galactic Currency Exchange," Biffa said simply. "The ICE. The first stop on our tour."

He gently pushed a lever forward on the controls.

"And here's your proof."

The hovershoot glided across the plaza, a few yards above the surface, towards a huge display panel that stood to the left of the Currency Exchange. Various incomprehensible symbols were displayed digitally on the panel in red and blue. The hovershoot drew to a halt about ten yards away, so that a few of the symbols filled the entire front windscreen of the hovershoot, red and flashing.

"That's showing the exchange rate for pound sterling to the Za-Nakarian dollar," Biffa said. "You can't read the script, but the Professor can. Professor?"

Paranoid Dave and Toby looked desperately at the Professor.

"Let me see now..." he replied. He carefully removed his half-moon spectacles, polished them, and replaced them. "Ah. Yes. I see."

"What does it say?"

"Yes. No. Oh dear. I'm afraid the Za-Nakarian Dollar does seem to have somewhat, ah-hm, *tumbled*."

Paranoid Dave and Toby slumped back in their seats.

*

"I just don't get it," Toby said. "You can't just magic a

currency into existence and then get rid of it again. I mean a currency has to be backed by something, right? There has to be some value there?"

"Oh really?" Paranoid Dave threw a withering look. "Look at all the currencies on Earth. What are they backed by? The gold standard went out years ago. Now they're mostly bits of paper – and those are the good ones. A blockchain is all you get if—"

"Actually, the kid's right," Biffa said, cutting across Paranoid Dave. "Currencies *ought* to be backed by something. Those are the rules out here, in the rest of the Universe. Rules of the Exchange. The Za-Nakarian dollar is – *was* – backed by something."

"Yeah, what then?" Paranoid Dave turned to Biffa, arms still folded, bolshy.

"Ice."

"Ice?"

"Yeah, ice."

"What kind of ice?"

"The water kind of ice. To be precise: the Antarctic ice cap."

"The Antarctic ice cap? You can't back a currency with *that*."

"Sure you can. A lot of stored value in that ice cap." Biffa leant back meditatively and sucked on his teeth. "All that pure, pristine water, all in one place, all frozen and transportable. I can think of a dozen planets would pay big sums to have the Jagamath shovel it up and bring it over. And the Earth's leaders were quite happy to sign it away in advance, as a token of goodwill. As far as they were concerned, if anyone ever came and collected all the ice, then great – no more risk of sea levels rising."

"That's absurd," Paranoid Dave retorted.

"Yeah? Well, maybe you're right. But it doesn't really matter now anyway. The moment the Za-Nakarians bought the Earth, the Za-Nakarian dollar melted. Literally."

"But why?" Toby asked.

"Isn't it obvious?" Paranoid Dave replied, both appalled and impressed. He popped a toffee in his mouth and spoke as he chewed. "The Za-Nakarians buy the planet with an explicit plan to warm the climate. Toast the climate and you melt the ice cap. Bingo – the store of value disappears and the currency crashes."

"And the Za-Nakarian dollar crashes," Biffa added, smiling. "The black widow trap."

"Excuse me?" said Toby.

"Black widow trap?" said Paranoid Dave.

"*Latrodectus hasselti*." The Professor spoke up. "A species of spider famous for its mating rituals, hmm? The female eats the male after they have, ah-hm, *copulated*. I think what our friend means is that once a deal has gone through—"

"—the client gets eaten. You got it." Biffa smirked.

"Hang on," Paranoid Dave eyed Biffa suspiciously. "Were you behind this? Was it you, was it Rakemore Telfer, that set this… trap?"

"Oh you are so naïve. It's time to head for our next stop."

Biffa pivoted the hovershoot gently to the left and it glided smoothly back into the flow of traffic.

Biffa sat back down, and turned to face Toby and Paranoid Dave, carefully placing the palms of his hands together like a teacher helping some struggling pupils.

"I'm gonna tell you children what's really been

going on. I know the situation *seems* bad now – I understand that. But once I've explained things, you'll understand how truly awful it actually is."

31

Charlie felt bewildered.

First Mrs B had dissected her feelings for Dr de Haan. Now she was asking about her family.

Charlie felt like she'd been seated in a rollercoaster she hadn't been expecting to ride by someone she wasn't totally sure she trusted. With each 90-degree bend, and each 45-degree drop, she knew theoretically she should be OK, since thousands had done this before and survived. But another part of her felt sick with the lurching.

And yet a third part of her was thrilled. Something that needed to change was about to change.

"How old were you when you found out?" Mrs B pressed gently.

"About fifteen."

"Oh ay, a sensitive age, you poor dear. And how long had it been going on?"

"I dunno. Maybe ten years?"

"You poor dear," Mrs B said again, with sincerity, and paused a moment. "Were they actually married?"

"No, I don't think so. Honestly, I'm not really sure. She knew about us, we didn't know about her. For ten years."

"Did he have any children with her?"

"Yes. Three. Honestly, where did he find the

energy," Charlie asked without asking, staring into the fire.

"A second family..." Mrs B mused to herself. "How did he think he would get away with it?"

"I dunno," Charlie replied. "While we – mum and I – lived on Java, I guess it was simple enough. We were living in Jogjakarta and he travelled back to the UK a lot with work. So that gave him the opportunity. But when I was about eight, mum and I moved to England, and that must've made it a lot harder to keep secret. Still, he managed it somehow." Charlie managed a rueful smile.

"How terribly hurtful," Mrs B sympathised. "And yet he was your father. You loved him."

"*Adored* him. Doesn't every daughter?"

Mrs B paused to sip from her mug of tea. She followed Charlie's gaze towards the fire. As they stared at the same flickering flame, thinking about the same problem, it was as much of a bond as if they were looking into each other's eyes.

Outside, the fading light at the end of the short Ormilu day cast a strange green-ish, yellow light through the cabin window.

"So you had that worst of dilemmas, Charlotte," Mrs B resumed at length. "How do you love someone, whom you can't forgive?"

"Yeah, I guess that's about the size of it," Charlie replied. "Or how do you hate someone, whom you can't stop loving?"

*

Toby watched more skyscrapers pass by left and right. He'd only been here an hour, and he already hated

Golgotha more than any place he'd ever been.

"Let's figure this out together shall we?" Biffa said. "The Professor has probably told you two kids that the Golgothans have been in contact with planet Earth for years now?"

Toby and Paranoid Dave nodded.

"And that Earth's leaders refused for years to engage in negotiations?"

They nodded again.

"So while Earth's leaders were being rude, who do you think the Golgothans quietly made contact with round the side? And who was – *how shall I put this?* – a whole lot more accommodating?"

"Rakemore Telfer?" Paranoid Dave offered.

"Exactly. Turned out the Golgothans had been visiting Earth for a long time, for *millennia*. They were trying to recruit. The Golgothans will recruit anyone, by the way, so long as they know how to make money. The least racist bunch you'll ever meet. Just that they never found anyone on Earth worth recruiting... Until the Credit Crunch came along. So who do you think impressed them during that little farrago?"

"Rakemore Telfer?"

"Right again. The fact that Rakemore could help cause the worst financial crisis in seventy years, while still increasing profits *and* persuading taxpayers to pick up all the costs... Now that was talent worth recruiting."

Biffa paused for a moment to smile to himself, before continuing. "And it got better. When the next financial crisis came long, when *you-know-what* came along, Rakemore had governments so well trained that bailing the financial system out was the first thing they did. Before they even bought virus testing kits or hired more nurses. Can you believe it? Trillions – and I mean, *lots of them* – were pumped in so quickly, so quietly, people barely noticed. I mean the genius of it. Watching governments and central banks at that time was like watching a frickin' dog show. It was a case of, *which poodle can jump highest?* So who do you think got rewarded after that with a state-of-the-art Bodytron to keep next to their boardroom, while Downing Street got some left over Personalitrons, manufactured centuries ago. Who?"

"Rakemore."

"And who do you think first let the Za-Nakarians know about this new investment opportunity, by which I mean planet Earth?"

"Rakemore again… The dogs! I knew they—"

"Just a second, I'm not done yet. The fun bit's still to come. Who do you think structured the deal as a sale-and-leaseback, so that the G7 have to pay their first lease payment – oh yes, you guys have to pay a monthly lease for the right to stay on the planet you've sold – who structured the deal so that that first lease payment would fall *today* at 6pm?"

"Rakemore Telfer," replied Toby, getting the hang of it.

"And who – now pay attention closely to this – who set the monthly lease at £10 trillion? Of course £10 trillion is only a tiny fraction of the sale price, but let's be clear about this. The lease payment has to be made in pounds sterling. Who fixed that up?"

"Rakemore Telfer."

"My God – you utter worm," Paranoid Dave cut in. "You're telling us that the Earth has been sold for £1 and now we've got to pay a monthly lease of £10 trillion for the privilege of living *on our own planet?*"

"Umm? Err… let me think…" Biffa replied. "Yes."

"Why you…" Paranoid Dave advanced a couple of steps towards Biffa. Something inside him was about to snap. "You complete and utter—"

"Uh-uh-uh!" Biffa wagged his index finger at Paranoid Dave, who stopped two yards away. "You're forgetting to look on the bright side."

"The bright side?"

"Sure. You guys are actually in luck. I mean you need to borrow £10 trillion by 6pm tonight. It'll be tough, but actually I think it's possible."

"How?" Paranoid Dave shot back. "There isn't a country left on the planet that has that kind of cash. They all run on debt."

"That's correct. So it's just as well you've got me."

"You?"

"Yeah, me. Rakemore. We would be prepared to lend it. And the interest rate would be competitive too. Say about 40 – no, that's mean – call it 30 percent."

"Are you *serious?*"

"Sure – we like to help out where we can."

"Hang on, let me get this straight," Paranoid Dave said, his blood rising. "Having helped sell the planet to a bunch of aliens, and then having manipulated the currency market so that humankind receives precisely nothing for the sale—"

"That's not true, you get one pound."

"—you would then lend us the money to pay the lease payment to live on our own planet at a 30 percent interest rate. Have I got that right?"

"A few details are off, but yeah, that's about right."

Paranoid Dave had had enough. The thing inside him that was about to snap snapped. He advanced the last couple of yards and stood in front of Biffa, chest-to-chest.

"My God, I could wring your scrawny, filthy little neck right now. How could you do this *to your own planet?*"

His eyes alive with uncontrolled anger, Paranoid Dave lunged forward and stretched out to grab Biffa by the throat. But Toby had spotted the danger. He darted between them, his body just wide enough to put Biffa's neck out of range of Paranoid Dave's outstretched hands.

A moment later, Biffa's minders stepped in. They effortlessly lifted Paranoid Dave by the shoulders and deposited him back in his seat.

"A bit quicker next time if you please, gentlemen?" Biffa said to his minders, adjusting his collar and looking shaken. "If that wouldn't trouble you too much?"

The two minders returned to their seats, apparently unconcerned.

"You should be a little nicer, given how much you lot need me right now," Biffa said, pointing at Paranoid Dave. He turned back round to the front and, recovering his poise, his tone brightened. "Oh look, we've arrived."

"Where?" the Professor asked.

"Clearly your two boys here have outgrown kindergarten," Biffa replied. "It's time we showed them round senior school."

32

"Why's it so quiet here?" Toby asked quietly. "It's kind of creepy."

"I dunno," Paranoid Dave replied listlessly. "Maybe the market hasn't opened yet?"

Paranoid Dave, Toby and the Professor were following Biffa onto the main trading floor of the Inter-Planetary Exchange. The IPE. It was colossal. Cavernously large, like the largest hangar you've ever seen, bolted together with several more like it. Here and there, Toby saw huge amphitheatre-like spaces, sunk into the floor. *The trading pits*, Biffa had called them. All of which created a very strange impression, not least because this huge, half-subterranean world was actually located near the top of the largest skyscraper on Golgotha. They were probably a mile above ground level.

But it wasn't the size of the room, nor its location, nor the trading pits that most struck Toby at that moment.

It was the fact that no-one was moving.

As they brushed their way between the crowded ranks of Golgothan traders, none of them seemed to notice or mind. The traders were frozen to the spot. It was like walking through a photograph.

Biffa led them to the edge of one of the trading pits.

As they got closer, Toby saw that it wasn't round, it was hexagonal.

He peered over the edge.

Immediately beneath him was a hexagonal platform, about ten yards in width, that ran all the way round the pit. A series of booths filled the platform, each one packed with traders. One level below this platform was another, smaller hexagonal platform, which was likewise packed with booths full of traders. Peering deeper still, Toby could see another level beneath that, and then another. In fact there was a whole series of concentric hexagonal platforms disappearing down into the darkness below.

"Thirteen."

"Excuse me?"

"Thirteen levels down. Cute, huh?" Biffa said. "But it's that tower you want to watch. That's where the action happens."

Biffa nodded towards the centre of this strange space, where a hexagonal tower could be seen, rising up from the depths of the trading pit all the way to the top. All the booths in the hexagonal amphitheatre were angled towards the tower and all the traders were staring at it, quite motionless. Up and down the tower, Toby could see large digital display panels showing the stock prices. All the numbers were static.

"So the tower shows the stock prices?"

"Yes. But it's also where the market makers sit. The traders – your buyers and your sellers – are in these booths round the edge. The market makers in the tower match the buyers and sellers," Biffa replied. "Right, Rakemore are down on the fifth level. Follow me."

They followed him down into the trading pit, down a series of short staircases to the fifth level. Once there, they walked past four or five booths, until they reached the Rakemore Telfer one. Toby recognised it from the logo, emblazoned on the side in gold. Within it were a couple of dozen Rakemore Telfer traders, all wearing the same purple jacket, and all motionless.

"Looks like Rakemore Telfer has broadened its recruitment pool," Toby whispered into Paranoid Dave's ear. "Check out the octopus."

"An octopus? Where?" Paranoid Dave replied, only half-interested.

"Over there." Toby nodded towards a creature with two puffy, tired-looking eyes, lurking behind the other traders. It had at least eight sleeves in its purple jacket.

"Well, boys and girls," Biffa said, as he opened a low door in the side of the booth and ushered them in, "the morning bell should sound in another minute or so. It's gonna be a fun morning. Biggest of the year,"

"Yeah? Is that because the Earth is being IPO'ed?" Toby ventured.

Biffa snorted. His hand went up to his nose to muffle his amusement.

"Oh you're perfect. I should keep you as a pet. I mean you're about as dumb as a hamster," he added. "No, it's not because the Earth is being IPO'ed, numbnuts. These guys eat planets like the Earth in their tea break. What am I saying? These guys *will eat* planet Earth in their tea break, in three hours' time."

Biffa leaned nonchalantly against the side of the Rakemore Telfer booth, and folded his arms in the manner of a man at ease in his own environment.

"These guys trade moons and planets every day. That's their bread and butter. See behind me," Biffa thumbed over his shoulder to the neighbouring booth. Toby's eyes followed Biffa's thumb to see two hulking, beast-like traders standing motionless and glowering. "The Vort twins. For a pair like that, the Earth is a rounding error. It doesn't even qualify for a proper auction. We'll sell the stock directly into the secondary market. No, that's not what gets this place excited. You're gonna have to think bigger."

"You mean they're auctioning a solar system? A sun, lots of planets, moons, that kind of thing?" Toby asked.

"Oh, solar systems are always fun, they bring out the big spenders. But no. Bigger."

"Well what's bigger than that?" Toby asked, confused.

"He means a constellation, Toby," Paranoid Dave replied with a weary voice. "A whole collection of stars."

"Nice try, but no," Biffa replied. "Bigger."

"A *galaxy* then?" Paranoid Dave asked.

"That's a big trading day I grant you, but no. Bigger again."

"You can't mean…" Paranoid Dave stuttered uncharacteristically. "You don't mean a…"

"I do," Biffa replied proudly, "oh, I do. Today, you lucky schmucks, a properly big one is going down. And when I say 'big', I mean something way too large for your tiny imagination. Overnight they auctioned a galaxy *cluster*. The Aranoid Cluster."

"Jeez…"

"Secondary trading starts this morning, and that," Biffa continued, "is why the rudest creatures in the Universe – and believe you me, these are the rudest creatures in the Universe – suddenly look a little bit subdued. But don't worry, girls – it won't last."

Toby, Paranoid Dave and the Professor looked at

the vast sea of traders before them. At that moment a tremor passed through the crowd. Something was starting to happen.

"Ah", Biffa said. "Dinner time."

"What's happening?" Paranoid Dave asked.

"The opening bell is about to sound," Biffa replied as he led them briskly to a small office at the back of the Rakemore Telfer booth. The office was sunk, cave-like, into the side of the trading pit. Biffa held the door open. "You do *not* want to get caught on the dealing floor when that happens, not today. Inside, *now*."

The three of them trooped dutifully towards the small office with a puzzled look on their faces. Toby went last.

"Look," Toby started to ask as he approached the doorway, "is it really necessary to—"

But before he could complete his sentence, the gong reverberated around the trading floor, amplified by an over-enthusiastic speaker system.

Toby didn't have time to dwell on what he saw.

A wall of noise physically propelled him into the office and blew the door shut behind him.

The trading floor had erupted.

The group gathered at a large plate-glass window in the office. The sound-proofing reduced the ear-shattering din to a muffled vibration. Robbed of sound, the vision before them became acutely nightmarish.

They watched transfixed as the traders started screaming and gesturing at each other and the lights on the huge dealing screens flashed like a discotheque. They watched the Rakemore traders scramble onto the counter at the edge of their booth and start yelling at the market makers in the tower. One of them, wanting attention, grabbed a bin and started throwing empty cans at the tower. When they ran out, he started throwing bottles. And when they ran out, he threw the bin.

Toby tapped Paranoid Dave on the shoulder and pointed him out. Paranoid Dave turned just in time to see a metal chair flying back from the tower and knock the trader clean off the counter. He landed with his head smack on the floor. Even as he lay there, cans and bottles were landing on or near him. Detritus was being hurled in all directions, raining down from the upper levels to the darker, deeper levels beneath.

"What are they doing? They're like animals." Paranoid Dave stared, open-mouthed.

"It's like feeding time at the zoo," Toby observed.

"Only worse."

"I know. Isn't it great?" Biffa replied, a dreamy warm smile spreading across his face.

"Hmm… Why this open outcry system?" the Professor asked quietly. "Can't they use computers?"

"Oh they used to use computer-based trading, sure they did," Biffa replied. "And they've still got it, for some trading. But you know what? They missed the yelling. They missed the cut and thrust. So they brought back the trading floor." Biffa's face was alight with a luminous, nostalgic glow. "Glorious isn't it?"

T H U M P !

The group recoiled from the glass window.

Someone, or something, had picked up the octopus and thrown him against the window, his full bodyweight crashing against the glass. The side of his face was pressed against the pane, and one of his tired eyes was staring vacantly into the room, the pupil dilated with shock. Three or four of his tentacles were trying to suck onto the glass to hold himself up.

"What just happened there?" Toby asked, alarmed. "Can he see us?"

"Nope, two-way mirror," Biffa replied casually. "He can only see himself."

The octopus' strength failed, and gravity won.

His body slid slowly down the glass and fell out of view, slumping onto the floor outside.

"Goodness…" Toby said. "Shouldn't you go and see how he is?"

"Nah, he'll be alright," Biffa replied, with a faraway expression. "And if he isn't alright, he'll be dead. Either way, what can I do?"

"You can't just let one of your colleagues die out there? Then you'd be no better than an animal."

"No better, true," replied Biffa meditatively. "But a lot richer."

Toby looked around and saw one of the beast-like Vort twins in the next-door booth look briefly at the octopus, as he dusted his great paws together with satisfaction.

"Right, that's it!" Toby replied, standing up. "I'm going out to help that creature, even if you—"

Toby was interrupted by a tug on his sleeve. It was the Professor. He pointed at the glass. A single tentacle – hesitant and quivering – had come into view. It probed feebly this way and that before sucking onto the bottom of the window. The octopus started to haul himself back up.

"There – you see? Alive." Biffa smiled beatifically at the group. "I told you it'd be alright."

Toby sat back down, relieved, but only slightly. His next worry was Paranoid Dave who was strangely quiet. He was staring out of the window at the carnage. He didn't look angry, he didn't look paranoid. There was just a blank expression where his face used to be.

"Dave?" Toby called nervously, "Dave? You OK?"

"Who are they out there?" he replied quietly, from a million miles away. "Who are these creatures? And what are they even trading?"

"Oh they're just dismembering the Aranoid Cluster that's all," Biffa replied.

"What do you even mean, 'dismembering'?"

"Well, there's no-one rich enough to buy the whole system. And even if there was, what's the point of that? We need to break it up, *realise its value*. So the galaxies are being diced into chunks, securitised, sold off, traded, bought back, and sold off again." Biffa looked down at his watch, and then back up again. "First ten minutes of trading. I suspect some of the more choice solar systems have been sold and re-sold two or three times by now. I'm just talking about the profitable ones, mind. You know, good minerals, young-ish sun, maybe a nice virgin planet tucked away somewhere."

"My God, they're trading planets like real estate?"

"They *are* real estate. But that's the kids' stuff. That's for the losers in the south-west pit," Biffa thumbed dismissively to another part of the trading floor. "You're in the derivatives pit. Here we can *go short*."

"Go short? Short of what?" Toby asked.

"Go short. Sell shares that we don't even own. So if the stock price sinks, you make a profit." Biffa looked at Toby's uncomprehending expression and took pity. "Look. You sell a planet short when the stock price is, say, x-dollars. Then, if you've been smart, the stock price halves. At that point you—"

"—can buy the real stock at the lower price, deliver it to your buyer and you've doubled your money," Paranoid Dave concluded, fluently and lifelessly. "Module 7. The Professor's course. It was the last one before I quit."

"OK…" Toby replied, looking at Paranoid Dave and back again at Biffa, "So that's your speciality here?"

"Only when we're being nice," Biffa replied. "We're trading futures and forwards, CDOs and CMOs, options, Anti-Gravity Swaps. Hell, the gang are even trading Dark Matter Calls, which I thought had been banned, but apparently not."

"Dark matter *what?*"

"Call options on dark matter. Gives you an option to buy the stuff at a fixed price in the future, just in case they ever learn how to harvest it. That's if it even exists of course, which I'm not convinced about. Our octopus friend here was trying his hand. Or should I say sucker? Looks like one of his trades went bad."

Toby turned back to Paranoid Dave, who was still staring out of the window, looking both transfixed and strangely detached. Shell-shocked. Like a man who's seen something too awful to speak of.

Just then they felt the room vibrate from a particularly loud cheer.

A good trade must've gone down in the Rakemore Telfer booth. Right in front of them, Toby saw two traders trample over the octopus and chest-bump each other with violent machismo. And then – in a well-rehearsed victory routine – the pair fist-bumped and high-fived and yodelled a single word so loudly, they could hear it through the plate-glass window:

"MOTUUUUU!"

"What does 'MOTU' mean?" Toby asked.

"'Masters of the Universe'" Biffa replied, staring lovingly at them through the window. "And they are. Indeed they are."

The celebration continued. The two traders high-fived again and then head-butted each other with a sickening thump. Apparently uninjured, they both yodelled a second word even more loudly than the first:

"MOT-*FUUUUUUUUUUUUUUUU*!"

"And 'MOTFU'?" Toby asked.

"They put an 'F' in front of the 'U'," Biffa replied, snapping back to his old self. "Take a guess hotshot."

Biffa turned very deliberately to face Toby and the others, his face twisted into a look of sneering triumph.

He advanced a couple of steps towards Paranoid Dave, Toby the Professor.

*

"Now can you see why I wanted to show you this?" Biffa started. "You thought maybe I was the problem, you thought you were up against me? But you're not, I'm not. You're up against *all this*," Biffa swept his arm back to indicate the trading pit. "You could try getting rid of me, but what good would that do? Knock me down, and there are a thousand others to fill the spot."

Paranoid Dave stared listlessly at the floor.

"He's right, guys. We can't beat that, the system. Look at it," Paranoid Dave said without looking. "All that power, all that money in the hands of creatures who just don't they care. *Who have no soul*. We're stuffed. We might as well kick back on a sun-lounger and enjoy being burnt to a crisp," he concluded simply, like a broken man. "It's over."

"Come on, Dave," Toby remonstrated, "don't give in like this. There's surely something we can do. This isn't you."

"You're right, it isn't me. And you know why?" Paranoid Dave looked directly at Toby, his eyes momentarily alive again with a strange, sorrowful anger.

Toby shrugged.

"My whole life… I've dreamed my whole life of travelling in outer space. And now, by some mad miracle, I do it, I actually do it. Can you believe it? I'm here, I'm *in space*, I've travelled in outer-bloody-space, I'm visiting alien civilisations. And what do I find?" Paranoid Dave gestured again towards the trading pit. "*This*. This stinking bunch of feral… Ah never mind. Point is, it's hopeless."

Paranoid Dave's head slumped again beneath the weight of his own disappointment.

"Listen to your friend here," Biffa said, laying a hand on the shoulder of Paranoid Dave, who didn't even have the spirit to resist. "It's over. But if you would just open your eyes to see, it's also *a beginning*. Your planet is toast, yes. But there's a whole Universe out here to explore. You lose a planet, you gain a Universe. I'd call that a good trade."

Toby looked at Paranoid Dave's near lifeless form and started to feel angry.

"It's a good trade for *you*," he said, rallying. "Can you tell me this. What is *your problem* with the Earth? Why have you turned against your own planet? Why are the Golgothans – why are *you* – so determined to screw things up for billions of humans?"

"Ah kid, you wanna have a go at me," Biffa replied, unruffled. "I can understand that, you're hurt, you're angry. But you're missing the point."

"Which is?"

"We're the good guys. Oh I know, you don't want to believe it. But it's true – the Universe *needs* us."

"Yeah sure," Toby replied sarcastically, finding a rebellious streak he didn't know he had, "the way a bug needs a windscreen."

"Aw, don't be such a baby. We were getting on so well," Biffa smirked.

He walked back to the window and looked at the trading pit beyond, drinking in the anarchy.

"Look out there – *look at it*. The Universe needs trade, it thrives on it. That's what builds civilisations. When you trade, you get winners and you get..." he gestured at the trio without even looking at them, "...*losers*. But you always get more winners than losers. And the most important thing about trade? Trade needs *peace*. That's the real deal. We Golgothans, we frickin' love peace. But we do more than that. We *enforce* peace. Peace means certainty. Peace means money. After all, you can't IPO a planet in a war zone."

Biffa turned back to the trio and fixed them in his stare. He spoke with emphasis.

"There are no major wars in the Universe because we don't let it happen. Bad for trade. That's right, we – the grim Golgothans – we keep the peace in your pretty little Universe. Like I said, we're the good guys."

Silence.

Biffa looked at the three limp figures in front of him.

"You know what? I think it's time we got you girls home. You're in no state for the IPO. My guys here will get you back to the hyperspaceport."

Biffa nodded at his two minders who were standing impassively at the back of the office, and they nodded back. They were standing either side of a second door, one that Toby hadn't spotted earlier. It led to a corridor running under the trading floor. Biffa walked up to it, opened it, and paused.

"Do please try to cheer up," Biffa said, standing in the doorway. "It'll be over before you know it. The final investor presentation is in an hour, and then the IPO bell will ring an hour after that. And that's it. *Sayonara*. The Earth will be sold off to greedy shysters from all over the place. Which, come to think of it," Biffa grinned as he walked out, "is not so different from how it is now."

As the door swung shut behind him, Biffa's dry, malevolent laugh was the last thing they heard.

*

Reluctantly, slowly, the Professor and Toby got to their feet. Biffa's two minders were waiting for them at the doorway.

"Dave..." Toby tugged gently on Paranoid Dave's sleeve. "Dave... We're going now."

Paranoid Dave turned and looked at Toby with wide, vacant eyes.

"Dave... We have to go now..." Toby said.

He gently pulled Paranoid Dave up by the arm and led his broken friend towards the door.

33

Charlie started to wake up in her bunk from a deep, deep sleep. Her brain picked up indistinct noises coming from somewhere below, which gradually became more distinct, and then became definite.

It was Mrs B preparing breakfast in the cabin.

Day 2 on Ormilu.

Charlie felt good. Refreshed. She watched as Mrs B hung an old-fashioned kettle over the log fire. Then she turned comfortably onto her back, and let her thoughts wander back to her conversation with Mrs B the day before.

Something had changed. Something inside.

How do you love someone, whom you can't forgive?

Mrs B's question rang in her mind like a church bell. People re-create the patterns of their childhood. Of course they do. Charlie had always known that. She had a father who cheated on her mother. Sure enough, she – Charlie – years later ends up falling for a married man. A married man with children. But knowing why a thing is happening doesn't stop it from happening. She had fallen for Dr de Haan.

How do you love someone, whom you can't forgive?

Except that Mrs B had led her to another door. Very slowly, very carefully she had guided Charlie to another realisation, a deeper one. By lowering herself to her father's level – by trying to do something as harmful as him – Charlie didn't need to forgive him anymore. She was right back next to him, she had lowered herself to his level, right where she could keep loving him. It was suddenly so obvious.

And what will you do now dear? Will you stay in the past? Or will you gently thank it for its lessons, and move forward?

It struck Charlie: finding the answer was easy, formulating the right question had been the hard part. Everything made sense now. For the first time in years, Charlie could picture Dr de Haan in her head and feel... compassion. Maybe a little admiration too. Yes, definitely admiration. But not love, not that kind of love.

"Breakfast is waiting for you, dear. Poached eggs, grilled bacon and muffins."

Charlie started slightly. It was Mrs. B, standing right under her bunk.

"Oh thank you, Mrs B. It smells delicious."

"You're welcome, dear."

Mrs B paused as she looked through the window. Outside, Jaakko was visible, gathering the huskies together.

"I have to go out now for a short while. For a journey," Mrs B continued, trying not to sound mysterious, but failing. "I shouldn't be too long. A few hours. Will you be OK on your own?"

"I'm fine, Mrs B," Charlie replied. "Don't worry about me. It's just..."

"Yes, dear?"

"It's Toby and Dave I'm worried about. And the Professor."

"I know, dear. I am too."

*

Toby looked at his watch – slightly pointlessly of course – but noted that it said 8:30am. *Whatever that meant.*

London time?

Possibly.

Running out of time?

Definitely.

"Papers?"

"What? You again? You can't be serious?" Toby was beyond exasperated. "You know we haven't got any papers. We're trying to leave. In a hurry actually. What do you need papers for?"

"Because, young man," the all-too-familiar Golgothan immigration official removed his small round, gold-rimmed spectacles for emphasis, "those are the rules."

"Rules? You have a rule that says you need valid immigration papers in order to *leave?*" Toby ran his hand through his hair. Precious seconds were draining away. He could feel a sense of panic seeping into the back of his brain like floodwater under a backdoor.

He tried a new tack.

"How come you're working on the departures terminal anyway? I thought you were an immigration official?"

"I work, young man, wherever there are troublemakers. So, let's try again," the official said, replacing his glasses on the end of his nose. "Papers?"

"We don't have any papers," Toby turned to Paranoid Dave in desperation. "Dave! Dave – say something! We can't just put up with this. We haven't got time!"

"Haven't got time? Time for what?" Paranoid Dave shrugged his shoulders. "We've got all the time in the world."

"What?" Toby turned to the Professor. "Professor! Could you say something? *Please!*"

"Hmm? What's that? You're asking about the time?" The Professor was staring intently at his gold fob watch again, his brow furrowed in mid-calculation. He looked up. "If you're worried about time, I have to say, I really don't think we can solve our problems in the time available."

"*What?*"

"Do we not have the right papers to depart from the Bodytron terminal? Hmm?" the Professor continued, looking at the Golgothan official. "Well, rules are rules, alas. Are they not?"

"Ah! A little common sense. How refreshing." The official looked down at his clipboard. "I shall have to fill out another detention form for you all." He started scribbling on the clipboard ostentatiously.

Toby looked around desperately, wondering, hoping help might appear from elsewhere.

Nothing.

On either side of him were several queues of bored, tired-looking travellers, waiting to have their papers checked. In front of each queue was an imposing metal turnstile.

But then something caught his eye.

Some yards away an enormous, scruffy creature stood with his back to them, tools scattered around his feet. He was reaching up into the ceiling, trying to fix one of the lights. *Lights, lights...* Toby wondered to himself. Lights!

"Professor!" Toby tugged urgently on the Professor's sleeve, speaking out of the side of his mouth. "Look! Look who's over there!"

"Hmm?" the Professor replied. "Have you spotted Mrs B?"

"Eh? What's Mrs B got to do with it? No, look! It's our cellmate, the ogre. The, erm, what did you call him? *The Cenaphian!* He's fixing the light over there. Maybe he can help?"

"Oh yes, so he is," the Professor smiled indulgently. "How nice."

The Golgothan immigration official looked up from his scribbling.

"Right, that's the detention form completed," he continued. "I rather think there's been enough rule-breaking today, especially by you three." The official signed the bottom of his clipboard with an exaggerated flourish and then called out in a happier tone, "Guards! Take them away please."

"No."

"Excuse me?"

"I said, No," Toby repeated.

"You said *what?*"

"I said No. And I meant it. You're not going to arrest us. We've got a planet to save and we're simply not going to be stopped by your stupid paperwork fetish."

"I don't see what your wishes have to do with—"

"Hey you! You! Friendly Cenaphian ogre fellow. Yes, you." Toby had caught the ogre's attention. "They're going to arrest us and put us back in that cell. Only I'd like you to stop them, could you—"

Before Toby could finish his sentence, the Cenaphian had stepped over and, very obligingly, lifted the Golgothan official by his collar. The tiny official hung suspended in the middle of the departure terminal, wriggling harmlessly beneath the Cenaphian's trunk-like arm.

"This is an outrage, an outrage! Put me down at once! Guards! Guards, I say!"

The immigration official blew on a whistle and, as if by magic, a line of five or six guards came clattering along a small passageway off to the side. But before they could emerge into the terminal, the Cenaphian raised one of his huge ogre feet and stuck it bang in the middle of the doorway. The guards collided with it, like a line of bumper cars at a fairground ride.

"Quickly, dears, quickly – now's your chancc!"

Who the... A familiar Scottish voice called to them from the other side of the turnstile.

Toby looked up. On the far side of the turnstile, he could see the unmistakable figure of Mrs B. He looked at Paranoid Dave, who looked back at him and shrugged his shoulders.

"Mrs B – is that you? How come you're here? And why... Why are... Why is..." Toby was struggling to put his last question into words. "Why are you on the Professor's set of library steps?"

"Oh there's nae time for idle chat now, dear. We've got to get you out of there."

"But how? We still can't get through the turnstile?"

"Oh, but I think you can."

Before Toby could argue, the Cenaphian – who was still holding the official with his arm and blocking the guards with his foot – stretched his last spare limb towards the turnstile. With a deft flick, he broke the locking mechanism and suddenly the chunky metal gate was spinning harmlessly on its hinges like a child's toy.

Toby, who was suffering from sensory overload and wondering how Mrs B came to be in the hyperspaceport on Golgotha just when they needed her, had no idea what to do next. So he fell back on instinct. *Stay polite.* He held out his hand to the Cenaphian.

"Well, thank you very much," he said. "That was very, err... obliging of you."

The Cenaphian smiled shyly. He extended a giant paw towards Toby and shook his hand with surprising gentleness. The official, still dangling from the Cenaphian's other arm, was enraged. He swatted the air furiously with his little fists.

"You will... both be... detained..." he stuttered breathlessly, as he swiped away, "for... at least... a year... *e a c h !* "

"Tobias – this is no time to be playing with your friends!" Mrs B remonstrated sternly, from across the barrier. "I've come a long way to fetch you. Please come through now!"

Toby turned away quickly and made his way through the broken turnstile, with the Professor just behind and Paranoid Dave just behind him.

"That man," Toby said breathlessly, as he reached the base of the library steps where Mrs B was waiting for him, "is not my friend."

"Well then, dear, all the more reason not to play with him," Mrs B replied, straightening her glasses. "Follow me up, please."

*

Mrs B bustled her way to the small platform at the top of the library steps. With their burnished wooden handrail and rich red carpeting, the steps looked like they had landed from outer space. Which of course they had. Mrs B knelt down in front of the small red leather bench and hinged back the seat to reveal a gleaming set of elegant brass dials and controls. She started twisting a couple of the dials, and then flicked a single brass switch.

"The steps will just take a few moments to charge, and then we should be off."

"Off? Off where?" Toby asked.

"These steps, my dear, are going to take us to Ormilu."

"Ormilu? Where's—"

Pfft.

34

Toby blinked a few times as he came to.

He looked around.

He could see a hurricane lamp hanging low in front of him. Its warm yellow flame was flickering and dancing as if recovering from a passing draught. To his left was a large, tidily stacked wall of logs. To his right he could see an old wooden door and a couple of small windows on either side. He was in a woodshed. And through the frosted windows he could make out what looked like... *snow?*

The air was cold. Very cold.

Toby, who was still wearing the ridiculous floral pyjama suit he'd been given on Za-Nak – albeit with his own jacket over the top – shuddered. He felt something brush his arm. It was Mrs B, as she stretched and yawned. Below him were Paranoid Dave and the Professor, slumped on the library steps.

Where are we, and how did we get here? Toby thought to himself, as he struggled to dredge his memory back up.

"Well, gentlemen, welcome to Ormilu!" Mrs B said, as if reading his mind.

"Ormilu? Ormilu?" Toby repeated. "Oh yes, Ormilu... You did mention something about Ormilu..."

And that triggered it.

His memories came flooding unpleasantly back in, like a boisterous group of rugby players into a quiet village pub.

"Mrs B, please," Toby turned to his left, remembering that he needed to panic. "Mrs B you've got to help. The Professor and Paranoid Dave. They've given up. Dave doesn't seem paranoid anymore and the Professor doesn't seem to care. You've got to get us back to London! *Now!*"

"Oh my dear," Mrs B replied soothingly, "I think you need to calm down."

"Calm down? Mrs B – our planet's about to be auctioned and millions of gigatonnes of CO_2 are about to be released into the atmosphere. How can I calm down?"

"Well, let's go back to London then."

"We can?"

"Of course, just as soon as you tell me your plan?"

"My plan?"

"Yes, your plan."

Toby's face looked wild and blank. No words came out.

"Ah, no plan. I see." Mrs B stretched comfortably. "Well if you don't have a plan, I suggest we come up with one. And there's no better place for thinking than Ormilu. Isn't that right, Professor?"

The Professor, who had just stood up and was stretching his arms above his head, gave an indulgent nod.

"Exactly," Mrs B continued. "And besides, there's someone here who's very much looking forward to seeing you."

"Seeing me? But I don't know anyone on Ormilu. I

don't even know where Ormilu is. Who is he?"

"*She*," Mrs B continued, "is already an old friend. Follow me."

*

The first breath of outside air hit the back of Toby's throat, clean and crisp. He looked momentarily at the scene beneath him, through eyes that were already starting to water from the cold. They were half way up a steep hillside and there beneath them was a breathtaking snowscape of frozen lakes and pine trees. The pine forest spread over fold after fold of gently rolling hills towards the far horizon.

It was fresh and purifying. Toby felt his spirits lift despite himself.

About thirty yards away Toby could see a log cabin. Above its chimney, wisps of wood smoke hung vertically in the air in a slowly turning spiral. To one side of the cabin, a tall, broad, hooded figure was cutting wood.

"Don't dawdle, my dears – you'll catch your death of chill!" Mrs B called out briskly, as she led the way across the snow-covered ground.

Toby briskly clapped his arms around himself three or four times and set off for the cabin. Still wearing only the floral beach shorts, his legs were the coldest.

As they approached the cabin, the hooded figure put down his axe and slowly rested both hands on the handle. He had the unhurried, deliberate movements of a true outdoorsman. He slowly drew back the hood to reveal a chiselled, weather-beaten face. It was human and handsome. He stared at them as they scuttled along.

Even in the brief instant that their eyes met, Toby felt his soul had been looked into.

*

They reached the cabin. Mrs B thumped against the door with her fist. The door opened, and they quickly bundled in. In a second, before Toby even had time to adjust to the indoor light, a pair of arms had thrown themselves around him, and he found his nose pressed close to the side of a sweetly-scented neck. It smelt of soap and water.

"You're safe! Thank God you're all safe!"

It was Charlie.

"How are you, Toby?" she said, leaning back to look at him, and then hugging him again. "I've been so worried about you."

Toby was caught completely off guard. He wondered quickly if he should say something heroic. Or perhaps a tone of nonchalant calm? Or, more likely, gush about the dangers he had just survived…

But before he could dither any longer, she turned away and threw her arms around Paranoid Dave with the same tenderness.

Paranoid Dave barely reacted.

Charlie unclasped her arms and stepped back to look at him critically.

"What's wrong, Dave? You look like you've seen a ghost."

He didn't reply. Charlie took him by the arm and drew him towards the roaring log fire.

"Come and sit here, tell me what happened." She sat down on a worn, comfy-looking sofa, guiding him down next to her with quiet forcefulness. "Tell me about Za-Nak? Tell me about *Golgotha?*"

Paranoid Dave lowered himself slowly onto the sofa, staring into the fire like a zombie.

"It was awful. The things we've seen. Awful…"

"I'm listening," she replied firmly. "Tell me."

And so he did.

Toby sat himself down on a sofa opposite and watched Paranoid Dave falteringly tell their story, while Charlie listened, her eyes wide with protective concern. As he watched them, Toby's mind wandered vacantly. And as it wandered, it started to wonder why Charlie looked different. She wasn't wearing make-up, that was one thing. Another was her hair. She was wearing a white, rollneck sweater, over which her mocha-coloured hair hung loose and a little messy, like she'd just been outside. Her eyes were bright and a rosy hue was just visible on her cheeks. She looked at ease, like she'd been here days. *Does this look suit her better, or worse?* Toby had no idea how other people saw her. He had lost perspective. Because to him, she had done something he didn't think was possible – she had become even more beautiful.

"Tea, Tobias?"

"Eh?" Toby gave a start. Mrs B was looking at him, with a knowing smile on her face.

"Oh yes, thank you, Mrs B. Yes please."

"Here you are, dear. And please take a shortbread. Jaakko makes them."

"Jaakko? Who's… Hang on, is he the one cutting wood outside?"

"That's right."

"He seems rather…"

"Mysterious?" Mrs B asked.

Toby nodded.

"Yes, well, it's not for everyone, this life," Mrs B mused. "He has no company here, except his huskies."

"So why is he here?"

"Oh, we'll get to that soon enough," Mrs B said, turning away. "Now, David, biscuit?"

Toby sipped his tea meditatively, and dunked the shortbread in it. It wasn't at all bad. In fact, it was rather good. He looked around. The log cabin was warm and inviting. Toby felt himself being lulled into a soporific state.

His eyes followed the Professor as he walked over to the fire. Carruthers was there, in a small basket, his head resting comfortably on the edge. Just like Charlie, he looked every bit at home. But as the Professor knelt down to stroke his chops, Carruthers' nose twitched a few times and he released a little hedgehog sneeze. The Professor scooped him up in an old cloth and took him to a second sofa, opposite Charlie and Paranoid Dave, whereupon the hedgehog released a couple more sneezes, before settling happily on the Professor's lap.

Despite everything, Toby's eyelids closed comfortably of their own accord.

*

A few moments later – *was it just moments?* – he opened them again, sleepily. Nothing had changed. Paranoid Dave was coming to the end of their story. Charlie was still listening. The Professor was still on the sofa and Carruthers was still on the Professor, and Mrs B was still bustling about the room.

"...and so the IPO is due to happen soon," Paranoid Dave continued. "That's the next thing. Maybe that's the last thing. Once that's happened, we'll never be able to buy the Earth back. It was due to happen in a couple of hours' time. But that was, I don't know how long ago? Criss-crossing the Universe, it's hard to keep track of time…"

Time, time… Toby repeated to himself, still half asleep.

Time…

Time!

He jolted himself awake.

"Time! We haven't got time!" Toby sat bolt upright on the sofa. "What are we doing here? We're wasting time. Our planet's about to be trashed, we've got to do something!"

Toby stood up. The others all stared at him.

"What is it? Why is everyone so damn… *calm* suddenly? Am I the only one who cares anymore?"

"No, no, you're right, something must be done," the Professor said agreeably.

"Then why aren't we?" Toby blurted back. "Am I living in a different reality to you all? This is so confusing."

"Don't be confused, dear," Mrs B replied. "Let's clear the air. Go ahead and ask everything on your mind."

"Right," Toby said. "Good. I've got at least three questions. In fact, make that four—"

"Ah, four questions, excellent," the Professor interrupted, clapping his hands. "Every good answer starts with a question."

Toby blinked and wondered for the umpteenth time whether the Professor was indeed the genius Mrs B claimed him to be, or actually a bit simple.

"So, the first one," he continued, shaking off that last thought and trying to focus. "Where are we? I mean, really, *where*? And why are you all so calm? That's two. And my third question. What *are* those library steps? And – four – if they can do what they seem to be able to do, why did we ever bother with that rusty Personalitron? Oh, and five, what's with that damn watch of yours?"

The Professor looked up from his fob watch, which he had been studying again.

"These are fair questions, hmm?" the Professor replied calmly. "Not the correct ones, of course, but fair."

"And the good news," Mrs B picked up cheerfully from the Professor, "is that they all have the same answer. More or less."

"Which is?" Toby crossed his arms testily.

"Do please sit down again, dear. You look so theatrical standing up," Mrs B replied. "That's right, the sofa will do."

Toby sat down bolshily next to the Professor.

"Now, Ormilu, dear, is what we call a 'safe planet'."

"A safe planet?"

"Yes. You know the concept of a safe house? From spy novels, that sort of thing? Well, Ormilu is a safe *planet*. It's our secret place. No-one else comes here. We make do with what we find here, and the rest we bring ourselves. That way we can escape attention."

"You mean, no-one knows we're here?"

"That's right," Mrs B replied. There's no Bodytron or Personalitron terminal. So we always travel here with our own—"

"Bodytron?"

"Not a Bodytron, dear, they're library steps," Mrs replied, as if stating the obvious. "It's the Professor's personal means of travel. Let's leave it at that for now." Mrs B sipped her tea with a sort of finality that confirmed there would be no more discussion of that particular topic.

"We had to let you travel in the Personalitron," the Professor said, "so you could get close to the world leaders and to Woola. You see, hmm? And then find out the Za-Nakarians' real plan."

"Which you did admirably," Mrs B continued. "But the main reason we find Ormilu so calming is because... How shall I put this Professor?

"Because time is moving faster," said the Professor.

"Much faster," said Mrs B.

"About twenty times faster," said the Professor.

"Twenty times faster? But that's a disaster," replied Toby with alarm. "I mean, have they already released the carbon dioxide back on Earth? Is it all over already?"

"On the contrary," replied the Professor looking at his watch again. "Because time is moving faster *here*, it's moving more slowly *on Earth*. Let's call it relativity. I believe that's the normal term, hmm? For every twenty minutes we spend here, chatting and thinking, that's about one minute on Earth."

"And the Professor knows that because he has a relativity watch. He will have set it while on Golgotha using Standard Universal Time. That's the—"

"Can you just, err, slow down a minute?" Toby said, with his hand on his forehead. "What is a relativity watch and how can time possibly be going faster here?"

"Ah! Fascinating question," the Professor replied. "Well, Ormilu is travelling slower through space relative to the Earth, much slower. It takes a little explaining, but this means that time has sped up. How much faster? That's what the watch is for. Great Uncle Claude made it. Designed it himself."

The Professor withdrew the gold fob watch from his waistcoat pocket and, with the same hand, deftly flicked the lid back on its hinge. Toby shifted closer on the sofa to get a better look. Paranoid Dave, showing a hint of life, got up from his seat and came to look too. The gold frame had tiny dents and scratches here and there which spoke of a well-travelled device, while the face was designed with the elegance of an earlier age.

"Do you see here the main dial? That's telling the time on Earth, like any normal watch. But look at this small dial lower left, hmm?"

Toby strained his eyes in the low light of the cabin, and saw nothing.

"Hang on," said Paranoid Dave with growing interest. "Is there a hand there, spinning, like, insanely fast?"

"Oh yeah," Toby said, "it's like a... like a tiny propeller blade."

"Correct! That shows how fast seconds are passing on Ormilu, *relative* to Earth. Now to the third dial. Ah yes. Great Uncle Claude's great innovation. The relativity regulator. You see here?"

The Professor pointed to the bottom right of the watch face with his index finger. As Toby's eyes flicked between the watch and the Professor's hands, he couldn't help noticing a strange similarity between them. The joints of the Professor's fingers were ornery and his skin was flecked with age spots.

"By adjusting this, I set the relationship between the other two dials, hmm? My notebook please, David?"

"Sure – here it is," Paranoid Dave replied, fishing it

from his jacket pocket.

"Good. So I've jotted down the main settings..." the Professor mused out loud as he leafed to the back of his notebook. "Ah, here we go. I turn the regulator anti-clockwise through 80 degrees, like so..."

The Professor pulled out the crown of the watch, adjusted it, and then pushed it back in.

"Ah, wonderful. Now look. You see? The main dial shows the time on Ormilu – while the smaller dial now shows how quickly time is passing on Earth. As you can see, very slowly."

"OK..." said Toby warily, as he looked at the needle on the smaller dial, which was now barely moving. "I think I get this. But what about Za-Nak and Golgotha. How do they compare?"

"Oh, they're actually similar to Earth. Time passes at about the same speed. No, in terms of our journey, it's just Ormilu where time is appreciably different."

"That's why we come here occasionally," said Mrs B. "The Professor and I. In order to think, you sometimes need that little bit of extra space—"

"—and time," the Professor concluded.

Charlie put her hand on Toby's shoulder. He looked up at her and she looked back with a gentle, reassuring expression. She gave his shoulder a brief squeeze.

*

Toby felt himself unknotting.

Some very taut thing inside him had been released. He got up from the sofa and crossed over to the window. Jaakko was still outside. A group of huskies was milling around, while he fed them titbits. Beyond, the breathtaking, snow-spectred wilderness of Ormilu seemed more inviting than ever.

"So, you understand now how time moves more slowly here?" Mrs B asked form behind his shoulder.

Toby nodded.

"Yes, Mrs B," he replied, rejoining the group. "It seems crazy, but I have to accept what you're both saying."

"Is there anywhere else on Ormilu time, Professor?" Charlie asked.

"Oh plenty of places, yes," the Professor replied cheerfully. "And some places go even faster. I know one place, you see, where 60 seconds pass in a single Earth second—"

"Professor!" Mrs B said warily, as if to warn him off a topic.

"What? What is it? Why are you *Professoring* him?" Paranoid Dave asked.

"Ah yes. Mrs B would rather I don't tell you about Ph'Estoun. No."

"Why not?" Charlie asked. "Mrs B, what's wrong with Fest— With whatever you call it?"

Mrs B rolled her eyes with resignation.

"Because, dear, some places don't need to be discussed. Particularly the foul ones. And Ph'Estoun is just about the foulest. It's a disused mining planet."

"And the home of The Fever," the Professor wagged a warning finger enthusiastically.

"*The* fever?" Paranoid Dave asked.

"Ah yes, Ph'Estoun Fever," the Professor continued cheerfully. "The most virulent disease in the known Universe."

"*Shut up!*" Charlie said.

"You have no idea," Mrs B said, rolling her eyes again.

322

"How virulent?" Paranoid Dave asked, his normal curiosity starting to return.

"Ah well, that's the question, yes," the Professor replied, clearly on a favourite topic. "It's caused by a hypermorphic cluster virus, hmm? Well, I say *virus*, but it actually appears to be a whole new kind of life form. Part fungus, part bacillus, and err, part... Part virus. Let's just say it makes SARS-CoV-2 seem like, well, a common cold."

"Sars-cov-*what?*" Toby asked.

"Not Sars-cov-what, dear", Mrs B replied helpfully. "*You-know-what.*"

"Yes," the Professor continued, "Ph'Estoun Fever can adapt to different hosts, different threats. It has a cluster genome, so it's really several lifeforms bolted together. Quite ingenious, you see? If an immune system manages to target one part, it just discards that component and carries on replicating. Different parts allow it to flourish in any number of, err, hosts. Animals, plants, fungi, and so on. It's so virulent, it can even cross the carbon boundary. It's been known to infect silicon-based lifeforms, it's even been known to crash computers. Can you imagine? A genuine computer virus, haha!"

"Hang on, Paranoid Dave said, "if it's so virulent, then surely it... Surely it, like, kills every host in minutes and then dies with them?"

"Ay, but that's its clever side," Mrs B replied, getting drawn in despite herself. "It's quick, but not too quick. You display symptoms after an hour – you're infectious after three hours – incapacitated after five – and then die a lingering death over the next six to ten days. During that time your body is ejecting infectious spores more or less continuously—"

"—from boils and buboes all over your body!" the Professor added gamely.

"It doesn't stop until all life on a planet has been wiped out." Mrs B concluded.

"OK… Nice…" Paranoid Dave replied. "But that's still my point. The virus dies with the planet. I mean, in evolutionary terms, that's a pretty dumb strategy. Surely?"

"Do you know what, Dave?" Toby said, "I think we get the gist. I think we've all had enough virus discussions to last a lifetime. Can we move the—"

"Just a moment, Tobias," Mrs B said, holding up a hand. She had fully given in to the topic now. "Your friend has asked a valid question. You see I'm afraid the virus doesn't die with the host. It enters a dormant state. It can survive outside a living organism for months – ay, for years for all we know."

Mrs B paused for a moment, wondering at the sheer malevolence of it. "More importantly, the virus flourishes in the wee beasties in which it first evolved. The catfish of Ph'Estoun. They're entirely unaffected. Them and the four or five other species that survive on the planet. Of course, all travel to Ph'Estoun is strictly banned—"

"—which is precisely why bandits and outlaws go there, hmm? To escape unwanted attention," the Professor added.

"Naturally they run a terrible risk," Mrs B continued, "and, if they ever manage to leave, the next planet they travel to could become infected."

"So why doesn't the intergalactic council just blow the planet up and be done with it?" Paranoid Dave asked.

"Oh they couldn't do that," the Professor looked

almost appalled. "They'd be sending space debris across the Universe, some of it impregnated with the most dangerous—"

"Great. Thank you, Professor, Mrs B, David," Toby interrupted decisively. "But now we're going to change the subject. We need to get back on topic."

*

"Professor, Mrs B…" Toby continued. "You said you come to Ormilu to do your thinking. Good. But how does that work? Thinking is great and everything, but right now we need action, we need—"

"Uh-uh-uh!" Mrs B wagged a finger, "Let's not start panicking again. If your thinking is panicked, your actions will be too. A right action can only come from a right thought. And a right thought comes from asking the right question. Ormilu," Mrs B said with emphasis, "is where we come to ask the right questions—"

"—and generally get our answers," the Professor added.

"Ok… How does that work?" Charlie asked.

"Hmm? Well, when you ask a question, you open a window in your mind. Do you see?" the Professor replied. "Show a little patience, and the answer will come fluttering in."

The Professor made a little fluttering motion with his hands, like a bird, and chuckled.

"Professor…" It was Charlie. "You said Toby asked fair questions, but not the correct ones – what did you mean?"

"Well I think we should ask the question that's really on our minds," the Professor replied.

"Like, how can we stop those bastards trashing our

planet?" Paranoid Dave asked, with more of his usual spirit.

"Ah, that's much better dear," Mrs B said approvingly. "A little rude, but on the right lines."

"Well then, how?" Paranoid Dave asked.

"One good question normally leads to another," the Professor said.

"Well, they hold all the cards," Paranoid Dave said, folding his arms, "and we hold none."

"That wasn't a question, dear," Mrs B said.

Paranoid Dave was about to protest, but Charlie held up her hand, and stood up.

"Maybe we need to understand them, the Golgothans. See things from their point of view…" she said, starting to engage. "Maybe we need to ask *why* they want to help trash the planet?"

"Greed?" Toby ventured.

"Yes, greed," Charlie continued. "And where you find greed, what else do you find…"

"…Fear?" Paranoid Dave offered.

"Ah!" the Professor clapped his hands. "We might be getting somewhere."

"Greed and fear," Charlie mused. "So I guess we should ask, how can that be turned against them? Will that help?"

"Oh I should think so," Mrs B said, glancing at the Professor.

"Well…" Toby started tentatively, "we do know one thing. The Golgothans are going to be presenting their plans for the Earth to investors at a conference an hour before the IPO launch. So I guess they'll be nervous about that going well?"

"That's right," Charlie added with a hint of excitement. "They'll be afraid of that going wrong.

Surely?"

"I think that's a very fair question," Mrs B replied.

"Sure it is," Paranoid Dave said, folding his arms. "But I'm sorry to tell you Charlie, Mrs B – you two don't know what it's like over there. On Golgotha. Those investors, as you're calling them, they're *animals*. They eat planets like Earth for breakfast. They'll sell it off, dice it up, trade it in small chunks, until no-one knows who owns which bits, it'll be—"

"David," the Professor held a hand up, smiling kindly. "It's the Golgothans' fear that we need to focus on, not our own. Hmm?"

Mrs B promptly clapped her hands and stood up in the middle of the group.

"Well, I think we've made an excellent start. But I also think, my dears, that maybe it's time we all went outside for a little air? Clear our heads a little."

Mrs B looked over to the Professor, who nodded quietly.

"It's time Charlie and I showed you Ormilu. I think you might enjoy this."

35

The sleigh had a bell on it, of course.

It tinkled prettily as they whooshed along a path carved into the hillside. Toby looked down to his right, where the sparkling snowscape lay before him. He could see icy lakes and forests, fading to a far horizon where the frozen snow and the frozen sky seemed to merge into a continuous, soft white vapour – like seeing the boundary where reality becomes dream.

"Do you want to take the reins?" Charlie asked, her eyes wide and bright.

"Err, sure. Thanks," Toby replied, taking them awkwardly in his huge leather mittens. "What do I do with them?"

"Oh nothing much. The dogs will just follow Jaakko's sledge anyway." Charlie smiled and nodded towards the sleigh in front. Jaakko was seated on the front bench with Paranoid Dave and Mrs B seated just behind. "But the huskies like to feel some tension on the reins. It lets them know we're still alive."

Charlie laughed, and nudged Toby with her shoulder.

"Oh right, of course. That's nice," Toby replied, struggling to shorten the reins in his mittens.

"By the way, who is Jaakko? And why did he come here?" Toby asked after a short pause.

"Oh sure, that's simple," Charlie replied. "He was escaping prison back home."

"Prison? What had he done?"

"His wife was seduced by another man. So he murdered him."

"He *what?*"

"Murdered him. Shot him dead. Strange, because he's actually the gentlest man."

"Oh, I see," said Toby, trying not very successfully to maintain the cool that might be expected of a man who'd survived a trip to Golgotha. "But is he, is he… Are Paranoid Dave and Mrs B safe with him?"

"Oh yes, completely," Charlie replied laughing. "Mrs B told me the whole story. It's extraordinary, I'll tell you another time. But Jaakko wouldn't hurt a fly. That's why he came here."

"Because there are no flies?"

Charlie laughed.

She seemed to be doing a lot of that. Toby wondered what this was, this change in her.

"His plan is to spend twenty or thirty years here, and then return home," Charlie continued. "Only a year will have passed on Earth – but he'll be unrecognisable by then. Something like that."

Toby nodded and looked warily at the hooded figure on the sleigh in front.

The path started to crawl uphill. The speed of the sleigh dropped and the huskies strained hard against the slope. Toby looked sideways at his companion.

"You know, Charlie, you seem…" Toby paused. "Different."

"Me – different? What about you!" Charlie retorted, with a mischievous glint in her eye. "But of course you *are* different, I mean this isn't even your real body, right? Or at least not your original one." She prodded his cheek with her mitten playfully.

"I know. It's nuts," Toby replied. "Well, that's my excuse. What's yours? What's happened to you?"

"Me? Oh, Ormilu happened, that's what. I love it here. The simplicity. It's magical."

"Yeah? OK. But is that all? I mean you seem so much calmer?"

Charlie was quiet for a few moments.

"Actually I've been doing a lot of thinking the last couple of days. And talking – with Mrs B, I mean. She's remarkable actually. She just has this way of..." Charlie paused to think, "...reading people. The way a mechanic might read a car. She lifts the bonnet, spots a problem, reaches in and fixes it."

"What problem?"

"Ha! That would be telling. Anyway I think... I think it's going to be OK now," Charlie replied.

"OK... But what about Earth? I mean – for whatever mad reason we've found ourselves at the centre of the greatest crisis our planet has ever faced. I know getting stressed probably doesn't help. But what choice is there? What's your formula for being calm *about that*?"

"That's easy."

"OK. And?"

"I have faith in you."

"In *me?*" Toby recoiled, giving an inadvertent yank on the reins. The huskies bridled and Toby quickly loosened the reins again. "If you think I've got the answers to all our problems, then you are deluded. I can't even ask the right questions!"

Charlie laughed – a clear, pure, disarming peal of laughter that rang across the frozen air like their sleigh bell.

"You know, Toby, you've changed too. Seriously. At the start of this you barely wanted to get involved."

"True…"

"And now look at you. You're involved and you're… You're *driving* things."

"Driving things? Is that what you call it?" Toby looked at the reins lying limply in his hands. "I'm just stressed."

"Stressed? No, I'm going with feisty."

Charlie dropped her voice, and turned on her seat to face Toby directly. Her tone was somewhere between tenderness and pride.

"They didn't succeed, did they Toby? The Golgothans. They tried to break you, and they didn't. You've shown more fight than any of us, and you've shown it just when we gave up. The Professor saw something in you from the start. I see it too now."

Toby was about to protest, but Charlie put a mitten to her lips and then pointed to the path ahead.

Their sled was approaching the crest of the hill. As they advanced higher, the forest dwindled away and an icy wind lashed their faces with increasing force. The snow had been blasted clean off the ground, exposing the frozen earth beneath. The few trees around them were stunted and weather beaten. Mrs B and Paranoid Dave's sleigh had already stopped on the crest.

Toby and Charlie's sled pulled alongside and, as they did so, Toby realised it wasn't a hill at all.

It was a cliff.

*

There before them was a frozen ocean.

In every direction, to the farthest horizon, lay hundreds of miles of sheer, flat sea ice.

All five of them stood and stared at it. A few wisps of snow could be seen here and there rising off the surface and swirling in the wind. This small flicker emphasised the granite stillness of the scene. It was a view bereft of detail. Toby struggled with the confusion of seeing both so much and so little.

He turned to his left and saw Paranoid Dave staring at him and Charlie. There was a strange, quizzical look in Paranoid Dave's eye, like he was seeing something for the first time. Then he nodded briefly at Toby – there was a friendly, accepting look in his eye – before turning back to face the ocean.

A moment later, Toby heard Charlie's voice in his ear.

"It's amazing here," she said. She was leaning very close to make herself heard, her lips almost against his skin. "But desolate."

Toby gave a simple nod in reply.

"I like Ormilu," she continued, enunciating her words clearly against the icy wind. Toby felt his skin tingling from the warmth of her breath. "But I prefer where we come from."

Toby turned and looked at her. Their eyes were only a few inches apart.

"Shall we head home?" she asked.

"Sure."

*

Toby stared into the warm, flickering fire. He was back in the log cabin. His whole body was enjoying the excess of heat the way you do when you've had an excess of cold. His face still tingled from contact with the fresh Ormilu air. As the others chatted, he stayed silent, revelling in the deep relaxation that was washing over him.

And yet his brain felt strangely clear and his senses heightened. The clarity of Charlie's voice as she talked about life on Ormilu, the taste of the hot cross bun Mrs B had given him, the little wrinkles in Carruthers' tiny nose as he sneezed – everything was brighter, sharper, clearer.

He noticed he wasn't the only one feeling better. Paranoid Dave seemed like his old self again. He started asking the Professor how many other safe planets there were, and whether they could be sure they hadn't been tracked.

"Are you sure you're OK, dear?"

It was Mrs B.

Toby turned his gaze from the fire to see her eyeing him closely.

"I'm good thanks, Mrs B," he replied. "Actually, I've never felt better."

"Ay, that's good," she replied.

Achoo!

Carruthers gave a tiny hedgehog sneeze.

"Only don't you be getting too relaxed. We cannae stay here forever. Ormilu is just a pause in the action, not a—"

ACHOO!

Carruthers gave a surprisingly emphatic sneeze.

"Oh my Heavens, the poor wee critter," Mrs B exclaimed as she turned to look at the hedgehog. "It's a pity he has to take all his bally germs with him as he criss-crosses the known Universe." She sipped on her tea meditatively and continued talking to no-one in particular. "That's one use of the Personalitron, no need to take any nasty germs back with you. True, you take all your germs when you're ejected. But not when you're re-inserted."

Toby looked across at Mrs B, and tilted his head. *Why would she mention that?*

"Ha!" the Professor exclaimed. "There's an interesting thought for the engineers. Hmm? No more germs. But could they distinguish with certainty between the healthy cells and the unhealthy? Only send these cells across, not those cells?"

The Professor paused to chew on a mouthful of toasted bun.

"After all, so often a harmful thing actually turns out to be helpful, and a helpful one turns out to be—"

"Sorry to interrupt, Professor," said Toby, interrupting. "What was that you just said, Mrs B?"

"Excuse me, dear?"

"What did you just say?"

"Oh, I just said it's a pity we have to take these wretched germs with us, when we—"

"That's it," Toby said staring into the fire again, his eyes suddenly wide.

"That's what, dear?"

"My God, you're brilliant. That's how we do it."

"How we do what?" said Paranoid Dave.

Everyone was staring at Toby.

He turned to face them.

"It seems so obvious now. Of course the Golgothans are insecure. They're scared of everything. Why else do they pile money on top of money?"

"I'm not following?" Paranoid Dave replied.

"Professor, can I see your watch for a moment?" Toby sprang to his feet and crossed to where the

Professor was sitting.

"Of course," the Professor replied, pulling his fob watch from his waistcoat pocket.

Toby took it from him and studied it intently. The others had all stopped in their tracks and were watching Toby. His lips moved silently as he performed a few quick calculations in his head.

"Guys..."

"Yes?" Charlie replied eagerly.

"What?" Paranoid Dave asked.

"I mean it's completely daft. Actually it's so daft it's embarrassing. Let me start again: have any of you come up with a sensible, realistic plan?"

Toby paused to look as his four friends. They all stared back at him, shaking their heads slowly, with a look somewhere on the spectrum between desperation and excitement.

"...then you'll have to make do with mine. I think I know how maybe, just maybe, we can beat the Golgothans at their own game."

"You do?"

"Are you serious?"

"*Shut up!*"

"Yeah, maybe," Toby replied, with a light in his eyes that, just then, seemed mesmerising. "But first I need to check a couple of things."

"What?" Paranoid Dave asked.

"Professor – I think I'll need to borrow your library steps?"

"You're most welcome," the Professor replied.

"And, Mrs B..."

"Yes dear?"

"I need you to tell me all about Ph'Estoun."

36

As the time sped past on Ormilu, there had been an hour or so of peace back in London. *That thing* in the sky had passed on. The mid-morning sun was streaming down. People were daring to look up again.

But not for long.

Morley was standing beside his stall, a warm mug of tea in his hand, thinking maybe he needn't throw away *all* of his Woola merchandise after all, when the next bulk carrier started to pass overhead.

But this time, once he started looking up, he stayed looking up.

It was mesmerising.

As the colossal, bulbous nose cone approached, the thin morning clouds parted either side of it like a net curtain. Its scale, its awesome buoyancy, the sleek gunmetal grey – Morley couldn't tear his eyes away.

*

And he wasn't the only one.

Not so very far away, Seamus and Declan were in the park, kicking their heels, and wondering if it was acceptable to go to the pub at ten in the morning. Just as they were persuading themselves it was fine, since they would only order a coffee – at least to start with –

they saw it too.

And as they stared, something started to happen.

All the way down both sides of the carrier, a whole line of flaps opened up, like gunports on an old-fashioned warship. A few seconds after that, huge metal nozzle-like things appeared from each opening, like so many cannon being run out.

Instinctively, Declan and Seamus flinched.

What now?

*

Most of London flinched with them.

Down a street that was about midway between them and Morley, the four remaining members of the TARP team had been ambling along, not quite sure what to do with themselves. As they watched the huge nozzles appear on the spaceship, they instinctively ducked for cover against one of the buildings and – slightly pointlessly – unholstered their pistols.

They waited, tense and expectant.

But nothing happened.

The spaceship carried on gliding, and the huge nozzles just sat there, insouciant to the anxiety of the Londoners beneath them.

One by one, the four TARP members relaxed their grip on the pistols. If those nozzles were some kind of gun, there wasn't anything they could do about it. They re-holstered their pistols, a little sheepish.

*

The truth was, the four TARP members felt lost.

They had lost contact with the authorities who had

dispatched them, they had lost their two leaders, who were currently dangling naked in a couple of big glass tubes, and they had lost their sense of purpose.

And now this.

Whatever these spaceships were up to, they felt pretty sure it wasn't anything good. And even worse, they had this nagging feeling that their mission had more to do with helping the spaceships than hindering them.

In a word, they weren't sure they were the good guys anymore.

TARP-3 stood back up and re-holstered his pistol.

"Sod it, guys, let's go to the pub."

37

Toby took the old service revolver in both hands with a feeling somewhere between awe and anxiety. It looked antique but lethal. It was freshly oiled and the steel was freezing cold against his fingers.

The thing that most struck him, however, was the weight.

Jaakko nodded at Toby.

Toby took the revolver in his right hand and immediately felt his arm sag. Jaakko had just given him the Professor's gun from his army days – *who knew?* – which he kept in a secret compartment under the library steps. *There's plenty of power in the Webley Mark VI, I can assure you, hmm?* the Professor had said. Toby looked across to the woodshed. Through the frosted window he could just make out the forms of the Professor and Paranoid Dave. In the next window along, he could see Mrs B and Charlie in the main cabin.

"You – target – shoot."

Jaakko spoke with uncharacteristic wordiness. He – a convicted murderer – was giving Toby a crash course in how to shoot. *I mean, why not?* Toby thought to himself.

Toby looked at Jaakko's pitted and weather-beaten face and then at the target. It was a large log about twenty yards away. He lifted his right arm to shoot, and found the log to be a lot smaller and a lot further than it first appeared.

"Safety catch – switch off," Jaakko said, in what was probably his longest speech that year.

Safety catch, of course. His arm trembling under the weight, Toby flicked the catch off and drew back the hammer with his thumb. Out of his right eye he was aware of Mrs B watching him from the log cabin; out of his left eye, Jaakko. Focussing forwards he could see the target sight on the revolver wobbling either side of the log. He couldn't hold his arm up any longer, he would have to shoot.

Wincing, and almost not daring to look, he squeezed on the trigger.

Crack!

The penetrating noise of the shot fractured the brittle Ormilu air.

And, to the astonishment of everyone watching, the log jumped like it had been stung and fell back into the snow.

*

As she watched the log jump, Mrs B was peering over the top of her reading glasses.

"Not so bad, not so bad. He's not going to win Bisley, but it'll do for now. Right," she said, pushing her glasses back into position and looking at a list in her hand, "where were we?"

"The first aid kit," Charlie replied matter-of-factly, tapping a small plastic briefcase on the table in front of her. "With additional bandaging."

"Ah yes, you've got those, good," she said ticking

her list twice. "And the field glasses?

"Check."

"Gumboots – two pairs?"

"Check and check."

"And one relativity watch – gold, with chain?"

"Check."

"Right, that's everything on the list. So…" Mrs B lowered her glasses again, and peered at Charlie. "What else might they need for a journey across the Universe?"

"Do you think we should pack these, Mrs B?" Charlie said, gingerly holding up Paranoid Dave and Toby's floral beach shorts, which had been left on a hook near the door. "I mean, the clothes they were given on Za-Nak. You never know, I mean, it might be really hot where they're going?"

"Oh my Heavens, what on Earth would they…" Mrs B started. And then she stopped and sighed. "Ay, you may be right. They might find some use. We dinnae have much else to give them, the poor souls. Best pop them in."

*

From the woodshed, Paranoid Dave watched through the window as Jaakko propped the log back up on the bench from which it had been shot, and then signal to Toby to move five yards further back for his next shot.

"Do you think Toby will actually need to use that, Professor?" Paranoid Dave asked. "I mean, seriously?"

"Ah yes, no. Not at all. I'm sure you'll both be fine, hmm?" the Professor replied from above. He was at the top of the library steps. "Now, shall we return to the dials?"

"Definitely. The dials. Let's do it."

While Toby was learning to shoot outside, and Mrs B was assembling the equipment with Charlie in the log cabin, the Professor was in the woodshed with Paranoid Dave, giving him a lesson in how to fly a 3rd generation teleportation device in the 7th dimension. Paranoid Dave walked back up to the top of the steps and knelt down next to him in front of the small, padded bench. It had been hinged back to reveal the gleaming set of brass controls.

The Professor reached into his jacket pocket and produced the leather-bound course notebook.

"Now, here at the back, I've jotted down the settings needed for some of the most obvious locations." The Professor pointed at a lengthy and rather mysterious set of coordinates in the notebook. "For example, here are the coordinates for the hyperspaceport on Za-Nak, you see?"

"OK..." Paranoid Dave replied cautiously. "That's where we're travelling first, right? To drop you guys off?"

"Correct. But where you and Tobias are going after that..." the Professor tilted his head to peer at Paranoid Dave over the top of his half-moon spectacles, "...I don't know the settings, you see? Yes. Yes, I've never been. Not many people have. Not in the last few decades. So..." The Professor pushed his spectacles up to the bridge of his nose and turned back to the dials, "we're going to have to guess."

38

As he came to, the first thing Toby became aware of was the smell. Not so much a smell as a stench – a cloying vapour that coated his mouth and throat like a thin film of oil.

The second was quickness of breath. He was heaving fast, shallow breaths of this vapour into his lungs. *Only fifteen percent oxygen*, Mrs B had told him.

And then gravity. He tried to stand up, and slumped straight back onto the steps. He was thirty percent heavier than on Earth.

Ph'Estoun.

And that was the good part.

The bad part were the scavengers. The outlaws and fugitives Mrs B told him about, who came to Ph'Estoun because it was the one place where no-one would follow them. No-one sane anyway.

And the really bad part was *where* they'd landed: on a hillside. On a boggy, exposed, uncluttered hillside. They were about as visible as it's possible to be within the faintly misty air of Ph'Estoun.

Damn.

Toby looked up at Paranoid Dave, who was lying next to the bench, still unconscious. Toby forced himself to his feet, and nervously scanned the landscape below him for any signs of movement. He reckoned he could see about a mile, maybe two.

Directly below the hill and to the right, maybe a few hundred yards away, were buildings. The former mining settlement, that looked more or less like Mrs B had described. A town of broken, charred, derelict buildings that stretched away into the mist. Away off to the right, he could just make out a cluster of towers, each with a huge winch at the top, like you would see above a coalmine. All was still and lifeless.

He looked to the left. He could see what looked to be a sort of forest. Its trees, if that's what you could call them, were starting to envelop the town at the edge.

And beyond all of them – beyond the forest, beyond the town, disappearing in the mist – he could see a swamp. *The* swamp.

Toby gave an involuntary shudder. The place gave him the creeps. Just like Mrs B said it would.

"Obdurite."

"Eh?"

"Obdurite," Paranoid Dave repeated, rubbing his eyes, and sitting up. "The Professor told me all about it."

"What about it?"

"Ph'Estoun was apparently its richest source. Still is, technically. They mined the obscurium here, refined it, smelted it, sold the obdurite for gazillions, and…" Paranoid Dave nodded towards the swamp, "…dumped the spoil in the lake. Didn't quite land us in the right spot, did I?"

"Hey? Oh… Yeah. It's not perfect. But we can manage."

"We were supposed to land next to the swamp. In – out – job done. *Damn it.* Now instead, we have a set of beautifully polished Edwardian library steps materialising elegantly on the crest of a hill, visible to every—"

"Dave!" Toby interrupted him and placed a hand on his arm. "We've done our best. We'll just have to adapt. Ph'Estoun time is running about sixty times faster than Earth, remember? I'll go first, you stay here to guard the steps. Once I'm done, we switch. We've got enough time. OK?" Toby paused and Paranoid Dave nodded. "Good. You got the binoculars?"

Paranoid Dave held up the Professor's pair of antique field glasses, which was hanging round his neck. He heaved himself up onto the small red leather bench, collapsing his large bulk onto it.

"Wow… Gravity's the big winner on this planet," he grunted, as he sucked in a deep lungful of fetid air. "And you – you got the Professor's gun?"

Toby nodded and reached into his jacket pocket. He pulled out the Professor's old service revolver. It was now as heavy as lead, literally.

Toby took a moment to compose himself. *They had to make this work.* He made his way down the steps, his legs shaking slightly from the effort, and stood poised on the bottom step. He looked down to check he was wearing the gumboots Mrs B had given him – he was – and planted his foot onto Ph'Estoun for the first time. The boggy ground yielded beneath his boot, releasing a small, sulphurous belch.

Toby paused to scan the surroundings. The stillness of the scene was as uncanny as the smell. Toby turned back behind. Paranoid Dave was already holding the field glasses to his eyes.

"Can you see anything? Any movement?" Paranoid Dave asked.

"Not a thing."

"Nor me," he replied, lowering the field glasses. "Then go for it. And good luck."

Toby nodded. He sucked his boot out of the mud and took his first effortful step towards the derelict buildings, towards the swamp beyond. Toby felt horribly exposed as he squelched heavily over the boggy ground. Progress was sluggish. And yet he dreaded reaching the derelict buildings.

After a couple of hundred yards, the ground became firmer underfoot. Toby found he was on the crumbling remains of what must have been a paved surface. Dry ground. In an attempt at running, he lumbered forward and pressed himself up against the corner of an old warehouse. Just beyond, a street stretched downhill towards the swamp.

Toby turned back to look at the library steps. He could see Paranoid Dave still scanning the area with the field glasses. Toby waved at him. Paranoid Dave lowered the field glasses and raised his thumb. *All clear*.

Toby broke cover and started running – lumbering – down the street as fast as he could, the Ph'Estoun mud gradually being shaken from his boots. He could see the forest wasn't just surrounding the town, it was attacking from within. Tangled, stumpy trees – all branch and no leaf – were thrusting up through the pavements and through the road. He could see more trees piercing through roofs and out of windows; he could see walls fractured and displaced, leaning against the trees that were attacking them. Whole buildings were being propped up by the very things that were making them collapse.

After reaching the end of the block, Toby drew up

against another wall. He leant over, hands on knees, panting heavily, and wanting to wretch. Best of all, a splitting headache had come on hard and fast. He turned to look back, but Paranoid Dave was no longer in view. And nor was his destination.

Toby was in the town proper. He was on his own.

He pulled out again from his cover and started down the street again. At least it was downhill. He shifted left and right to avoid the trees, jumping clumsily over the ruptured road surface where the roots were thrusting through. The road started bending round to the right. As Toby followed it, the swamp came back into view, much closer this time. Toby ducked into an open doorway and – before he had time to check the building he had entered – collapsed down onto his knees, breathless.

After a moment or two, something next to his knee caught his eye. It was yellow and dusty with age. It looked like… Like some kind of plastic space rocket. It was a toy, a child's toy. He looked around. There were aisles and shelves, half-collapsed and mostly empty, but with some stock still visible. He was in a toy shop. A toy shop on Ph'Estoun. It made Toby shudder for no reason he could put his finger on.

He looked out through the broken window. Ahead he could see the swamp, stretching away into the mist. There were a few branches poking out, and some kind of wispy, brownish plant was growing over the top of it. He squinted, searching the shoreline for the pier that the Professor had promised. In the dull grey light, he could just make it out. It was a derelict wooden thing, sitting low to the swamp surface. There was still just enough of it standing to do what Toby needed it to do.

He strained his eyes and strained his ears for any

hint of movement or noise. Still nothing, thank God.

OK...

Just another hundred yards to go. Toby pulled himself back to his feet and stepped out through the doorway.

This time he didn't run.

Staying close to the buildings on one side of the street, he edged his way towards the swamp and towards the pier.

*

Paranoid Dave kept the field glasses pinned to his face. He scanned the hillside and the edge of the forest.

Nothing.

Then he turned towards the swamp. That's when Toby came back into view, just a yard now from the start of the pier. Even at this distance, he could see Toby's movements were hesitant as he stepped onto the dilapidated wooden structure.

Paranoid Dave scanned along the pier and onto the lakefront road. Nothing else was moving. He slowly swung to the right until he could see the warehouse that Toby had first reached.

Still nothing.

So far, all clear.

He was about to check the forest again when something caught his eye. He trained the field glasses back on the lakefront road. Something moved. It might've been nothing, just a trick of the light. It was at the farthest end of his field of view.

He adjusted the focus. He tried to locate it again, without success until...

There – again.

Movement.

Something – someone – was darting between the buildings.

And also over there. Something else was moving.

And over there. Several blocks *behind* Toby, a third movement. This time he got a clearer glimpse. A creature was scuttling along the road, keeping low against the warehouses but very clearly following Toby's path towards the pier.

Paranoid Dave followed it carefully with his field glasses, until *another* movement distracted him from the corner of his eye. A couple of creatures were darting out of the forest.

Paranoid Dave felt sick to his stomach. The whole lakefront had come alive with a furtive scurrying and scuttling, like they had disturbed some old, rotten log and the insects were scattering.

Only these creatures weren't fleeing. Five, six, maybe more of them were *converging* on Toby. It was like they were in league together, as if some hidden signal had been sent between them. In no more than a minute or two these scavengers would reach the pier and any escape route for Toby would be cut off. He trained the field glasses on Toby again. He was edging forward along the pier, oblivious to the danger behind.

With the scavengers gathering behind, the only way off the pier would be the swamp. And that meant certain death.

Paranoid Dave made a quick decision.

He flung back the bench he'd been sitting on. He had only seconds to make a quick calculation, and then only one shot at it. No second chance. He twisted two of the dials by the tiniest degree, somehow keeping his hands steady as he did so. He turned a third dial through 180 degrees. He flicked a couple of switches. Paranoid Dave looked up momentarily at the lifeless grey mantle of poorly illuminated cloud that formed the only weather that was ever seen on Ph'Estoun, mumbled the briefest of prayers, and pulled the brass lever at the centre of the controls.

*

Toby edged cautiously forward along the pier. The boards creaked perilously with each step. He stumbled momentarily but regained his footing. He drew in a breath and pressed forward.

He reached the end of the pier.

No further to go.

The swamp here should be deep enough. Toby knelt down and started to roll up the sleeves on his left arm. As he did so, he felt the hairs on the back of his neck go up on end. A sense of dread was creeping up his spine.

He turned round, and that's when he saw one of them.

One of the scavengers.

His eyes fixed onto it. It stopped, reared onto its hind legs and stared back. Toby and the creature were frozen in a look of pitiful empathy just for a moment. Then it lurched forward onto all four legs and started sprinting across the last twenty yards to the foot of the pier. The violent movement was a signal to the others. Six or more scavengers broke cover all along the lakefront and started hurtling forward, converging on the same point. Scavengers of all descriptions – two-legged, four-legged, even an eight-legged alien.

Toby's brain froze. He raised his gun, but the

revolver was shaking so violently, he couldn't aim at anything.

He took a step forward with his right leg to try to steady himself, but as he did so, his leg sheared clean through a broken plank. Toby suddenly found himself flat on the deck, his right leg dangling helplessly just above the swamp, while his left was splayed out awkwardly to the side. He was jammed in between the two solid planks either side, barely able to move. The revolver had slipped from his hand and was balanced precariously at the edge of the pier, a foot out of reach.

Toby looked back down the pier. The scavengers had reached the far end. Their combined bulk filled the full width of the pier. They knew their prey was trapped. Their advance was slow now, and menacing.

Toby's situation was hopeless. Certain death lay in front, it lay behind, and it lay beneath him.

It was suddenly so simple. Everything hinged on *now*.

It wasn't supposed to, but it did.

There was no suspense anymore, no more dread, no more waiting. His own life must surely end – but Paranoid Dave still had a chance. Here, in the pestilential bog of Ph'Estoun, the Earth had never felt so worthwhile, and Dave had just become its last chance. This was his story, Dave's story, and Toby suddenly saw the part he had to play. He had to reach that gun, he had to shoot as many of the scavengers as possible. If he killed enough, Dave still had a chance.

A lifetime of doubts and hesitations faded away and, in the eye of the crisis, a moment of pure lucidity descended on Toby.

Jammed in between the planks as he was, he looked at the revolver, twelve inches beyond his reach. He would have to take it in one clean grasp. The slightest nudge and it would topple into the swamp. A strange power surged through Toby and, with a strength he didn't know he had, he levered himself forward with his left arm. At the same time he threw his right arm up into the air, forced his body to move a foot forward, and landed his hand directly on the revolver's grip. He grasped it gratefully and levelled the revolver at the advancing creatures in one swift, unhesitating movement.

Still jammed between the planks, Toby took aim at the largest target. He flicked the safety catch off. As he pulled back on the hammer, his hand was steady, the gun felt light.

He squeezed the trigger.

Crack!

The revolver bucked in his hand. The deafening noise of the gunshot ricocheted off the derelict buildings, and the creature on the far right of the group toppled screaming into the swamp.

One bullet fired, five left.

The remaining scavengers stopped momentarily in their tracks to assess this new risk. Toby took the opportunity to fire again – *Crack!* – and another one collapsed lifeless onto the decking. The surviving scavengers realised their error and surged forward with a wild desperation. They knew their best chance was to overrun Toby as quickly as possible.

Toby did a quick count: there were still six alive. He couldn't hit them all, not with his four remaining bullets.

It didn't matter. He raised the revolver again, steadier than ever, and took aim at the next one.

Crack!

Another scavenger slumped dead.

There was very little time now. They were just twenty yards from him. He took aim a fourth time – squeezed – and a fourth scavenger bucked and fell. And then very quickly he shot again – it was impossible to miss now – and another went down.

One bullet left, but it was all over for Toby. The lead scavenger was just ten yards away. He could maybe knock that one out, but there were two more coming up just behind.

But Toby never got to take his final shot.

Just as his finger was about to squeeze on the trigger, his arm was thrown wide. His whole body was shaken by a thundering vibration in the pier, while a strange groaning, rending noise echoed through the air.

On the far side of the scavengers, maybe twenty yards away, he saw something materialise on the pier.

It was the library steps.

In a single fluid movement, just as the steps appeared, Paranoid Dave bounded off them. It was a miraculous movement. Paranoid Dave seemed to jump even as he was materialising – like he had started to run down the steps before they had even left the hillside.

Toby watched awestruck as Paranoid Dave landed on the pier and ran headlong at the scavengers from behind, weaponless, screaming and flailing his arms like a madman.

And then a fist – or a paw, or a foot, or a blunt weapon – Toby never got to see – landed on his face, and he passed out clean.

Oblivion.

Again.

39

Biffa walked nervously up and down the empty conference suite, checking every place setting with anxious precision.

The chairs had been chosen carefully. A very low seat with four armrests for this investor. One with a high neck rest for that investor, and a basket behind to curl his tail. One chair was inside a glass tank of water.

Woola watched Biffa from the corner of the room, looking slightly bored. His elbow was propped up on the edge of his aquapod and he was resting his head on his flipper, blowing a few idle soap bubbles into the conference suite. He couldn't wait to get off Golgotha and back home to Za-Nak. This planet was just so joyless. His digits tapped compulsively to the tune of *Scotland the Brave*, which he couldn't get out of his head.

"What are you staring at? Hey, you!" Biffa barked at him. "Why don't you do something useful? Go check the presentation deck is working OK!" The terrible thing about the future, Biffa had learnt to his cost, is that technology is just as apt to glitch there as it is in the present.

"OK, OK…" Woola replied bolshily, as his aquapod glided to the front of the conference suite. "Glmm tring chachala vling, vrang-sang," he muttered under his breath. (*Keep your hair on, Grandad.*)

Woola pressed a button on the lectern. High up, in the centre of the room, a small holographic image of the Earth flickered to life. As it rotated slowly on its axis, a huge image of a Za-Nakarian holiday maker appeared beneath it. The Za-Nakarian was reclining in a gleaming bronze aquapod – head back, a pair of jet-black shades on his nose, and a drink in one flipper. The bronze aquapod had a fetching pair of silver stripes running all the way round it.

"*Lala-luuuuuuu!*" Woola exhaled appreciatively (*Ni-iiice!*)

"Quit fooling around! Get back to the first slide." Biffa barked. "The investors will be arriving any moment."

Woola clicked another button, muttering under his breath, and a holographic image of the Solar System materialised.

*

A few minutes later and the investors were filing into the conference suite in a steady stream.

They were an impatient and surprisingly dishevelled-looking rabble. Biffa stood at the door with an obsequious smile on his face, exchanging unpleasantries as they entered.

"Hello!… Nice to see you again, how are the wives and kid?… Ah, they're starting to eat each other? That's too bad… Hello! Yes, this way, please come in… Hello again, how are you?"

"**** off!"

"Of course I will, just as soon as the presentation is over. Your seat is over there… Hello, this way, please!… *Oh, it's you two.*"

Biffa pulled up short, looking even more tense than before.

The Vort twins had just stomped into the room. Rakemore Telfer's neighbours from the trading floor. They were hulking, gorilla-sized creatures; they were so strong, even their muscles had muscles. The first one paused in front of Biffa and looked at him like breakfast. He leaned forward menacingly close to Biffa and, reaching with his left paw, took hold of Biffa's cheeks. He closed his digits and Biffa's lips protruded comically.

"Aww, would you look at that cute liddle face?" the creature boomed in a mock baby voice. Everyone in the room stopped and looked. "It's my fave-wit liddle fwend fwom Wakemore Telfer."

"Hello Dor-Vort," Biffa squeaked.

"Has my teeny liddle fwend got a teeny liddle planet to sell today? Hmm? Has he? Aww, you're such a sweet liddle puddy cat!" Dor-Vort said, squeezing a little harder.

Biffa's eyes bulged in their sockets and swivelled towards his two minders, who were standing either side of the main entrance. He jerked his head in a gesture that clearly indicated now was the moment to come and save him.

Only they didn't. They stayed exactly where they were and folded their arms.

"Now would you look at that? My liddle fwend wants his big fwends to come and wescue him. Isn't that the sweetest thing, Vor-Dort?" he added, addressing his twin.

"There's just one problem," Dor-Vort continued, abruptly dropping the baby voice. "Our company bought their company and, hey presto, suddenly I own those guys. Isn't life strange?"

Dor-Vort moved his grip from Biffa's face to his throat instead. He proceeded to lift Biffa bodily off the ground with a single arm. His muscles rippled under the brown matted hair.

"Get this," Dor-Vort continued. "I didn't sleep last night. Nor did Vor-Dort. We were up all night for the auction. And this morning, we've been trading our position. We've torn strips out of Aranoid. We've already made fifty billion, *net*. It's been profitable, it's been exciting. But now we've broken off from that to come to your little auction. So to summarise…"

Dor-Vort lifted Biffa even higher, straightening his arm to full extension. Biffa was now so high, the holographic image of Uranus spread in a grey arc across the middle of his tortured face.

"…we're tired, we're grumpy, we're even richer than before, but not as rich as we could be. So your itsy-bitsy little IPO better be worthwhile. You hear me liddle puddy cat?" Dor-Vort said, resuming his baby voice.

"Yeees," Biffa squeaked.

"You suckers better have left some upside for investors. Because, if you haven't, liddle puddy cat is gonna learn just how high—"

Dor-Vort suddenly released Biffa, who fell to the floor with a sickening thud.

"—a dead cat can bounce," Dor-Vort concluded, dusting his paws against each other.

He ostentatiously stepped on Biffa's wounded frame as he made his way to a seat in the front row.

His twin, Vor-Dort, leaned down, picked Biffa up by his collar, set him on his feet, and went to join his brother. Biffa looked around to see all the investors' tired, fidgety eyes turned on him with a slightly, but not particularly, surprised expression.

"Hahaha!" Biffa laughed sycophantically, holding up his unsprained wrist to point at Dor-Vort. "He's an old friend. We love joking."

*

As Toby came back round, his eyelids blinked into the open position, and then blinked straight back shut again. The light hurt. He winced with pain, as a fierce headache started settling in behind his eyes. His hand went up automatically to the side of his head, where he felt a large lump under his hair.

He tried to muster his thoughts.

Where am I?

What just happened?

"You're probably wondering where you are and what just happened?" a voice said to him, slightly God-like.

"As a matter of fact I am," Toby replied automatically, thinking how much his head was hurting.

"And your head probably hurts?" the voice said, obligingly.

"As a matter of fact it does."

"I can make that pain go away," the God-like voice continued. "That was quite a blow you took, young man. But we're off Ph'Estoun now, so you're—"

"Ph'Estoun!" Toby's body shot bolt upright like an electrocuted corpse. His hand thrashed around for the Professor's revolver, which it found in his jacket pocket. *Scavengers.* Toby looked around wild-eyed for danger.

"Hey, hey, hey – easy now – put that thing away. You've still got a bullet left."

Toby looked up to see Paranoid Dave a couple of steps above him, gesturing for calm.

"Please don't shoot me, Jeez, I don't deserve it..." Paranoid Dave continued "...not after what I've done for you."

"Oh sorry," Toby replied sheepishly, starting to calm down. As he looked around, he could see they were in some kind of hospitality suite. It was a little bit glitzy. It didn't look at all like Ph'Estoun.

"Painkillers?"

"Thanks."

"They've certainly worked for me – so far," Paranoid Dave said, as he dropped two pills into Toby's outstretched hand.

"Where are we?" Toby asked, as he popped the pills in his mouth.

"We're on Golgotha – at the Inter-Planetary Exchange. And we're still on track, more or less."

"What... What happened? I sort of expected I might be..."

"Dead?"

"Yes."

"You gave it your best shot," Paranoid Dave replied. "I reached the pier in the nick of time. And in just the right spot, which was a small miracle."

"That was skill."

"No, it was a miracle."

"But how did you beat the scavengers?" Toby asked. "You didn't even have a gun. *That* must have been a miracle."

"No, that bit was simple. I just bundled them into

the swamp. Come on, I rushed them from behind, on a set of library steps that had popped out of nowhere. It was a cakewalk. They were so confused, they'd have probably tied my shoelaces if I'd asked them. Anyway, here we are," Paranoid Dave continued, reclining against the bannister, stretching his left arm out to steady himself, "back at the Inter-Planetary— *Aaaargh!*"

He broke off, crying with pain.

"*Damn*, shouldn't have leant on that…"

Toby watched as Paranoid Dave cradled his left arm in his lap. He had been mid-way through bandaging it. Blood from a wound had seeped through and left a dark red ring in the white cloth. Gingerly, Paranoid Dave wound the remainder of the bandage around his arm. Gripping the loose end of the adhesive tape in his teeth, he picked up a pair of scissors in his right hand and cut the tape. He pulled the tape fast around his forearm, screwing his forehead with pain. Once it was secure, he leaned back against the steps, panting, a thin film of sweat on his brow.

"Did you… Did you manage to…"

"Yes. Yes I did. Here on the forearm." Paranoid Dave weakly raised his bandaged arm.

"A catfish?"

"Yes."

"And me… Am I?" Toby looked down at his legs.

"No. That's the crazy thing. They didn't want you," Paranoid Dave replied. The bravado had left his voice now. "After I pushed the scavengers into the swamp, there was a feeding frenzy. God, it was horrible. I just had to dip my arm in, and one of them immediately… *Urgh.* But as for you, with your plump, dangling leg? They weren't interested."

"Right…" said Toby, trying to take everything in. "So only one of us is infected."

"Right. Only one of us. What do we do?"

"I'm not sure. This wasn't exactly the plan," Toby replied, pulling the Professor's relativity watch from his pocket and toying with it in his hands. He tried to think what the Professor would advise right now.

"How long have I got before symptoms start to show?" Paranoid Dave asked.

"Mrs B said an hour after the initial bite…"

"…which probably means about half an hour from now? Or does the time difference on Ph'Estoun affect the calculation?"

"No," Toby replied, looking at the watch again. "What matters is time *as we experience it*. The Professor explained it. So symptoms in half an hour from now, then you become infectious another two hours after that."

"So by then I have to get back to Za-Nak, back to the Personalitron and back into my real body?"

"Correct. Unless of course you want to infect the whole of Golgotha *and* Za-Nak," Toby replied. "And die in the process."

"Not particularly."

"I thought not."

"Right then," Paranoid Dave continued, "we better get on with it. We better find Biffa?"

"Sure…" Toby replied. "But not until we have a plan."

"Well we had a plan. We were both supposed to get infected. How do we carry it through with only one?"

"That, David, is a very good question," Toby replied. "Really."

Toby stood up and immediately felt light-headed as

the pain behind his eyes throbbed back to life. He steadied himself with a hand against the bannister, then walked slowly down the steps and round to the side of them. He ran his hand carefully along the lowest board. He found the small catch he was looking for and a panel in the side of the steps sprang open.

"How do we carry through this plan with only one of us infected?" Toby muttered to himself as he started rifling through the clothes and others bits that Mrs B and Charlie had packed for them.

"Hey, what are you doing down there," Paranoid Dave said, trying to peer down between the bannisters. "What are you up to?"

"I'm trying to ask the right question..." Toby said in a distracted voice, as he sifted through their belongings. He fastened on Paranoid Dave's pair of floral beach shorts and stared at them with a strange intensity.

"Hang on, I recognise that look," Paranoid Dave said. "You've thought of something, haven't you?"

Toby didn't reply.

"What is it?" Paranoid Dave persisted. "What are you doing?"

"Hmm? What am I doing?" Toby replied, as he continued to stare at the beach shorts. "I'm improvising."

40

Biffa mopped a thin film of sweat from his brow.

He and Woola had been going the best part of an hour. They had covered the whole prospectus. Woola had started them off with his usual charm act, covering the attractions of planet Earth – the untapped minerals, the stable weather, docile population, and what was commonly known by planetary investors as the "triple tick".

Oxygen at about 20% – *tick.*

Gravity at about $10m/s^2$ – *tick.*

Relative time within +/–1.5x Standard Universal Time – *tick.*

Woola had handed over to Biffa to do the dull-but-important regulatory bits. The Endangered Indigenous Aliens plan (EIA) and all the other stuff necessary to keep the do-gooders happy, and lull the investors into a nice, sleepy sense that Rakemore Telfer had everything nicely covered.

Which was basically true.

Rakemore Telfer *did* have everything covered.

The investors had lapped up the lush holograms of tropical glades glistening, beaches sparkling, and ice-sheets calving. They were in the perfect place for the final phase of the presentation: the financials.

Biffa had presented the forecast profits of "Za-

Nakarian Resort 987 plc", as they had re-named Earth. He had shown them boring tables and seductive graphs, he had shown them pie charts, bar charts, and histograms – all of which demonstrated irrefutably that, despite the occasional dip (inserted into the forecasts to make them look realistic), this was an investment that was going to go up and up and up.

Only another couple of slides to go. Then there would be some questions, which would probably involve more humiliation from Dor-Vort and his grotesque twin, but that didn't matter, because the auction bell would ring in thirty minutes and after that, it was done.

The *quadrillions* would roll in.

98% to the Za-Nakarians, 2% to Rakemore Telfer.

And the best thing about two percent? It was low enough to keep the spotlight off Rakemore Telfer, but high enough to mean wealth beyond extravagance. Two percent of quadrillions equals *trillions*. Not bad for one average, middling-sized deal on the IPE.

And what was even better than Rakemore Telfer earning trillions from this deal? Biffa's own two percent bonus. Because two percent of trillions still equals *billions*. Lots of billions. This was Biffa's first IPO, and it was his own planet, and he was about to become one of the richest humans who had ever lived.

Biffa's attention wandered.

As one half of his brain droned through his discounted cashflow model, the other half was cherishing those *billions*. Biffa would be coming back to planet Earth and he would be letting everyone know exactly how rich he was. Not for him, the quiet retiring existence of the modest billionaire. No way. Biffa was going to buy himself fame, he was going to buy himself power and, above all, he was going to buy himself *love*. His philanthropy would be legendary. His new foundation for curing some-disease-or-other would be the best funded in the world, his pop star friends would be the most popular in the world.

A small smile sneaked into the corner of Biffa's lips as he continued to drone at the investors.

"...and as you can see, we can look forward to an acceleration in free cashflow up to Year 30. We conservatively forecast that climatic disturbance costs then start to increase, leading to probable abandonment of the resort by Year 40. At that point the mineral strip can commence, and finally the atmosphere suck. This creates a small but helpful uptick in the final years of our DCF model..."

*

"...that brings us to the conclusion of today's presentation," Biffa intoned. "Are there any questions?"

"God that was boring!" Dor-Vort boomed, rubbing his eyes. He turned to his twin. "What did you think of it, Vor-Dort?"

Vor-Dort muttered back. The twins briefly debated the issue in their own dialect.

"Vor-Dort says it's persuasive. He says we should do it," Dor-Vort said. "But you know what I think?"

"What do you think, Dor-Vort?"

"I think you're slimy, I think you're ugly and I don't trust you."

"I am slimy, Dor-Vort, I am. And ugly too," Biffa replied. "Even so, the IPO?"

"We're in," Dor-Vort replied casually. He leant

back and swung his legs onto the desk. "We'll be taking ten percent of the opening tranche at the strike price."

Biffa put on his serious, responsible face, and inclined his head in acknowledgement to each of the twins.

But inside Biffa was laughing.

He was rejoicing, he was jubilating, he was high-fiving himself. He was dancing a little jig, and clapping his feet together in mid-air to the tune of *Singin' in the Rain*. If the Vort twins were in, the others would follow. They knew the investment was now protected by a couple of the nastiest creatures in the financial universe.

"Thank you. Are there any other questions?" he said, maintaining a magnificently unsurprised tone. Around the room the investors were nodding approvingly to each other.

Nearly there, Biffa thought to himself, *nearly there.*

"No more questions?" Biffa said, successfully imitating the solicitous but slightly bored tone of a lecturer who doesn't expect any questions because there's really nothing to question. "In which case, the investor presentation has now come to a conclu—"

"Oh, are we late? I hope we're not late?"

There was a scuffling sound behind Biffa's left shoulder.

He turned to see two horribly familiar figures. The Professor's friends, the clowns – looking even more clown-ish than usual. Both were still wearing the floral beach shorts and shirt Biffa had organised for them on Za-Nak. But now they were both wearing a bright red cape as well.

"Who are these schmucks?" Dor-Vort barked.

"Err, they are the err… That's to say, the err…" Biffa stuttered.

"We're your entertainment package," Toby interrupted helpfully. "To conclude the presentation, we're here to show you what the simple, grateful folk of planet Earth are like and to show you a few of our local customs."

Toby swept his cape back as he took a deep theatrical bow before his audience, in the manner of a wandering minstrel at the start of his show. He crossed one leg elegantly in front of the other, he swept both his arms wide, and bowed his head almost to his knee.

"I think you'll find us…" Toby resumed, as he stood back up. "No, you say. How will these smart, sophisticated people find us, Barnabas?"

"Derr… Umm…" Paranoid Dave looked at Toby with a big dumb, uncomprehending expression on his face. "Derr… *Quaint?*"

"That's right, Barnabas!" Toby clapped his hands with delight. "Quaint!"

"Huh, huh, huh!" Paranoid Dave let out a braying laugh, his shoulders heaving up and down with the noise. As his face creased in laughter, a livid red boil just above his lip bulged uncomfortably.

"Are these guys for real?" Dor-Vort barked. "What the Hell's going on here?"

He looked round the room. Biffa's face was gurning in an awkward smile, like this was all part of his plan. Some of the investors were starting to snigger.

"Let's hear them out, Dor-Vort," a watery, electronic voice boomed out from a speaker. It was the investor in the water tank. "This'll be a laugh."

"Grng ya la-la," Toby said in his worst Za-Nakarian towards the water tank. "*Thank you.* We're also here to say how much the people of Earth are looking forward to welcoming you to our humble planet."

Toby took another bow, even deeper and more sycophantic than the one before.

"Bow, Barnabas, bow," Toby hissed from somewhere below his own knee.

With an idiot grin on his face, Paranoid Dave put a hand on either side of his beach shorts, pulled them outwards, and bobbed up and down in a curtsy.

"Now!" Toby clapped his hands. "My friend Barnabas would like to share with you some of the local delicacies that we have brought with us, wouldn't you Barnabas? Barnabas? What are you... Where are you going? Barnabas! Come back here... BARNABAS!"

Paranoid Dave had lolloped clumsily towards one of the desks and picked up a translation earpiece, which he was staring at in dumb fascination. When Toby barked at him, he panicked and popped the earpiece in his mouth. He turned round to stare at Toby with wide, nervous eyes.

"Barnabas, give that back AT ONCE!"

Slowly, nervously, Paranoid Dave dropped the earpiece from his lips onto his open palm. He placed the saliva-drenched article back in front of the investor, who stared at it with seven degrees of disgust.

"Barnabas – concentrate, please. The delicacies!"

Paranoid Dave timidly pulled a small backpack from his shoulders and passed it to Toby.

"Thank you, Barnabas, that's better," Toby said, before turning to the investors. "Ladies, Gentlemen, alien beings of the Universe – we are now going to serve you with the rarest delicacies of the Earthling diet. First of all, I present to you..." Toby announced, as he pulled out the first item and held it up, "the potato crisp!"

It was the bag of crisps from the Squirrel & Acorn, that had been half the way round the Universe with him.

"And now…" said Toby, pulling out the second item, "the exquisite toffee!"

It was Paranoid Dave's half-eaten pack of toffees.

Lastly, Toby pulled out a small stack of paper plates. He passed them all to Paranoid Dave.

"Serve our guests, please Barnabas."

Paranoid Dave enthusiastically took the items from Toby and lumbered across to the first investor. He put one of the plates down and placed a toffee on it and then a single crisp. He gave a short, braying laugh of delight, licked saliva from his fingers and moved onto the next desk.

"Well that's very helpful, you two, thank you," Biffa said, trying to regain control of his meeting. "Now if we could resume the present… I mean if we could conclude the presentation… I mean if we could—"

"Shut up, Biffa," Dor-Vort butted in. "Tell me why this idiot is looking so bloody unhealthy? What's wrong with him?"

All eyes turned to Paranoid Dave. He looked up and gave a big imbecilic smile, and continued to give a single crisp and a single toffee to each investor.

"There's nothing wrong with him…" Biffa replied hopelessly, having not the faintest idea what was going on. "But now you mention it—"

"Actually, he does have a minor ailment," Toby continued. "He has a fever, but it's not yet contagious, so all should be well. Barnabas – please continue."

Paranoid Dave arrived at Dor-Vort's seat.

"Just a minute – stop right there!" Dor-Vort held up a hairy, muscular paw. He leaned forward to examine him more closely.

Paranoid Dave grinned gormlessly and held out a single, rather unappetising crisp. Dor-Vort looked at it with reluctant fascination, the way people look at gross-out pictures even when they don't want to. His paw reached out and took the crisp from Paranoid Dave. And then Dor-Vort looked again at Paranoid Dave. The boil above his upper lip looked ripe and puce against the sweaty pallor of his complexion.

"Do all humans look this gross?" Dor-Vort boomed with disgust. "I mean, I know Biffa is unusually ugly, but at least he's not covered in boils."

Biffa smiled awkwardly.

"Quite right, Dor-Vort, I am obscene. But no boils. Let me have them ejected."

Biffa gestured to his two minders. The two thugs at the side of the room stood up and started walking across.

"Well, perhaps that is sensible," Toby said soothingly. "This particular fever is new to us on Earth. I believe he isn't contagious yet, but safest is best."

"Hang on," Dor-Vort boomed, as the two minders advanced towards Paranoid Dave. "*Which* particular fever?"

"Hmm, which?" Toby repeated innocently. "Now what was it? I think the Doctor said… He seemed in such a hurry… What was it again? *Ph'Estoun Fever*, could that be it? Yes, yes, that *was* it."

The entire room went numb.

Toby might as well have opened the door and ushered in the Four Horsemen of the Apocalypse. In fact, as far as his audience was concerned, he had.

The two minders stopped exactly where they were. The audience froze. One investor's face was left contorted – upper jaw to the right, lower jaw to the left – with a toffee stretched in between.

"*W H A T ?* " boomed Dor-Vort.

Paranoid Dave looked slowly round the room, his mouth hanging open, his eyes baby-like and uncomprehending.

"Grab them! Eject them! Get them out of here! *Now!*" Biffa squeaked at the minders with high-pitched outrage.

The two minders looked at Biffa and shook their heads.

"You what? *You what?*" Biffa squeaked again. "You're FIRED!" The two minders merely shrugged their shoulders, but stayed planted to the spot. No-one seemed able to move, like they'd all stepped on a landmine, and merely to move would unleash Armageddon.

"I really don't think there's any need for these theatricals," Toby said to Biffa in a tone of gentlest rebuke.

"What the Hell is going on?" Dor-Vort boomed, looking with total disgust at the crisp he was still holding between his fingers.

"Well, it's quite simple," Toby replied, unphased. "A stray Carillion flea entered one of the Personalitrons that the Golgothans gave us to use—"

"*Personalitron?* They gave you a bit of junk like that?" Dor-Vort boomed, switching his gaze to Biffa.

"Oh yes, we're very grateful," Toby replied. "Well, we *were* grateful. Until this particular flea brought this… particular fever. That was rather unfortunate.

But it shouldn't be too serious, it's just a small outbreak, nothing for seasoned investors to—"

"How small?" Dor-Vort interrupted.

"Oh not too bad, all things considered," Toby replied. "The authorities have imposed a universal curfew. They are quite confident they can contain it on just four of the seven continents. So we're looking at perhaps a 50 to 75% mortality rate. Tourism from Za-Nak remains our priority of course. We estimate that can restart in – let's say – twenty Earth years from now?"

Toby paused for a second and looked sympathetically at Biffa.

"Your cashflow model might still work after that?" Toby said with parental kindness. "Provided, that is, that none of the endemic species develop immunity and continue to host the disease. I mean like the catfish on Ph'Estoun. Provided that doesn't happen, there's really nothing to worry about." Toby paused. "For twenty years… Or so."

"I don't believe you," Dor-Vort barked. "Is there a Medilator in this room?"

"Yes…" Biffa replied, "…YES!" He suddenly realised this was his chance to expose their ridiculous trick. "Yes, there's one in the first aid cupboard over there." Biffa pointed to the back of the hall.

"Get it."

"Of course," Biffa replied. He ran to the back of the room, passing between the motionless, terrified investors. He pulled a small white device from a cupboard and ran back. And as he ran, a little confidence returned. *This has to be a trick,* Biffa reasoned to himself, *it has to be.*

"Pull your sleeve up, *'Barnabas'*," Biffa barked at

Paranoid Dave.

Paranoid Dave, who was starting to feel nauseous and slightly faint, fumbled with his cuff. Before he knew it, Biffa had grabbed his sleeve and yanked it up his forearm. It revealed a large red boil that looked ripe to burst. But Biffa wasn't in the mood for any more deceit. He clamped his left hand around Paranoid Dave's forearm, and jabbed the Medilator, probes first, directly into the base of the boil.

The Medilator gave a series short beeps, and then a final, extended beep.

Biffa looked down at the display and read the diagnosis.

And then his universe crumbled.

His hopes, his dreams – *his career* – fled his body like a departing soul.

His face sagged and what little blood there was left in it drained clean away.

"So it's true," Dor-Vort said, looking at him.

Biffa nodded vacantly.

"Yes," Toby replied calmly. "But like I said, I don't believe Barnabas has reached the contagious stage. I really didn't want to bring an infected entertainer to this event, but there aren't many healthy ones left on Earth. We've still got two hours to get him back in the Personalitron. Please don't be alarmed."

Don't be alarmed.

The investors nearest the front heard a furtive rustling behind them. Looking behind they could see the back row had quietly, rapidly got up from their seats and were starting to edge their way from the room.

The remainder furtively glanced at each other. A couple of chairs squeaked against the floor a little louder than intended, as some of them tried to stand up unnoticed. Then a couple more. Dor-Vort threw the crisp away in front of him. The investor who had started chewing the toffee spat it out noisily, and started pulling desperately on the bits still clinging to his gums, giving little strangled yelps of panic as he did so. The investor who had been using the earpiece – the one which Paranoid Dave had chewed – pulled it out, threw it across the room and started screaming. All the investors under the flight path of the infected earpiece started screaming.

And then *all* the investors started screaming.

And running.

In the panic of the stampede, some of the investors found themselves bumping up against a bewildered Paranoid Dave, and started pushing him around between themselves in disgust and horror. Dor-Vort and Vor-Dort joined the stampede. They stopped for a second a few feet from Biffa.

"Trying to trick us were you?" Dor-Vort bellowed at Biffa above the noise. "Trying to palm off an infected planet at an inflated price? *You little worm.*"

"No, Dor-Vort, no!" Biffa pleaded. "I had no idea… What am I saying… It's not true. These are a pair tricksters. There's still time to stop the IPO and clear this up—"

"Stop the IPO? You must be kidding. Rules are rules. The bell will ring in five minutes from now. That gives me, and all the others, five minutes to get the word out. And believe you me, we *will* get the word out. We're going to make sure every investor from here to the Singularity has heard what you've tried to pull. Your IPO is *toast*," Dor-Vort boomed. "So is Rakemore Telfer and so – if I wasn't worried you might be infected – would you be!"

Dor-Vort's clenched fist arrived just a few inches from Biffa's face and hung there for a second, bulging and shaking, like a bull mastiff straining on its leash. Biffa stared at the fist, the face, *the fury*—

And promptly soiled himself.

Dor-Vort lingered a moment longer, then ran for the exit with his brother just behind, the room shuddering from the thump of their feet.

*

What no-one noticed in the melee was Toby quietly picking up the Medilator and following Dor-Vort out of the room, just a few feet behind.

*

When they saw Toby behind them, Vor-Dort and Dor-Vort instinctively stopped, backed up against the wall of the corridor and made menacing gestures at Toby.

Unphased, Toby disinfected the two probes of the Medilator. Then he pressed them against the skin of his forearm, and presented the display to the Vort twins. A single flashing green light gave the 'all clear'.

The Vort twins visibly relaxed.

"I think you and I need to talk," Toby said calmly.

"What do you have in mind," Dor-Vort asked warily.

"What do I have in mind?" Toby mused. "On our planet, we call it justice."

41

A deep bass rumble tumbled down from the sky.

It boomed through the streets of London, thunderous but not thunder. The sound pulsed louder and louder, before retreating again. It was like nothing of this world.

*...boom – Boom – BOOM – BOOM – **BOOM** – BOOM – BOOM – Boom – boom...*

Everyone knew it came from the spaceship that was gliding overhead. It shook Londoners to their conscience, as if God had just cleared his throat, and judgement was coming.

*

Seated next to his stall, Morley peered upwards at the spaceship. And then down at his watch: 10:30am. The thing had been gliding unhurriedly over his head for 30 minutes – and it was *still there*, stretching on and on, with the strange nozzles visible the entire length of it. Morley wasn't the anxious type, but he couldn't stop glancing at it, like some teenager obsessing about a pimple. And now as he looked, he heard – he *felt* – the deep rumble descend down from the Heavens and shake him to his core.

A few streets away, Seamus and Declan stopped

dead in their tracks as the rumbling started. They exchanged a brief glance, pulled their coats tighter around themselves and hurried onwards to the Squirrel & Acorn.

Before the doorway of that very tavern, the four remaining members of the TARP were paused anxiously as they looked up to the Heavens and listened to the rumbling.

*

*...boom – Boom – BOOM – BOOM – **BOOM** – BOOM – BOOM – Boom – boom...*

As they looked, to their horror, huge jets of gas violently burst from the nozzles all along the side of the spaceship. The gas jets were white-ish in colour, each one surging outwards to reach a couple of hundred yards from the spaceship before dispersing into the morning air. A second or two later the violent hissing sound of escaping gas reached them at ground level.

As they continued to watch the gas spurting from the spaceship, the remaining members of the TARP team, Seamus, Declan, Morley and all of London had the same thought.

Was the gas poisonous?

Was this how it was all going to end?

Was this how the story of humans on Earth was going to conclude, in a pall of poisonous gas released from the underside of a vast spaceship?

Here, today, *now?*

*

And then, as suddenly as they had started, the gas jets stopped.

*

The good folk of London couldn't know it yet, but what they had just witnessed was a Jagamath bulk carrier following standard protocols prior to unloading a gaseous cargo. And not just any carrier, but the flag carrier. It was clearing its vents, checking its expulsion motors, and preparing for the full discharge.

And it wasn't just happening in London. Synchronised to within a second, the same events were observed up and down the Greenwich meridian, and indeed under the three other orbital paths around the planet that the bulk carriers were following.

But even as the gas jets stopped – *temporarily* – the deep bass rumbling continued.

*...boom – Boom – BOOM – BOOM – **BOOM** – BOOM – BOOM – Boom – boom...*

42

Paranoid Dave breathed in deeply, counted to three, and exhaled slowly. The growing nausea he was feeling momentarily abated.

Very quietly, very gently he pushed on the door in front of him. It yielded to his touch. Pushing the door ajar, but no further, he leaned his head round the side to peer into the small, darkened room in front of him.

Paranoid Dave had good reason to be nervous.

He was at the backdoor to the Vort twins' office. They weren't people he wanted to bump into, not now they knew about his fever. As he looked in he could see their office was identical to the Rakemore Telfer office they had visited earlier. At the other end of the small room was a two-way mirror and a small door. Through the two-way mirror he could see the back of the Vort twins and, beyond them, the trading pit.

But strangely enough, it wasn't those figures who unnerved him. He could see two other silhouettes *inside* the office.

"Hello, dear, do come in. You're a wee bit late. We were worried you were going to miss the action."

"Mrs B…" Paranoid Dave leaned with one hand on the back of a chair, weakened by the shock. "You're supposed to be back on Za-Nak? What is it with you and surprise visits?"

"Don't make a fuss, dear. I've come to make sure you're ok."

"How did you even get here?"

"Oh, that was easy," the Professor replied. "We took the Bodytron from Za-Nak." He smiled genially, before leaning down and starting to fiddle with his leather briefcase.

"And then the Professor guided us to the closest booth to the Rakemore Telfer one," Mrs B continued. "Now please tell us, how did things go on Ph'Estoun, how... Oh my dear, you look terrible."

Mrs B stood up and started moving towards him.

"No, wait, wait," Paranoid Dave held up his hand. "Don't come any closer. I mean, I don't *think* I'll be infectious for another hour or so. According to our timings. But what if we're wrong?"

"Yes, I see," Mrs B said, as she reluctantly retreated. "If we're wrong, then we're likely to destroy life on one, possibly two, planets."

The two of them looked at each other with alarm.

They were distracted by a movement on the floor. They looked downwards.

It was Carruthers.

"Ah yes, you see," the Professor said, "my hedgehog. He's most reliable about these things..."

They watched as Carruthers calmly padded across the room towards Paranoid Dave and nudged his nose against Paranoid Dave's leg.

"...and it would appear that all is well, hmm?" the Professor smiled affably.

Paranoid Dave dropped effortfully, gratefully to his knees. Relief washed through him. He was amazed at how pleased he was to see the creature. "So I'm not infectious yet, eh Carruthers? Just as well." He gently stroked the hedgehog under his chin.

Paranoid Dave looked back up. "So where's Charlie? Didn't she come with you?"

"Actually, no," Mrs B replied. "She left us. She took the Personalitron to London. She was a wee bit mysterious about it actually. She said there was—"

"Ah, look!" the Professor interrupted, gesturing to the two-way mirror. "Trading has started!"

The three of them turned to watch the trading floor.

They looked first at the enormous display panel on the central tower. Scanning down the columns and columns of numbers, Paranoid Dave soon spotted it.

Planet Earth.

Trading in planet Earth had just opened on the Inter-Planetary Exchange on Golgotha.

There was a small neon image of a green and blue planet rotating next to some flashing red numbers. Most of it looked incomprehensible, written in Golgothan script. But like all the other planets being traded, two of the numbers were written in the local currency and the local language, English. One showed the stock price and one showed the market capitalisation – the total value of the planet.

"So dear, did the plan work? Did you get the word out?" Mrs B asked, peering at the numbers. "Do they believe the Earth is infected?"

"Yes, I think so."

"And so what's the plan from here?"

"Well that's the thing, Mrs B," Paranoid Dave replied. "I don't actually know."

"Well, whatever it is, it seems to be working," the Professor added.

"How? What do you mean?"

"Look. Look at the numbers, hmm? They're falling.

Rather fast."

And they were.

Paranoid Dave and Mrs B looked at the display panel.

£103trn

£103 trillion. A lot of money, but already a lot less than the quadrillions the Za-Nakarians had allegedly paid for the Earth.

£87trn flashed up and disappeared.

Then £83trn.

Blink

£80.5trn

Blink

£78.7trn

The price was tumbling faster than the screen could keep up.

Just a few yards ahead, Paranoid Dave could see the Vort twins trading furiously. They had jumped up onto the counter at the front of their booth and were yelling across the trading pit at the market-makers in the tower opposite.

"What are those two doing?" Paranoid Dave wondered out loud.

"Who are they?" Mrs B asked.

"A couple of the nastiest thugs in the IPE," Paranoid Dave replied. "And they just happen to own the office we're standing in. But what I don't get is why they're trading? I thought they wanted nothing to do with this IPO?"

The Vort twins clearly weren't getting the attention they wanted. While Dor-Vort started shaking his trunk-like arm in anger, Vor-Dort picked up a passing refreshments seller and hurled him at the tower.

"My God. They're *shorting* it. They're short-selling

shares in the Earth," Paranoid Dave quietly whistled. "Toby must've persuaded them, the clever, bloody rascal."

Paranoid Dave peered to his left. It was the Rakemore Telfer booth. He recognised their bright purple jackets. An eerie calm lay over them. No frenzied activity, no shouting, no hollering. Nothing. All of the traders were simply watching the stock price, hypnotized. Paranoid Dave followed their gaze and saw the numbers continuing to drop with each flash.

£38.3trn.

Blink

£31.2trn.

Blink

£20.9trn.

The descent was *accelerating*.

He looked around for Toby. In the confusion of the trading floor, with bodies pushing, tentacles waving, he couldn't see his friend. He looked back at the display panel.

£8.97trn

Blink

£5.01trn

Blink

£2.05trn.

Blink

£1.10trn

It was falling so fast, the value of the Earth was *halving* with every blink.

Paranoid Dave scanned the trading floor again. Still no sign of Toby. He looked back at the screen. The value had changed from trillions to billions.

£51.6bn

Blink

£5.05bn
Blink
£591m
Blink

The stock price was now decreasing by a factor of ten with every flash.

*"*The power of fear…" Mrs B said in a hushed tone of pure awe, "…right there."

"It certainly is," Paranoid Dave replied, his mouth open and his head spinning.

The three of them stared at the two-way mirror, as the red and white artificial light of the display panel flickered across their faces. They were stunned, mesmerised, as if watching some magnificent but terrifying spectacle of nature.

£6.94m
Blink
£497,000

The screen blinked again.

"*My God*" Paranoid Dave said out loud in disbelief. "It's almost at the value of the flat."

He rolled that thought around in his feverish mind some more.

"We could sell the flat – which we don't technically own, but hey – we could sell the flat and use the money to buy the whole of planet Earth. Which has lots of flats in it. As well as other things. This is madness. The price can't go any lower…"

And then Paranoid Dave had a thought.

A thought which made him panic.

He remembered Module 7 of the Professor's course, on derivatives.

"This can't go any lower! The Vort twins will need to short cover, right Professor? They need to buy back the stock in order to… to crystallise their profit. That's right, isn't it Professor?"

"Ah, well, yes, I suppose technically—"

"And that will drive the stock price back up, won't it?" Paranoid Dave continued breathlessly, feverishly. "Or worse, someone else will try to pick it up at this bargain price. Maybe someone worse than the Za-Nakarians?"

"Hmm, yes it is a poss—"

"We've got to buy it now. But what the Hell with? Professor, Mrs B – have you got any money on you? Damn, where's Toby…"

Light-headed, panicked by the thought that this was their only chance to buy the Earth back for a song, Paranoid Dave pressed his face to the plate-glass window, desperately trying to spot his friend.

He still couldn't see him. He would have to go out there, onto the trading floor, Ph'Estoun Fever or not.

To Hell with the risk.

He *had* to get out there now. He *had* to find Toby. They *had* to buy the Earth back.

*

"David?"

"Eh?"

"David Pendragon Smith?"

"Yeah?"

"May I present you with…" Toby paused. "Hang on, we better shut this door. Don't want anyone disturbing this historic moment."

Toby pulled the door shut behind him.

He had entered the small office just as Paranoid Dave was about to leave.

"Let's start again... David Pendragon Smith?"

"Yeah?"

"May I present you with..." Toby started rummaging in his pocket and then paused. "Just a moment – were you about to go out there? Onto the trading floor?"

"Excuse me?"

"You. *In your condition?* Were you about to go out there?" Toby scrutinised Paranoid Dave's face intently.

"Me? No? *Nooo*... I was just, you know, stretching my legs."

"Yeah?" Toby replied, looking suspicious. And then he brightened. He rummaged in his pocket again and drew out a bit of paper. It look scrunched and a bit scruffy. "Right, let's get to the point. It's quite an important point after all. David Pen— Hang on. My goodness! Professor, Mrs B – *you're here?* How wonderful. How did you even get here?"

Mrs B and the Professor gave Toby a quick wave and gestured to him to carry on.

"Yeah? OK, you're right, get to the point. OK..." Toby drew in a quick breath and rattled his words out. "David Pendragon Smith, may I present you with—"

Toby held the scruffy bit of paper out with both hands.

"—*planet Earth.*"

Toby pressed the docket into Paranoid Dave's open palm.

"Right there. In your hand. Purchased for one pound. On the nose."

Paranoid Dave stared blankly at the piece of paper in his hands.

"Just as well it was so cheap. That's all the money I had," Toby added cheerfully.

Paranoid Dave turned the docket round in his hands, his face still blank. He looked at it upside down, back to front. He shook it slightly, he held it up to the light. He couldn't process it. On one side the docket was written in Golgothan; on the other it was in English.

Planet Earth trading as Za-Nakarian Resort 987 plc
Stock holding: 1,000,000,000 (one billion) shares
Percentage of issued share capital: 100%
Unit price: £0.00000000089
Total consideration: **£0.89**

"But it says 89p here?"

"Does it?" Toby replied, looking again. "So it does. Oh well, they can keep the change."

"Can I just check a couple of details here…" Paranoid Dave said uneasily. "Did you just cut some kind of deal with the Vort twins to short the Earth's stock?"

"Mmm, kind of. I'd call it an understanding, not a deal. I wanted to buy a planet, they wanted to screw Rakemore."

"And through their shorting, you've now been able to buy planet Earth back?"

"Yep – that's about right."

"Every single share."

"Correct."

"For 89p?"

"Uh-huh."

"O h   m y   G o d ! "   Paranoid Dave looked at Toby. "You did it…"

"Correction: *we* did it. Couldn't have done it without you." Toby pointed at one of the riper-looking boils forming on Paranoid Dave's skin. "No buboes, no deal."

Toby and Paranoid Dave stayed locked in a silent stare for a moment longer, before both realised a spontaneous moment of uninhibited physical expression was about to burst over them.

Paranoid Dave threw his arms up.

"WHO-HOOO-HOOOOOO! We did it! We beat those suckers!"

Toby reached up and met Paranoid Dave's two outstretched palms with his own.

"M O T U, baby!"

"MOTU? *MOTU?*" Paranoid Dave replied with outrage, and then yodelled with the full force of his lungs…

"MOT–*F U U U U U U U U U !*"

He threw his arms wide, and the pair collapsed into a victory hug.

"Oh my dears, you've turned out to be quite wonderful," Mrs B exclaimed as she threw her arms around them both.

"Ah, yes, bravo," the Professor added, as he affectionately patted their shoulders. "Bravo. Really splendid. Hmm?"

"Hang on," said Toby as he extricated himself. "Where's Charlie?"

"Charlie?" Paranoid Dave echoed. "Yeah right, I was wondering about her too."

"Ah yes, I was just saying," Mrs B replied. "She took the Personalitron back to London in a hurry. She was a bit mysterious. She said there was one thing you'd forgotten, Toby."

"One thing I'd forgotten? What, what was—"

"Well that is strange!" The Professor interrupted. "Whatever are they doing now?"

"What is it? What can you see?" Paranoid Dave asked, following the Professor's gaze through the two-way mirror.

Trading appeared to have stopped.

An eerie silence had descended on the trading pit. The traders all seemed to be watching a smallish vehicle that was threading its way carefully past the front of the booths towards them. It looked like a cleaning vehicle, the kind of thing you might see clearing leaves from a street. The vehicle stopped directly in front of the Rakemore Telfer booth. Out of the tiny cabin, a tiny contractor stepped out. He was wearing a small brown coat, like an old-fashioned janitor. He carefully unhooked a large articulated black plastic hose and dropped it over the edge of the Rakemore Telfer counter.

The Rakemore traders watched him in a kind of hypnotic trance.

A moment later, the Vort twins jumped over their counter and ran to pick up the end of the hose. They pointed it towards the Rakemore traders like firemen in front of a burning building. A moment after that traders ran across from all directions and lined up behind the Vort twins, holding the hose in a long line. Nothing came out of the hose, but the whole line of traders started braying like stags in the rutting season:

Hwuh – Hwuh – Hwuh – Hwuh – Hwuh…

Throughout the entire trading pit, the other traders started stamping their feet to the same rhythm. The traders on the same level, the traders on the levels above, the traders below, right down to the thirteenth level, all of them braying and stamping to the same rhythm. As they did so, the strange, unexplained hose bounced up and down. The beat accelerated, and the noise rose towards a deafening pitch—

HWUH – HWUH – HWUH

Trading stopped, stock prices stalled, the whole pit was vibrating to the same deep, stentorian braying, which accelerated towards a climactic, ear-shattering roar—

HWUUUUUUUUUUUUUUUUH!

At that moment, the small brown-coated janitor, who was standing by the side of his vehicle, pulled down on a lever. As he did so, a jet of sludgy brown liquid erupted from the hose in a powerful, messy arc over the Rakemore Telfer booth.

"I don't believe it," Paranoid Dave said. "Is that what I think—"

"Manure," Toby said, slack-jawed.

It turned out that the smell of ordure was roughly the same at this end of the Universe as at the Earth end. With a look of feral joy, the Vort twins and another twenty traders behind them directed the jet back and forth across the booth, spraying strips of brown across the Rakemore traders, across Biffa. Strange to behold, none of them moved. They didn't run, they didn't cower, they didn't duck. They soaked up the humiliation like the victims of some religious sacrifice.

"But why?" Paranoid Dave asked. "I mean they're scum. I get that. No-one wants to see them punished more than me. But their reputation is shot, their bank is bankrupt, and now *this?*"

"It must be some kind of ritual," Toby replied. "Look at Biffa."

The pair looked at one particular Rakemore trader as he transformed from arch nemesis to broken man right there in front of them, beneath a hail of manure.

"And we never even learnt his real name," Toby added. "Guess it doesn't matter anymore."

"Toby…" Paranoid Dave said weakly, resting his hand on Toby's shoulder for support. "I feel ill. I think I've seen enough for two lifetimes. Can you get me out of here?"

43

An orderly wheeled Charlie out through the circular door of the Personalitron.

She sat up on her gurney and looked around carefully. Definitely London. She recognised the terminal, she recognised the body silos, she was back under Downing Street. She had made it back from Za-Nak. Step 1 complete. Now came the hard part. The really hard part. Charlie needed a helicopter, and she needed it fast.

She spotted a clock on the wall.

11am, local time.

Just enough time. Maybe. There was only one person in London, who could help her right now. *Dorothy*. Dorothy Overend – the security dragon under Downing Street, who had a soft spot for the Professor, and who had rescued their mission when she let them through to the Personalitron the first time. Everything depended on whether she could find Dorothy, and Charlie wasn't at all sure how to.

Meanwhile a small flotilla of orderlies in hazmat suits had gathered around her, looking confused and faintly outraged through their plastic visors. They had no idea who she was, and she had no idea who they were. She definitely couldn't see the person she was looking for.

"Excuse me, Madam, but this appears to be an unauthorised use of the Personalitron."

"Really? I'm terribly sorry. I thought Woola's dad had—"

"Woola's *who*? Never mind. Our protocols require that we take you to the Head of Security."

"The Head of Security? Promise?" Charlie smiled to herself, reclining back on the gurney. "That would be just perfect."

*

The landlady of the Squirrel & Acorn looked at her two latest customers intently.

"You two back again I see," she said. Her gaze was stern and steady while, just a few inches below, her jaws chewed gum ferociously.

"So we are," Declan replied, avoiding her gaze.

"What do you want? The usual?"

"Err, no, just a soda and lime," Declan replied.

"And for lofty?"

"He'll have the same," Declan said. The landlady looked towards Seamus. He nodded in agreement, and dropped his gaze.

Behind them, the Squirrel & Acorn was filling up rapidly.

About an hour earlier a news flash had gone out. It was delivered by the same kind but stern-looking Government offiical as the day before with the same message – namely that everyone should get themselves near a television or wireless for another press conference.

The result was that once again, a mere 24 hours after the whole world had last tuned in, switched on and dropped out, it was getting ready to tune in and switch on again. And everyone was experiencing that same need to hear whatever had to be said in the company of others.

"Excuse me, but would these two seats be taken?" Declan asked at the last table with any spare seats.

"Nah, you're alright. 'elp yerself, mate," a broad cockney accent replied. "I mean, we did need 'em. But not anymore," he added with a sorrowful look.

Seamus and Declan nodded in gratitude and sat down nervously. The four other occupants of the table were hulking, manly figures, all dressed identically in grey t-shirts and black combat trousers.

Seamus nudged Declan, and whispered in his ear. Declan's eyes lit up with recognition.

"Excuse me, sir, but have we met before? My friend Seamus thinks he recognises you. Are you regulars here?"

"Nah, we're not regulars at this pub," the cockney replied, taking a generous gulp of ale from his pint glass. Then he looked up, with a moustache of froth across his upper lip, "We did raid it yesterday, though."

"Ah that would be it," Declan replied. Seamus threw his arms up with recognition.

"Yeah, sorry about that. Just following orders, like."

Seamus leaned across to Declan and whispered in his ear again.

"Seamus says he met two other very fine gentlemen, friends of yours. He's wondering where they are?"

"Ha, so are we," TARP-3 sighed. "That's Jason, our gaffer, and Jake. They travelled into space and we've never heard from them since. No idea where they are."

"Ah, but that's terrible." Declan leaned across as Seamus whispered something else in his ear. "Seamus says you shouldn't worry. He always reckoned they were from there anyway."

"Yeah, is that so? That's a thought... It's a funny old universe," TARP-3 said, holding out his hand. "The name's Jim by the way,"

"Declan. Nice to meet you," Declan said.

"And I'm Jack," TARP-4 said, holding out his hand. "Nice to meet you. Declan."

"And I'm Josh—"

"'old up, 'old up. Something's 'bout to 'appen." TARP-3 interrupted.

The TV screen was flickering as it transitioned back to the studio.

*

Paranoid Dave paused for a moment at the doorway.

He looked at the sky above London, or what little he could see of it, and then at his watch.

11:15am.

He thought about Charlie and the mission she was now on. Either she would be successful, or she would fail. Heads or tails. Either way, he couldn't change it, that was someone else's coin toss.

But there was something he could change.

He looked through the glass in the door. No queue. He reckoned he had ten minutes spare. Not much, but enough.

He hadn't come to this particular location for the Professor, nor for Mrs B. He hadn't come here for Toby, nor for Charlie. Especially not for Charlie. He hadn't even come here for the sake of the planet, nor for the billions who lived on it.

He had come here for *him*.

For David.

David Pendragon Smith.

He looked at his watch again.

Sod it, he thought, *the world can wait.* And he pushed through the door.

44

Toby stared out of the window of the taxi.

London was bathed in midday sunshine. A few luxuriant white clouds were hanging in the sky, little blemishes daubed across an otherwise spotless blue canvas. Toby held up his right hand and rotated it slowly in the slanting sunlight. He looked at the texture of his skin in a way he had never bothered before. He experienced a simple pleasure in stretching his fingers and relaxing them again. He was back in his own body and it felt good. Amazing even.

Then the taxi rounded a corner, and the perfect blue sky suddenly looked a little less than perfect. Mostly because the fearsome flank of a Jagamath bulk carrier had come into view.

At the same time, the rumbling noise from the carrier approached another crescendo.

…boom – Boom – BOOM – BOOM – **BOOM** – BOOM – BOOM – Boom – boom…

Toby was back in London. *Good.* But the bulk carriers were still very much here, and now they were making threatening sounds. *Bad.*

Very, very bad.

Toby could kick himself.

How did I forget something so obvious?

Great that he had got himself and Paranoid Dave

safely from Golgotha back to Za-Nak. Great that Woola's dad had helped get them from Za-Nak back to London in the Personalitron, back into their own bodies. Great that Woola's dad was even now disposing of Paranoid Dave's diseased second body. Even better that they had managed to buy the Earth back. Good job all round.

But how were the Jagamath supposed to know all that?

They had a delivery to make and a reputation to uphold. Until the legitimate owner of planet Earth came along – *with proof of ownership* – they were going to make that delivery. Of course they were.

Toby pulled out the Professor's watch and checked the time.

11:30am

Thirty minutes to cargo release.

Too late for him to do anything. All they could do now was hope Charlie succeeded.

"Don't worry yourself, dear," Mrs B said, sitting opposite him in the taxi and reading his thoughts. "She'll manage it, she'll pull it off."

"You think? *Really?*" Toby replied warily. "I don't know what makes you so confident?"

"She had faith in you, I believe," the Professor said. "When you doubted yourself. Before you even had a plan."

"True…"

"So maybe it's now your turn to have faith in her, hmm?"

Toby smiled faintly.

"And in any case, we want you to focus on the press conference," Mrs B added.

The press conference.

Set for 12pm. The exact same time as the cargo release. Toby gave a momentary shudder. It was either going to be a moment of pure joy, or utter despair. Either Charlie succeeds, the booming stops and the bulk carriers start to leave. Or Charlie fails and the Earth gets gassed to extinction. No in-betweens.

"Do the press know where to come?" Toby asked.

"Oh yes, Dr de Haan has taken care of that," Mrs B replied. "They'll be there. And all the world leaders with them."

"Them as well?" Toby sucked in a deep breath. It triggered a thought. "Professor, could I borrow your notebook? I just want to have another look at the—"

"The last module?" the Professor said. "'Nine ideas for rescuing capitalism from itself'?"

"Err, yes, that one."

"Yes, yes, I see. But no," the Professor replied, smiling. "David has the notebook, I'm afraid."

"Does he? Oh... Where is Dave by the way?"

"We sent him ahead," Mrs B replied.

"To get the venue ready," the Professor added. "For the press conference."

"Oh right... Makes sense I guess," Toby replied. He wondered which room the Professor was planning to use in the house on Cleremont Avenue. The conservatory seemed the most appropriate.

Toby looked out the window again.

The bulk carrier was still there, and still rumbling.

*...boom – Boom – BOOM – BOOM – **BOOM** – BOOM – BOOM – Boom – boom...*

*

Dave heard the front doorbell ring. He quickly

switched off the hoover and bundled the machine into the dining room. He checked his watch: 11:35am.

He surveyed his surroundings. Not perfect, but it would have to do. He made his way to the front door and caught sight of himself in the hall mirror. He double-backed to get a better look. He ran his hand over his chin. This would take some getting used to. One small trip to the hairdresser was one very large change for Paranoid Dave.

The doorbell rang a second time.

Dave went to the front door, lifted the latch and pulled it open.

"Hi there. Journalist or world leader?"

"Journalist. BBC. May I come in?" Behind him a camera crew was arriving at the top of the stairs with a small mountain of equipment.

"Of course. Dining room, please – down the hallway, second on the right."

Dave was about to shut the door again, when another figure appeared at the top of the staircase. He was blond and slim, with puffy eyes and a generally hungover look.

"Journalist or world leader?"

"Journalisht. From the Shvenska Dagbladet," he said in a sing-song Scandinavian accent.

"Hang on… Don't I know you?"

The journalist looked a little sheepish.

"Just a second", Dave continued. "You're the one who bar-dived onto the Downing Street shecur… security detail?"

"I wash a little annoyed they had shold the planet."

"Yeah? And then you changed your mind once Woola turned up?"

"I did, yesh." The journalist hung his head.

"And now you've changed your mind again, seeing as Woola's disappeared and left us in a big pile of poo?"

"I have, yesh." The journalist's head lowered even further.

"Well, turns out you were right the first time. Never mind. Down the hallway, second door on the right."

Before Dave had even shut the door, the bell rang again.

He pulled it back open.

"Yes? Journalist or world leader?"

"I am the President of Brazil."

"Ah yes, of course," Dave replied, straightening up. "A world leader. To the sitting room, please. All the way down the hall, door at the end."

"The people of Brazil thank you."

"They do? Well that's very kind of them," Dave replied, feeling surprisingly chuffed. "But I'm afraid they'll have to stay outside."

"Excuse me?"

"Your security guys," Dave said pointing to the dozen tanned, chiselled and slightly humourless characters in suits and shades who were standing behind the President. "We're expecting a lot of people. They'll have to stay outside."

*

Toby shifted round on his seat.

The taxi had just driven clean past the turning to Cleremont Avenue.

"Professor," Toby said, "what's going on? That was the turn-off to your house, wasn't it?"

"I am just taking you to where you must be going,"

a very calm voice replied from the front of the cab. As it spoke, two vaguely familiar eyes fastened onto Toby's gaze in the rear-view mirror.

"Really?" Toby replied, slightly unnerved and trying to place those eyes. "And where's that exactly?"

"It is where the gentleman professor said for you to go."

"Oh I see." Toby turned to the Professor. "We need to get to the press conference, Professor. At your house. Surely?"

"Hmm? Oh, yes, yes quite. But no. We *are* going to the press conference. But it won't be at my house."

"OK... Where is it then?"

"Somewhere nice," Mrs B replied, folding her hands in her lap. "That's all you need to know."

Toby leaned forward, feeling more than a little exasperated. He tapped on the glass behind the cabbie's head.

"Excuse me, Mr taxi-driver? I've had a really trying 24 hours. *Please* could you tell me – where are we going?"

"Ah, but I cannot be breaking the confidence of this gentleman and this lady. I am in their service," the cabbie replied, looking at Toby in the mirror. The taxi stopped at a red light. The cabbie pulled the glass back with one hand, and turned to face Toby. "But I can say that it is very good to having you back and to finding you safe."

"YOU!" Toby exclaimed.

"Yes," the Professor said, "it is our friend. Most interesting, don't you think?"

"You're the cabbie who was driving the TARP team. Err... Aftab isn't it?"

"It is I. And yes, it was also I who drove the

assassins. And so you see, I have been most concerned about you."

"Well that's very, um, thoughtful of you," Toby replied, leaning back in his seat. "What a coincidence you picked us up."

"Not entirely," Aftab replied as the taxi started to move again. "I have been waiting near Downing Street, hoping that you would be safe. And so it is."

"Funny, because I think you said you'd pray for us?" Toby said. "Must've worked."

"Indeed," Aftab replied, with transcendent calm, as he swung the cab into a gentle left turn. "And the assassins? Are you knowing what happened to them? Their leader was, I believe, very lost."

"Oh, that guy?" Toby replied. "You don't need to worry about him. He's found himself alright. Last time I saw him, he was delivering spa treatments to stressed travellers on Za-Nak."

Aftab tilted his head, not understanding.

"It's a long story. Let's just say, his assassinating days are almost certainly over."

"This is very good to hear. Very good," Aftab replied. "And the very large spaceship above our heads. Are you managing to help with this?"

"Ah, that? Well, we've err…" Toby paused and momentarily caught Mrs B's eye. "Yes… Yes, that's being dealt with as we speak. It's going to be OK."

Aftab looked in his wing mirror, applied his indicator, and gently brought the cab to a halt on the curb.

"Well then," said Aftab, as he applied the handbrake and turned slowly in his seat. He fixed his deep, soulful eyes onto Toby. "Everything is working out as it should. *Inshallah*."

Toby had reached his destination.

45

The doorbell wasn't ringing anymore at Flat 21, No. 144 Eden Park. There was no need, Dave had put it on the latch. With the comings and goings, it was swinging open and shut like a catflap in a gale.

"Journalist or world leader?" Dave asked wearily, as he swatted away the back end of a lighting rig being carried past his face.

"Я лидер свободных русских людей!"

"Right? Really? That probably means world leader perhaps? Oh hang on, I recognise you. Golly, you look a bit short in real—"

"His Excellency is telling you," a very young, very handsome interpreter interrupted testily, "that he is the leader of the free Russian people."

"*Can't be many of them,*" Paranoid Dave muttered under his breath.

"Excuse me?" The handsome interpreter pouted with indignation.

"Of course. World leader. Down the corridor, door at the end. But I'm afraid this lot will have to wait outside. No room." Paranoid Dave gestured to the interpreter and the bodyguards behind the Russian President.

"Невозможно. Я хожу везде со своим переводчиком."

"His Excellency says that's impossible. He goes everywhere with me."

"Does he indeed?" Paranoid Dave folded his arms. "Very well. But the goons stay outside. Next!"

"Hi there," said a cool voice with a North American inflection.

"Journalist or world leader?" Paranoid Dave asked.

"World leader."

"Yeah? Which one?"

"I'm from some place you've never been to most likely. Left of Greenland, just up from the USA."

"Ah, Canada. Always been meaning to visit. Sitting room – down the corridor, door at the end."

"Thanks."

"Pleasure. Next?" Dave said. "Oh! It's you."

*

Toby was first up the stairs, panting from the effort. The queue for the lift was too long, and he was excited to get to the top. He leant for a second against the wall to get his breath back.

Toby looked up and saw Dave. He did a double-take.

"Wow, Dave, you look…"

"Different?"

"Different."

"You like it?" Dave stepped forward into the lobby and turned slowly on the spot.

"Sure," Toby replied. "You look… *different.*"

"Yeah, you said." Paranoid Dave had a strange look in his eye. "I reckoned it was time to move on."

Toby looked him up and down.

Dave's hair had been cut back to an orderly, sober

length. He had brushed it and combed it and created a tidy parting just left of centre. His beard had gone. He was even wearing a dark suit, with a pressed white shirt, open at the neck. It was still Dave. He was still pudgy, his eyes were still small, and his skin was unnaturally pale where his beard had been. But there was no doubting it. With the suit, the open-necked shirt, he cut just a bit of a dash. He looked handsome.

"But why, Dave?" Toby asked. "I mean you look great. But why the change?"

"You've got a set of G20 leaders to convince, right Toby? You're PR, remember? And Charlie too. She's beautiful, she's smart, she's articulate..." Dave's voice trailed away for an instant. "You'll both do great on TV. So you don't want some troll in the background distracting everybody. So there you have it. I tidied up."

"OK... I get it. I think."

"So," Dave said, snapping back to the present, "where are the Professor and Mrs B?"

"They're downstairs, waiting for the lift." Toby replied. As he did so, the booming sound pulsed towards another crescendo.

"Damn, can you hear that?"

...boom – Boom – BOOM – BOOM – **BOOM** – BOOM – BOOM – Boom – boom...

"Oh that? Don't worry about that," Dave replied confidently. "Charlie'll fix it. Right! We've only got five minutes. Come and help me round up the world leaders. We need them all in the sitting room."

"For the press conference?"

"Yeah, but... Not exactly. Come on!"

*

Dave pushed his way through the front door and down the hallway, weaving between the throng of visitors. The first door he pushed open led to the bathroom, where he found the Prime Minister of India moisturising in front of the mirror. Dave unceremoniously flushed him out, shooing him down the corridor towards the sitting room. Then he checked Charlie's room – empty – and his own room – also empty.

Even in the chaos and confusion, Toby quietly noted how clean and tidy the flat looked. And roomy too.

*

"Right, this is the spare room," Dave said, as he paused for a moment. He looked Toby in the eye. "It's your room, Toby. If you still want it."

Without waiting for a reply. He swept the door open.

As he did so, he revealed two figures sitting on the bed.

It was the President of the United States, sitting next to the President of France. Their knees were turned towards each other and she had one hand resting in his. She looked down demurely as she recognised Dave.

"Oh hey there you guys! How y'all doing?" the US President asked breezily. His eyes twinkled and his perma-grin stretched comfortably along its favourite wrinkles. He patted the bed with his open palm. "Why don't y'all sit down and we can get comfortable?"

"No, Mr President, we are not going to get comfortable," Dave replied briskly, as he strode towards the bed. "I was quite clear. I said all the way down the hall, to the last door at the end. The sitting room. Not second door on the left. Come on, out now!"

"Mais fais pas comme ça!" the French President spoke up. "Mon dieu, you look 'andsome without that beard. Asseyez-vous! Je vous en prie."

"And you too, come on, out you go – shoo!" Paranoid Dave insisted, clapping his hands. "Shoo, shoo."

Reluctantly, the two Presidents made their way to the door and down the corridor, with Dave shushing from behind. The French President pouted, the US President grinned and Dave clapped his hands, like he was driving a pair of geese from the wrong shed.

The two Presidents remembered to let go of each other's hands just before they entered the sitting room.

*

"The sitting room."

There before Toby was the slightly surreal sight of the world's foremost leaders, assembled in the sitting room of Charlie and Dave's flat. They were gathered around the room in small knots and gaggles, talking animatedly to each other, quite oblivious to the two young men standing at the doorway.

"Damn…" Toby looked on in disbelief. "The leaders of the G20."

"Yep," Dave replied. "With India, the US and France back in, you've got the set. All twenty."

"Hang on, no, not twenty. Just nineteen," Toby replied. "We're missing Germany."

"Eh?"

"Otto never left Za-Nak, remember?" Toby said.

"Too scared to use the Personalitron."

"You're right. Pity. He was my favourite."

"One question: why the G20 all of a sudden? Why not the G7 like before?"

"Oh it's always like that. It's all about the G7 when things are going well, and the G20 when they're not," Dave replied. "Anyway, we need to get to our last stop. The dining room."

"You mean the press conference?" Toby replied, with a sinking feeling. Just at that moment, perfectly audible amidst all the confusion around them, the booming noise from the Heavens crescendoed again.

*...boom – Boom – BOOM – BOOM – **BOOM** – BOOM – BOOM – Boom – boom...*

"Yep, the press conference," Dave replied, as he pulled the sitting room door shut behind them.

Toby watched as Dave produced a key from his pocket which he placed in the lock.

"Don't want that lot disturbing our little moment of fun, do we?" he said, as he turned the key and then slipped it back into his pocket.

"Hang on, did you just do that?" Toby asked in amazement. "Have you just locked the leaders of the G20 behind that door?"

"G19," Dave corrected.

"But... But... You can't just lock the world's most powerful leaders in your sitting room!"

"I haven't," Dave replied with perfect poise. "They're standing right here."

That strange glint was back in his eye, as he winked at Toby.

"The press conference," Dave continued, "is this way. Shall we?"

46

Two dozen microphones were poking out of the podium, like a small electronic hedgehog. A few feet beyond it, the BBC producer and his cameraman were adjusting their equipment.

Beyond that, there were two TV lighting rigs.

And beyond that, chaos.

All across the dining room, journalists were jostling and jockeying to get a view. A few desperate ones had climbed onto the narrow windowsill and were clinging to the curtain rail for balance. Others had been swamped and all Toby could see was a single hand held in the air, clutching a dictaphone. The dining table had been pushed against the opposite wall, and more journalists were piled on it, squawking and elbowing like seabirds at a clifftop colony.

"We're on air in one minute," the producer said, making himself heard above the din. He was a lanky fellow, with long brown hair down to his shoulders and a gentle but slightly stressed-looking face.

Toby gave a start. He looked at the podium in front of him and up at the clock on the far wall. 11:59am.

The producer gestured to the journalists to quieten down and – bit by bit – they took notice. The room started to turn silent.

"You guys ready?" the producer asked, turning back

to Toby and Dave.

"Not really," Toby replied, feeling sick to his stomach.

"Sure we are," Dave added.

And then something happened.

As the silence in the room grew, the booming from the bulk carrier became more apparent.

...boom – Boom – BOOM – BOOM..........

And then it stopped.

The room really had fallen quiet by now, as all ears strained to listen to the sound of...

Nothing.

Toby looked at Dave, with a pleading inquiry in his eyes.

Had Charlie done it?

Or was Armageddon about to be unleashed?

Dave smiled back calmly and pointed over Toby's shoulder towards the window.

Toby turned around. Through it he could see the underside of the bulk carrier passing overhead. As he looked more closely, there was no doubting it. The vast vessel was pivoting upwards.

It was leaving.

"Fifteen seconds," the producer said.

Toby turned back to face the camera. This weird weight, that he hadn't even realised he was carrying – the weight of the whole world – starting lifting from his shoulders. And his shoulders started floating up behind it. He had the sensation he might drift up to the ceiling of their top floor flat; his hand went out and took hold of Dave's arm.

"10 seconds."

Toby spotted two faces at the back of the room. There was no reason he should spot them at that precise moment, but he did. Between the blindingly bright TV lights, and across the huge press of journalists in front of him, he saw the Professor and Mrs B. They were smiling, beaming at him. And the Professor was carrying a small hedgehog in his arms, which just seemed the most natural thing in the world at that moment. Toby smiled back, confused, amazed, happy.

The producer, who was squatting down beneath the main camera, gestured frantically to get Toby's attention. In a kind of delirium, Toby spotted him and watched him counting down from five with his fingers.

FIVE

FOUR

THREE

TWO

ONE...

As he mouthed 'One', the producer rearranged his index finger and thumb into the pistol shape and pointed at Toby.

This was it.

Toby was live and he was about to speak truth to billions.

It was exhilarating.

*

The TV screens in the Squirrel & Acorn flickered as the view transitioned to press conference proper and two young men appeared on screen.

"Blimey, TARPs," TARP-6 said, "them's the youngsters we were chasing. Do you think Jason and Jake are with them?"

"Sssh, George," TARP-3 said. "The kid's about to

start talking."

Someone over by the TV turned the volume up, while the entire pub went silent. The one on the right – the ordinary-looking one – was ready to talk.

Suddenly his voice could be heard across the Squirrel & Acorn and, indeed, the whole planet.

"24 hours ago," the ordinary-looking bloke started, "we learnt that the Earth had been sold…"

He paused and leaned into the mic.

*

"…*Oops*."

Toby straightened back up.

"I'm here to tell you that was a really dumb idea.

"Why was it a dumb move?" Toby asked rhetorically, while wondering where all these words were coming from. Speeches were not his thing.

"Well…" he pressed on. "Remember watching Woola splash about in Loch Ness? That wasn't just PR. That was Woola checking out his future holiday destination. The Za-Nakarians wanted to turn the northern and southern latitudes of Earth into a tropical resort. A *temporary* tropical resort."

And so Toby told the whole story.

He told everyone about Za-Nak and about the Za-Nakarians. He told them about their love of holidays and their love of daylight hours. He talked about their powers of hypnosis. About their holiday planets and about their use of climate control. He explained what the bulk carriers were, what they were carrying and when they were going to dump it. He told everyone about the Personalitrons that had been given to planet Earth, and the Bodytrons that hadn't.

And when he was done talking about the Za-Nakarians, he moved on to the Golgothans. He described the whole towering edifice of confusion and double-dealing with which they'd fooled Earth's leaders. The IPE, the IPO, the ruinous lease payments, the fake currency, the crazy Antarctic connection, *the black-widow deal*. He told them how the Earth's value had shrunk to the price of a bag of crisps.

The words flowed. Toby felt like he was at the centre of the Universe. He felt as if time and events were circling around him, in motion and – at the same time – perfectly still.

And so Toby arrived effortlessly at his conclusion, without even realising that he had a conclusion to arrive at. But he did and he did.

"So that's what happens when you sell something," he said, *"you give up control.* We lost control of our planet the moment we sold it. Honestly, the Za-Nakarians and the Golgothans could now do what they wanted and they'd find a way of making it legal."

Toby paused and reached for a glass of water. He took a sip and cleared his throat. He wanted the next line to count.

"But you know what? Before we get too angry with them, let's remember this about the Za-Nakarians. They were only planning on doing to the Earth what we're already doing. Just a bit faster."

He paused again for another sip of water, leaving that last thought like a little island in people's minds, perfectly moated.

"So," he continued, "we all got duped. But the question you're probably wondering is: *where are we now?* What are the spaceships going to do to us? Who owns the Earth? Well…"

Toby paused stopped, mid-sentence, as something occurred to him.

"...my friend Dave here is going to answer that. And by the way, it's him that you want to thank for saving the planet. Seriously. Him and our other friend, Charlie, but she's not here right now. Anyway, Dave?"

"Thanks, Toby," Dave replied with perfect self-assurance, as he stepped closer to the cluster of microphones. "Well the short answer is, you can all wake up and pretend it was a bad dream. It's all been fixed."

*

No-one in the Squirrel & Acorn could believe what they were hearing.

They wanted to laugh with relief. They wanted to yell out in anger. They wanted to say sorry. They wanted to be furious, but they felt complicit, so they wanted to cry. In the event, no-one said a word and no-one looked at each other. They stayed glued to the TV.

They watched as the stocky, handsome bloke in a suit started talking. *Must be the money man*, they were all thinking.

"I could go into the detail of how we fixed this," the handsome bloke said, "but you know what? Let's just say we duped them back. The thing you all want is *proof* that we fixed this. Fair enough. Let's look at the spaceships. Err, excuse me?"

The handsome bloke appeared to lean away from the mic and gesture to someone off camera. He leaned back into the microphones.

"We're just gonna adjust the camera and have a quick look at the bulk carrier over London. Let's see where it's heading."

The camera started to pan towards the window. They saw a couple of journalists scrambling off the windowsill to get out the way. A second or two later, the exposure was adjusted, and the TV screen showed the view from the top-floor flat.

The viewers in the Squirrel & Acorn, most of whom had spent most of the morning looking at their feet, could now see the undeniable reality of a Jagamath bulk carrier. They watched transfixed as it departed southwards from London along the Greenwich meridian and climbed slowly upwards.

But there was more.

As the camera continued to refocus, it showed not just one, but *three* bulk carriers departing along the meridian. End-to-end, they described a vertiginous arc stretching from the lower atmosphere up towards space.

The furthest one was starting to pierce the Earth's stratosphere into space beyond.

No-one in the Squirrel & Acorn, nor anyone else, had ever seen an object in the upper atmosphere larger than a speck. From the dawn of time until now, it had just been an endless shimmering blue, or cloudy, or grey, or something, or anything. But not this. Not three insanely large megastructures climbing sedately into space. It defied all sense of reasonable expectation, like seeing a mile-high tsunami, or a mile-wide hole to the centre of the Earth.

Gasps rang out around the Squirrel & Acorn. There was a clatter as one pub-goer went out cold. Someone dropped a pint glass.

47

While the camera and everyone's attention was focussed on the window, a small commotion broke out at the doorway to the dining room.

Toby peered between the TV lights and spotted three figures entering. The two heads at the back he couldn't quite make out, but he knew the one in front. It was Charlie. He could see the black sunglasses perched on the gorgeous mocha hair. He watched as she flexed her way effortlessly through the press of journalists, slipping between them like water.

As she emerged out the front of the crowd, and before she could even set eyes on him, Toby threw his arms around her neck and hugged her tight.

"You're safe," he said. "Thank God you're safe."

He held onto her a moment longer, drinking in the scent of her hair. Just as they were separating, Charlie spotted Dave and pulled up short.

"Dave," she exclaimed, "my God you look…"

"Different? Yeah, I know. Toby's done all that stuff already." Dave looked at Charlie with that strange glint in his eye again.

He and Charlie shared a lingering look, during which they communicated Toby-wasn't-quite-sure-what thoughts.

"So how did you *do it*, Charlie?" Dave asked,

breaking the moment. "How did you persuade the Jagamath?"

"Oh, you want to know about my little adventure?" Charlie asked.

"Too right," Toby replied. "How did you even get into that bulk carrier?"

"Yeah, that bit was quite tricky," Charlie replied. "I had a pretty good idea where the docking bay would be. The Professor and I spotted that the first time we saw a carrier. And then, once I had a helicopter, the rest was easy."

"A helicopter?" Toby spluttered. "How do you get one of those in a hurry?"

"It just fell into my lap," Charlie replied, with an impish smile. She looked at Toby and took pity. "Let's just say that, once I arrived back under Downing Street, I got lucky. The one person I needed to be there was there. And she helped me."

"*Who?*" Toby and Dave asked simultaneously.

"She's here right now," Charlie said. "Ask her yourself."

Charlie stepped aside, just as a rotund lady with steel-gray hair thrust her way out of the crowd, dragging behind her a pudgy bald man in a Hawaian beach shirt and shorts.

"Dorothy!" exclaimed Toby.

"Otto!" exclaimed Dave.

"Ah ze young people. Ze heroes! Vunderful. Otto is very happy!"

Otto took Dave's hand in his own pudgy grip and pumped it enthusiastically. Then he grabbed Toby's.

"Otto – it's so good to see you safely back on Earth," Toby said, in a quavering voice as his hand gyrated up and down. "Germany will be... very pleased."

"Yah, yah me too. He is so pleezed zat ze young people have all returned safely to ze planet, yah?"

"Dorothy," Toby said, turning to her, "thank you for helping us. Thank you for helping Charlotte. We owe you a huge—"

"Stop waffling, young man," Dorothy replied. "Your press conference is about to re-start."

"Err… right, yes."

"All you need to know is that we found the Jagamath perfectly accommodating. Once we'd established a few ground rules."

"Dorothy," Charlie continued, winking, "is a force of nature. You try saying No to her, and then you'll learn."

"Excuse me…" the BBC producer bobbed up between them. "We're back on air in one minute."

"One minute? Right…" Dorothy turned to Otto. "Come on, you big baby. We can't have you on TV, not with that shirt on."

Dorothy started tutting and fussing with Otto's shirt, as she pushed him back into the crowd.

"Yah, yah, Otto iz a little bit ze big baby. Big baby Otto!" the Chancellor replied, holding up a single index finger. "Otto likes ze beach clozing!" was the last thing they heard as he disappeared back into the crowd.

Charlie, Dave and Toby looked at each other for a moment, and were about to collapse into laughter when the producer bobbed up between them.

"Make that 30 seconds," he said, as he bobbed back down again.

"Right, I better get out the way too," Charlie said, wiping a tear of suppressed laughter from her eye, and starting towards the crowd.

"You're going nowhere," Dave replied. "There's a spot for you right there, the other side of Toby."

Charlie shrugged her shoulders and took her place next to Toby. The room had quietened down again, leaving just a residual hum of excitement from the sight of the bulk carriers.

"Well, what do you think of it?" Charlie whispered out the side of her mouth.

"Excuse me?"

"The flat. Your room. Will you take it?"

"Err, are these microphones on yet?"

"Do you care?"

"Not really."

"So?"

"Like it? I *love* it. Of course I'll take it," Toby replied. "And me? Do I pass?"

"Let me think…" Charlie leaned forward to look past Toby. "What do you reckon, Dave, is he in?"

"Go on then," Dave replied. "Providing he remembers to do his washing up."

"What's the rent?" Toby asked.

"Ten seconds!" The producer was starting to look stressed, and was nervously pulling his long hair back over his ears.

"Hmm… We'll settle for one percent of planet Earth. Paid annually," Charlie replied.

"Seriously? How about I just give you the whole thing?" Toby whispered.

"You'd give me the world?" Charlie whispered in Toby's ear.

"Five seconds!" The producer started counting down with his fingers.

"Yes," Toby whispered back.

Four

"Will you two stop gossiping?" Dave said.

Three

"We're done," Toby replied.

Two

One

"Right, well, welcome back," Dave said briskly. "First of all, a quick introduction. Here's Charlotte – but you can call her Charlie. She's the one that persuaded those bulk carriers to leave."

*

The camera shifted slightly to the right to focus on the girl with the long mocha hair.

"She's another of the ones we were chasing," TARP-6 commented. "Wow. Pity we didn't catch 'er."

"Don't be daft, George," TARP-3 replied, shaking his head again. "*Thank God* we didn't catch 'er. She just helped save the planet."

"Oh yeah, good point."

*

"So now you'll be wondering who owns planet Earth?" Dave continued. "The answer to that is simple: we do. And here's the proof."

Dave pulled from his pocket the sale docket. As the journalists strained to see the crumpled bit of paper, the buzz of noise in the room increased in intensity, like gas starting to escape from an over-pressurised system.

"This, to be precise," Dave continued, as he tried to smooth out the wrinkles between his palms, "is a sale receipt issued by the Inter-Planetary... Never mind all that. Let's just says it confirms that we have purchased all the outstanding shares in planet Earth."

Hands all across the dining room shot up. Cameras started to flash manically.

"Now I'm going to pre-empt your next question. You're probably all wondering if we're going to give it back? Yeah?" Dave asked, as he strafed the room with his eyes. "Well I'm glad you're all thinking that, because the answer is… Yes, we will. But—" He stabbed a single pudgy finger into the lectern. "On one condition."

He paused.

"Come again, *ten* conditions."

The buzz in the room dialled up another few decibels.

"What are the conditions?" he continued. "Well, we want to make sure the financial system is stabilised and the global economy starts to work for the good of the global population and for the, well… For the globe. It's not actually that hard to do. You just need to stop the— Excuse me? *Excuse me?* Can we quieten down please?"

Dave paused theatrically while the noise subsided slightly.

"Thank you. As I was saying. You just need to stop the alcoholics running the off-licence. By which I mean, you just need to stop the financiers and company bosses writing their own rules. So we've created this list of ten simple measures—"

"I thought there were nine?" Toby whispered out of the side of his mouth.

Dave made a calming gesture to Toby with his open palms.

"—*Ten* simple measures that the world's leaders

must agree to implement," he continued, raising his voice against the hum of noise in the room. "The world's leaders – I mean all of them, not just the G7, or the G20, but all of them – need to sign this!"

Dave pulled from his jacket pocket a second piece of paper and waved it above his head.

"*The Ten Demandments*!" he declared.

The buzz of escaping gas in the room exploded. The press pack broke out in a furore of disbelief and excitement and camera clicking and hand waving. A volley of questions hit the front of the room like a missile strike. So many, so loud, Toby and Dave didn't have a chance of hearing them. Adding to the pandemonium, the world leaders had managed to escape from the sitting room and were trying to bustle their way into the press conference through the door at the far end.

"Our message to the world's leaders is simple," Dave shouted into the mic. "Sign these and you can have the planet back!"

In amongst the combustible mix of confusion, outrage and excitement, little notice was taken of the Professor and Mrs B who were weaving their way through the crowd, handing out copies of Dave's conditions.

"The Ten Demandments?" Toby yelled into Paranoid Dave's ear, just making himself heard. "When did we call them that?"

"Made it up just now," Dave yelled back. "Cute, don't you think?"

*

Seamus, Declan, the remaining members of the TARP

team and everyone else in the Squirrel & Acorn watched the TV confused and dazed.

Nothing made any sense anymore. The world had been saved, but they sensed it would never be quite the same again.

They watched as the three youngsters – who just then seemed to be the most powerful people on the planet – started taking questions. The tumult subsided just enough to catch the end of the first question.

"...summarise? Can you tell us which is the single most important measure here?"

The handsome bloke in the suit stepped up to the mic again.

"Yeah, sure we can. It's probably the first one. It's about human welfare and how we're going to measure it from now on. Let me explain..."

*

"...GDP as a measure of welfare is past its sell-by date. Long past. In fact, in the developed world it's started to become a measure of *dis*-welfare. And environmental damage. Why in Hell do you guys..." Dave raised his arm to point over the top of the journalists to the world leaders at the back of the room. "...why do you guys compete with each other to increase something that's making everyone miserable *and* screwing the planet?"

Dave paused for a moment to look at Toby, who nodded encouragement to him. He pressed on.

"Well from now on, you won't be. You're going to start reporting quarterly to your populations on a new welfare index. Only this one will be made up of the things that people actually care about. Levels of environmental quality in your country, levels of racial equality, levels of educational attainment, reported levels of crime, per capita levels of income *and*..." Dave jabbed his index finger into the air, "income equality. It'll take some time to figure out the detail, to balance these things against each other, but we'll get there."

"If this idea's so sensible, why hasn't it been done already?" another journalist yelled out.

"Probably because rich nations are stuck in some kind of ego-fest about who's got the highest GDP number," Dave replied. "But that stops now."

"Great, I think we're all agreed on that," Toby added, smiling. "Next question?"

Toby pointed to a raised hand towards the back of the room. And then realised it belonged to the Prime Minister of Great Britain. He was crammed onto the dining table at the back of the room. His head was pressed against the ceiling, and he was staring at Toby from a funny angle.

"Item Number 10 on your sheet," the Prime Minister started in a slightly smug, I-think-I've-caught-you-out sort of tone. "It seems to be blank. Could you explain?"

"Err, Dave – can you explain?" Toby asked.

"Yeah, the Tenth Demandment," Dave replied. "We left it blank in case we think of something later. A way of making sure that if you do anything dumb, or misapply the other Demandments, we can write another to fix the problem. Think of it as an insurance policy. Neat, don't you think?"

"But granting this 'Tenth Demandment'..." The Prime Minister twiddled his fingers in quote marks. "...That's madness, that would be like writing a blank cheque."

"Really?" Toby replied.

"Yes."

"How wonderful. Well that's settled then. Right," Toby said, winking at the Professor who nodded back approvingly, "one last question. Yes, you, sir?"

Toby had picked out the Scandinavian journalist. The one whose bar dive had captivated the world 24 hours earlier. Anders Salvgoda.

"Do you know whatsh going to happen to all that carbon dioxide? Will they releash it into shpace?"

Toby looked towards Charlie, who stepped straight up to the mic.

"I'm really glad you asked that," Charlie said brightly. "As a great man once said, 'every good answer starts with a question.'"

"Excoosh me?"

"No, that CO_2 is not going to waste. I've just returned from one of the bulk carriers, from the flag carrier in fact. That consignment of CO_2 has already been pre-paid by Rakemore Telfer and the Za-Nakarians. So we thought, why waste it?"

Charlie paused to look at Toby, who stared back at her blankly. He had no idea where this was going. First Dave, now Charlie. Completely off-script. And the glorious thing was, he wasn't worried anymore.

"All those bulk carriers you can see, they're not just disappearing into space. They're heading to the Moon. *Our* Moon. They're going to release the CO_2 there."

A gasp of amazement rang out around the dining room.

And across the Squirrel & Acorn.

And the rest of the planet.

"But why?" asked the Scandinavian.

"Simple," Charlie replied calmly, not especially

*

And so the most bonkers 24 hours in Toby's life drew to a close at a summit photo with the world's most powerful leaders in front of an audience of billions.

But right then Toby didn't care anymore about the billions or the G20 or the TV cameras or even the bulk carriers taking their cargo of carbon dioxide up to the Moon. Because what mattered to him right then, in the midst of all the madness and the bedlam, was this strange feeling of peace that had descended on him.

He had found a place to live and a set of friends.

And the best bit was still to happen.

As the flashes went off and mere anarchy was breaking out amongst the journalists in front of them, and the whole world was teetering somewhere between joy and anger and relief and shame, he felt Charlie's hand slip into his and give it a squeeze.

He turned to his left and there she was, smiling.

THE TEN DEMANDMENTS

Professor Artemas C James

Edited by David Smith
(aka 'Paranoid Dave')

Download your FREE copy at:
www.squirrelandacorn.co.uk/10-demandments

Join us on our Facebook page:
Facebook.com/squirrelandacorn

Follow us on Twitter:
@squirrelacornuk

Find out more about the author and our forthcoming
publications on our website:
www.squirrelandacorn.co.uk

SQUIRREL &
ACORN PRESS

Printed in Great Britain
by Amazon